**I didn't know who they
them get away with brea**

I got in my car and drove off. As I turned right toward Keele Street I saw a tan-colored Dart, parked on Kane Avenue. It was right in my rear-view, sitting at the side of the road. I drove onto Keele, then made a quick U-turn and looped back to Donald, a street that paralleled mine, one block over. I parked on Donald, facing my backyard neighbor.

My street does not have a back lane. My back yard butts against the back yard of a house owned by another family. I knocked on their front door. Nobody was home. I walked around to their back yard and hopped their back fence into my own back yard, then climbed into my basement, through a small window I always left unlocked, and went upstairs. Now all I had to do was sit quietly and wait.

As it happened, I didn't have to wait long. Within a few minutes, I heard the rumble of a fat V8 outside my living room windows. I peeked through a slit in the nearly closed drapes and listened as the car's engine stopped two doors away. I never saw the car.

Perhaps I was wrong. Perhaps they were just visiting a neighbor down the street. Perhaps. A minute later, two men in suits, walking slowly, stopped on the sidewalk in front of my house. They spoke softly, looked around to see that nobody was watching, then they came up the driveway to the side door.

I looked around, wondering where to hide. I wanted to nab them inside the house, to catch them red-handed, and not just chase them off. I needed to know why they were in my house, what they wanted. These were not kids and not common thugs. These men were here with purpose.

A phone call in the middle of the night sends a police officer on one of the most perplexing cases of his career.

Detective Sergeant Ian McBriar is called to investigate a death that seems to have no motive and an obvious suspect that has no alibi. The deeper he goes, the darker the trail of death becomes.

Set against the backdrop of 1974 Toronto, Ian must also prove his love to the woman he has come to care about and to her son who has come to look on him as a father.

Death Works at Night is the second exciting instalment in the *Ian McBriar Murder Mystery* series, the story of a Metis police detective who conquered bigotry, prejudice, and his own personal tragedies to succeed.

KUDOS for *Death Works at Night*

In Death Works at Night by Mauro Azzaon, Detective Sergeant Ian McBriar is trying to solve a murder. He doesn't think the girlfriend did, but she's the most logical suspect, especially when the bodies start racking up and she's been either married to or living with most of them. But she has no motive, or at least none that Ian can find. *Death Works at Night* is the second book in the Ian *McBriar Murder Mystery* series, and like its predecessor, it's a fast-paced, hard-hitting, police-procedural mystery. The plot is strong, with a lot of clues that don't make sense until the end. And the murderer is a real surprise. Just my kind of book! – *Taylor Jones, Reviewer*

Death Works at Night by Mauro Azzano is a follow-up story to Azzano's first book, *The Dead Don't Dream*. We get reunited with the characters we met in the first book and get to meet some fun new characters as well. There were a few things that I wondered if I would have understood if I hadn't read the first book, but overall, it's an excellent effort by this talented author. Azzano's characters are well-developed and three-dimensional, and the plot is intriguing. *Death Works at Night* is a fast-paced page turner with some surprising twists and turns. There's a lot of little things you'll miss if you don't read it carefully, so you'll want to put it on your shelf to read over again. – *Regan Murphy, Reviewer*

ACKNOWLEDGEMENTS

To Alison: Any woman who can make me laugh, and who laughs at my jokes, deserves recognition. Any woman who can put up with me for as long as you have, deserves a medal. Thank you for your support and love.

To Michael and Jennifer: Thank you for being helpful when I was unsure of how to promote my works, and thank you for your patience.

To my other family members: Thank you for giving me the resolution to finish what I started, and thank you for giving me the tenacity to ignore those who didn't think that I could.

To my friends in uniform: The dedication goes deeper than most people can imagine. Your experience, skill and dedication are a lesson for us all.

DEATH WORKS AT NIGHT

By

Mauro Azzano

A Black Opal Books Publication

GENRE: MYSTERY-DETECTIVE/SUSPENSE

This is a work of fiction. Names, places, characters and incidents are either the product of the author's imagination or are used fictitiously, and any resemblance to any actual persons, living or dead, businesses, organizations, events or locales is entirely coincidental. All trademarks, service marks, registered trademarks, and registered service marks are the property of their respective owners and are used herein for identification purposes only. The publisher does not have any control over or assume any responsibility for author or third-party websites or their contents.

DEATH WORKS AT NIGHT

CHAPTER 1

*I*t's a warm, sunny Saturday afternoon; my brother and
*I walk to the movie theatre where our mother works.
The marquee out front reads* High Noon *ends* Tues.
Below that a poster in the ticket window reads Coming
Wed. – The Quiet Man.

*Our mother, in her beige uniform with red piping and a
red pillbox hat, smiles her smile, takes us into the theatre
and sits us up front. The Maple Leaf Theatre is only half
full, and the owner lets us in for free when there are empty
seats. He likes mom, and letting us in keeps her happy.*

*The theatre goes dark. A distant sound—like a playing
card on a bicycle spoke—emanates from the projection
room. The screen lights up. After the cartoon we will finally
see the western everyone in town is talking about.*

*A bell rings in the lobby behind me. It rings again, in-
sistent. Before I can turn back to look, Karen's voice comes
over the theatre's speakers.*

*"Hello?" she says. "Yeah, he's here, hang on a sec.
It's for you. Ian. Ian, wake up, it's for you."*

ᘓᘓᘓ

I sat up.

Karen handed me the phone and slid back down under
the warm sheets.

"Hello?" I wheezed, still half asleep. I listened to the

man at the other end of the phone, trying to focus on what he was saying. I nodded, forgetting that he couldn't see me nod.

"Fine," I mumbled. "I'll be out front in ten."

I crawled out of bed and shuffled, shivering in the cold air, to the clothes I laid out over a chair for just these calls.

I put my suit on, clipped my tie onto my shirt collar, and combed my hair. Karen lifted her head and squinted at me.

"Everything okay?" she whispered.

I nodded.

"We have a dead body, that's all," I whispered back. "Go back to sleep, hon." I kissed her nose.

"What time is it?" she mumbled.

I squinted at the clock radio. "Three thirty."

"Will you be long?"

"I don't think so. I should be back in time for breakfast."

I tugged the covers up under her chin and kissed her cheek.

"Get some sleep. I'll tell you all about it in the morning."

I drank a glass of milk, stepped out my front door, and locked it behind me.

On the sidewalk, a young man in a pale gray suit paced beside a navy Dodge Polara, puffing frantically on a Craven A. I walked down my porch steps and nodded. He opened the passenger door, tossed the lit butt onto the sidewalk, and balanced on the toe of a shiny black shoe, crushing the cigarette to a powder.

I rubbed my eyes involuntarily. "Hey, Walsh. What do we have tonight?"

He smiled and walked around, sliding behind the wheel. I got in the passenger side.

He started the engine and pulled out onto the street. "A dead guy in Leaside, boss. Woman says she came home from work and found her common-law husband dead."

"Do we have a cause of death?" I asked, rubbing my face, trying to wake up.

Walsh smiled and glanced over at me. "We think it may have something to do with the knife sticking out of his back."

Despite myself, I laughed at the statement. "Something to start with, then. Any witnesses?" I was wide awake now and thinking clearly.

He nodded. "Yeah, we're talking to them now."

Walsh glanced left and drove briskly north to Eglinton Avenue, turned right onto Bayview, and left at a street called McRae. There were almost no cars on the roads, and we made good time.

The skinny police tires made a hissing sound as they crossed streetcar tracks and chirped when he turned over white road paint. Walsh looked around constantly, watching for cross traffic.

Leaside was a working class, residential neighborhood. Old Toronto ended right here and, to the north, new homes—ostentatious houses and oversized ranch-styles—claimed their space on the map.

To the south, toward downtown, apartments were smaller, buildings were taller and the roads less inviting, feeling more like a path out of town than a part of the neighborhood.

Walsh drove too fast, his youth and his impatience evident in his driving style.

He screeched right onto Millwood, a curving, quiet street with clusters of small, low apartments separated by the occasional single house. This was not the kind of street you'd expect to generate a murder. Then again, in this job I'd come to expect almost anything. We turned left onto a street named Airdrie Road and stopped behind a yellow cruiser, its emergency flashers warning passersby that a crime had been committed. Two uniforms on the sidewalk were setting out sawhorses and caution tape, blocking off the entrance to a three-story walkup.

A black Ford station wagon, the coroner's car, sat across the street, almost invisible in the dark.

Back on the sidewalk, a handful of people milled around, shivering in bathrobes and sweat suits.

Walsh led me past them, up the front steps, through the small lobby, and up a zigzag stairway to the second floor. A third uniform stood outside an open apartment door. The door's latch was shredded, as was its doorjamb.

The uniform nodded in recognition.

"Hey, Ian." He smiled. "Constable Walsh." He frowned.

Walsh shrugged. The uniform crooked a finger at me and pointed carefully at the broken latch and the deadbolt, intact, above it. I looked for a moment, comprehending his meaning, and grinned.

"Got it. Thanks, Perry," I said.

Walsh looked at me, puzzled. "What'd I miss?" he asked, curious.

I thought for a second. "Tell you later." I wanted him to work for the answer.

I followed Walsh into a small one-bedroom apartment. It reeked of stale cigarettes, burnt steak, and beer. I got out my Moleskine book and started making notes.

A pair of constables held measuring tapes and numbered cards for the photographer, standing around a dead man like construction workers around a hole.

In the bedroom, a female constable was crouched beside a small, painfully thin woman with short, teased blonde hair and a sleeveless shirt hanging over worn jeans. She looked about thirty-five, with thick makeup and smeared mascara tracing the creases around her eyes.

She seemed to be in shock. She sat on the bed, hugging her knees, her head down.

The officer asked soothing questions, trying to comfort her, but the woman only grunted short answers.

I walked past the bedroom to the coroner, who was leaning over a small dining table. He was looking at a crumpled body on the floor—a man in a rough plaid shirt and white pants, lying in a small pool of blood.

The man was curled up in the fetal position; he could have been asleep except for a green-handled dinner knife sticking straight up out of the right side of his back, behind his arm. I knelt down and spoke softly, as if loud voices might wake the corpse. "Doc, how's it going?"

"I'm fine, Ian," he said, also softly. "Better than our friend, here. Single stab wound. We'll know more later, though."

I nodded and said a quiet "Hail Mary" for the dead man's soul, then I walked back to the bedroom. Walsh followed. The female officer met us at the doorway.

I smiled. "Hey, Eve."

"Sergeant McBriar." She nodded. "The woman's name is Rhonda Clark. The victim is her boyfriend, Ed Hereford. She says she got home from work, the door was kicked in, and she found him like this. She called us right away and claims she didn't touch anything, claims she doesn't know who could have done this. There are a few signs of a struggle—a chair knocked over and a broken vase. She wrinkled her nose. "But something smells funny, Ian."

I smiled. "You don't buy it, huh?"

She shook her head. "Something's fishy. This doesn't feel right."

"Did either of them give us any trouble before this?" I asked.

"Neighbors say they fought a lot—they drank. They lived together, but they weren't married."

Walsh snickered. "More of that going around," he joked.

I glared at him. He shrank back, embarrassed at the blunder.

"Thanks, Eve." I said. "Get the witness details and go home." I motioned Walsh to follow me into the hall. He trailed me like a moping puppy. I poked my pen into his chest and stared at him. "Listen," I hissed quietly. "You comment on my private life in public again and I will break your jaw. Am I clear?"

Walsh nodded sheepishly and looked up at me. "Sorry. Won't happen again, Ian."

"Detective Sergeant McBriar," I snapped.

"Detective Sergeant McBriar," he repeated meekly.

I went back into the apartment bedroom and squatted beside the blonde woman.

"Hi. You're Rhonda?" I asked softly. "I'm so sorry for your loss. Can I help you at all?"

She shrugged her shoulders and looked up at me with sad eyes. "I don't know what I'll do. I loved Ed. He was my best friend. I miss him already."

I made notes, quietly nodding as she spoke. She looked up at me.

"What happened?" I asked. "When you got home, what did you see?"

She looked around at the apartment, what little she could see from the bedroom. She poked her chin at the front door.

"I got home and the door was like that," she said, matter-of-factly.

"I called out to Ed, but there was no answer. So I got Annie to come in with me. That's when we found him like this." She looked up at me again.

"Who's Annie?" I asked quietly.

"Annie Ross—my next-door neighbor."

"You called us right away?" I asked, confirming her statement.

She nodded.

"Was anything missing, anything taken, out of place?" I asked, trying to sound concerned.

She shook her head. "Me and Annie looked to see if anything was gone. We didn't find nothing." There was a definite maritime accent that I picked up in her speech.

"Do you have somewhere to go? Anyone you can live with for a while?"

She seemed surprised by the question. Her face flushed. "Why can't I stay here? It's my place, after all," she snapped.

I shook my head. "Sorry, but we'll be here for the next few days. You might accidentally disturb something that will tell us who did this."

She looked around the bedroom nervously, thoughtful. "What if I just sleep in here, and stay out of the living room?" she asked, hopefully.

I shook my head again and smiled a consoling smile. "Rhonda, our forensic team needs to do their work. Trust me, they'll find out who did this to Ed. They always find things people don't realize they left behind. That's what they do."

Her eyes shot to the kitchen, and she stared at the sink for a minute before looking back in my direction. She leaned her head back, staring at me. "When you find the guy who did this, what will happen to him?" she asked.

"Why do you say it's a guy?"

"Just figured. I sure couldn't 'a kicked in the door."

It sounded too shifty, like an evasion. I nodded, making mental notes, and smiled softly at her. "Why were you coming home so late, Rhonda?"

"I work late," she said, "Cleaning offices. I work the six p.m.-to-two a.m. shift."

"Where do you work?" I asked warmly.

"Them new buildings up on Don Mills—IBM, Kodak, and all them."

"Do you take the bus home after work, or do you drive?"

"Nah, I don't drive. I get a ride home most nights."

"So Ed would usually drive you home?"

"No, Ed was a baker. He started work ten at night."

"He wasn't working last night, though, was he?" I pointed out.

She paused and looked away. "Yeah, shouldn't't've been home."

I had hold of something tangible now, I felt, and moved gently forward.

"Who drove you home tonight, Rhonda?"

She stared at me for a long time. "Gustavo. Mr. De Melo, my boss." She seemed hesitant to give up the information.

"Did he come up here with you?" I asked, firmly.

"No," she lied.

I could hear it clear as a bell.

"Does he often drive you home?"

"Sometimes. He drives right past here to go home."

Also a lie; I could hear that in her voice. Her eyes darted around nervously.

"Where is Mr. De Melo now—at home?" I persisted.

"No, he's going away on vacation today."

"When exactly is he leaving, do you know?"

"No, I don't know." She sounded unsure of her answer.

I wanted her to stew for a while, so I excused myself and joined the two uniforms by the body.

One nodded to me. He leaned close beside me, whispering so I could barely hear. "Figure she did it?" he asked.

"Uh-huh. Not solo, though," I mumbled.

"You think the boyfriend caught her with the boss?"

"Smells like." I frowned. "Where's the cutlery?"

The uniform pointed to a drawer under the kitchen counter and pulled it open with a pencil.

Inside were a dozen or so assorted spoons, forks and knives, scattered loosely and mixed in with a dirty can opener and a few odd cooking utensils. The cutlery was all green-handled, like the knife in the dead man. This was an open-and shut case, I thought. Should I tell her what I think happened, or let her sweat? I decided to let her sweat. I wanted to find her accomplice. I just knew she had one.

Walsh was taking witness statements from the neighbors. Most of them were in the hall by now, talking casually, swapping stories about other gruesome sights they'd seen.

I asked him to point out Annie, the one who'd found the body with Rhonda.

Annie was a pear-shaped woman in her sixties, who waddled like a duck when she walked. She was wrapped in an Indian-blanket bathrobe, which came to her knees, and clutched a discolored mug filled with some kind of soup.

Looking at her, I doubted she could have kicked her slippers off, much less kick hard enough to break the door.

"Hi, Annie. I'm Detective Sergeant McBriar," I said. "You came in here with Rhonda earlier, is that right?"

Annie nodded. "Yeah." Her voice was like a rusty gate.

"Can you remember how long it was from when Rhonda knocked on your door to when you called us?"

She shook her head. "I don't remember, actually," she creaked. "It wasn't long, though, I don't think."

"Is Rhonda a close friend of yours?" I asked.

"No, I barely know her. I figure she knocked 'cause she knew I was awake."

"How would she know that?"

"You can hear inside the apartments from the hall. I guess she heard me walking around."

I smiled politely. "Are you usually up at this time of night?"

She wrinkled her face, insulted. "I got a day job. I got woke up by the noise next door. Rhonda knocked after I heard the noise."

"There was a disturbance at Rhonda's before she came to get you?" I asked. It confirmed my suspicions.

Annie nodded. "I heard yelling and screaming, then it went quiet. But by then I was wide awake."

"How soon after that did Rhonda knock on your door?"

"I dunno. Not long, ten minutes, maybe."

"Roughly what time did she come to your door?"

"About a quarter to three, I guess. Yeah, I'd say about a quarter of three."

I thanked her and went back to Rhonda's apartment. The neighbors had all gone home, some trying to get to sleep, others resolving to get an extra early start on the day, along with juicy gossip for the water cooler, I guessed. The female officer waved me over.

"Rhonda has a cousin named Paulette up in Richmond Hill, who might take her in for a few days," she said

We called Rhonda's cousin. She agreed immediately to put her up so I got a uniform to drive her, with instructions to note the address and a description of the cousin.

The female officer helped her pack, making certain that no evidence was taken, and walked Rhonda out, shielding her from seeing the dead man.

I looked at my watch. Five-fifteen. I wrote this in my Moleskine notebook: *5:15 a.m., Tuesday, September 24, 1974.*

The photographer left, the coroner took the dead man away, and the uniforms prepared to seal up the apartment.

Walsh, wanting to make amends, came meekly up to me. "Sergeant," he started. "Why did you suspect her right away?"

"She referred to him in the past tense," I explained. "Usually, when we break the news that a loved one is dead, people still refer to them in the present tense. 'Ed is a great guy,' or 'I love my Wilfred,' or 'John wants dinner on the table every night at six.' They only use the past tense if they already knew the victim was *in* the past tense, already dead."

Walsh nodded at that. He thought for a moment and frowned. "What did you see at the front door?"

I smiled and walked him to the broken doorjamb. "Look." I pointed. "The door latch is broken, but there's a deadbolt above it that isn't. It must have been unlocked when the door was kicked in. Why would you bother kicking in the door if it wasn't even locked?"

He frowned and stared at the door, trying to come up with a plausible explanation. "Maybe the killer wanted to get in and just kicked the door without checking if it was open?"

I shook my head. "You're coming here to kill someone: why would you kick in a door instead of trying it first? You'd lose the element of surprise if you kicked it more than once. Also, if you kick the door in, you're not paying a social visit. And if you came here intending to stab somebody, wouldn't you bring your own knife? Why trust that your victim would have something right at hand that you could use? Finally, if you came over and *then* decided to kill him, why kick in the door?"

Walsh watched me explain it, fascinated, then shook his head slowly and sighed. "You think they kicked in the door after they killed him to cover up their motive?"

I nodded.

"Jesus," he mumbled. "They don't teach you everything at the Academy, do they?" He looked up at me, his curly strawberry-blond hair and freckles making him look like a young Robert Redford. "You're very good at this, aren't you, Sergeant McBriar?"

I smiled. I was sure he didn't realize what a real compliment he'd paid me. "Call me Ian." I grinned. "Unless you piss me off again," I added.

"Thanks, sir." He grinned back. "Ian."

☙☙

At six in the morning, he dropped me back at home, chirping the tires as he sped off up the street.

I opened my front door and crept quietly into the kitchen. Karen came around the corner from the bedroom, wearing flannel pajamas, and wrapped her arms around me.

"Morning, sweetheart," I whispered. I kissed her nose.

She looked up, worried. "Hey you. Are you okay?"

I nodded. "Woman killed her live-in, we think. I don't know who helped her, but I'm pretty sure we'll find out soon."

"Why did she kill him?" Karen asked.

I frowned. "He didn't make her breakfast. Let's make sure I'm not next."

Karen smirked. "Nut. I'll take you up on that, anyway."

We talked, eating and sipping coffee, for the next hour.

Karen showered and dressed then got Ethan up and dressed for school. I made him breakfast, packed his lunch, and got him ready for his day.

"Do you need anything else, sport?" I asked.

He shook his head. "Can you make my friend Alan some lunch, too?" he said. "He likes my lunches."

"What does he bring for lunch?" I asked, amused.

Ethan shrugged. "He doesn't have lunch," he said simply.

"Doesn't he get hungry?" I asked stupidly.

Ethan nodded. "That's why he eats some of my lunch."

I stared at him for a minute. "Okay," I said. "I'm walking you to school today."

Karen kissed us goodbye and left just before eight, her Beetle whistling down the street, the engine sound fading as she turned the corner.

I unloaded my gun and left it in my dresser, then I walked Ethan across the street to his school.

Three hundred children raced into the building at eight-thirty. I stood in the middle of the hall like a rock in a river, with a stream of young heads rushing past me at waist height.

Ethan waved at one, a thin young boy his age who stopped in front of us. "Hey, Alan," he squealed.

The other boy looked at me, the way I've seen suspects look at me.

"Hi," he mumbled.

Ethan tugged my arm and giggled. "This is my pops. He makes my lunch."

I squatted down to child height. "Hi, Alan." I smiled. "I hear that you don't bring lunch with you?"

He shrank back, as though I'd discovered a terrible secret.

"It's okay." I smiled. "I just want to know if I can help. Do you have any brothers and sisters?"

He shook his head. "No," he chirped.

"Does your mom work?"

He nodded, slowly.

"Is she home now? Do you live near here?" I asked.

The boy shrugged.

I got his address. He wasn't sure what street number the house was, but it was just around the corner, and he lived on the ground floor. He described the truck owned by the family upstairs, then he and Ethan ran off to class. I sighed and debated, briefly whether I should meddle in this boy's home life.

Of course, I should.

I walked around the corner, knocked at a door by the garage, and waited for an answer. I heard movement on the other side of the door, but nobody came to open it. I knocked again, more insistent.

A shadow moved over the frosted window in the door and stayed there.

"Hello?" I called. "I'm looking for Alan's mom."

The lock clicked loudly and the door swung open. Inside, a woman stepped out of the dark and faced me.

She was very attractive, dressed in a maid's smock with a big purse slung over one shoulder. She looked like Ava Gardner, I thought, but with flaming red hair. She was curvy, with an hourglass figure and a bosom that strained at her buttons.

My eyes opened wide despite myself. I smiled. "Hi, my name is Ian McBriar," I stated. I stretched out my hand.

She looked behind me, ignoring my hand. "Is Alan all right? He isn't hurt or anything, is he?"

I shook my head. "Don't worry, ma'am, no, he's fine. I'm concerned about him, though. Our boy, Ethan, mentioned that he doesn't bring lunch with him to school. Is there a problem?"

She glowered at me, indignant. "I need to get to work.

I'm sorry, but I can't talk. I have to be at work in half an hour."

"Would you like a ride? I don't mind. We can talk as I drive you," I offered.

A split second later, it sounded like a bad idea. I suddenly hoped she'd say no.

She looked at me warily. "How do I know you're not some just kind of creep?" she asked.

I pulled out my ID and showed it to her. I waited as she read it, slowly. "I'm a police officer. As I said, I'd just like to talk to you about Alan, that's all." I shrugged.

She waited outside on the curb while I drove up in the Fury, and I opened the door to let her in the passenger side. She gawked at the radio and the magnetic gumball—it proved that I really was a cop, after all.

"So what kind of policeman are you?" she asked curiously.

"I'm a Detective Sergeant in homicide. Can I ask why Alan doesn't bring lunch to school?"

She looked at her white tennis shoes and sighed. "Times are tough. I barely make ends meet. Sometimes I don't have time to make lunch."

She played with a ring, spinning it around on her finger.

"Does your husband work?" I asked.

She sneered. "No. He's been in jail for two years. Bastard did nothing for us, anyway."

"Where are we going?" I asked, pulling out onto the street.

She sighed. "I work at the Holiday Inn up by highway 401, in housekeeping."

"Do you enjoy your job?" I asked.

She smiled sadly. "Not bad. Lets me do my own thing. I just wish it paid better."

"Look." I sighed. "Alan seems like a nice kid. I just want to make sure he's okay. Would you mind if I made lunch for him too when I make Ethan's?"

"*You* make his lunch?"

She said it as though I was just bragging.

I shrugged. "Usually, yes."

She stared at me, calculating something. "You married, mister?" she asked, grinning.

"Working on it. Why?"

"You're not just trying to get into my pants, right?"

I blushed a deep red and grinned. She laughed out loud.

"I'm only trying to help out Ethan's friend, ma'am," I said. "That's all."

"Vivian," she purred.

I nodded. "Vivian."

We drove on, not speaking for a minute. Finally, at a light, she looked up at me. "Look, if you want to give Alan lunch, that's fine with me. I appreciate the help. Lord knows, I need all I can get."

"Great." I stopped at the back door of the hotel. "Ethan will like that, too. Anything in particular he likes, any allergies or dietary restrictions?"

She laughed a husky laugh. I got a warm rush hearing it, and that made me feel somehow guilty. "You sound like a doctor," she chortled. "No, he'll eat anything."

She opened the door and slid out. She leaned back in, bending deeply to retrieve her purse. Instinctively, I glanced at her cleavage. I could see down her smock, past her bra to her navel.

She grinned as my eyes met hers and wagged a finger at me. "Naughty."

I shrugged sheepishly and watched her walk gracefully away. No matter how hard I tried to forget it, the image of her round, pale breasts and wiggling hips stayed with me all day.

CHAPTER 2

I pulled into the 52 Division parking lot about thirty seconds ahead of Walsh and waited beside my car. He screeched to a halt and followed me into the detectives' room. Walsh veered off to talk to a secretary.

My old partner Frank was telling the detectives a joke. "So the brother says, 'Well, you know how grandma loves to chase squirrels...'" His voice trailed off, and the men laughed.

I nodded at him and sat down at my desk. Frank sat facing me in a plastic chair. "Detective Sergeant McBriar."

I nodded. "Detective Inspector Burghezian." It was a standard routine we'd perfected.

"So, kid, how's the rookie?"

He grinned. I sneered slightly. "He pissed me off already," I said. "He made a crack about Karen and me not being married."

Frank scowled. "Want him beat up? I got friends."

I smirked. "Thanks, but I've already threatened him. I'm sure he won't do it again."

Walsh walked toward us. Frank stood and glared up at him, nose to nose. "What's this I hear about you insulting the sergeant? Are you out of your mind, Constable?"

Walsh turned pale and took a short step back. I frowned so as not to giggle.

"I—I'm sorry, Inspector. It was just a joke, that's all, a bad joke. Sorry, sir."

Frank's eyes fixed on Walsh for ten seconds, then he sighed and glanced at his watch.

"Coffee truck will be here in five. Get us each a Danish, squirt." Walsh mumbled another apology and dashed out the door.

I shook my head. "Anything to get a free pastry, huh, Frank?"

He chuckled and rubbed his nose, watching Walsh stand outside in the cool air. "Gotta keep the young ones on their toes, you know." He turned back to face me. "So when do we come over for a barbecue? Helen's been bugging me to ask you."

I smiled and nodded. "How about Sunday after next? Karen said she'd like to see you guys more often."

Frank nodded. "Following Sunday afternoon it is. How's Ethan doing?"

I thought of Vivian's round breasts. "Good." I thought of her swaying hips. "He's enjoying grade one."

ᥱᔕᥱᔕ

Rhonda Clark, I learned after a handful of phone calls, worked for the True-Bright Janitorial Company, owned by Gustavo De Melo, the man she said had driven her home.

Gustavo was not in his office. He was going to spend a few days with his daughter's family in North Carolina, but nobody seemed to know where he was right now. His van was at his office and he wasn't at home. Maybe Rhonda knew where I could find him. I found the scrap of paper with the phone number for Rhonda's cousin.

Walsh sat across from me, proffered a Danish on a plate, and left. I nodded thanks and called the number on the paper. The phone rang twice and a voice, a copy of Rhonda's voice, spoke. "Hello?" she said tentatively.

"Hi, this is Sergeant McBriar; can I speak to Rhonda, please?"

"Sorry, she's not here." She seemed apologetic, but also irritated.

"Do you know where she went? Did she say when she'll be back?" I was starting to worry now. Walsh came back with two coffees and sat in the plastic chair facing me, mirroring my frown.

"I have no idea." The woman sighed. "She was here at breakfast. I dropped our daughter at work and when I got back she was gone. I mean, her clothes are here and she left her work shoes, but she didn't leave no note or nothing. Is there something I should know? Should I worry about her?"

That started alarm bells ringing in my head. "Why do you say that, Mrs…"

"Flaherty. Paulette Flaherty. Jim said there was something queer about Rhonda. Jim—my husband—he said she was always lookin' over her shoulder. He'd know, I guess."

"Why do you say that, Paulette?" I used her first name to put her at ease.

"He's a policeman, same as you. He gets a feelin' about people, you know. He's usually right. Like when they wanted to come and sell us aluminum siding, and they says it wouldn't cost us nothin'. But Jim saw they was fishy, and soon as they heard he was a policeman they took off."

I grabbed a pad and started writing notes. "Does Jim work out of our Division? I don't recognize the name," I said.

She chuckled. I could hear her shuffle in her chair. That meant she was getting comfortable. "No, son. He's with the York Regional Police. He worked for them since we moved here, boy." Her accent got thicker and her slang more obscure as she spoke.

"Where did you move here from, Paulette?"

"Corner Brook, son. The rock. God's country."

I could hear her smiling.

"Gee, you're a Newfie?" I joked. "I'd never have guessed." She laughed—a deep, phlegm-stained laugh—and sucked in a lungful of air.

"Did Rhonda come from Newfoundland, too?" I asked, trying to sound casual.

"Yah, 'course then her name weren't Clark, it were Wilkins," the woman tossed out.

I sat straight up. Walsh's eyes widened and he shrugged, mouthing "What?"

"Which was her maiden name, Paulette? We just need it for our records, of course," I said, matter-of-factly.

Walsh moved the Danish away from my pen and watched me.

"She were born Clark, but then she married Cam Wilkins. Course, that were after she married the Partridge boy, but they was both real young then."

I rolled my eyes, flabbergasted. "Does that do it for husbands, or do I have to start a new page?" I groaned.

She laughed again, this time coughing so hard I thought I might have to clean my phone.

"No, that'd be it. She married Isaac Partridge when they was seventeen, but it were no good. She got annulled from him and married Cam Wilkins, but he got sick and died. That were when she came out to Toronto, 'bout the same time as us. We don't see her much, except now she got this trouble, 'course. But Jim says we help family, so we're helpin' her."

I nodded for Walsh to wait. He sat back, patiently listening to me.

"Listen, Paulette, thanks for talking to me. Can you have her call me when she gets in? I should be here till about noon." I gave her my phone number, had her read it back, and hung up.

"Okay," I started, looking at Walsh. "It sounds like we might have a black widow on our hands."

He frowned. "Sergeant?"

"Our Rhonda was married twice, then she shacked up. Her second husband and her boyfriend are dead, and now her boss is missing. See any common threads?"

"All the men in her life end up dead?"

Walsh stated the obvious. I handed him the page with the names of her husbands along with the scribble *Corner Brook 10 years ago* written on it.

"Follow up with the NC on this one," I ordered.

"You mean the Mounties?" he asked, hesitant.

"No, squirt, I mean the Newfoundland Constabulary. They're the law on the Rock."

"Oh, right, sorry." He shook his head. "Forgot."

He walked away to telephone Newfoundland. I noticed Frank standing a few feet away, amused by this exchange.

"Inspector Burghezian," I started formally. "May I help you?"

He chuckled and sat down in the plastic chair Walsh had warmed. "Well, Sergeant McBriar, how is it having the dumb help assigned to you?"

I leaned back and smiled. Nobody around could hear us. "Was I like that five years ago? Tell me I wasn't that goofy—was I, Frank?"

"Worse." He smiled. "You were trying *so* hard to be Joe Friday. You never wore the same suit two days straight to prove that you had more than three in your closet. Your shoes were too shiny, and your shirts were always crisp." He grinned in satisfaction. "Total keener."

I looked down the hall at Walsh, struggling to get a long distance line, and sighed. "Think he'll come around and become a good cop?"

"Why not?" Frank smiled. "You did."

I sighed again. "Should I go easier on him, then?"

"Nah." Frank shook his head firmly. "Half the fun in this job is bossing around rookies."

༺༻

Frank, Walsh, and I walked to our local diner for lunch. Rhonda Clark hadn't called me, and there was no answer when I called Paulette back just before twelve.

The NC would send us a copy of the file they had on Rhonda Clark/Partridge/Wilkins/Clark, but it was coming by regular mail and wouldn't be here until Thursday or Friday. I sat in the booth, my back to the counter, facing the window. Walsh ogled the new waitress as she poured coffees at the next booth.

"So, squirt, what do you think about this case?" Frank asked him.

Walsh shrugged. "I agree with Ian, sir. I think she's a serial murderer."

Frank sat up and looked back and forth at us. "Man killer? You think we got one of those?"

I wrinkled my nose. "Yeah. Smells funny. She says she came home to find the door kicked in and the boyfriend dead, but it doesn't add up."

"Ian figures the door was kicked in, but only after our victim was killed," Walsh added. "Also, he was killed with a knife from the kitchen, not one brought in by the killer." He seemed intrigued by this detail.

I leaned forward. "I'd like to know why the victim wasn't at work. Our suspect says he worked nights, as a baker. If she's telling the truth, then why was he home?"

"Maybe he was home sick?" Walsh offered. "She wouldn't expect him to be home. She'd assume he was at work."

"Could be," I said. "He's home sick, she comes in with the new squeeze, gets surprised, and they fight. New squeeze stabs the boyfriend and takes off, kicking in the door to give her an alibi. Good thinking, squirt."

"Patrick, sir. Detective Constable Patrick Walsh," he corrected.

I smiled. He was defining his territory. That was good. "Patrick it is."

CHAPTER 3

At three-fifteen, I stood outside the main entrance to Ethan's school, waiting for the bell to ring. Right on time, the red metal bell on the outside wall rang like a fire truck, and two minutes later a horde of young children raced out into the school field.

Ethan and his friend Alan, sticking together like Siamese twins, ran up to me, giggling. "Hey, Pops." Ethan jumped up and down, "Can Alan come over and play at our house?"

I smiled and rubbed the top of his head. "Sure, sport, if it's all right with his mom."

The two boys raced down the grass to my house and thundered up the front porch steps. Off to one side, I saw Vivian, in a tight pencil skirt and matching sweater, shuffling toward me.

Before I could decide what to do, she waved at me and motioned me over to her.

I walked slowly in her direction, smiling politely. I was not sure what she wanted. "Hi, Vivian. Nice to see you again."

She grabbed my arm and pulled me around to face the street. "Thank you for making Alan's lunches," she said. "I want to have you with coffee, and I won't take no for an answer."

She led me toward her house. It suddenly dawned on

me where we were going. "Where would you like to go for coffee?" I asked, playing dumb. "Should we drive there?"

"No, don't be silly," she said.

She giggled and tugged my arm close to her, her left breast rubbing against my elbow. It was not an unpleasant feeling. We crossed the street and stopped at her front door. She opened the door to her apartment and pulled me in behind her, then closed and conspicuously locked the door.

"Sit. Get comfortable," she ordered and dragged a coffee pot onto the gas burner.

I sat at the Formica dining table and waited politely for the coffee to perk. I decided to take the lead in the conversation. "So how is Alan doing?" I volleyed. "Ethan really likes him. They're good buddies."

She clattered around the small kitchen, arranging a tray with biscuits, cream, and sugar, and carried it through to the coffee table by a loveseat behind me.

"Yeah, they get along great," she said, almost as an afterthought. "Do you take anything in your coffee?"

"Just black for me, thanks," I mumbled.

"You like it hot and steamy, huh?" she joked.

I said nothing.

"Come. Sit here," she ordered. I raised myself up and sat at one end of the love seat.

She slid herself to the center cushion, inches from me, and poured coffee.

"Nice weather we've been having," she said, out of nowhere.

"Yeah, it's been a warm month. Hope it continues," I answered mechanically.

She fanned her face with her hand and fluttered her eyebrows. "Gosh, it's hot in here," she huffed. "Do you want to take your coat off?"

I shook my head. It was not that hot. "I'm fine, thanks."

"Well, I'm boiling," she said and peeled her sweater up over her head, throwing it onto the floor beside her.

She was wearing a thin, silky blouse underneath. I looked down and saw that she absolutely was not wearing a bra. She slid closer to me and wrapped her arm around my neck, pulling me close.

"So," she cooed. "You like what you see?"

I stared down at her olive eyes and inviting lips. For a fleeting moment, I wondered if I could have a brief affair, if I could "graze in a different meadow," but still keep Karen. Just for that moment.

No, I couldn't live with myself doing that. Karen was better than that. I was better than that, no matter how enticing the idea was.

I smiled sadly. "Look." I sighed. "I can't. I'm sorry. You're an extremely attractive woman and if I wasn't attached, I'd be more than willing, but I couldn't do that to Karen. She doesn't deserve that."

She looked up at me, gauging my answer. "What if she never finds out? She wouldn't have to know," she offered.

"I'd know," I argued. "I would always be thinking of it, no matter what I told myself."

She slowly uncurled her arm from my neck, stood up, and smoothed her skirt. She picked her sweater up off the floor and carefully brushed it off, her lovely, shapely back clearly visible through her shirt the whole time. I got the distinct impression she was trying to change my mind. She came closer in that moment than she would ever know.

"I'm not a tramp, you know," she whispered. "I'm just a normal woman, you know, and I need a man every once in a while. Is that so bad?"

In that moment, I felt terrible for her. I felt bad that I'd rejected her, but also sad that she was trying to seduce a near stranger.

"I know what you're going through," I said softly. "I was alone for a very long time, too."

She turned to me and smiled, the smile a waitress gives to one who complains about the food.

"Yeah, you're a good guy. I get it. Listen, if you don't

want the coffee, I understand. You probably have to be somewhere, right?"

I shook my head and reached for the coffee cup. Now that the air was cleared, the tension gone, I felt at ease with her. "Alan's a cute kid. You must be very proud of him."

She seemed to relax, too. Her shoulders sagged somewhat and she smiled warmly back. "I do the best I can for him." She sat on a chair across from me, pulling her sweater back on. "Listen," she said, leaning forward. "Please believe that I'm not just some hose-bag, okay? I mean, yeah, I like men, but it's hard to meet anyone nice in the hotel, you know?"

I frowned and put my cup down. "Why is your husband in jail?"

"Check fraud," she said flatly. She shrugged. "He doesn't like to work for a living."

"That sucks." I grimaced. "And it doesn't set a good example for Alan."

We talked for about an hour. They were from Elora, just outside Toronto, and they had been here for a year when her husband was arrested for the umpteenth time and put away for a long stretch. It seems that writing bad checks was one thing, but he had sold newspaper subscriptions door-to-door and, when the subscribers paid by check, he had "kited" the amount and changed the payee name to his own. The judge threw the book at him.

✺✺✺

Around five o clock, I walked home and started dinner. Alan and Ethan were playing with GI Joes and watching TV in the basement. Karen would be home soon. My mind bounced back and forth between thinking of Karen—her long dark hair cascading around her as we made love—and Vivian's filmy shirt exposing her round breasts and curvy back. I had to focus. I tried to think of the case: where was

Rhonda? Why did she run off? And when would she be back?

Where, also, was Gustavo De Melo? He had driven her home—I was certain he had gone up to the apartment with her, and I thought he might have been the one to kick in the door. I still figured he was sleeping with her, but I couldn't confirm that until I spoke to him in person.

A whistling sound in the driveway—a Beetle—brought me out of my deep thought. Karen came up the steps one at a time, humming softly to herself.

"Hello?" she called.

I came out of the kitchen. "Hi, in here," I answered. "How was your day?"

She wrapped an arm around me and kissed my neck. "Fine."

In that one instant I knew I'd made the right decision.

"What's for dinner, chef?" she asked and kissed my neck again.

I turned to face her. "Chili con carne. Are you hungry?"

She looked into my eyes and frowned. "What's wrong? Work go badly?"

I shook my head. "We lost a witness. She's run off somewhere. I think she could be our killer."

Karen frowned at me. "Be careful, okay? I worry about you."

Ethan and Alan came thundering up the stairs, panting. "Hey, Pops," Ethan squealed, "Can Alan stay for dinner? He says your food smells yummy."

"I suppose, but maybe his mom already made dinner?" I asked, trying to keep the image of Vivian's breasts out of my mind.

"If not," Karen added, grinning warmly, "does she want to join us? It'd be nice to meet one of the other moms. What do you say, sweetheart?"

I mumbled something—I can't remember what—and Karen smiled.

"Great. Let's do that then," she said. "Alan, call your mom and I'll talk to her, okay?"

Vivian showed up a few minutes later, wearing a thicker blouse and a looser skirt, and introduced herself to Karen. The four of them sat at one end of our dining table, talking while I finished making dinner. I brought out dinner rolls and butter then steaming bowls of chili and drinks for everyone. It felt like working in my father's restaurant again, except that I knew what both these women's boobs looked like. That was my guilty secret—I kept it to myself.

Dinner was pleasant. Karen and Vivian talked about work, children, and life in general, and I dutifully poured milk and wine and refilled the bread bowl. Around eight o clock, after coffee, Vivian thanked us for the meal and walked home, hand in hand with Alan. Karen stood at the door waving then, as they turned the corner, she stepped back, closed the door, and glared at me.

"What?" I asked, puzzled.

"You know damn well what," she snapped. "You were ogling her the whole time she was here! You think I didn't notice? Why don't you run over and ask her for a date—I'm sure she would be amenable to a quick leg-over. Go on—catch up to her, why don't you?"

She stormed off to the bedroom, slipped off her shoes, and removed her earrings. She undressed and put on a pair of flannel pajamas, all the time scowling. I watched her with amusement, at her fuming about what she'd misunderstood, and realized again just how much I loved her.

She saw me smiling at her and sneered at me, furious. "Well, what are you waiting for, dumbass? I'm sure that little redheaded tramp would be happy to jump you. You don't have to settle for just me, you know. I'm sure she'd offer you sex."

I gave Karen a warm, loving look. "She did," I said simply. "I turned her down."

Her face fell, and her mouth dropped open. "What? When?" she barked.

"This afternoon, after school. She said she was lonely and offered me a good time. I said no."

Karen glared at the hall toward the front door and fumed. "Why, that filthy bitch. Thinks she can steal my guy? I should go right over there and slap her silly!"

I started to laugh, which was possibly the wrong thing to do, but I was amused at the about-face Karen made. She saw me laughing and scowled at me, then her face softened and she smiled.

"You said no, huh?" she asked. I nodded. She thought for a moment. "Were you tempted to say yes?"

I shrugged. "I'm a guy—what do you think?"

She wrapped her arms around me and hugged me. "Why did you say no, then?" she asked, softly.

I kissed her nose. "Because I love you."

She kissed me gently then leaned back and kneed me in the thigh.

I bent over in pain. "What was that for?"

Karen wagged a finger at me. "For even thinking about it." She looked down at my thigh then poked her finger between my eyes. "Sorry about that. But don't ever think that thought again."

In that moment, I realized how committed I was to spending my life with her. She would find out exactly how I felt soon enough.

CHAPTER 4

Thursday morning was warm for late September, but the wind blew around the dust in the air and made it hard to walk without squinting.

I pulled into the station parking lot and sat in my car until nine o clock. At one minute after nine, I walked into the detectives' room and sat at my desk. Five minutes later, Walsh scrambled in, straightening his hair and tugging at his jacket.

"Hot date?" I asked.

He grinned. "I met this girl—a woman, really—who likes cops. I flashed my ID and she bought me drinks."

I sighed. "Any word on our missing suspect, Rhonda?"

He sniffed slightly. "I called her cousin's place. Rhonda showed up last night. She said she'd been out looking for a place to live. Apparently she decided that she doesn't want go back to that apartment after all, so she went looking for a new one."

"You don't buy it, do you?" I asked.

"No way." Walsh shook his head. "She was adamant before about wanting to get back there, but now she's looking for a different place to live? I think she was out with the new boyfriend."

"Speaking of which," I said. "Have we heard yet from the elusive Mr. De Melo?"

Walsh pulled out his notebook and started to read. Frank wandered over and nodded to us.

"Oh, hello, Inspector," Walsh said. "No, no news there. His office staff is just two people, and they know his routine like clockwork. He goes to visit his daughter and her family in Raleigh around this time every year, and he always drives down. However, his truck is at his office, and he hasn't called in since Tuesday."

"He works nights," I said, playing devil's advocate. "Maybe they just missed him?"

"I thought of that." Walsh shook his head again. "He calls them at five every night, then at eight every morning— his way of making sure they're in on time and not sneaking out early."

I leaned back and rubbed my eyes. Karen had become very excited by me being propositioned by another woman and showed me just how excited the previous night. Maybe it was her love for me. Maybe she was just marking her territory. In any case, I was exhausted.

"Tell you what," I said. "Let's interview Rhonda before she takes off again, and then we'll look for Gustavo. He's got to be around here somewhere."

We called Paulette to be sure Rhonda would be home. She was still sleeping, we were told. Walsh drove us to the cousin's house in Richmond Hill. It was in a nineteen-fifties planned community, a wide suburban road with a sweeping curve that made it look like the street went on forever. The Flaherty house was one-half of a duplex, separated from the other side by a neat, low hedge on a trim lawn. Walsh pulled his Polara into the driveway, behind a York Regional Police cruiser, and we knocked on the side door.

The door was opened by a large man in a police uniform. He had wavy salt-and-pepper hair in a tight mat, a thick push-broom moustache, and thin gold-rimmed glasses. He had the arms of a bouncer and the build of a lumberjack. In any gathering, he would look formidable. He glanced at our badges and smiled.

"Sergeant McBriar, Constable Walsh, please come in. I'm Jim Flaherty. Rhonda should be out any moment.

Please. I made coffee." His voice lilted, an Irish tenor, which sang as he spoke.

We shook hands and sat in the living room, me in a flowery wing chair and Walsh straddling two cushions of a plump, sea-green sofa. Officer Flaherty appeared from the kitchen with small dishes, cups, spoons, and forks on a tray. A moment later, a slight woman, a fortyish brunette version of Rhonda Clark, followed him with a pot of coffee and a tray of sliced cake. We stood politely. She introduced herself as his wife, Paulette. She was a pretty, petite woman with the perpetual expression of someone who helped the needy—a soft smile and a slightly pained expression, like the nuns I knew.

We introduced ourselves and quietly let her pour coffee and serve cake.

"Thanks very much for seeing us." I gave them a warm, disarming smile. "We just need to talk to you and to Rhonda and clear up some loose ends, that's all."

Jim scowled and leaned back.

"Something wrong, officer?" I asked.

"Jim," he corrected. "Y'know, in Newfoundland I used to work with me uncle pumpin' out sewage tanks. I come to recognize crap from quite a distance all right."

"Okay, Jim." I smirked. "Straight to the chase. Where did Rhonda go yesterday?"

He smiled softly and nodded at me with respect, remembering something. "You're the one what got shot a year ago—April, was it?"

His wife stared at me, as though seeing a ghost. I smiled at her. "March of last year—four bullets to the chest and shoulder. I'm fine now, though," I explained.

He leaned forward. "Takes balls to come back after that. Good on you, Sergeant," he grunted.

"Ian," I offered.

"Ian." He smiled. "Rhonda's sure upset about Ed's death, but I think something's not right."

"How do you mean?" I asked.

"She's more vexed by maybe losing her job than by Ed's passing. That don't ring true. What do you think?"

I shrugged. I wouldn't share my thoughts much around Rhonda's cousin. I wasn't sure of her loyalties. I took a bite of the coffee cake and frowned. "You made this? It's extremely good." I smiled at Paulette and took another bite.

Officer Flaherty beamed and sat up straight. "I made it—always enjoyed cooking. It relaxes me."

"Could I get the recipe?" I asked sincerely.

He squinted, thinking. "Trade you recipes," he countered.

"Apple cheesecake?" I offered.

He grinned. "Done."

From the back of the house, I heard a shuffling sound. Rhonda walked out to join us, clutching the collar of a plaid flannel robe, scuffing pajama pants on the floor behind her.

I stood up politely, and Walsh did too, not quite sure why I was standing for just her.

"Hi, Rhonda," I said. "How are you doing?"

She shrugged sadly and sat on a dining chair, slightly behind her cousin.

"Okay, I guess," she mumbled.

"We just need to ask you a couple of questions," I soothed. "You're doing okay? Do you need anything from the apartment—something that we can bring you?" I asked, trying to put her at ease.

She shook her head.

"Should we call your boss to explain why you're not at work?" Now I wanted to make her worry.

"Paulette called my work." She sighed. "Gustavo's not in. I don't know where he be."

The Newfie accent got stronger being around her cousin, I noted.

"Have you worked for him long?" I asked casually, jotting in my notebook.

"Why?" She appeared wary.

I shrugged, as though it was inconsequential. "I have a

list of questions I have to ask, that's all. Like, how long had you known Ed?"

She looked down, thinking. "I met Ed about two year ago." She shrugged. "He were divorcing his wife. I liked him. I let him move into my apartment." She took a coffee mug from the tray and poured herself a half cup. She sipped slowly, looking down, thoughtful.

"How long have you worked at this job?" I asked, again casually.

I examined a piece of lint on the end of my pen, as though it were more important than the question. She relaxed slightly, easing back into the chair and adjusting her feet.

"I got the job 'bout that time. Gustavo ran an ad in the paper for cleaners what could work night, so I called. I like it, goin' to them fancy offices and ridin' the elevators and such." She smiled at the memory.

It seemed to me that, when her hair was done and she wore makeup, she would probably be a fairly attractive woman. I tried to play that angle.

"Must be tough, a pretty lady like you, living with a guy like Ed."

She fluttered her eyelids and grinned, her teeth flashing under her dark eyes. "Bless your heart, no, he were a gentleman, were Ed. He liked his drink, but then what man don't? Nah, he were fine."

Walsh leaned forward to talk. I half wanted to swat him and tell him to shut up, but I thought it would do less damage to let him ask his question.

"Did Ed have any enemies?" Walsh asked gruffly. "Anyone threaten him?"

Rhonda shook her head twice.

"Was he doing anything illegal?" he grunted. "Was he selling drugs or something?"

Rhonda shook her head emphatically.

"How about his ex-wife? Was she possessive?" I asked softly. I would be the soft cop today.

"Not a bit, son. She didn't want nothing of his stuff."

I glared at Walsh and he leaned back. "Sorry, that's not what I meant," I corrected. "Did she resent him living with you?"

Rhonda thought for a moment and shrugged. "Nah, she were fine with it. She got her a new man, too."

I wrote some notes, letting the room get quiet, then smiled at the Flahertys. "Would you good people mind if we spoke to Rhonda alone? We'll be brief."

Jim nodded and stood, taking his wife's arm. "C'mon, hon," he lilted. "Let's go for a walk."

They walked out the side door and onto the sidewalk. I watched them head down the street for a minute, then I turned to Rhonda. Walsh had no idea what I was going to say.

"So," I started, "How about telling me what really happened?"

Rhonda slid back a little in her seat, moving away from me. She glanced at Walsh then back at me, looking for an escape route, then shook her head, slowly. "I don't understand. What do you mean," she said unconvincingly.

I leaned forward. "You don't really expect us to believe that story about finding Ed like that, do you?"

Walsh looked back and forth between us, wisely saying nothing.

"Who kicked the door in—De Melo? Or did you do it?" I shook my head. "No, you're not nearly strong enough. It was De Melo, wasn't it?" I stared at her, a cold, unfeeling stare.

She shrank farther back into her seat. Walsh just kept looking between us, fascinated.

Rhonda started to say something, then she shook her head and turned bright red with anger. "It's not what you think!" she snapped. "He was already dead! We didn't do nothing to him!"

"Okay." I leaned back and put my notebook down on the arm of my chair. "Tell me what did happen, then."

She leaned forward, stared at her slippers, and ran her fingers through her hair, slowly, thinking about what to say. "Gustavo likes me. He's all alone, now his wife's gone, and he likes me. He's fun to be with, you know? We'd go to my place after work some nights. Ed didn't seem to know, nor care if he did." She hunched her feet up onto her chair and hugged her knees. That told me she was scared of what was coming next. "So anyways, me and Gus, Gustavo, went up on Tuesday, and the door's open a crack. First thing is, I thought Ed done left it open, the silly git, but then we sees that the television's on, and all we sees is white on the screen, cause he watches the CBC and they go sign early, you know?"

The detail in her statement made me think this part was true. She wasn't that inventive.

"Gustavo looks in and we sees Ed there, lying like you found him, dead."

"Did you check to see if he was really dead?" I asked sharply. "Did you call an ambulance?"

Rhonda shook her head and looked up at me, tears in her eyes. "He were cold, been dead for hours, I figure. So I says to Gustavo, if the cops come now it'll look like you done it, so go. We argued. He didn't want to just run off. He says we should tell you fellas exactly what happened, but I didn't think you'd believe us. So I told him to close the door and then kick it in, so's it'd look like we got robbed. Then Gus leaves, and I calls Annie over so's it'd look like her and me found Ed together."

I believed that version, as far as it went. I didn't think it was the whole truth, however. "That's why Annie heard a commotion? You and Gustavo were arguing?"

She nodded and slid her feet down to the ground. I picked up my notebook, opened it to an earlier page, and stared at a blank sheet. She couldn't tell, though.

"We contacted the Newfoundland Constabulary about you," I said, pretending to read. "We heard that you were married twice before living with Ed."

She would assume I got the information from else-where, not her cousin.

"I were young—too young," she said firmly. "I married Zack Partridge 'cause I were pregnant. He done right by me, but the baby didn't take. I lost it at four month, so we broke up. Then I married Cameron, but he got the consumption and died. Too bad—he were a good man. He worked for the government, and he made good dough. We lived good."

She stretched her legs straight out and arched her back, fluffing her hair like a pin-up girl in one of those garage calendars.

Walsh ogled her. I glared at him.

"You moved out here about ten years ago, is that right?" I asked.

Her pajama top opened slightly, revealing a slim, pale shoulder. Walsh focused on her skin, moving his eyes from her neck to her armpit. I glared at him and rolled my eyes. Rhonda saw none of this.

"I come here just after Paulette and Jim did. They said it were a lovely place to find work. Weren't no work back home less you fished for cod, so I come away," she said.

"Did you always do this kind of work?" I asked.

She sat up straight and shrugged. "I worked in a dry cleaner's out here, for a long time after Cameron passed, but they done closed. After the benefits ran out I needed a way to pay the bills. I got this job."

She fumbled around in the pockets of her bathrobe, fi-nally pulling out a battered pack of cigarettes and a brass lighter. She dragged a bent cigarette out of the pack, straightened it somewhat, and stuck it into her mouth. Hunching down, she lit the end carefully then leaned back and blew a cone of blue smoke into the room.

"How long have you been seeing Gus?" I asked.

I wanted to sound as casual as possible when talking about her lover.

She shrugged. "I dunno. A year, maybe. Don't get me wrong, Ed were okay, but Gus—" She snickered then beamed. "He's got a way of makin' the stars come out, you know?"

Walsh's eyes widened. Even quickly glancing at him, I could tell that he was mentally undressing Rhonda. I ignored him and leaned forward.

"Do you have any idea who could have done this to Ed?" I asked softly.

She shook her head.

"Where's Gus now?" I asked. "He's not at home, he's not at work. We can't find him. Is he okay? We're worried about him."

Rhonda hugged the robe tight around her, the cigarette dangling from her lips like a floppy white noodle. She thought for a while, wrinkling her brow before speaking. "He got this room in an apartment block. A few times we went there, you know, when Ed was home. It's not much, but it were private, and it were close by." She looked up, tears in her eyes, showing more emotion at revealing her love nest than she had for Ed's death.

"Where is it? Does it have a phone?" I asked.

Walsh got his notebook out.

She shook her head again. "Like I said, it ain't much. It's just a room in a building, is all." She took Walsh's notebook and drew a rough map of the apartment. "I ain't too good with writing and numbers and such, but here you go," she mumbled.

She handed me the notebook and explained where it was, describing the building at length. What she described was a building which had been an elegant place to live thirty years ago, but had declined after years of neglect—a brick building near Bayview and Davisville, with curving masonry balconies overlooking the street. She described their room and told us how to get into the building without a key.

The Flahertys came back in as we were getting ready to leave. Jim Flaherty pulled me aside and lowered his voice.

"Everything okay? She a suspect?" he asked, worried.

I shook my head. I didn't think his family was in danger, in any case. "I think she got in over her head, but there's no evidence she did it," I said.

It was not a lie, just not the whole truth. He needed reassurance more than he needed to worry right now, I thought. He nodded, unconvinced. He was a good cop. He knew exactly what I wasn't telling him.

"Want me to keep an eye on her, then?" he asked.

I understood him precisely, too. I nodded.

⌘

After Walsh and I got into the Polara, I reviewed my notes. "Could you try to be a little more discreet?" I grunted.

"How do you mean, boss?" he asked, genuinely puzzled.

"You were mentally undressing her," I lamented. "It was painfully obvious."

"No." He laughed. "I was way past that. I was already in the hotel room ordering breakfast."

I shook my head. He chirped the tires and pulled out into traffic.

We drove to the apartment building on Rhonda's map and parked in a side alley. I checked my watch—eleven o clock. The front security door was locked, as we'd been told to expect, but with my car key I slid the latch over and opened the lock in about five seconds. Even better, to anyone walking by it would just look like I was unlocking the door.

Walsh followed me down a hallway to the back of the building. It was paneled in a good oak veneer, but it had seen better days. The carpet, a dark patterned shag, had bald spots where thousands of feet had scuffed it over the years. It made the dimly lit hall seem even less inviting.

Walsh stayed close behind me as we looked for a gray

metal door that Rhonda had described. We walked through into a short corridor and stopped at a wood door at the end of the corridor.

I felt along the top of the doorframe and found a key, as Rhonda said I would. I opened the door, put the key back, and went in.

Thirty years ago, this was probably the maintenance man's office.

It had a toilet on one wall, a small kitchenette with a desk along another wall, and a window area, which would have been occupied by a sofa and chair in the past.

A double bed was placed there now. In the bed, face down, was a large man with pale brown skin and a bald head, dressed only in gray boxer shorts and a faded orange T-shirt.

Great, I thought, *another dead body*. I didn't want to disturb any evidence, so I approached him cautiously. As I got close, he groaned and rolled over. Walsh and I both jumped involuntarily.

The man opened his eyes and saw us. He sat up and roared with anger. "What! Who are you? Get out! Get out!" he growled and flailed his arms at us.

Walsh stepped back and let him rant—the right thing to do. I got out my ID and held it in front of me. The man looked blearily at the badge and sank back onto the bed.

"Mr. De Melo," I barked. "I'm Detective Sergeant McBriar. This is Detective Constable Walsh. We've been looking for you."

He looked at us for a moment then shook his head. "I got to pee."

He staggered to his feet and stood at the toilet, urinating. He smelled drunk. I looked around. There were empty rum bottles, pizza boxes, and coffee cups in a metal garbage can by the foot of the bed.

The man came back, casually adjusting the waistband on his boxers, and sat on the edge of the bed as though this was an everyday visit. He rubbed his face with a pair of weathered, hairy hands and sat up straight to look at us.

"Yup. So?" he asked me, a puzzled look on his face.

I stared at him, scowling. "Do you know why we're here?"

"Probably that thing with Rhonda." He looked at his watch. "Shit, I should go to work."

He tried to stand up, but I pushed on his shoulder and he tumbled onto the bed. Walsh stood back, not knowing what I'd do next. It added to the threat I wanted De Melo to feel.

"You have any idea how much trouble you're in?" I snarled. "You tampered with evidence. I think you may even be responsible for Ed's death. What do you have to say for yourself?"

He shimmied back along the bed, scared, his shoulders scuffing the concrete wall. "We didn't do nothing. I was with Rhonda when we found Ed, that's all. We didn't do nothing. We just found him like that." He was whining now, almost whimpering.

"You kicked in the door after you found him," I yelled. "That put us on a wild goose chase. You've been hiding for two days. That smells guilty to me. Right, Constable?"

Walsh grunted.

De Melo sat up, leaned forward, and made a globe with his hands, a sign that he was trying to formulate a story as he was telling it.

"You don't understand. We found the door kicked in. We came back there after work, because—" He looked around, thinking. "Because Rhonda forgot her purse, and we went back for it. That's when we found Ed." His voice was rough, harsh, a slight Portuguese accent barely there.

"Wrong on all counts," I sneered. "You were humping Rhonda at her place while Ed was at work and here when Ed was home. She told us." I hissed the last sentence.

He winced.

"She told us how you kicked in the door after you

found Ed, to make it look like a robbery. Why would you do that if you weren't guilty?" I asked, almost daring him to prove me wrong, or call Rhonda a liar.

He fidgeted, looking around for something on the bed. He finally found it, a crumpled pack of cigarettes, the same brand Rhonda had smoked an hour before. He poked his finger into the pack, rooting around until he found a lone cigarette, and stuck it into his mouth. He stood up, almost casually, and picked up a pair of pants from the chair. Reaching into a pocket, he retrieved a small lighter, lit the cigarette, then put the lighter away, and let the pants fall to the bed. He sat down and leaned back on his outstretched arms, thinking.

He stared at me, defiant. "You think I killed Ed?" he sneered. "Bullshit. Why would I kill him?"

"How about the fact that that you were banging his girlfriend?" Walsh snapped. "That might piss him off, don't you think?"

De Melo glared at Walsh, his huge brown eyes spitting anger at the young man. De Melo blinked slowly, deliberately then stared at me.

"You," he barked. "You gonna let this kid talk to me like that? You have any idea who I am?"

I smiled. Statements like that came from unimportant men, trying to sound important.

He scowled, an angry, irate scowl. I stared back at him for a minute, still smiling softly. He realized that I wasn't going to back down and his expression faded, slowly changing to mild fear.

"I know exactly who you are," I stated firmly. "You are someone who was there, where Ed Hereford died, someone we've been trying to find for two days. Why are you hiding?"

He leaned forward and rubbed his head, his hairy knuckles sliding over his smooth scalp. He rested his wrists on his knees and looked up, defeated, then sucked on the cigarette some more.

"Look," he started and glanced down at his hands.

That told me he was remembering previous actions. This would probably be something approaching the truth.

He gazed up at me. "Yeah, me and Rhonda. She's a good woman, she really is. Ed's a moron. He doesn't deserve her. She's really pretty, you know. She dressed up for a party a year ago, and that's when I noticed just how pretty she is. Ed just drank and talked about golf with the guys. I asked her to dance. That's when it started between us."

He was referring to the victim in the present tense. That told me he almost certainly didn't kill him, so I shifted my questioning and softened up.

"What really happened the night you found him? The truth now—I'll know if you're lying."

He sucked on the cigarette one more time, stubbed out the lit tip, and tossed the butt into the sink. "We went back to her place, same as most Tuesdays. Ed was supposed to be at work. The door was open, and we found Ed, just like you did, on the floor. We checked to see if he was still alive. He was cold. I tried to roll him on his back, but he was stiff. I couldn't even open his hands, so I left him there, with the knife in him.

"Rhonda started screaming at me, yelling that we had to do something. So she says, 'Let's make it look like we were robbed.' We messed up the living room a bit, and she said I should kick in the door, and so I did, then I got out of there. I hid in the stairwell, and I could hear her knock on the next-door neighbor's, asking her to look in with her, and then I came here and got drunk. I didn't want to go home, and I sure couldn't go to work. I just wanted to come here and be alone for a while."

I wrote down his statement automatically, all the while thinking about what he'd said. "Why Tuesday? Did you always see her on Tuesdays?"

He reached back, patting the bed, looking for another cigarette. He couldn't find one. "Tuesdays, the bakery sells a special rye bread." He sighed. "Ed goes in early on Monday nights, so we knew he'd be out of the way. By nine in the morning, he comes home and I'm long gone. Except this Tuesday," he added sadly.

I looked around at the room. De Melo seemed at ease here, unafraid of being discovered.

"Why did you come here?" I asked. "Weren't you afraid of being disturbed or found out?"

He stood up and shrugged. "I own this building. It's my own private room. The super knows to leave me alone."

"Did you ever bring Rhonda here?"

"A few times, but she didn't like it here. Besides, her place is nicer, and it's got a shower."

He grinned a sly grin, just a man eager to brag about his love life.

"Gustavo, go home." I sighed. "Don't disappear again. We will need to talk to you later."

"Why?" he asked stupidly.

"Because—" I spoke loudly, nose to nose with him, "we have a murder to solve, and you are already guilty of tampering with a crime scene. You want us to arrest you now?"

Walsh whipped out his handcuffs and dangled them playfully. De Melo shook his head and got up. He pulled on his pants, threw on a heavy shirt then a worn corduroy jacket over it, and fumbled for his keys. He chose a silver ignition key and started for the door.

"One sec," I said, puzzled. "How did you get here?"

"In my car," he answered.

"Your truck is at your office. We didn't know you had a car," I stated.

He shook his head, confused.

"Take your car to 52 Division. You know where that is? This morning, please?" I said firmly.

He shrugged and gave a slightly embarrassed nod.

We got into Walsh's Polara and headed back to the station.

Our dispatcher said that the Newfoundland police file

on Rhonda had arrived. That would make for interesting reading, at least. The pathologist had also finished his autopsy on Ed, and that report was sitting in a manila envelope on my desk.

I read the report, a three-page account of Ed's last hours of life. He had eaten a bowl of chicken noodle soup, along with some bread. He had washed that down with a fair amount of whisky and sedatives. Together, that would have made him very drowsy, possibly unconscious.

I shook my head at the notations on the side of the page. "Good lord." I mumbled. I handed the report to Walsh. "He would be so spaced out that he wouldn't be able to fight back. He was a fairly big guy, but this much booze and drugs would have incapacitated him."

Walsh looked at the report, flipping back and forth between the pages, picking out details. "So a woman could have killed him, then?" he asked. "You figure Rhonda looks good for this?"

"Hell, yes. Who else can you imagine that wanted him dead?" I looked at my watch. "Lunch?"

CHAPTER 5

I made some personal phone calls after lunch, checked with the Flahertys that Rhonda was behaving herself, then I went home.

I would cook something nice for dinner. We'd watch TV and snuggle in bed together. I set the table and tossed a salad before Karen got home. Ethan was out back, playing in the driveway beside the garage. This was the time to set my trap. She wouldn't suspect a thing.

Karen raced up the driveway, screeched to a halt just up from the sidewalk, and opened the driver's door. From the front window, I could see her long, slender legs pivot out of the car as she placed her feet gently on the ground. She looked up at me looking at her, smiled, and waved hello.

I listened with schoolboy anticipation as her heels clacked up the porch steps to the front door.

"Hi, honey, I'm home," she joked.

I put down the bread I was cutting, wrapped an arm around her waist, and kissed her—softly, passionately, with an emotion I didn't always show.

"What was that for?" she gasped. "Everything okay?"

"Yeah, fine." I smiled. "Dinner's almost ready. Hungry?"

We talked about her day, Ethan's teacher and the barbecue in ten days. I waited for a lull in the conversation and sprung my trap.

"Hey," I said. "Since we're heading into winter, I thought this weekend might be the last time this year we could have a picnic. What do you say—a day in the country, fresh air? Huh?"

Karen smiled, reading me like a book. "What have you got up your sleeve, Ian? What are you planning?" She leaned forward, waiting.

"Me? Nothing. I mean, I just thought it might be nice to go out into the country, that's all."

She stared at me for a moment longer then picked at her salad. "So this 'nothing' picnic, when is it?" she asked, casually.

"I dunno, how about Saturday? It's supposed to be good weather. We could do it then, huh?"

"Bull," Karen said. I was crestfallen. "Still," she added, "let's pretend that I don't smell a setup and we'll go with that, okay?"

Ethan looked at us and just shrugged.

I grinned. She didn't believe the picnic story. It didn't matter, anyway.

"Great, I'll make sandwiches—we'll have a fun day out there. In the country, I mean."

ぐろくろ

I walk up the steps and round the landing to Rhonda's apartment. The door is open. Ed sits at his dining table, a lit cigarette in one hand, a glass of rye in the other. He looks up, bleary-eyed.

I say something.

"I'm sick," he slurs. "I'm home 'cause I'm sick." He takes a swig of the whisky, his eyes red and swollen, then he puts the cigarette in an ashtray and rubs his face with one hand.

I walk behind him to the kitchen counter and pull a green-handled knife out of the drawer.

He stares at the glass of rye, ignoring me. I speak again, and he looks up at me.

"Just like her," he grunts. "Just like her. Why would she do that to me?"

I jab the knife into his side. He stares at me, puzzled, and looks down at the knife.

"Why?" he asks. "Why would you do that?" He slides off the chair, curls up, and dies.

☙❧

I sat up in bed, sweating. I had no idea what the dream meant. It was important, I knew, but I had no idea why.

Karen grabbed my arm and pulled me down beside her. She hugged me close. "Shh. All better?" she whispered.

"Much better now," I agreed.

☙❧

Friday morning, I sat in the parking lot of 52 Division till ten after nine. Fifteen minutes later, Walsh came in, a file folder under his arm. He smiled broadly and sat across from me, placing placed the folder on my desk. "Guess where I've been?" he smirked.

"Does it involve a woman?" I asked sarcastically.

"Kinda." He grinned. "Rhonda's first husband, the teenager. They got annulled, not divorced."

"Sure." I shrugged. "She's Catholic."

"Right. You are too, Ian. Sir. But then she married…" He opened the folder. "Cameron Wilkins. He worked for the Department of Highways, and he died of 'complications due to intestinal cancer.' He had a family history of cancer, and he'd been diagnosed with it in the past year. However, there's a twist." He pulled a slim silver pen out of his jacket and pointed to a line on the report. "One doctor said that he probably had some years left. Another said he was on borrowed time. I placed a call to the doctor who said he had lots of time, and he remembers the case. He said that he was highly suspicious that Cam died like that. He's been treating people for thirty years, he says, and that case still bugs him."

Walsh lifted a Xeroxed page from the folder and handed it to me. "The doctor did say that he thought the death was suspicious. He said it reminded him of another death from a decade before, also in the Corner Brook area. This was a guy who was a heavy smoker—seems to be a theme there—and he died in about fifty five. The man was doing okay for years, but all of a sudden he died. Doc says it was odd, but the body was cremated, so he let it drop."

"Nice work, Patrick," I said. "I'm impressed." I went on to a different topic. "Are you available for a while tomorrow morning, around nine?"

"Sure." He shrugged. "No problem, boss."

"Good. Drop by my house. Bring that report with you, if you would."

I made some more personal phone calls and cleaned up some paperwork then left early. At three fifteen, I met Ethan and Alan at the school yard.

"Hey, guys," I said. "Do you think Alan would like to have a sleepover tonight? You two can camp out in the basement. I'll set up the tent. What do you say?"

The two squealed with delight at the prospect.

I called Vivian at home and asked if she'd mind having Alan sleep over. It was fine with her. Then I asked her to join us for breakfast, around eight-thirty. She would love to, she answered.

I explained this all to Karen when she got home. She gave me the look you give someone who's just run over your cat, but I hurriedly explained that she should trust me, that I was doing all this for a good reason. She said okay, but I felt like I was on a short leash.

We had dinner, watched TV, and listened to a pair of six-year-old boys playing with GI Joe dolls until they exhausted themselves. The boys went to sleep. We did too, eventually.

∽∾∽

By six-thirty on Saturday morning, I was dressed and poaching chicken breasts for sandwiches. At seven fifteen, Karen came into the kitchen, dressed in tight jeans and a deep V-neck sweater. I stared at her cleavage. I assumed that's why she wore the sweater—staking her territory.

By eight o clock, both boys were awake, watching cartoons. I made eggs and pancakes and put on a large pot of coffee. I figured the house would get very busy, very soon. I was right.

Just before eight-thirty, Vivian stood at the front porch and rang the bell.

Karen opened the door, smiling politely, and ushered her into the kitchen. Vivian was in a slim skirt, with a fluffy wool sweater and a tortoiseshell head band which pulled her red hair back like a flame trailing behind her. I did my best short order cook impression, whipping up breakfast for all five of us. By nine o clock we were all laughing and smiling, munching happily on seconds of everything. The boys were almost comatose from excitement and maple syrup. The doorbell rang again. I stood up before Karen could turn around.

"I'll get it," I sang. I reached the door in two steps and let Walsh into the front entryway.

He nodded at Karen, then his eyes fixed on Vivian and opened wide. "Hi. Who's your lovely friend?" he purred. He was just short of salivating on my carpet.

"Patrick, this is Vivian. Vivian, Patrick. He's a detective in our squad."

They shook hands, slowly, purposefully. Their eyes never left each other.

I asked a couple of aimless questions about work, and

he answered them as though he'd invented policing, with a brashness and authority clearly intended to impress Vivian.

I then asked if he'd mind walking her and Alan home, as we had an errand to run. He looked at me as if I'd given him the keys to the Ferrari. He agreed, casually offering to take them both out for lunch later. The three left, and the house went eerily quiet. Karen smirked at me, satisfied.

"You orchestrated that well." She grinned. "Nice going, you're out of the doghouse."

"Thanks." I smiled, looking at the front door. "You think they'll be okay?"

"She'll eat him alive," Karen joked.

I chuckled. "Serves him right—do him good."

❦❦❦

By ten-thirty, I'd loaded up a huge picnic lunch, and some papers I refused to let Karen see, and we drove north on Highway 400, away from the city and up toward the sparse rural area known affectionately as "cottage country."

After about forty minutes of driving, Karen was perplexed as to why I was going so far from home for just a picnic. I headed east through the sleepy village of Holland Landing and zigzagged up to the northernmost tip of Warden Avenue, the bustling Toronto street which, this far north, was now just a deserted gravel road. We rolled past dairy farms, sheep farms, sod farms and wheat fields, Ethan pressing his nose against his window, ogling the scenery.

"Will you please tell me where we are going?" Karen asked, exasperated.

"Georgina," I explained.

"Another girlfriend?" she sniffed. "Should I have dressed up?"

"You look fine. Georgina isn't a she, it's a town," I soothed. "We're almost there."

We drove past the half dozen houses that made up the

village of Georgina, turned east, and then north again at a sign that read *Fairbank Avenue*. It was lined with large flat lots, populated by modest, well-kept houses, nestled behind hedges and split rail fences—the summer homes of accountants and lawyers.

Fairbank Avenue ended at a T-intersection. Across the street Karen could see Lake Simcoe, the stiff breeze of this cool day whipping up gray waves that splashed onto the sandy beach just a few yards away.

Ethan gasped at the view. "Can we go over there, Pops, can we, huh?"

"Ask me in an hour," I answered cryptically.

I turned right and paralleled the lake. Ethan was still gawking at the waves. A few seconds later, I turned into a narrow, curving, tree-lined side street.

"Who lives here?" Karen asked. "Some rich Mafia friends of yours?"

I smiled. "I don't know who owns the place," I said.

I took a scrap of paper from my pocket and read an address. It was three houses down, on the water. I pulled into a narrow driveway, parking behind a huge, pale-purple Buick Electra.

From the Buick stepped a woman in a skirt suit the same color as the car, with matching purple shoes and a purple suede purse.

She was in her fifties, slim—a Jackie Kennedy with bobbed strawberry hair under a purple hat.

She met me and reached out a hand. "Mr. McBriar? Right on time, I see. Hi, it's nice to meet you."

I took her hand and introduced Karen and Ethan.

"Hi, Audrey Rogers. They call me the lavender lady. It's my favorite color." She shrugged. "Come, I'll show you around." She turned on a lavender heel and marched away from us.

I looked behind me at the property. It was the size of a regular house lot. At the street end of the angled driveway, a hedge on either side gave privacy from the road. The driveway bisected the lot front to back, ending at a bungalow. The lot had a big maple tree, also shielding the bungalow from the street. The bungalow, clad in neat white siding, had a short porch leading out from a front door down to a flagstone path facing the driveway.

"Shall we go in?"

The woman went into the bungalow. I followed, Ethan's hand in one hand, a silent Karen's in the other. We stomped up the steps and followed Audrey inside. She rattled off details about square footage, kitchen appliances, and plumbing upgrades. I ignored this completely. I was stunned by the view of the lake from the living room window.

"There are two bedrooms—here and here—and your bathroom is there."

The woman waved her arms expansively. Karen ignored her and walked straight past the sofa and chair that framed the living room to the same large picture window. It looked onto a rolling lawn then on to a short beach. On one side of the lawn was a barbecue and a swing set, on the other was a flagstone path leading to a small boathouse and a dock.

Karen's mouth was wide open.

The "lavender lady" was still talking. "I see you've noticed the view. Of course, that's one of the best features of this property. The house is insulated, so it would be a marvelous winter retreat as well. You can get a foldout sofa bed in case you have guests. What business are you in, Mr. McBriar?"

"I'm with the Toronto Police Department."

"Right, you did say. As I told you last time, my parents were not inclined to sell until my father broke his hip, so we hope it will go to a family that will love it as much as we have."

At that, Karen's eyes shot up and glared me. For the first time, she realized what I was doing.

"How much are you asking again?" I asked casually.

"Twenty eight," the woman said, matter-of-factly.

Karen was now staring straight at me.

"Does that include the furniture?"

"Well, for that we could negotiate." She smiled, waiting for my rebuttal.

"Will you take twenty five for everything?" I asked.

Audrey frowned and looked at me, formulating her answer. "This is a waterfront home. These lots are rare, getting rarer every day, you know," she scolded.

"Yes, but it's been on the market all summer, and if you wait any longer, you'll have to hold it over the winter," I said. "Also, its neighbor sold for twenty four ten weeks ago."

She nodded coyly. "You do your homework, don't you?"

"So, what do you say? It's a good offer."

Audrey looked at me, her poker face still trying to read me. "Don't you need to arrange a mortgage before making an offer?" she asked cautiously.

I shook my head. "I would be writing a check. Financing is not an issue."

Karen's eyes widened. She gasped. "Excuse us," she barked. She dragged me off to one corner and pulled my face down to hers. "Ian, what the hell are you doing?" she hissed, her nostrils flaring as she snorted at me.

"I'm buying a cottage," I informed her. "Why, what's wrong?" I gave her my best stupid smile.

Karen stared up, studying me. She furrowed her brow. She did that when she was puzzled.

"Don't you like it?" I asked, playfully hooking a finger into the vee of her sweater.

She looked around again. The cottage was cozy and only slightly smaller than our house. A kitchen window looked out to the driveway and front yard. Hanging from the tall maple tree were two ropes and a plank that made up a swing. Beside the kitchen, a round dining table was corralled by four chairs. Between them and the living room, a wood stove on a brick base stood alone, solid and black.

The window in one bedroom let the pale sunlight stream onto a Persian carpet. Out on Lake Simcoe, a single white sailboat skipped over the choppy waves, leaning away from the wind.

I imagined us fishing on the dock, sailing a small boat, spending long hot summer days on the water, having Frank and Helen up for the weekend. It felt right—totally, completely right.

Karen seemed to be thinking the same things. She seemed to be gazing out, mentally walking the back yard to the beach.

"So," I asked again, "Don't you like it?"

"We've got our house the way we want it." She sighed. "Life is fine, it's going well. Aren't you happy with how it's going for us?"

"Sure," I agreed. "But wouldn't it be nice to have somewhere nice to go? Somewhere like this?"

She sighed, almost moaning. "But why, Ian? Why this place? Why a cottage?"

I glanced out to the back lawn and leaned down to her, face to face. I pointed at the window. "Imagine when Ethan has kids. Where should he take them? Imagine when we're old and want to retire somewhere quiet. Can you think of a better place in the whole wide world than right here? Now tell me, sweetheart, what do you think of this cottage?"

Karen's eyes welled up. I took a half step back. I'd said something wrong. "It's paradise," she whimpered. "It's beautiful."

I grinned and led her back into the living room and turned to Audrey. "So, is it a deal?"

She smiled widely. "I don't think Dad will let it go for twenty five. I could go to twenty seven, but no less."

"Including furniture," I stated, firmly.

Audrey thought for a moment then nodded. "I'm sure you'll love it as much as we do." She smiled. "When did you want possession?"

"Let's say January first, nineteen seventy five. We'll

start off the last quarter of the century here. How's that?" I nodded at Karen, who smiled back and nodded, still slightly stunned.

Audrey nodded again and pulled out some forms. "Just over three months—very good. What name will we put on the bill of sale?"

I nodded at Karen. "Please make it out to Karen Prescott."

Karen stepped back and stared at me, furious. I had no idea why. "What are you doing?" she snapped.

"Buying you a cottage?" I answered.

"You were buying it for you, you said. Why would you put it in my name?" she snapped again.

"Do you really need to ask? Because I love you," I answered softly.

Karen looked at Audrey and grimaced, a professional, pasted-on smile. "Would you excuse us, Audrey? Ethan, stay inside." She stared at me. "You—come."

She grabbed my jacket and dragged me out onto the back lawn, slamming the door behind us.

I looked down, shuffling leaves with my foot as she spoke. Audrey and Ethan watched us through the window, the thick glass muffling our voices.

Karen flapped her arms like a pelican. "What kind of an idiot are you?" she yelled. She slapped my arm to punctuate her words.

I spoke softly, even though, inside, they could hear none of what I said.

I reached forward to hug Karen, but she pushed me away. She walked in a circle then clenched her fists against her temples. "Ian, what am I going to do with you?"

I just smiled. Silently, I went down onto one knee. "There's a simple answer to that. You could marry me."

I pulled a small black box from my pocket, tilted my head back, and opened the box. She jumped back, covering her mouth with her hands.

"Karen, will you be my wife?"

A moment later she nodded. I took the ring from the box and put it on her finger. She stretched her hand out, admiring the diamond, and I stood up. Karen threw herself at me, covering my face in kisses.

We walked back in a short while later. Ethan was puzzled. Audrey was teary-eyed.

"A slight change." I grinned. "Please make it out to Karen McBriar."

"That's so romantic," Audrey sniffed. "So, so beautiful. I wish you all the very best of luck." She paused for a moment, frowning. "You could still go twenty eight with the furniture, right?" She was serious.

"No, but I'll invite you to the wedding."

She shrugged, defeated.

We filled out some paperwork—Karen went through it in no time. When I said that I'd lured Karen there for a picnic, Audrey suggested we have it at the cottage. She left us the key and drove off, giving us her best wishes. For a long while, we all sat on the sofa, just looking out at the water. I found some wood and lit a fire in the stove. The day was chilly, but the stove warmed us up in no time.

Ethan ran through to the smaller bedroom, gushing about weekends, friends he would have over, and all the fun things to do at "his farm." Karen brought in the picnic hamper from the car and set it on the dining table. I found a percolator and coffee in the cupboard and glasses for the juice we'd brought for Ethan.

We munched on sandwiches and potato chips, gazing out at seagulls soaring on the gusty wind. After lunch we went for a walk on the lawn. Ethan swung between our outstretched hands.

I took off my shoes and socks and dangled my feet in the lake. The water was cold, but it was now our water, our dock, and our lake. Karen sat beside me, hunching her knees up to her chin against the chill. She leaned against me and kissed my cheek.

I smiled. "What was that for?"

"It's a lovely ring." She stretched her hand out again. "How did you get my size right?"

"You have a signet ring you wear on special occasions. I borrowed it to compare," I confessed.

We sat on the dock for a time, my arm around her shoulder, looking out at the water. Ethan floated leaves and twigs off the dock, watching with fascination as the wind blew them under the dock, only to reappear later below me.

By four-thirty, the sun went low and we were getting cold. I put out the fire. We took our picnic things back to the car. I handed Karen the key Audrey had left us. She took one last look at the living room, sighed, and locked the front door. It felt like leaving an old friend.

She held the key out to me as we walked to the Fury. I shook my head.

"No. You keep it. It's your cottage," I insisted.

She looked down at the brass key in her hand and grinned. She clutched it tight then carefully added it to the other keys on her ring. "I own a cottage," she mumbled, shaking her head. "Unreal."

We headed back to town, Ethan bombarding us with questions about the cottage—whether we could live there full time, how many school friends could come stay at once, and if we could get a dog, because it could swim in the lake.

Karen threw her arm over the seatback and talked to him, the way my mother used to with us on car trips. Ten minutes later he was asleep.

I suggested we celebrate the day by going out to dinner. Karen thought that would be nice. I suggested a small Greek restaurant on Mount Pleasant, reminding her that we'd gone there the day I showed Ethan the house we now lived in.

It seemed a fitting end to a perfect day. I'd started off by pairing up my rambunctious constable with the lusty Vivian and ended it by buying a cottage to give my fiancée as her dowry.

The word hit me as I parked by the restaurant—fiancée.

I was now attached. I froze in my seat. "Hon," I started. "You realize you'll now have to introduce me as your fiancé, right?"

She grinned, delighted at the thought. "Right—you, too." She giggled. "I'll just have to tell the girls at work, of course." She held up her hand and wagged her ring finger. "This is on for keeps."

We ate a light dinner and strolled down Mount Pleasant, window shopping for nothing in particular, and all the while my mind was on the cottage, with Ethan again between us, talking about a sailboat and seagulls.

We headed toward home, and I automatically turned on my police radio.

"Fifty-two-four-eight to dispatch," I said mechanically. "Any messages?"

"Four eight, stand by," came the response.

I perked up. Karen watched me, curious. I waited.

"Four eight, hold," the dispatcher reiterated. "Detective, here you go."

Walsh's voice came on, crackling and distant—a telephone patch-in."

"Sergeant, can I meet you right away, sir?" he said politely.

"I'll be home in ten," I answered.

"Meet you there, then. Bye." The background hiss of his phone faded away.

I pulled into my driveway. Karen and Ethan went inside, and I stood outside, waiting for Walsh.

A minute later, he showed up, clutching a handful of paper and a file folder.

He nodded over my shoulder at my garage. "Doing some mechanical work, boss?" he asked.

I turned my head and saw a pale light on under the garage door. It appeared to move around.

"What the hell?" I mumbled. "Come with me."

We walked softly up the driveway to the garage. I heard voices, low, whispering.

Walsh reached into his jacket for his revolver. I frowned and shook my head. He drew an empty hand back out. Quietly, I reached down and grabbed the garage door handle, then pulled it up with all my might. The big folding door rumbled up, exposing the entire garage.

Inside, a pair of teenage boys stopped dead, as though that made them invisible. They had screwdrivers and pliers on the seat of my Fiat. They'd already taken the faceplate off my AM/FM cassette player. One boy moved first. He rushed around to the far side of my car and ran down the driveway. The second tried to follow him. Walsh got to that boy and swung an arm into his neck, clotheslining him. His legs flipped comically up and he landed on his back as Walsh stood over him, making a fist. The boy cringed and stayed put.

I turned to go after the first boy. He was at the base of the driveway, moving fast. He glanced back and sneered. He thought he was home free.

I ran track in high school. Natives are fast runners, so I ran track. I was tall, skinny, and very fast. I took off after the boy. Five houses away, he was still running at an amazing speed, the energy of youth and fear of getting caught propelling him. Twelve houses away, he could hear me closing on him. I could see his ears turn red as he struggled to keep his pace up. He tired quickly and started to stagger. He spun around, pulled something out of his back pocket, and held it up. He pushed a button on the knife, and a shiny blade flipped out. He pointed it at me, menacingly.

"Piss off, asshole," he sneered. "Piss off. I'll use this, ya know. I'll stab ya."

I rested my knuckles on my hips, grinned, and shook my head slowly. "You have no idea what a big mistake you just made, kid."

I walked slowly back to my driveway, holding the youth's right arm twisted behind his back.

His jacket, torn and dirty, was over his head. His jeans were dusty. His sneakers, which I'd pulled off his feet a block back, were in the gutter. I didn't want to make this easy for him in any way. He walked gingerly, barefoot, staggering in pain on the rough sidewalk.

Karen was beside Walsh, telling him that police were on the way. She glowered at the youth on the ground. It seemed that if she could get away with kicking him, she would. A minute later, a yellow cruiser drove up. Two uniforms got out slowly and strutted menacingly up to us. The senior man, clearly enjoying this, sauntered over to me, adjusting his gun belt as he did. He was older, burly, and at least my height.

"Hey there, Sergeant McBriar," he said.

The youths guessed who I must be. Their eyes widened.

"Evening, Gerry." I handed the knife to the uniform. He sneered and pocketed it. "Arrest them both; charge them with illegal entry, burglary, and destruction of property. This one, assault with a deadly weapon." I twisted my youth's arm slightly and he winced in pain.

The officer scowled at the pair and shook his head. "You two are in such deep shit," he growled. "You have any idea who this man is?"

The one I held started to shake, terrified. His knees buckled. I propped him up, seeing something in him that reminded me of a much younger me, and felt a touch of pity.

"Listen, mister," the youth whimpered. "We were just messing around. We don't want to rip you off. Honest. I'm real sorry, so sorry. I'm very, very, very sorry."

I believed him. Still, I glared at the boy. He shrank, expecting me to hit him.

"Gerry," I growled. "Take them to lockup. Keep them overnight. Then call their parents."

Gerry nodded to his partner, a copy of Walsh in uniform, who cuffed them, thrust the pair into the back of the cruiser, and watched them.

I turned my back to the youths and spoke softly to the

uniform. "Scare them shitless then let their folks take them home tonight."

Gerry glared over at the pair, as though I'd told him something terrible. He nodded. "Figure they just need some smartass lessons?" he mumbled.

I shrugged. "The one with the knife reminds me of me. The other one's a hanger-on. They don't seem like criminal types, but use your judgment. Shake them up. Hell, it's not like they did anything terrible. Just stupid kids, that's all."

"You're letting them off easy then, Ian?" he grunted.

"We've all been young and stupid, huh, Gerry?"

He winked so the boys couldn't see it. "Why do you think I became a cop?" He went back to the cruiser and opened the passenger door. His partner, now behind the wheel, nodded, waiting for instructions. "Sergeant said to beat them up if we have to," he bellowed.

The boys cowered in the back seat and the cruiser drove off. I chuckled softly and walked back to check the Fiat. The boys hadn't gotten very far. They had done no damage. I had the radio faceplate back on in no time and locked up the garage.

Walsh followed me into the house and sat at the kitchen table, putting the stack of papers in front of him.

"Now, where were we?" he joked. "Right—Rhonda Clark." He handed me a sheet of paper. "Her second husband died of cancer, like I said yesterday. The interesting thing is, the doctor I spoke with, who said there was that case he'd seen some time back, the heavy smoker who died? Apparently that guy owned a dry cleaner's. Remember Rhonda said she worked in a dry cleaner's when she first moved out here?"

I leaned back and nodded. "Very good, Patrick, very good." I picked up the top sheet of paper. "But why the urgency to tell me this now?"

"The doctor I spoke to is in Toronto this weekend for a wedding. I know you don't like to be bothered on Sundays, so I figured I'd just talk to him myself. Okay with you?"

"You're doing well, squirt," I said. "Go, ask him all the right questions." I checked my watch. "Have you eaten dinner yet? I can whip you up something, if you like," I offered.

"Thanks, but I have a date." He stood up. "Thanks for that, too." He left, whistling to himself.

CHAPTER 6

*R*honda is at the dry cleaner's, behind the counter. *"Hi," she says. "Something to drop off?"*
I hand her a bundle of clothes. She throws it over her shoulder, onto a larger bundle behind her.

"No problem," she says. "Come back Monday." She hands me a green slip of paper then reaches under the counter and puts a glass jug on the counter, yellow liquid sloshing in it. "Here you go." She smiles. "See you again."

❧❧❧

I sat up, sweating through my tee shirt. The room was not that warm. I looked down. I hadn't woken Karen. I squinted and the numbers on the clock radio stopped dancing. Four in the morning. *Go back to sleep.*

At seven in the morning, I dressed for church. I made coffee for Karen, to have when she woke, and put my prayer book and rosary into my jacket pocket. I would take Communion at Mass, so I wouldn't eat until I got back. I always observed the required fast before Mass.

As I slurped down the last of the coffee and rinsed the cup, I heard a sound coming from the back of the house. Ethan, in his flannel pajamas, ran through, clutching a piece of heavy drawing paper.

"Hi, Pops," he chirped.

He thrust the paper up toward me. Scribbled on it, in crayon, was an inverted V sitting on a square, with a green clump to one side. It was a very good drawing, but I played dumb.

"What is it?" I asked.

"It's my farm. Can we go back there today, huh? Can we, Pops, huh?"

I blinked back tears and squatted down to his level. He grabbed me tight around the neck and hugged for dear life.

"Okay, Pops?" he pleaded earnestly.

Another noise, behind Ethan, caught my attention. I looked up to see Karen, wrapped in my bathrobe, prominently wiggling her new ring. She grinned. "Yeah, Pops, what do you say?"

"Could we invite Frank and Helen?" I offered. "Make it a whole day shindig."

She nodded enthusiastically and wiggled her ring again. "I haven't told her about us yet. It could be a fun outing, for sure. What do you think?"

I kissed her nose. "Call them—I'll be home by nine," I answered and kissed her again, properly.

⁊⁊⁊

The Mass at Immaculate Conception was short. It was the twenty-sixth ordinary Sunday of the year, and so no special service was held.

I took Communion, sat in my pew, and prayed for a while, then right after church I came home. I already knew what I would find there.

Frank's car was parked across my driveway, hastily, as if responding to a burglary.

Helen was in the kitchen, giggling like a schoolgirl, admiring Karen's ring, both women finishing each other's sentences. Frank sat apart from them, silent, with a look that cornered animals have.

He brightened up as he saw me and stood, reaching his hand out. "Congrats, Ian, best wishes," he said. "I am sure you two will continue to be happy together."

Helen rushed up to hug me and kissed me on the cheek. "You romantic." She giggled. "What made you think of proposing to this gal right now?"

I smiled and hugged her back with one arm. "It seemed like a good time." I shrugged. "I figure after a year and a half, she's a keeper."

Helen giggled again and grabbed Karen's left hand, examining the ring like Aladdin admiring his lamp.

"It's lovely," she said. "I wish you both all the happiness in the world." She sat back down. "So when's the wedding? Do you need help planning it? Have you picked a matron of honor?" This last question was said slowly, carefully.

Karen snickered. "I would love for you to be my matron of honor," she said.

Both women hugged, giggling.

"More importantly—" Frank leered. "Where's the honeymoon?"

Karen shook her head. She hadn't told Helen about the cottage. Frank looked at us, puzzled.

"What do you two have planned for today?" I asked.

ତେ

We took the Fury, cruising through Georgina, up Warden Avenue, and along the curving lane to the driveway between the hedges again. I half expected to see the lavender Buick, but I just parked where it had been the day before. Frank and I were in the front seat, Karen, Helen and Ethan in the back. We all tumbled out and stood in the front yard for just a minute. Frank looked around, his mouth open, staring at the maple tree, the swing that Ethan was now attacking, and the cottage just beyond it. Our cottage.

"This is yours," Frank mumbled. He stared at me and repeated it firmly. "*This* is *yours*."

I nodded. He shook his head.

"Want to go inside?" I asked.

"Can we, please?" he asked, his voice child-like.

Karen proudly unlocked the door—her door. She took Helen on a tour of the cottage, both of them cooing at the wood stove, the quaint kitchen, the furniture. Frank, oblivious to them, walked slowly over to the living room window.

Through the window, the sky was partly cloudy. Patchy white clouds, like cotton candy, sailed east to west along the lakeshore toward the town of Barrie. Rays of sun, poking between the clouds, alternately shone on the lake and the lawn, as if deciding what to spend their light on.

Frank stared, silent, for almost a minute. Ethan grabbed his hand, finally, and tugged it. Frank looked down, distracted.

"Uncle Frank, come out with me," he pleaded, jumping up and down.

Frank smiled at him, nodded to me, and let himself be led out onto the back lawn, toward the dock.

From the window I watched Ethan point out the boathouse, the gulls, and a pair of speedboats racing each other to the far side of the lake. Frank nodded, smiling, as Ethan spoke. A few minutes later, they came back in, cold and slightly windblown.

"So, how do you like it?" I asked.

Frank frowned and pulled me aside. "Ian, this is unbelievable. Amazing. Can I rent it from you sometime?" he asked, serious.

"No." I said firmly.

Frank was crestfallen. His face sagged.

I shook my head "I owe you my life, Frank. You can stay here whenever you like."

He stepped back. The statement clearly stunned him. "Really?" he asked, incredulous. "For sure?" he reiterated, to be sure he hadn't misheard me.

"For real. Honest. Any time you like. For free," I confirmed.

Frank grinned like a child. "I love you, man. But I'll kill you if you ever tell anyone that."

"Your secret is safe with me, Frank. Want to grab lunch?"

Karen, Helen, and Ethan set the table, while Frank and I made a "burger run" to the village of Jackson's Point, a mile down the road. Frank insisted on buying and, within twenty minutes, we returned, struggling in with bags of fish and chips, burgers, and all the trimmings. We sat at the table, my table—Karen's table—watching the view as though we'd never seen anything like it before. I know I hadn't.

Frank told Ethan that in winter, some people went ice fishing on the lake, and others went cross-country skiing. Frank had cousins in Barrie, a half hour away. He'd always loved this area, he said.

"So is this where you want to spend your honeymoon, or what?" he asked, his eyebrows arched.

I glanced at Karen. She straightened up and grinned. "Actually, we were thinking of getting married here," she said. "Helen, what do you think?"

Helen put down her food and looked around. She nodded. "Lovely," she said. "Leave the details to me."

She and Karen giggled again. Frank and Ethan played at the swing on the maple tree for a long time, laughing madly.

We all drove back to town, singing camp songs like eight-year-olds, giddy from the day's fun. Frank and Helen went home, hugging like teenagers.

Karen called her parents to tell them we were engaged. I'd spoken to Karen's mother on perhaps a dozen occasions before—mostly when they had come to visit Ethan. This time, she asked Karen to put me on the phone, and she bombarded me with questions. She wanted to know if I would take care of her daughter, if I was good for her. I told her she'd have to let Karen answer that.

She cried softly as we spoke, sniffling that she was very happy for us, and that they would, of course, be here for the wedding. I pointed out, with Karen's approving nod, that we were thinking we'd hold the ceremony at Karen's cottage on the lake.

That stopped her crying. I explained how it was that Karen had a cottage, and suddenly all the questions changed.

She asked about my family, and was I actually "a real police officer?" She seemed impressed by the answers. I was amused that I'd grown so much in her view by just buying some real estate.

Then I called my father and told him the news. He said he would come whenever we wanted and hinted that he might ask me to return the favor, when he and Pam Krieger married. I wished him all happiness and agreed.

We ate a light dinner, since lunch was still sitting heavy, and went to bed early. I lay there with Karen draped over my chest. I caressed her spine, listening to her breathe slower and slower as she drifted off. It had been a memorable weekend. I fell asleep.

∽∾∽∾

Rhonda is behind the counter. I try to hand her a bundle of clothes, but she just shakes her head.

"No," she says. "Not today. No laundry today."

She hands me a bottle of yellow liquid. "Here," she says. "You'll need this."

∽∾∽∾

I parked at the 52 Division lot before nine and walked straight to my desk.

Frank was telling his morning joke. "If you did, you'd get this shooting pain…"

The men groaned at the punch line. I sat at my desk and checked my address book for something.

Frank sat across from me. "The cottage," he started. "I could chip in for new furniture if you like. What do you think?"

"Forget it." I shook my head. "You're our guest, but it's our cottage."

Frank grinned and leaned back. "Have it your way." He chuckled and watched me, curious. "What are you looking for, Ian?"

"The shrink's phone number—it's here somewhere," I mumbled.

He sat up straight. "Still having flashbacks to the shooting, kid?"

"No, that's gone," I mumbled. "I'm having dreams about the dead guy's girlfriend. I've never dreamt of live people, not this way. I'm trying to figure out what it means." I found a business card and smiled, triumphant. "Ha. Colleen Feldman. Here we go."

"Can I come, too?" Frank asked excitedly.

"She's married," I scolded.

"She's real cute," he cooed.

"You're married," I countered.

He sighed, "Say hi for me," and walked away.

ಐಐ

Colleen had an office across the street from New City Hall, a block from Old City Hall.

I parked in a "Police Vehicles" spot at Old City Hall and walked down the street to Colleen Feldman's office. From my car, I could almost see her up on the fifteenth floor, at the corner of Queen and Bay Street. I checked my watch. I was a few minutes early.

I got out of the elevator and sat in the anteroom, staring out the glass wall to the street below. From here I could see people walking past the reflecting pool at New City Hall, shuffling quickly in the cool air.

A door beside me opened and an attractive bronze-haired woman stepped out. She looked like Rita Hayworth, I thought, or Maureen O'Hara, or maybe Gene Tierney. I stood up.

She reached out a hand and I extended mine to meet it.

"Doctor Feldman. Thanks for seeing me again on such short notice," I said.

"Colleen, please. No problem, Ian. How can I help you?"

She waved me through the door and we sat in her office. It was stark, modern, with a potted fern in one corner and a wall of diplomas beside it.

A pair of fat goldfish swam in a tall tank, climbing and diving as they chased each other. She waited for a minute before speaking.

"Watching these guys really calms you, don't you think?" She spoke softly, holding a notepad. "Ian, just look at them for a while. Breathe slowly." Her voice soothed.

I shook my head and smiled. "No need to hypnotize me, Colleen. I just have some technical questions for you."

She grinned and put the notepad on the desk beside her. "Fair enough. Go ahead."

I leaned forward and clasped my hands together, hanging them between my knees. "I often dream of the victims, the ones whose murder cases I work," I started. "Once the case is solved, those dreams go away."

She had the notepad in her hand again. "I see. Go on."

"This is different." I frowned. "I'm dreaming of a woman who might be a killer. She's trying to tell me something, but I don't know what."

"Is she someone you know?"

Her voice, calm and even, settled me. It was meant to, of course.

"Yeah." I nodded. "I've even interviewed her. I know where she is—staying at the house of another cop, of all things. But I just have no idea why I'm dreaming about her," I ended emphatically.

"Are you attracted to her?" There was no hint of prurience in her tone, just clinical curiosity.

I laughed. "No. My partner is. But I'm not."

She sighed and looked out the window, thinking.

"What are their names?" I asked.

She puckered her lips. "Pardon?"

I pointed at the goldfish. "Your fish. What are their names?"

"What makes you think they *have* names?" she teased.

"Your name is on the office door and on your desk." I smiled. "Your trays are labeled 'inbox' and 'outbox.' You work alone in this office, yet you meticulously label things. Therefore, you'd be likely to label the goldfish. So what do you call them?"

"Do you think that makes me compulsive, then?" she asked, amused.

"No, just organized. I'm a detective. I don't judge motivations, only actions."

"What would *you* call them?" she countered.

I took a scrap of paper and wrote something. "Now, tell me their names," I challenged.

"Sigmund and Carl," she answered sheepishly.

I held up my scrap of paper. It read *Carl-Sigmund*.

"Good trick. How did you do it?"

"A racing driver might call his dog 'Andretti.'" I shrugged. "A chef might call his cat 'Escoffier,' and a singer might call his canary 'Caruso.' An analyst would name her fish after Jung and Freud."

"True," she said noncommittally. "What would you call these fish?"

I leaned back and thought for a moment. "Don't overthink it," she warned. "First ideas, Ian."

"Sam and Philip," I said quickly.

"Why?" She spoke softly again.

"Sam Spade, Philip Marlowe."

"So," she thought aloud. "I name my fish after real analysts. You'd name yours after fictional detectives. Do you think that means something?"

"Prove that Freud was real," I challenged.

She smirked and bunched up her shoulders in surrender.

"'The debt we owe to the play of imagination is incalculable,'" I quoted.

"I'm impressed," she said. "Most people can't quote anything by Jung."

"Back to the reason for the visit, doc," I said. "The woman in this dream I had?"

She frowned and made a note on her pad. "How often have you had the dream?"

"Just twice, but both times it was the same. She was working in a dry cleaner's. I came in with laundry and she handed me a bottle of yellow liquid. Why yellow liquid? What does that mean?"

Colleen looked out the window at nothing in particular, then she pinched the bridge of her nose with a thumb and forefinger and scratched her forehead—the universal signals for deep thought.

"Yellow liquid. You're quite specific about that. What do you think the liquid is?"

"I dunno." I shrugged. "Urine, nitroglycerin, lemon juice, bleach—I just don't know."

"How about this?" She leaned forward. "Next time you have the dream, ask her."

I hadn't thought of that approach. I rolled my eyes in embarrassment. She smiled.

"I like that. Thanks, Colleen." I got up to leave.

"Any excuse to charge the Department," she joked, standing as well. "I'm late for a meeting, sorry, I have to go."

෴

I went home just before six. A quick call to forensics told me that Gustavo De Melo's car was clean—nothing relating to Ed Hereford's death; lots of janitorial supplies, of course, and an extensive collection of cigarette butts, but nothing else.

Walsh had left me a message that he was tracking down some lead or other, and he'd see me in the morning. That said, I'm pretty sure I saw his Polara outside Vivian's house.

We ate dinner, talked about the cottage, and watched TV. Karen flipped through the Canadian Tire Catalog, looking for shower curtains that would "go nicely in our place."

When she said those words, she looked over and smiled at me with a warmth that said just how much she loved the sentiment behind the gift.

I had a nagging thought in the back of my head. If I had that dream again, would I remember to ask what was in the bottle?

I needed to talk to someone about it. I called Frank.

"Hey, kid, what's up?" he sang, as Helen passed him the phone.

"Frank, I need to talk. Got a few minutes?"

"Sure, Ian. Want me to put on coffee?" He sounded cheery, but I heard the concern in his voice.

I walked the three blocks to his house and bounded up the porch steps, two at a time. For five years now, three as his partner and two more as his colleague, I'd leaned on Frank for support, groused, whined, grieved, and laughed with him. He was the closest thing to a big brother I had in the city and the best friend I had ever had. All these thoughts ran through my head as I got to the top of his porch.

Frank opened his door before I could knock, wearing orange plaid pants and a lime green golf shirt. I stepped back at the visual assault.

"Hi, Frank," I said. "Bowling for the Jamaican team, are we?"

He frowned and raised one eyebrow dramatically. "You just came over to insult me? Bye, Ian."

He half closed the door then reopened it, smiling. I sat in his kitchen, clutching a mug, and staring at my coffee as if I was reading tealeaves. "I get these dreams, Frank," I started. "I dream about the cases I work. You ever get that?"

He shrugged and hooked a thumb over the back of his belt. "Yup. All the time. Goes with the job, I suppose," he said matter-of-factly.

"Even now that you're driving a desk?" I asked.

"Yeah," he drawled, leaning forward and resting his elbows on the table. "I still visit some crime scenes with my team. I still see the blood stains, the bullet holes. That's your question, Ian? Does it ever go away?"

"Maybe." I bobbed my head. "I visited Colleen Feldman."

He smiled at that. "And you didn't want me along. Bastard. Still having nightmares?"

"No. I asked her about this dream. It had a woman with a mystery bottle." I skipped the details. "Colleen said I should ask the dream woman what the bottle means. Do you ever do that? Do you ever talk to the dreams?"

Frank stared at the kitchen wall for a long time, recalling, then he faced me. "I had this one dream over and over for a long time. I tried to change what happened in it, but I couldn't. I finally figured out what it was trying to tell me. There was nothing I could change, but after I figured that out, the dream stopped."

"Was it a case we worked on?" I asked, curious.

"No," he answered curtly.

"Something from before we met?"

"Yes." The short answers told me I was in sensitive territory. I shrugged, puzzled. "Do you want me to drop this?"

He sighed and stared at the wall again, thinking for another long time.

Then he leaned forward. "You asked me once why I never went back home, back to Pennsylvania," he started. "I was not an only child." He looked down at his coffee and sighed. "My brother was two years younger."

The word 'was' gave me chills.

"I enlisted in 'sixty-one. He signed up two years later," he said softly. "I was sent to 'Nam in 'sixty-four; spent a few months sitting on a beach, getting drunk, then our unit went to the bush." He hunched his shoulders, rubbing one hand around his coffee mug. "We went in with Aussies, the SVA, the French—all good guys, all soldiers, all heroes. Me, I just carried their knapsacks."

I didn't believe the last part, but I nodded.

"I spent two years in the jungle," he hissed. "Two years. You know what it's like to live on shit and Spam for two years? Two years waiting for some local to shoot you, slit your throat, or hack you to death? And I was one of the lucky ones." He snorted, rubbed his face, and winced. "You want a drink?" he asked casually, looking out to the living room liquor cabinet.

"No, Frank, no, I can't." I shook my head. "I'll sit with you here and talk all night if you want to, but please don't ask me to go down that road."

He shrugged and went back to staring at his coffee mug.

"So Woody, my little brother, decides he should help mankind, you know, the usual hippie crap. He was the smart one in the family—like you, a college boy." He rubbed his nose and sniffled. "We were named after presidents. Dad is a lifelong Democrat. I was named for FDR, and Woody was named for Woodrow Wilson." He snickered again and sipped his coffee. "He wanted to follow in my footsteps. He was in second year at Penn State, studying Medicine. Medicine, for Christ's sake. He wanted to be a surgeon. We were so proud. But I went over there, so he joined up too, went in as a medic."

He slid his coffee away and wrinkled up his face. "December fourth, nineteen-sixty-five, he was cleaning up after a really shitty firefight. The VC had fragged his CO. It was chaos. They had dead and wounded everywhere. Woody sees this kid lying there, moaning, and rolls him over to see what he can do. The VC had booby-trapped this kid with a bunch of lemons—hand grenades—and as soon as Woody rolls him over, they both get blown to hell. We didn't get enough back to bury. My father hasn't spoken to me since. He blames me for Woody getting killed. I can't say as I can really fault him, you know?"

He stared at me, the Green Beret now as emotionally naked as I'd never before seen him. Helen came in from the living room. She'd heard everything. Of course, she already knew the story. She stood behind Frank and hugged him. He reached up and caressed her hand.

"What was your dream?" I asked softly.

Frank sighed and reached for his coffee. That said he was coming back to the present, mentally.

"I dreamt that I was with him when it happened. So many times, *so many* times, I had the dream that I was behind him, calling to him, screaming for him to stop, but every time he'd roll the kid over. Every time they blew up."

He smiled slightly. "Once, I dreamt that I got there first, that I rolled the kid over. But the kid didn't blow up—he just smiled at me. And then Woody touched him, and they still both blew up." He pushed back from the table and stretched his legs.

"Did you figure it out?" I asked. "What did the dream mean, in the end?"

"He was meant to die." Frank sighed. "Nothing could change that. He was supposed to do just exactly what he did. He had saved dozens of lives, and the universe wanted his life in exchange." He swigged a mouthful of coffee, put the mug down, and leaned back, frowning. "So that's my story, Ian. Now you know. What about you? What's bugging you?"

I thought that my worries would seem insignificant compared to his and shrugged, apologetically. "I dreamt of our dead guy's girlfriend."

"Yeah?" Frank nodded. "Go on."

"She worked in a dry cleaner's in Newfoundland and then one here, before working as a cleaner. In my dream, I bring in some clothes to get laundered, and she hands me a bottle of yellow liquid. I have no idea what the bottle is, or what it means. Colleen said I should ask the dream woman what's in the bottle. What do you think?"

"I dunno." Frank scratched his cheek. "Cleaning fluid? Dry cleaner's—cleaning fluid?"

"Sure," I said. "It's a dry cleaner, after all. Cleaning fluid makes sense."

"Maybe it's beer," Frank offered. "Maybe it's not really a bottle, but something else. It just looks like a bottle."

"I dunno," I grunted. "Look, I'm sorry I bugged you." I stood up. "I should get some sleep and see if anything comes of it. I'll let you know."

Helen poked Frank in the back, smiling. "Tell him," she hissed.

Frank smiled at her and nodded. "After all, since you're here, there is some other news. Good news." He grinned. "You know how much we love Ethan. Did you ever wonder why I got so attached to him so quickly?"

I shrugged. "He's a nice kid."

Frank nodded. "We always wanted kids. We tried, Lord knows, we tried. We've tried for years to have a baby. Six years, and no luck."

"I'm so sorry," I said sadly. "I didn't realize."

"Well, yeah," he drawled. "We didn't know what to tell anyone, but—"

"I'm pregnant," Helen interrupted.

I slammed back down onto the seat. My mouth dropped open. "What? When?" I asked, incredulous.

"I'm four months along." Helen beamed. "I just went for a checkup. Everything's going well."

"We were waiting until we were sure," Frank added. "Now we're sure. Now we can tell people. Starting with you."

"When did all this happen?" I asked stupidly.

"I'd say around four months ago," Helen joked.

"Wow. I guess, congratulations, you two," I mumbled. "So you're due in, what? March, then?"

Helen nodded.

"Should I keep this to myself, or what?" I asked.

"Give Karen our love." Frank smiled. "Go home. Get some rest."

I grinned broadly and hugged Helen. I shook Frank's hand, patted him on the back, wished them both the very best, and walked home, feeling uplifted, joyful.

ℰↁℰↁ

Karen squealed at the news. She ran to the phone and talked with Helen for a long time. They laughed and chortled and planned then wished each other a good night and hung up.

I tucked Ethan in, closed up the house, and went to bed. Karen slumped over my chest, caressing my arm, and talked about Helen and the baby, excited and bubbly at the news.

A minute later, she yawned, took a deep breath, and fell asleep. I lay there for a while, listening to her breathing, feeling her lungs rise against me. I caressed her back through her sleep shirt, softly rubbing her spine, pausing over each and every vertebra. I fell asleep, too.

CHAPTER 7

I walk into the dry cleaner's, holding out a bundle of clothes. Rhonda stands behind the counter, writing on a scrap of paper. She looks up at me and shakes her head.

"Not today," she says.

I drop the clothes on the floor.

"Here," she says, reaching under the counter to hand me a bottle of yellow liquid.

I hear a noise. I must have spoken.

"I don't know, love." She shrugs. "It's not my bottle. Take it. It's what you're lookin' for."

I take the bottle and look at it carefully. For the first time, I see a label on the side of the bottle. I squint to read it, but the letters move and change, from script to block to something foreign. I ask Rhonda something.

She shrugs and lights a cigarette. "No idea. I can't read it neither."

∽∾∽

I made breakfast, then lunches for Ethan and Alan. Karen sat on my knee, nibbling at my toast and sipping my coffee as I peeked down her robe. At eight-thirty I drove to work. Frank and I exchanged quick looks across the floor, snickering like friends after a schoolboy prank. I went to my desk to review some reports.

Frank sat across from me and nodded. I nodded back, silently.

"Not a word," he said softly.

"About?" I asked.

"Helen."

I smiled in agreement and leaned forward, serious. "I spoke to the woman in the dream." I shook my head. "No help. I did get to hold the bottle, though. There was a label on it, but I couldn't read what it said."

"At least we know it's a real bottle." Frank shrugged and stood up. "So what are you guys doing for dinner?" he asked.

"Eating with you two?" I offered. "Three," I corrected.

Frank grinned like an idiot.

I called Karen at work to tell her about dinner. She agreed, but she seemed distracted, distant.

"Something wrong, hon?" I asked.

"It's delicate," she said, slowly. "I don't know how to ask this."

"Gee," I joked. "That's 'cause we barely know each other?"

She laughed; I could hear her lean back in her chair. "How do you feel about Ethan?" she asked simply.

I answered in a second. "I love him like he was my own son."

"Enough to adopt him?" There was a long silence as she waited for my answer.

"Adopt him?" I echoed. I certainly felt like a father toward him. If I adopted him, I could honestly call him my son, and not have to tell people that I married his mother but he was not mine. "That sounds like a wonderful idea," I said at last.

There was more silence on the other end.

"Karen? Sweetheart, are you okay?" I asked.

"I'm crying," she sniffled finally.

"I'm sorry, did I say something wrong?" I said stupidly.

"No, of course you didn't. That's why I'm crying, you idiot."

"See you at home, hon," I offered.

"See you there, Pops," she answered.

I could hear her smiling over the phone.

෧෨෧

The police department had a lawyer for personal and family matters. I looked up his number, explained my situation, and asked what I needed to do to adopt Ethan.

He said he would send me the required documents, then he made an appointment for us to visit him. Walsh arrived and brought me up to speed with his interview of the Newfoundland doctor, as well as some details he'd read in the autopsy report.

Captain Van Hoeke called us into his office later that morning. I sat across from him, Walsh trailing meekly behind me.

"So," Van Hoeke started. "Where are you two in the Hereford case?"

I nodded to Walsh, and he opened his notebook. "The doctor I spoke to Sunday said that he'd treated Rhonda's second husband—Cameron Wilkins—before he died. He had suspicions about the man's death, but not enough to raise alarms. Turns out that Rhonda didn't really like her husband much—good guy, but boring as hell—so losing him was not a huge deal. She didn't get a payout, however, so I don't think she bumped him off for the money. The interesting thing is, we talked about another suspicious death some years before—another fellow who also passed away faster than anyone thought he should."

"Any connection between the two men?" I asked.

"Doesn't look like it." Walsh shrugged. "The first death was a guy who had a dry cleaner's, the second, Cameron Wilkins, worked for the government in Newfoundland.

They may have known each other—I mean, Corner Brook's not a big town—but apart from that, who knows? The doctor worked as a missionary in Africa somewhere for a few years after this incident. They looked at him, too, to see if he had a motive, but he's clean."

"What about our current victim, Ed?" Van Hoeke asked.

"Ed Hereford *didn't* die in the wee hours of the morning, sir," Walsh stated. "The pathologist figures he died around eight in the evening, based on rigor mortis. The forensics team found prints from Ed, Rhonda, and Rhonda's boyfriend, Gustavo De Melo in the apartment. They also found three other sets of prints. One belonged to our witness, Annie Ross. One belonged to the caretaker. They had a broken stove, and he was in to fix that." He flipped to the next page. "That leaves one unidentified palm print. It's a smaller hand, and it's only on the dining table and the drawer where the knives are kept."

"What does that tell you?" I asked, smiling slightly.

"Is this some kind of test, Sergeant?" Walsh asked.

Van Hoeke leaned back, watching us.

"It's a question. What does the placement of the unknown prints tell you?" I repeated, slowly.

He thought for a moment. "It means that they were familiar with the apartment. They knew where things were stored."

Walsh grinned, pleased with himself.

"Good. You get to keep your job. Anything else you'd like, Captain?" I asked.

Van Hoeke shook his head. "Keep me posted. I want this case closed as soon as possible, gentlemen."

Walsh and I stood to leave.

"Ah," I said, remembering. "Captain, are you available next Sunday afternoon?"

He frowned. "Some special event, Ian?"

"We're having a barbecue. I wondered if you and Rebecca would care to drop by."

He smiled broadly. "Should I wear my dress uniform?"

I shook my head. "Just come for good eats, sir. By the way, do you keep kosher?"

Walsh shot him a look of surprise.

Van Hoeke smiled. "Whatever you make will be fine." He waved us out of his office.

Walsh looked over his shoulder at the Captain's closed door. "Van Hoeke's a Jew? Really?" he sneered.

I stopped and glowered at him. He stepped back a half pace, nervous.

"He flew Hurricanes in the war. He was shot down twice, injured four times, and went back up anyway. He is one of the bravest men I know," I hissed, poking his chest. "You have no idea how much respect every man in this building has for him."

"Why did they nickname him Captain Hook, then?" Walsh asked, curious.

"It's not meant as an insult," I answered. "It's a nickname given in respect. Any one of us would walk through fire for him—anyone—knowing that he's right there beside us. Remember that."

Walsh nodded sadly, with the look a dog gives you after you scold it.

"By the way, you're invited, too," I added. "Bring a date. I don't suppose that will be a problem?"

Walsh smirked.

I nodded. "Come on, squirt, let's get an early lunch."

༄༅༄

Later, as I sat at my desk, a secretary handed me a manila courier envelope. I took it home.

Ethan came home from school with Alan and ran out to the backyard. They kicked around a soccer ball for a few minutes then went downstairs to watch TV.

I opened my manila envelope and read the lawyer's

forms. It all seemed straightforward: Karen and I would agree to raise Ethan, there were some documents to notarize, and then we'd be done. Except. Except that I had to get permission from Ethan's natural father. That one page form stopped me dead.

His name had been mentioned perhaps five times in the year and a half that I'd known Karen. Now, I would have to get him to agree, or Karen would have to get him to agree, to me adopting Ethan.

I decided to do nothing till Karen came home. It would be stupid to barge ahead without talking to her first. I made dinner and called down to ask if Alan wanted to stay and eat, but he and his mother were going out for dinner, he said. No surprise as to who was taking them. At least Vivian was chasing Walsh and not me.

დოდ

At five-forty, a familiar mechanical whistle filled the living room as Karen's Beetle rolled up the driveway, her shoes tick-ticking as she walked up the porch. A moment later the door opened. "Hi?" she called.

"Kitchen," I answered. "Dinner's almost ready. Hungry, sweetheart?"

She tossed her purse onto the sofa and walked through to the kitchen. She wrapped her arms around me and rubbed my stomach.

"Hey, you," she purred and playfully nibbled my ear. "What are we eating?"

"Chicken and rice, with bread pudding just for Frank," I answered.

She gazed up at me. "What's wrong, love?"

I shrugged. "A form I have to get filled out. A call to make, too. I really don't want to."

She flipped through the stack of papers on the kitchen table and stopped on the same page I had.

"Ah," she said, understanding. "Do you want me to do it?"

I shook my head. "It should come from me. It's what a guy would expect."

❧❧❧

Frank and Helen came for dinner, Frank saying little, mostly beaming at his wife. They left early when she started to feel tired.

After dinner, Ethan went downstairs to watch *Happy Days*.

Karen fished an address book out of her dresser drawer, undid the elastic that held it closed, and ceremoniously presented it to me.

"Do you want to be here when I call?" I asked.

"No." She shook her head. "I want as far from him as possible; the farther the better."

She went downstairs and sat with Ethan while I dialed the number. It was long distance, a six-one-three area code—Ottawa.

I waited for the call to go through, collecting my thoughts and steeling myself. The phone rang twice, then a voice like Lee Marvin came on.

"Hello?" it growled.

"Hello. Pierre Guy Marchand, please," I said, in my best policeman's voice.

"Who shall I tell him is calling?" the voice asked.

I thought of *The Dirty Dozen,* the boot camp scene with Lee Marvin shooting out the climbing rope below Trini Lopez. I imagined this man in fatigues, cradling a machine gun.

"Tell him that Detective Sergeant Ian McBriar of the Toronto Police Department wants to talk to him," I answered gruffly. I didn't want to sound insecure or tentative with this man.

"One second," he grunted.

I waited for a minute. I could hear soft, muffled noises—walking and talking in the room. The phone may have been pushed onto a sofa cushion.

The muffled sound cleared and I heard a deep sigh on the other end, then a new voice.

"Yes?" the voice said, simply.

It was impatient, irritated, that one word stating that he was far more important than I was. He sounded like a mix between Vincent Price and Clifton Webb, effete and haughty all at once.

"Mr. Marchand, we've never spoken before," I started, politely.

"Of course not. Why would we?" he snapped back.

"Karen Prescott and I are getting married. I want to adopt Ethan. We feel it would be better for him to be part of our new family."

"No," he answered immediately. "You can't."

"I can't what?" I asked, irritated.

"I said no—period," he snapped, his voice rising.

"Listen," I said. "You want what's best for Ethan, don't you? Surely it's best for him is to be in a—"

"I said no," he repeated firmly. The Vincent Price voice became even higher, more shrill.

"But, be reasonable," I started. "You—"

The phone clicked, a dial tone came back. I went downstairs. Karen was looking at the TV—not watching it, just staring at the screen. She looked up sadly.

"So?" she asked, seeing the answer on my face.

I shook my head. "Option number two." I shrugged. "We'll do it without his permission. That's that."

"Is it that easy?" Karen asked, searching my face for some reassurance.

"Should be," I lied. I smiled, but it didn't feel right.

ତ୨ତ

On Wednesday I called a family judge I knew. The judge asked me, in careful language, whether Karen and I were really married.

I pointed out that she'd recently agreed to marry me, but we were, as yet, not legally married. That would make it harder to adopt, she said.

She was pleasant and sympathetic, and said she'd do what she could, but ultimately we'd have to prove that Ethan would be better off with us than with the man who left Karen.

That was it. I'd find a way to get Ethan. I wouldn't give up. I'd find a solution.

Walsh sat across from me, holding a thick bundle of paper in a yellow folder. He must have been there for a couple of minutes, but I didn't notice him.

"Sorry, do you have something for me?" I asked.

He smiled and opened the folder. "Didn't mean to derail your train of thought. I keep thinking this doesn't seem right." He shook his head. "Ed was drunk and drugged when he was stabbed. He died around eight at night, right?"

I nodded. "And you're wondering if Rhonda knew he was drunk before she left for work?"

Walsh leaned back, surprised that I was thinking ahead of him. He sighed. "I should have expected you'd figure that one out. Sorry, Ian, the hubris of youth, I guess."

I tilted my head back, curious. "Hubris? Good word. Where'd you go to school, Patrick?"

"I went to Saint Andrew's College, then U of T for my Psych degree."

"Why did you become a cop? Your family's not exactly blue collar, right?"

He grinned sheepishly and looked out at the front reception area, formulating his answer. "I never wanted to be a banker." He shrugged. "My family has always been in finance. I didn't want to do that. I wanted to do something real with my life. How about you, Ian? You were all set to wear a Roman collar, I hear."

"That was then," I said. "After I lost my mom to a drunk driver five, six years back, I couldn't become a priest. The only way to find peace was to solve crimes and ease my pain that way."

He nodded slowly. "Ever regret not taking the cloth?"

"You should ask Karen that one." I grinned. "No, I take that back. I got the girl and the secular life, but at heart I'm still a guy in a cassock, trying to do good works."

He tapped the file folder. "So what happened, then? Do you think Rhonda did it?"

I shrugged. "What did she do? Stab him, go happily off to work, then eight hours later bring the boyfriend back and act surprised? How many ways do you think that plan could go wrong?"

He furrowed his brow and pointed at the pathologist's report. "Yeah, so what *do* you think? She left him at home drunk, went to work, then someone else came by and knifed him? That's almost as improbable, don't you think?"

I leaned back. I hadn't thought of that possibility. It didn't sound likely. "We're only considering her role on this one." I shrugged. "Did Ed have any enemies that might have done this?" I stood up. "Let's find out."

We called the Flaherty's home. Paulette said that Rhonda was in the back yard, helping clean up the garden for the winter. She would put tea on for us, she said.

The York Regional Police cruiser was gone, replaced by a baby-blue Maverick. We knocked at the door and Paulette let us in, smiling. Last time we were here, I'd noticed a subtle aroma in the house—cinnamon. I'd put it down to Jim Flaherty's coffee cake.

There was now a definite smell of nutmeg. The kitchen, clean before, was immaculate now. There were no pots or pans out, nothing out of place. We went into the living room.

Paulette set out tea and cake for us. It was store-bought, not Jim's—a letdown. She left us alone and went downstairs to finish some chores. Rhonda would be in shortly, she said.

Rhonda came in the back door, pulling off a pair of yellow garden gloves, and curled up, facing us on the La-Z-Boy, tucking her feet under her. She leaned forward to grab a cigarette from a package on the coffee table and her shirt billowed open, flashing a pale brown nipple. Walsh noticed it immediately, of course.

He lunged forward, his elegant gold lighter already aflame as he moved. She leaned forward with the cigarette in her mouth, and he got another look. Their eyes met; both knew what the other was thinking. Rhonda smiled at him, pleased. Walsh sat back, also pleased.

"Thanks for seeing us on short notice," I said, breaking the spell. They both looked at me. "Rhonda, we wondered if you could fill us in on some details, now that you've had time to settle down?" I asked, glaring at Walsh as I did.

He leaned back, silent.

"When you left for work that night, was Ed already drunk?" I asked, my voice as neutral as I could make it.

"No," she said. "He di'nt drink on work days, just on the weekend. During the week, he di'nt drink at all."

"But—" I pointed out. "He had a large amount of whisky in his system. Did he ever drink after you left for work?"

"I don't think so."

She leaned forward again, tapping the end of her cigarette into the ashtray. Walsh's eyes were fixed on her shirt as she did.

"Did he have any enemies?" I asked. "Did he owe anybody money?"

Rhonda snickered. "Ed? He di'nt spend money. He di'nt hang out with rough folk, and he di'nt play the horses or nothin'. No sir, he were a hard workin' guy. He just worked at the bakery and he drunk on weekends. No funny stuff." She took a puff of her cigarette and looked down sadly.

"So, why did you start seeing Gustavo, then?" I asked.

"He were lonely." She shrugged. "First off, I was just

tryin' to make him feel better. His wife went back to Portugal two year back, when her mum got sick. He only got the one daughter in North Carolina, an' his wife got lonely for the old country. So she goes to see her ailin' mother and gets herself a younger fella back home, tells him she's stayin' there. So I treat him to some lovin', and we get goin' from there."

She stretched out, her arms behind her head, arching her back. I couldn't tell if Walsh was going to jump on her or faint. He sat completely still.

"When you went out the other day," I said. "Did you go see Gustavo at that apartment building?"

"Yeah." She shrugged. "He were lonely. So were I," she said matter-of-factly.

"Was he drunk when you went over there?" I asked.

She grinned sheepishly and stretched. "Not too drunk."

Walsh's eyes widened.

I decided to change the direction of the questions before Walsh booked a hotel room.

"Why did you want to stay in the apartment? Wouldn't it have seemed ghoulish after what happened to Ed?"

"Girlish?" she asked. "You mean like, no guys?"

"*Ghoulish*. I mean like creepy. Why would you want to stay there at all?"

She looked down sadly and shrugged. "I ain't got a lot of things. What I'm wearin' is Paulette's. I wanted my own stuff, is all."

I sighed. The answers she gave all made sense, sounded true. I believed she might be innocent. Still, there was the handprint that we couldn't identify.

"Who else visited you there? We think that people other than you and Ed were there," I said, not wanting to tell her too much.

She shrugged. "A couple of the gals from work come by, and Paulette did once or twice, and Paulette brung her daughter Cynthia. Nobody else as I can think."

I leaned back, smiling. I couldn't think of anything else

to ask her. I turned to Walsh. "Detective Walsh, do you have any questions you'd like to ask Rhonda?"

He sat up straight, alert at the mention of his name. "No, not at the moment. But if I do think of anything, can I call you? I can take you out for a coffee, or something, and discuss it?" he added tentatively.

Rhonda nodded, and grinned broadly. "Sure. Sounds good."

We thanked Paulette for the tea and walked back to the Polara. I sat in the passenger seat, reviewing my notes. Walsh adjusted the rear view mirror, checked his hair, then started the engine.

"So, do you ever sleep alone?" I asked, casually.

"Not if I can help it." He smiled. "Why? Is there a problem?"

I shook my head. "What do you look for in a woman?" I suddenly realized the raunchy answers he could come up with and regretted asking. I shook my head. "No. Forget it. I don't care."

He glanced over at me, reading my mind, and roared with laughter. "So," he asked, "how did you behave when you first dated Karen?"

I smirked. "None of your damned business, Patrick."

He roared again.

CHAPTER 8

The lawyer we used for personal affairs was not exactly a glitzy Avenue Road powerhouse. The attorney, although competent, operated out of a nine-story building at Bathurst and Wilson, a narrow brick monolith that crammed two rows of basic offices on each floor.

Karen and I took the elevator to the fifth floor and turned right, following the signs to a polished teak door. Inside the door, a small anteroom kept us to one side of a counter.

I sat Karen in one of the wing chairs flanking a coffee table, and pushed a button on the counter to announce our arrival.

A door opened on the other side of the counter and a portly man with a thick black beard came out. He smiled and stretched out a hand. "Ian, nice to see you," he sang. "Come, come inside. You're Karen? I've heard a lot about you, young lady. I see Ian was not exaggerating." He reached over the counter and clutched her hand. "Steven Machtinger," he said. "A pleasure."

He turned, limping slightly, as he reached for the doorknob and disappeared through the door, opened a similar one on our side of the counter, and ushered us into his office.

It was a cozy arrangement. He had a big wooden desk, completely clear except for one piece of paper and a telephone. We sat facing him in a pair of burgundy leather chairs that could have been plucked from a British gentle-man's club.

Steven picked up the piece of paper and placed it in front of me, unceremoniously. "The man you asked about is not very cooperative," he stated. "To be blunt, he's a schmuck." He shrugged. "I spoke to his lawyer—he's rea-sonable, but Marchand isn't. If you can get him to sign this, you'll have no problem getting the adoption. The biggest issue is, he's a dog in a manger. He doesn't want to raise the child, but he doesn't want anyone else to have him, either. As I say, he's a schmuck."

I looked at the form. It seemed straightforward. Marchand would just sign the bottom of the page, his law-yer would witness it, and that would be that.

On the other hand, it looked like a map for someplace just beyond my reach. I had no idea how I could convince Ethan's natural father to allow the adoption. I handed the form to Karen. She held it like it was made of glass, about to break. She sighed and handed it back to me.

"If we can't get him to agree," I said, my voice waver-ing, "Would it be easier to arrange if we were married?"

"It would." Steven nodded. "You could argue that you've been the boy's effective parent for a year and a half now, and that he views you as his de-facto father."

Having him refer to me as a father made be blush. I al-so felt, more than I had felt before, more than I thought I could possibly feel, that I would do whatever I had to for Ethan.

We thanked Steve for his time and headed back down to the car in silence. Karen bowed her head, thinking. "Any idea what we can do, then?" she asked sadly.

"Yeah," I answered. "Leave it with me."

Pierre Guy Marchand was now squarely in my sights.

జుస్తిజు

Friday was a wrap-up day for me. Working with Frank

had made me careful to finish up my paperwork before clocking out for the weekend. We also had the barbecue on Sunday afternoon, and Karen wanted it to be a special affair. I called the True-Bright Janitorial Company. Gustavo was in the office. This time, he was sober.

"Sergeant McBriar? How can I help you?" he asked, getting straight to the point.

I heard a door close and the background noise vanished. He didn't want his staff to hear him talking, apparently. At least that meant he probably wouldn't lie.

"Last Wednesday," I started. "Did Rhonda come see you in your maintenance room?"

"Yes. We had sex," he answered, bluntly.

I hadn't expected that. "How long did she stay?"

"A couple of hours. She also wanted to know if I had an empty apartment for her."

"Do you?"

"Not right now." He sighed. "But I will on the fifteenth. I told her that if she could hold on till then, it was hers."

"For free?" I asked. It wasn't meant as a slur, but perhaps it sounded that way.

"For cheap. I'm not *that* stupid," he snickered.

"Look," I said. "We think Ed died long before you found him—much earlier in the evening. When did Rhonda show up for work that night?"

"Same as always—around six, six-ten."

"Did she seem different in any way? Was she nervous or distracted?" I asked.

"Nah. She was just like every other day—always cheerful, always works hard."

"Did she talk about Ed being drunk when she left?"

"She almost never talked about him." He sighed. "Except once. They had a big fight a few months ago."

"What about, did she say?" I scribbled notes quickly.

"Yeah, she said he was drunk and making moves on her cousin."

"Paulette?" I asked, curious.

"Yeah, that's her. Came over to say hi one time and Ed was all over her, Rhonda said."

I heard the snick-snick sound of a lighter then "paah" as he exhaled cigarette smoke.

"She said Paulette was really pissed about it, but she didn't tell him so to his face," he added.

"Do you think he could have gone further? Maybe followed Paulette home?" I was reaching, but it couldn't hurt to ask.

"You'd have to ask Rhonda. I can't see it, though. I think he just took a shine to her 'cause he was drunk and she was at his place. Like I said before, Ed wasn't a creep, just boring."

I sighed. This gave me something to work with, anyway. "The night Ed died, was Rhonda at work the whole time? She didn't leave work at all?"

"No." He was emphatic. "One of the other girls was off with a broken ankle. Rhonda worked a whole floor by herself all week. She did a hell of a job, too."

I imagined Gustavo, sitting in a small office, leaning back and smoking. He was a man who was comfortable in his own skin, one who'd found his level and either risen or sunk to it.

"Listen," he asked. "Can I get my car back? I'd really like to go see my grandkids, okay?"

I grunted. "Okay. I'll release it. Leave us the phone number where you're staying in North Carolina, though. We may need to ask you more questions."

"Fine, I'll be back in a week. You want I should bring you back some Budweiser?" he cackled, amused.

I smiled at the offer. "Thanks. I couldn't take it, but thanks anyway."

He hung up. I told impound that Gustavo would come for his car, then I called Karen.

She would be at work for a few hours yet, so I told her I'd buy groceries for the barbecue on my way home.

Walsh sat across from me and nodded, waiting for me to get off the phone. "How are we doing, boss?" he asked earnestly.

"Gustavo doesn't have anything more on Rhonda. He says she was at work when Ed was stabbed. He wants his car back, though. Can you tell forensics I've released it?"

Walsh nodded again. "Sure. Anything else you need before I clock off?"

I shook my head. "No, go home. Got a busy weekend planned?"

He chuckled. "Yeah. I should be up and about for your barbecue, though."

"See you there, Patrick." I smiled. "Around one-ish."

He grinned and walked toward the door, making a detour to talk to one of the secretaries as she crossed his path. She giggled and smacked his arm, playfully. He straightened up and followed her to her desk, speaking softly and staring at her legs. She blushed slightly and smiled, nodding.

He was lining her up for the following weekend, I guessed.

Karen got home at the usual time, her heels dancing on the porch steps in a be-bop rhythm as she got to the front door. "Ian? I'm home" she called.

"Kitchen," I yelled.

She kicked her shoes off and padded into the kitchen. She wrapped her left arm around me, wiggled her ring finger, and squeezed my waist.

"Hey, you," she purred. "What's for dinner?"

"Meat loaf with baked potatoes," I answered. I bent down and peered into the oven. "Now," I added. "I have a truckload of food in the fridge, and in the basement fridge, so tomorrow I'll set up for the barbecue, okay?"

She inhaled the aroma of the baking beef and nodded. "Smells good. I'm starved." She slumped into a chair. "How was your day, my fiancé?"

I grinned. "Fine. No news on the dead guy. Still looking into it," I answered casually, distracted, as I stirred a pan of gravy.

Karen sighed again and caressed her ring, admiring it proudly. "One of the girls at work was on vacation last week. She almost fell over when I told her we were engaged."

"Did she have me in her sights?" I joked. "'Cause I'm kind of picky, you know?"

Ethan thundered up the stairs, Alan right behind him. "Hey, Pops, can Alan stay for dinner and a sleepover? His mom says it's okay."

I glanced at Karen. She smirked and nodded.

"Fine," I said. "Set the table then, guys. Tell her to come by for breakfast at nine. And clean up the mess downstairs, okay?" I added.

The pair thundered back down, racing each other to the basement.

Karen watched them head out of earshot. "Another hot date for Walsh, huh?" she said.

I shook my head. "Was I like that when we met?"

She smiled. "Yeah, but you went for quality, not quantity."

⋐⋑⋐⋑

Dinner was pleasant. It capped off the day well. Both boys ate heartily. Alan was still slightly amazed that I cooked at all, let alone that I cooked well.

I dug out some apple pie and ice cream for dessert and we finished the meal in silence, listening to the tinkle of spoons on bowls. The boys went downstairs to set up a pup tent and race Hot Wheels along the floor, while Karen changed into casual pants and slumped onto the sofa.

I brought coffee through from the kitchen, sat beside her, and rested her feet in my lap, massaging her toes.

"Penny for your thoughts?" I offered.

She shook her head and leaned back. "No, no thinking. Just keep doing that." She sighed. "Long day, I'm tired."

She leaned her head back and closed her eyes. I watched the dull glow of the TV, as the vaudevillian antics on *Sanford & Son* played out to a canned laugh track.

A half hour later, Karen was fast asleep. I slid out from under her and she rolled over, facing the back of the sofa, still asleep.

I went down into the basement. Alan was still sliding hot wheels cars up and down a track, running it through the pup tent, over a chair seat, then down to the fireplace screen. He rocketed the cars along the track so they left the road, sailing over the chair, then made a ting sound as they came to a stop at the metal screen. Ethan was asleep, curled up beside him. I spoke softly to Alan, who was yawning despite himself, and woke up Ethan enough to get both boys ready for bed.

I dragged the trundle out from under Ethan's bed and made it up. Alan crawled under his sheets and Ethan mechanically rolled into his own bed beside him. Both of them were asleep in no time.

I went back upstairs. Karen was still asleep, sighing softly. I slid my arms under her and lifted her off the sofa, feeling as if I was Clark Gable, carrying Vivien Leigh to bed in *Gone with the Wind.*

She woke up briefly, undressed, and settled immediately under the covers, the flannel—warm and cozy—putting her back into a deep slumber.

I washed up the dinner dishes, put away the dry plates and glasses, then I swept the front entry, and sat in the living room, thinking. I couldn't sleep.

On one hand, I was anxious to get to sleep. I might get more information out of the Rhonda in my dream, more insight into the mysterious bottle she gave me.

On the other hand, I felt restless. Karen wanted me to adopt Ethan. I wanted to adopt Ethan, as much for my need to give him a real family as for the desire to make Karen happy, and as a byproduct it would make Ethan feel even more loved. All my thoughts were jostling each other, each trying to get to the front of my mind at the same time. I shook my head. It was all too much.

I put on my pajamas and warmed up a saucepan of milk. At least that would help me sleep.

It was a cool evening, the three-quarter moon in the sky looking like a pale cookie with a bite taken out. It faded and shone, passing behind clouds and reappearing, paying peek-aboo with me.

I sat on the front porch, my knees up at my chest and my feet warm in fuzzy slippers, sipping my warm milk. As a child, I used to look at the sky and wonder if anyone was out there, looking down, watching me as I watched the stars.

A sound made me tilt my head. Karen, her tartan robe tight around her, sat down beside me.

"Hey, you," she whispered. "Can't sleep?"

I smiled and kissed her softly on the lips. "Hi," I said. "Did I wake you up? I'm just thoughtful."

"I still have that penny for my thoughts." She nudged me. "What are *you* thinking?"

I shook my head. "Lots of things. The dead guy's girl-friend, mostly."

"Is she cute?" Karen asked, smirking.

I grinned. "Not particularly. Walsh likes her, though. I dream that she still works in a dry cleaner's, and she's try-ing to tell me something. I think it may be important."

Karen frowned and rested her head on my shoulder. "Be careful, okay? You can only be hurt so many times and come back. Last year was hell."

I slid my right arm around her shoulder and hugged her. "Don't worry. This isn't like last year."

Karen scratched my knee. "What else are you think-ing?" she purred.

"Ethan. He can't get caught in this battle between Marchand and me. I won't let that happen."

Karen clutched my arm and tugged me close, smiling. "Good. Right answer."

I yawned, and the world suddenly got darker, colder, later. I got up, helped Karen to her feet, and we went to bed. She fell right to sleep. I was awake, thoughtful, for a moment. Then I slept.

ოექ

I enter the dry cleaner's. I pause at the door, thinking that I have to ask something. I can't exactly remember what, though.

Rhonda is behind the counter, smoking a very long cigarette. She nods at me. "You don't get it, do you?" she says. "Here."

She hands me a bottle, filled with clear yellow liquid. I unscrew the cap and sniff the contents.

I say something.

"Yeah." She shrugs. "I think that's why he died."

ოექ

I sat up, sweating. The dream, so vivid just a second ago, started fading the moment I woke up. I strained to remember the details, but it was like grasping fog. It got weaker and farther away the more I clutched at it.

Karen turned over and opened one eye. "Are you okay, hon?" she whispered.

I nodded. "So close. So damn close. I just need to get a handle on this thing." I sighed and squinted at my alarm clock. Three-thirty-five a.m. Too early to get up. I went back to sleep.

ოექ

Saturday mornings had a regular routine in our house.

Ethan was keen to have Alan take part in it. It began with cartoons: *Yogi's Gang* then *Bugs Bunny*. After that, stop for breakfast, usually pancakes and eggs.

This morning, however, I'd asked Frank and Helen to join us, so I set up the dining room with an extra leaf in the table and draped a huge white tablecloth over it. I pulled two kitchen chairs, out to complement the original six, and cooked while Bugs Bunny outsmarted Elmer Fudd.

Right on time, just before nine, Karen answered a knock at the door. Frank and Helen, cheery and rosy-faced, took off their coats and piled into the living room.

"Hey, Ethan," Frank said. "How are you doing?"

"Fine, Uncle Frank." Ethan jumped up and down with glee. "We got pancakes. Pancakes! Yaay! *Pancakes!*"

Frank looked at him, solemn. "So what's for breakfast?"

Ethan giggled. "Pancakes."

Frank nodded, still solemn. "You sure? What are we eating?"

This banter went on for a good two minutes, until Frank finally broke out into a wide grin. The joke had run its course.

"So." He turned to me. "Where are we in the Ed Hereford case?"

"Pancakes," I answered. "Today, Frank, the subject is pancakes."

Karen and Helen leaned in close, whispering to each other, occasionally glancing at Frank or me, and smirking. I went to the kitchen and got the coffee going then back to the dining room and set the table for eight.

Frank counted plates. "Two extra spots?" he asked, puzzled.

"Alan's mom and a guest should be here shortly," I answered.

Frank raised one eyebrow. "Really. Anyone I know?"

I smiled. "Sarcasm. Very good."

Right on cue, another knock at the door, and Karen

opened it again. I could hear her greeting Vivian and Walsh casually, with no hint of surprise or wonder that they'd shown up together. The pair piled into the living room. Walsh froze when he saw Frank.

"Inspector, hello—I didn't expect to see you here, sir."

"Hi," Frank drawled. "Of course, why would I be at the home of my best friend?"

Frank's eyes moved over to Vivian. She was wearing a tight pair of slacks and an equally tight pullover. Frank stood slowly, as though getting up quickly might scare his prey. He glided over to her and reached out his hand.

"Hi, I'm Frank. Call me Frank, just Frank," he crooned.

I leaned over and whispered into his ear, "Easy, tiger," I smirked.

He frowned at me and sat back down.

I clapped my hands together. "Okay, everybody, let's eat."

Everyone gathered at the dining table. Karen and I ran back and forth, passing plates of food and cups of coffee from the kitchen to the dining room.

Walsh sat beside Vivian, sharing his time between wolfing down food and whispering to her. Frank sat between Helen and Walsh, instinctively protecting her.

I placed a plate in front of Frank, bowing with a flourish. He glared at it, unsure of what to do.

"What's this?" he asked, halfway between indignant and puzzled.

"Eggs Benedict, Frank," I answered.

"Is it good? I've never heard of this before."

"No, Frank, it's crap." I sighed. "All my food is crap."

He shrugged, embarrassed. "No, I just mean, you know, just, I never ate this before, is all."

He took a tentative bite of his eggs, with a liberal daub of sauce, and chewed it slowly. His eyes widened and he nodded, still chewing. "Mff. Goof," he grunted. He took another, larger bite.

"You're welcome," I said. He nodded again. I looked

over at Helen. She was staring at her plate wistfully. "Problem?" I asked.

"Eggs." She shrugged. "They make me kind of sick right now."

Karen stood up and swiftly took Helen's plate. Wordlessly, she went through to the kitchen and came back with a plateful of pancakes and a banana.

She placed them in front of Helen and leaned in close, whispering. "Bananas helped me with Ethan," she said.

Helen nodded thanks.

Vivian gasped at the interplay.

"You're pregnant?" she squealed. "Congratulations. When is it due? Is this your first?"

Vivian covered her mouth and snickered. Helen looked at Frank.

Frank glowered at Walsh. "You say one word." Frank aimed a finger at Walsh. "I use you for target practice."

Walsh grinned like an idiot and shook his head, waving his hands in front of him. "No sir. Not a word." He chuckled, leaned down, and attacked his food, smiling silently.

As we finished our coffee and leaned back, letting the meal settle, Frank looked out the window, thinking to himself.

"You doing all right, Frank?" I asked.

He shrugged. "Yeah. If you don't mind, we'll announce Helen's news tomorrow at your barbecue."

He smiled at Helen. She nodded and smiled back.

Walsh turned to Frank and leaned forward. "Inspector, do you have any insight into our case?"

Frank glanced at me for permission to talk shop. I nodded.

"Your dead guy had no enemies, no gambling debts, no pissed ex-wives, right?" he asked.

"Right," Walsh agreed. "And his live-in, Rhonda, was at work when he was killed. We got that from her *other* boyfriend, Gustavo De Melo. He's also her boss."

Frank snorted. "Busy girl. Any other news?"

"Some," Walsh said, getting serious. Vivian watched him, intrigued. "De Melo kicked in the door after he and Rhonda found the dead guy, maybe to make it look like a robbery gone bad. But we don't think either of them did it."

Helen leaned forward. "Why would she do that?"

Frank grunted, "Hmm?" and took another swig of coffee.

"Why make it look like what it wasn't? She must have known neither of them did it?"

Frank leaned back. "What are you getting at, hon?"

Helen shook her head. She was about to tell us something we should have thought of. "If my boyfriend and I found a body, why would I try to disguise the crime?"

The room went dead quiet. Frank stared at her. "Why?" he asked.

She continued. "What if each thought the other *seemed* guilty?"

Walsh shook his head. "But," he said. "We interviewed them separately. Rhonda would have told us if she thought Gustavo did it. He would have said the same about her. At that point, there would have been no point in covering for the other person."

Helen shook her head. "That's not what I'm getting at," she said, firmly.

Walsh opened his mouth to say something, but Frank glared at him and he closed it again.

Helen placed the heel of her hand firmly on the table, in a slow-motion karate chop. "I didn't do it, and we were at work when he was killed, so you didn't do it." She nodded, the idea becoming clear in her head. "If they called the police and said 'we came here to have sex and he was already dead,' it would cast a bad light on them. It would make them *seem* guilty. So the best solution was to make it look like they discovered him, but innocently. That's why they had to make it look like a crime as well as a murder. Otherwise, how could the boyfriend explain being there?"

Frank nodded. "So who did it?"

Helen smiled. "You're thinking the killer was this woman or the boyfriend. They're the only suspects you have. But they are the two people least likely to have killed him."

Frank frowned. "Why?"

"Because," Helen said. "Both had reasons to keep the status quo, right? Neither one benefitted from your victim's death."

Frank smacked his forehead with his hand. I just shook my head.

Frank nodded. "You couldn't just tell us who actually did it, could you, hon?"

Helen shrugged. "No, that's your job. You're on your own there."

CHAPTER 9

I spent most of Saturday preparing for the party. I had a large gas barbecue, plus one I'd borrowed from a neighbor, set up in the back yard. Plastic tablecloths, paper plates, and disposable cutlery were all lined up in baskets in the basement, so that after church I could simply set out everything for the event. Just before dinner, the phone rang. Karen answered, frowned, and handed me the receiver.

"Someone for you," she said, puzzled. "A man."

I took the phone from her. "Yes?" I asked.

"Hey, man," said the voice on the other end. "Congrats. From Dad, too."

I smiled. "Yeah, you bet. He told you?"

"Yeah, man. Called me on the road."

"Where are you?" I asked.

"Kingston. We'll be in Toronto tomorrow, man."

"Listen, we're having a barbecue tomorrow," I said, smiling at a puzzled Karen. "How many of you are there?"

"Busload, man. Busload," he said.

"Good, see you then. All my best."

"Who was that?" Karen asked, curious.

"Someone who wants to meet you."

She frowned. "He sounds like a thug. Is he another one of your criminal acquaintances?"

I chuckled. "You'll see."

၉၁၉

After church, I hurried home and made breakfast for the three of us. By ten in the morning, I'd set up the barbecues, assembled the tables beside them, and stapled down plastic tablecloths. It looked quite elegant.

I arranged the condiments, buns, plates, and cutlery in rows on one table, beverages on the other. Working in the restaurant with Dad was good training. Ethan helped us, glad to be involved. Karen cleaned the house, dusting and preening as though royalty were coming to visit.

By noon, with light wisps of smoke curling lazily from both grills, I was all set for company.

I donned my "Kiss the cook" apron, glanced up at the sky, thankful for the mild weather, then started on the first round of food. A half hour later, Frank and Helen sauntered up the driveway hand in hand. Ethan tackled Frank and gave him a big hug. Karen led Helen off to one side, both women talking over each other.

Frank strolled over to me and carefully examined the barbecues. "So, Ian, what's cooking?" he joked. He leaned down and sniffed at the closed lid nearest him.

"Hungry, Frank?" I asked.

"Hell, yeah. Anything good, kid?"

"Just for you, buddy." I took a plate and loaded on grilled potato wedges. Then I constructed a loaded burger and presented him the finished dish. He nibbled on a potato, then he took a bite of the burger and frowned.

"Problem?" I asked, puzzled.

"Are you completely incapable—" He paused, munching. "—of making mediocre food?" He took a larger bite of the burger and grunted, nodding approval.

I grinned and put an arm over his shoulder. "I'm flattered, Frank. Thanks."

He grunted again, munching happily. Within a few minutes, Walsh arrived, escorting Vivian and Alan. Next Captain Van Hoeke and his wife walked up the driveway, his arm around her waist.

They were in jeans and sweaters, clearly outfits they

were unused to wearing. I walked down to meet them part-way.

"Captain, wonderful to see you, sir," I said. "Rebecca, as lovely as ever." I gave her a peck on the cheek.

"Ian," She tilted her head expectantly. "How's married life?"

I grinned. "No idea. I'll keep you posted."

A half dozen or so more guests streamed in, dragging wives and girlfriends, and by one-thirty, the yard had two dozen people clustered around in small groups, eating and laughing. I was talking to one of the detectives, swapping stories about something or other, when we saw him. He was tall, huge, the color of milk chocolate, with wild afro hair that rippled as he took a step. He wore heavy prison jeans and a studded leather jacket with a metal eagle on the back.

He came through the suddenly silent crowd, oblivious to everyone else, and walked up to me.

"You Ian?" he asked in a thick Jamaican accent. I looked up at him and nodded. He turned, looked back down the driveway and yelled, "*Yep!*" the turned back to face me.

Walsh and Frank took up positions behind me, worried about what might happen next.

"Where you want?" the man asked, serious.

I frowned. "Here and now?"

Frank looked around for something to use as a weapon. From the base of the driveway, another man came up. He was my height, pale, slim, wearing a suit jacket, with a po-nytail and a shiny black goatee. He walked briskly up to me, stopped dead, threw his arms around me, and lifted me up.

"Hey," he said, in a Louis Armstrong voice. "How's my little brother?"

He let me down. I wrapped my arm around his neck and addressed the group, who collectively sighed in relief.

"Hey, everyone, this is my big brother James." I tugged at his ponytail. "Hungry, man?"

"Starved, bro," he hissed. "Got enough food for the band?"

I frowned. "They gonna play?"

"If they can eat, they'll play." He laughed. "Boys, come get it!" he called.

A handful of men, all wearing denim jeans, streamed up from the street and lined up to take food from the tables. They mingled with the other guests, talking about music, travel, and everything else. By two o clock we were one big group. James looked at his watch and winked at Karen.

He yelled something and his men headed, en masse, down to a Bluebird school bus parked across the driveway. They returned with a few cases, unpacked them, and, in ten minutes, set up a drum set, upright bass, and an amplifier.

One case became a small, low podium. James hopped onto it, put a mouthpiece into a shiny chrome trumpet, turned to the men behind him, and casually counted; "One, two, three."

They started to play. They belted out tunes by Duke Ellington, Tito Puente, Count Basie, and a string of others.

Within five minutes we were all bouncing to the beat or tapping in time. Captain Van Hoeke swung Rebecca around as the band played a soaring version of "Satin Doll."

After thirty minutes, the band stopped. Everyone cheered loudly—everyone. I turned around, stunned to see several neighbors, clustered at the base of the driveway, applauding the music. I waved them up to join us. Some did, others stayed back, too polite to crash the party.

James got down and made himself a plate of food. I smiled at Karen and raised my eyebrows in a silent question. She grinned and nodded.

I climbed up onto the platform, raised my hands, and waited till the crowd went silent. "Ladies and Gentlemen," I announced. "Can I ask you to give a big hand for my brother, James McBriar, and his amazing band, The Scarlet Pimpernels."

The crowd roared, even the people in my driveway.

"I would like to make an announcement," I called out.

I inhaled deeply. This was a one-way trip. I couldn't

take back anything I said now. The crowd stared at me, waiting for my next words.

"It is with great pleasure that I want to announce—" I paused, looking around. "—that Karen, the joy of my life, the light of my being, has agreed to become my wife."

The crowd was silent. Everyone stared at me. What had I said wrong? Karen stepped up onto the platform and took my arm. At that, everyone cheered. The men shook my hand, the women gave me a kiss. Karen accepted hugs, kisses, and best wishes from everyone as well, nodding and smiling as they clustered around us.

I turned back to see James shake Karen's hand and give her a peck on the cheek. "I know you'll be happy with this goof," he wheezed. "He's every bit as nice as he seems." James hugged me again and took my head in his hands. "You do right by her, man," he warned. "Elsewise, Dad said he'd come after you." He grinned broadly.

Everyone started eating again, smiling as they did.

James shooed us off the platform. He raised his hands, his trumpet swinging from his thumb. "I just want to say," he bellowed out, in a voice far too loud to be his. "My little brother Ian has always been a guy you could rely on, a guy who would always to do the right thing. I talked to Dad last night," He looked down at Karen and me. "And he says to keep on doin' the right thing. I'd like to dedicate this next song to my little brother's lovely girl, soon to be his lovely wife. Karen, this's for you, hon."

He pushed a plastic cone into the bell of the trumpet. His guitar man played a few notes and stopped. The crowd hushed. Then the guitar started again, playing the intro to the tune James had apparently chosen as our song. I agreed with the choice.

James held his trumpet at his side, then joined the guitar, his muted trumpet purring in the open air. Van Hoeke nodded at me. He recognized the tune right away.

James lowered the trumpet and sang the lyrics, his voice like Frank Sinatra over sandpaper.

"Someday, when I'm awfully low,
When the world is cold,
I will feel a glow
Just thinking of you
And the way you look tonight."

I took Karen's hand and danced with her, slowly, gently, as the people around us moved back to give us room. James played a refrain and put the trumpet down again to sing the next verse.

"Yes, you're lovely, with your smile so warm,
And your cheeks so soft,
There is nothing for me
But to love you,
And the way you look tonight."

The guitar played the refrain again, and the music stopped. Karen and I stood still, surrounded by people, every one of them silent. She reached up on her tiptoes and kissed me, gently.

"Hey, you." Her eyes were moist. "The answer is still yes."

I grinned like an idiot, hugged her tight, and kissed her forehead. Everyone applauded. I looked around and saw that Frank was pointing at himself.

I smiled and nodded. "Ladies and gentlemen," I bellowed. "Can I ask you to turn your attention to my good friend, Frank Burghezian. Frank?"

Frank shooed James down from the platform and stood up on it. "Today is a day for great joy," he started. "I wish my friends Ian and Karen all the happiness in the world." He clapped loudly and the crowd followed him with another round of applause. "In addition to the good news from my friend Ian, I'd like to share some good news of my own." He looked at Helen, who smiled broadly, biting her fist in front of her mouth. He continued. "I'd just like to say that in a few months, the world will be blessed by the birth of one more Burghezian." He grinned. Everyone gasped. Helen smiled and made a peace sign. He frowned. "Huh?" he asked.

She mouthed the word "'Two."

"Two," he repeated. Then the significance of that hit him. *"Two? Twins? Two? Two!"*

He leapt off the platform and rushed over to Helen, hugging her gently.

Everyone laughed. He didn't notice them as he cradled her in his arms. "Twins," he whispered.

Helen laughed. "Yes, silly. Twins." They hugged again.

The crowd went, "Awww," in unison.

The band started up again, and James sang a jazzy rendition of "We're Having a Baby."

ԇ๛ԇ๛

James and the band were back on the road, headed for Detroit to a gig. They all thanked us profusely for the food. I'm sure some of them hadn't eaten a proper meal in weeks. They also happily took almost every scrap of leftover with them. I took that as a compliment. James gave Ethan an old trumpet as a gift. Ethan spent hours trying to get a sound out of it, finally blowing something between a middle C and a charging elephant.

James had done a number of card tricks that kept us all amazed. He had loved magic for as long as I could remember. He was smooth, engaging, and kept everyone guessing until the end of the trick. That was part of what made his band successful, I realized. He could make an audience anticipate the next trick, the next song, the next chord then wow them with the unexpected.

ԇ๛ԇ๛

It was almost seven o clock by the time everyone left. Captain Van Hoeke and some of the others helped clean up. I returned the second barbecue to my neighbor, along with my thanks and a bowl of potato salad. He said I could borrow it again anytime. Frank and Helen sat on our sofa, Helen with her feet up, Frank rushing back and forth getting drinks and pillows for her.

Frank was still in a state of shock. Finally, when we'd settled down, he turned to Helen and asked the question we'd all been thinking. "When did you find out we're having twins?" he asked, mystified.

Helen grinned. "Friday. I went for my regular checkup. The doctor wasn't entirely sure before, but he definitely heard two heartbeats Friday. Everything's still going well, don't worry."

"Don't worry," he snickered. "Easy for you to say. You're not worried like I am."

"No." Helen smiled. "I'm just pregnant, that's all."

Frank stared at her for a second then broke into a smile. "Sorry, I'm excited. I'm an idiot."

"That's why I married you," she answered.

Karen was staring down at her shoes, thinking. I watched her for a minute. She didn't move.

"I have a penny for your thoughts," I said. What are you thinking?"

She looked up at me, frowning. "Could we get married right away?"

I felt a rush of emotion—panic and excitement all at once. I shrugged. "Why do you ask?"

"I don't want Ethan to grow up a bastard," she said simply.

We were quiet, watching her.

I had never thought of him as one, but I understood her wanting to protect her son. "We can get married right away if you want, but later on I want to do it right—a big wedding."

"Deal," she answered.

Helen leaned forward. "Can I come, too?"

Karen grinned. "*Someone* has to throw rice."

Frank beamed. "So, 'The way You Look Tonight,' that'll be your song, huh?"

"Why not?" I answered, glancing at Karen. "It's appropriate, don't you think?"

Frank nodded. "Gershwin, right?"

"Jerome Kern and Dorothy Fields," I corrected.

"Dorothy Fields? Isn't she 'The Flying Nun' on TV?" he asked.

"No, that's Sally Fields," I answered.

He shrugged. "Whatever."

Frank and Helen left around eight-thirty. Frank carefully guided her behind the wheel of her car then ran around to the passenger side. As they drove off, Karen wrapped an arm around my waist and waved goodbye. Ethan was asleep in no time, his trumpet upright on the night table beside him.

Karen got into her sleep shirt, brushed her teeth, and climbed into bed. I put down the book I was reading and slid down beside her.

"Hey, you," she said. "So, still want to marry me?"

I sighed, and hugged her tight. "More than ever."

We both fell asleep.

ເຈເຈ

Monday morning was sunny and mild. I made lunches for Ethan and Alan, humming cheerily to myself. Karen and I took the morning off and drove to City Hall. Karen clutched our birth certificates and driver's licenses in a folder and we applied for a marriage license.

There was a three day wait, I was told, to get married in Ontario. On the plus side, we didn't need a blood test. After being in hospital a year ago, I hated needles.

We had lunch near her office, then I dropped her at

work. I headed to my car, still humming to myself. I alternated between "The Way You Look Tonight" and Gershwin's "S'Wonderful".

I sat in the Fury, still smiling, and turned on the radio.

"Fifty-two-four-eight for messages?" I asked.

Walsh's voice came on immediately, anxious. "Sergeant, can you call this number right away?"

He rattled a number off. I wrote it down. "Anything I should know about before I call?" I asked.

"It's important. Just call it, sir. Now," he said. There was a hint of panic in his voice.

I walked to a phone booth by the car and dialed the number. To my surprise, Walsh answered. "Ian, I need to talk to you," he started.

I heard traffic in the background. "Why not just talk to me on the radio?" I asked.

"I couldn't put this on the air," he answered. "Mrs. Burghezian called Frank at work. A male teacher has really upset her. She was crying, it seems."

"Not good." I frowned. "Where's Frank now?"

"He's on his way to 'kick the living shit out of him,' in his words," Walsh said. "I'm at a pay phone near her school. He was looking for a ride when I left."

I sucked air. "Meet me at the school. I'm on my way." I got into the Fury and put the gumball on the roof.

The flashing red light, as always, bought me space in traffic, the siren even more.

Helen's school was in the old East York area of the city off Coxwell Avenue, in a building that was the standard school design for fifty years—three stories of thick stone and small, wired windows, surrounded by a playground and a baseball diamond.

I screeched to a stop in the parking lot.

Walsh was pacing outside his Polara. We walked into the building, side by side.

Along one wide terrazzo-floored hall was a sign that read *Office*. We entered the double door below the sign. Sitting on a chair, weeping softly, was Helen. She looked up as she saw us, blushed with embarrassment, and straightened her skirt, an unconscious way of saying "I'm fine."

I crouched down beside her and whispered, "Hey, Helen, you okay?"

She shook her head and started to cry again. "He's such an asshole," she hissed. "I was just trying to do what's best for the kids, and he screamed at me."

"Who?" I asked. I was aware of a man beside me, a slight, balding man with glasses. He looked like Clarence the angel in *It's a Wonderful Life*.

"Are you a colleague of Mr. Burghezian?" he asked, a mild Irish accent coming through.

I stood up. "I'm Detective Sergeant Ian McBriar, a friend of Helen's."

He craned his neck to look up at me. "I'm Principal Taggart. I've already spoken to Mr. Frost. He was quite unreasonable, we feel."

"What exactly happened?" I asked. "Be clear, and make it fast."

"Mr. Frost wanted the children to run laps around the school field. One boy has severe asthma. Mrs. Burghezian told him so, and that she thought the boy should stay behind, but Mr. Frost refused. He became quite insistent and, when Mrs. Burghezian argued with him, he called her some very unpleasant names. He will be admonished for this behavior, of course."

"That may be the least of his problems," Walsh said. "Inspector Burghezian is on his way."

Helen looked at Taggart in surprise then at me. "Frank?" she said. It was enough. She covered her head with her hands.

"Don't worry," I said. "We're here."

"I'm afraid Mr. Frost is quite formidable. He was a heavyweight boxer," the principal warned.

"Great." I smiled. "That will buy him an extra five seconds of life."

The principal's eyes widened. He heard a sound in the hallway, and we all turned to see.

Frank stormed into the office, trailed by a young uniform who had driven him over.

"Helen?" he barked. The old Staff Sergeant came out, loud and clear. He squatted beside her.

"I'm fine. Let's go. Just take me home. Please," she sniffed.

Frank stood up and turned to the principal. "Where is he, Taggart?"

The principal bravely held up his hands. "Frank, be sensible. Let's all be adults here."

Frank pivoted and marched down a different hall, toward a sign that read Gymnasium. Walsh, the uniform, and I followed at a trot, three unlikely groupies. I turned to the uniform and pointed.

"Wait in the office, please," I said.

I didn't want any more witnesses than necessary. He stopped. Frank turned a corner and walked through a set of swinging doors, into a small gym. A burly man in shorts and sneakers was barking at a group of terrified young boys. He loomed over them, strutting back and forth, a basketball under his arm, belittling them one by one.

He lifted up the ball and threw it casually into the stomach of one boy. The boy staggered back, clearly hurt. Frank stood along one wall of the gym, waiting for the man to notice him.

A moment later the man turned back, glared at Frank, and stuck his hands on his hips. "What are you doing here?" he sneered and waved at the door. "Get out of my class."

Frank didn't move. "Tired of picking on pregnant women? Moving down the food chain to kids, huh, Frost?"

"I'm warning you, Frank," the big man said, waving a finger. "Don't push me. You'll regret it."

"Not really," Frank said, confidently. "You're just a bully and a gutless little chickenshit."

The boys snickered at the language.

The man glowered at them, upset at being ridiculed. He turned beet red and took a step toward Frank. "You take that back, you stupid moron," he barked. "Or I'll tear you apart limb from limb."

Frank tucked his hands under his armpits then started hopping and clucking like a chicken. The boys giggled— clearly they enjoyed seeing their tormentor being teased.

Frost glared at them. "Frank, you're just begging for a beating. Do you really want me to give one to you now?"

Frank snickered. "You couldn't beat an egg, you pussy."

The big man turned even redder and marched over to Frank. He was taller than me, and he clearly worked out. His shoulders were a squared line from side to side. He poked Frank in the chest with a thick finger. "Don't push me, little man. I know karate."

"Really?" Frank feigned surprise. "The Japanese chick? I banged her sister."

Frost roared and hauled back, swinging a wide fist. It caught Frank on the side of the head. Frank staggered and leaned sideways, his legs buckling, but he stayed upright.

Frank turned to the boys. "Who threw that punch?" he called. Obediently, they all pointed at their teacher. He smiled. "Good. You all saw it."

He straightened up and lunged forward to grab Frank in a bear hug.

The next three seconds happened in slow motion. Frank swung a short rabbit punch into Frost's throat, then he brought his heel up and stomped on Frost's left foot. Frost curled up his leg, wincing in pain.

Frank backed up slightly and kneed the inside of Frost's thigh, hard.

Frost, in obvious agony, bent forward. Frank stepped back and, with one swift kick, tried to punt Frost's face into the rafters.

Frost did a quarter backflip, landed on his shoulders, and slid to a stop, unconscious.

Frank smiled at the boys. "Class dismissed," he said.

He brushed himself off and walked casually back to the principal's office.

We followed, silent.

Frank grinned at the principal. "You may want to get some Band-Aids for Mister Frost." Taggart nodded. "And an ambulance. Good day."

He took Helen's arm and walked her out to her car. They left silently, the uniform trailing along behind them, leaving Walsh and me alone with Principal Taggart.

"So." Taggart sighed, looking back and forth at Walsh and me. "What do we do now?"

"Well." I shrugged. "First, I'd call an ambulance. Mr. Frost will be off work for a while."

Principal Taggart frowned. "You know, there will be consequences to this incident."

I smiled. "I agree. Mr. Frost attacked a police officer. We have witnesses."

We made notes of the incident, along with names and times, and left our business cards. Walsh and I walked out to our cars to talk, moving aside so the medics could wheel Frost's gurney past us into their ambulance.

He squinted at me and crooked a finger, calling me over.

I bent down close to him. "Yes?" I asked.

"Frank's a stupid ass. I'm going to get him for this," he wheezed.

I stood up and nodded. "Detective Walsh, follow the ambulance to hospital. I want this man charged with assaulting a police officer."

Walsh smiled and got in his car.

I leaned down again, right down close to Frost's ear. "Bad idea, stupid," I whispered. "Also, if you ever piss off Helen again, this will be nothing compared to what I'll do to you."

തെരുത

The clock on the Fury's dashboard said two forty five. I had to pick Karen up at five. That left me a little over two hours to kill. I wanted another look at Rhonda's apartment.

I drove up Bayview to Rhonda's place, not quite sure of what I'd find, just looking for inspiration. In the daylight, her building looked stark, the few shrubs around the brick walls sparse and dry. I walked up the steps to the front door. It was wide open. The caretaker was in the lobby mopping up, letting the breeze dry the floor.

He nodded at my badge and stepped aside to let me up the stairs. I padded up the steps, mentally picturing Rhonda and Gustavo, sneaking up the steps at two in the morning, holding hands, whispering, his arm around her waist as they entered her apartment.

I passed Annie Ross's door as I headed for Rhonda's. She would have heard them passing her apartment if she had been awake. The TV was on. I could hear a commercial playing and, a second later, I heard the clanging of dishes. Annie was home. I knocked on her door.

She opened the door, dressed in a purple velour track suit and sandals which did nothing for her appearance, a fuzzy ribbon pulling back her shaggy hair. She seemed at first shocked to see me, then she got a guilty look.

"Hi." I smiled. "It's Annie, right? Annie Ross?"

She nodded, her mouth slightly open in surprise. "Yeah, hi," she mumbled.

"Mind if I come in for a moment?" I asked cheerily.

She backed up slightly. I stepped past her and into the living room. I looked around, nodding. "You have a nice place here, Annie. You keep it tidy."

Her apartment was sparely furnished. A brown corduroy loveseat sat against one wall, facing a black and white TV on the other wall, with an oval coffee table separating them.

I noticed a pile of clothes in a hamper by the loveseat and some newspapers scattered on the coffee table. A withered dracaena plant hung limp in one corner.

"You're not at work," I said. "Are you off sick?"

She stared at me for a second. "Um, yeah," she said, absentmindedly. "Feeling sick."

"You're out of work, aren't you?" I asked bluntly.

She closed the door quickly behind me and leaned her back to it, nervous. Her body language said, *Don't let that information out of here.* "Look, I can't lose this apartment. I got no place to go." She sighed. "I'm only off for a couple weeks. When the strike's settled, we go back to work, but if the super hears I'm at home, he'll try to evict me. I pay half what a new tenant would pay. They'll use any excuse to evict me."

"He can't do that," I stated. "It's against the law. If you get hassled, though, just call me, okay?"

She smiled. Her shoulders sagged in relief and she leaned forward, moving away from the door. "Would you like some tea?" she asked, relaxing. "I was just about to put the kettle on."

I nodded thanks. "Have you lived here long, Annie?"

"Yup. Years now, since my Arthur died. I like it here. It's quiet, and it's on the bus route." As she talked, she moved to the kitchen and filled a kettle.

She placed it on the stove, gathered some cups and saucers from a shelf, carefully arranged them on a square wooden tray, and brought them through.

"How long were you married?" I asked, mostly so she'd open up to me.

"Twenty five years. Arthur was a machinist. He made a good living. Now the kids have grown up and moved away so it's just me here. I still got my job with the union, but like I said, we're on strike right now, so I'm home."

The kettle whistled, sending a plume of steam into the air. Annie emptied it into a Brown Betty teapot and brought the pot through.

"So," I said. "The night that Ed died, do you remember anything else? Something, anything you might not have thought was important?"

She shrugged and poured tea for us both. "Nothing that comes to mind, no."

I lifted my cup and took a sip. "Mm. Good tea. Could we go over that night again, though, now that the panic of the moment has passed?"

She nodded. "I was asleep. It was about two in the morning, maybe two-fifteen, and I heard yelling." She paused, collecting her thoughts. "I thought it was Ed and Rhonda fighting. I try to ignore them when they do that. But I heard a loud sound. I figure that must have been her door getting kicked in, and a couple minutes later Rhonda knocked on my door."

"Did you see anyone in the hall? Anybody in the stairwell?" I asked.

She paused, thinking, and sipped her tea gingerly. "I can't be sure, but you know, for some reason I thought at the time there was somebody in the stairwell. I don't know why. You know that feeling that somebody's looking at you? I had that feeling. But then we found Ed, bless his soul, and I forgot all about that."

I nodded. "Did many people come over to visit them, do you know? Anybody you've noticed that came to see Ed or Rhonda?"

She shook her head. "They almost never had visitors. A couple of times I saw Rhonda talking to this woman who looked a lot like her, but nobody else really."

"That was her cousin, Paulette. Had you seen her often?" I asked as casually as possible.

"A few times, in the evenings."

"Did she come alone or with her husband?" I was scribbling as she spoke.

"Both. Sometimes she was with her girl. I guess it was her girl. Very pretty thing."

I smiled. "Okay. That's all I need for now. Thanks for the tea. And listen, if they do try to evict you, call me. I have friends."

ତେ୨୦

At a quarter to five, I pulled up outside Karen's bank building, put the *Police Business* sign on the Fury's dash, and jogged up the steps to the lobby and past the security guard. He nodded in recognition as I took the elevator to the twelfth floor.

I opened the brass-handled door that read *Mortgages and Loans* and stepped into the waiting room of Karen's office. It was the first time I'd been there since I proposed to her.

A handful of women, standing behind a high counter sorting documents, looked up and squealed in unison when they saw me. I felt the way The Beatles must have on The Ed Sullivan Show.

They all gathered against their side of the counter, giggling and smirking at me. I smiled politely and walked to the counter to meet them.

Some of the ones I'd met before kissed me on the cheek, others squeezed my hand, and all of them wished us well.

A long, long two minutes later, Karen fought her way through from the back to the counter and smiled at me.

She grinned. "Hey, you. Be right out."

One of the women looked after her, turned to me, and nodded. "She's a lucky girl," she said.

"I dunno. I think I'm the lucky one," I answered.

They all giggled.

Karen appeared from nowhere and took my arm. "Come on, let's get you out of here," she said.

I nodded goodbyes to the women and waved. "Bye, all. See you later," I called.

They yelled "Bye," and "Good luck," as we left the office for the elevator. I sighed. I was tired.

"Long day, hon?" Karen asked.

The elevator opened and we stepped in.

"Yeah," I drawled. "Frank got into a fight at school."

She frowned, worried. "Ethan?" she asked, puzzled. "Ethan, you mean?"

"Nope. Frank took on a six-foot-six, heavyweight boxer."

"Oh, dear. No, don't tell me." She gasped. "Is he all right?"

"He's in hospital." I chuckled. "Frank's fine."

She stared at me. "You're idiots, you know. Aren't you boys old enough to know better?"

I shrugged. "Frank was provoked. The dummy made Helen cry. Served him right."

She frowned. "I'll call Helen when we get home," she said, firmly. "Let's go."

The door opened at the main floor, and Karen dragged me out to the Fury.

She was completely silent on the drive home, frowning and staring out the window. She stomped up the porch steps and into our living room, sat at the sofa, and dialed Frank's phone number.

I opened my mouth to speak, but she pointed at me. "Quiet," she ordered.

I sat down, smiling.

Her eyes lit up. "Hi, Helen? So, what happened?" She listened intently, staring at the carpet. "Uh huh, yeah," she said. "And?" A pause. "He said what? Well, yes, I'd have decked him, too." Another pause. "But you're fine, right?" She nodded. "Okay, then. Much love. Bye." She hung up and glared at me. "He sounds like a brute. Why didn't you punch him out, instead of Frank?"

I laughed. "Frank was doing just fine by himself."

Karen shook her head. "Men," she sneered.

℘℘℘

Tuesday morning, I knew roughly what I could look

forward to. I made lunch for Ethan and Alan, kissed Karen goodbye, and drove to work.

Frank was in the station house, telling a joke. "So," he said, "The guy says 'Shoot the dog! Shoot the dog!'"

The other detectives laughed.

Frank turned when he saw me, smiled, and nodded. "Hey, Sergeant. Have a good evening?"

I shook my head. "Karen reamed me out for holding your coat in the fight. I'm just wondering what Captain Hook is going to do about it?"

He got serious. "Yeah. I wondered about that. If we get shit for this, let me do the talking, okay?"

Walsh showed up a few minutes early for a change. We stood in a tight group, quietly discussing what to do when we were asked about the school incident. The consensus was to go with the simple truth: Frank was provoked, was attacked first, and defended himself.

By nine thirty, most of the detectives headed out to their respective assignments. Frank and I stayed behind, as ordered by Van Hoeke, dreading what we knew was coming. Shortly after ten o clock, he called the three of us into his office. It was that "sent to the principal's office" feeling all over again, just like at school.

Frank sat across from Van Hoeke, staring at him. Walsh and I sat behind him, the classic three-man V-formation for confrontations. The captain put a single sheet of paper on his desk and, ignoring Frank, turned to face me.

"First off, Ian, Rebecca and I want to thank you for a lovely time at your barbecue. Rebecca especially wishes you and Karen the very best." He gritted his teeth, picked up the paper, and glared at Frank. "You, what the hell was going through your thick little head?" he snapped.

"Captain, if I can just explain," Frank started.

"Shut up, Frank." the captain interrupted. "You walked into a school and picked a fight in front of a class of children. What in God's name were you thinking?" He turned to Walsh and me. "And you two—" He pointed at us. "Did neither one have a single brain cell between you to defuse this bomb?" His teeth clenched as he spat out the words. Walsh shrank back in his seat. The captain sighed and waved at the ceiling with an unblinking stare. "What am I going to do with you? We report to a review board now after these hijinks, you know. We just can't go around beating up troublemakers like we used to."

Frank was going to lose his job, I realized. He would be kicked off the force, and it was my fault. I hadn't stepped in to stop him when I could have. The same Frank who'd saved my life when I was dying in the street. I owed him everything; giving up my job would be a small price to pay.

"Actually, Captain," I interjected. "It was my fault, not Inspector Burghezian's. I should have been the one to respond to Helen's call, since he was personally compromised in the situation."

Walsh leaned forward. "Sir, I'm the one you should blame," he stated. "If I hadn't told Sergeant McBriar about the argument, he wouldn't have gone to the school. I should have been the one to stop Inspector Burghezian. I should have calmed him down before he left here."

I looked at Walsh, stunned that he was willing to take the blame for the fight.

He grinned. "What? I can always go back into the family business."

Frank shook his head and faced the Captain. "Sorry, Marty, but I won't let these guys take the rap for me. If you want to boot my ass out, do it. But Ian and Patrick are *not* to blame. It was my fault. Period."

I leaned forward. "No, Captain. I'm the senior officer to Constable Walsh, and I should have been the one to handle the situation. Frank was too involved, emotionally."

Walsh shook his head. "If I hadn't called Sergeant McBriar, he wouldn't have been aware of this at all, sir, so it was my fault."

Van Hoeke leaned back, a combination of amazement and amusement on his face. He waved his hand at the door.

"Are there any other people out there who want to take the blame for this, or is it just you Three Stooges?"

Walsh smiled. "Actually, there were five Stooges in all, sir, just three at a time."

"Really?" I asked, oblivious to the trouble I was in. "Two of them were brothers, right?"

"Three: Moe, Shemp, and Curly were brothers," Walsh said.

Frank stared at us, amazed at the inane chatter. "Anyway," he reiterated. "Fire me, not them."

Van Hoeke stared, silent, then he leaned forward, scowling. "On a completely *different* subject, do you know what Rebecca and I like to do in the evening?"

Frank sighed. "Martin, your sexual escapades don't interest me. Fire me, and let them get back to work."

Van Hoeke frowned at him and addressed the three of us. "As I was saying, we like to relax playing board games. Our favorite is Monopoly. Rebecca loves Monopoly."

"Great," Frank groaned. "Now we get to hear about strip Monopoly. Just can me now, Marty."

Van Hoeke ignored him and went on. "One thing we do to make the game more interesting is to change some of the rules. It makes the game more fun."

Frank groaned. "Bo-ring! Does this bus stop soon, Marty? Can we get on to the firing part now?"

Walsh's face lit up. He leaned forward. "Shut up, Frank," he whispered.

I stared at Walsh.

Frank, ignoring Walsh, shook his head. "Let's just get this over with, huh, Captain?"

"As I was saying," Van Hoeke continued. "We change some of the rules, especially with the Chance cards."

"Boring, boring," Frank moaned.

It dawned on me what Walsh had just figured out. "Shut up, Frank," I said. I stared at him. His mouth was open in amazement. "Frank, shut up," I repeated.

Frank looked at me, puzzled. It finally occurred on him

what the captain was telling us, and his face brightened. "I'm so sorry, Captain," he said politely. "Please go on."

Van Hoeke sneered at Frank and continued. "One rule change is the 'Get out of Jail Free' card." He paused, waiting till he was sure we all understood. "We use it just once. Period." He stopped and watched our reactions. We all smiled quietly. He picked up his telephone and dialed an extension. "Please ask him to come in." He hung up. "Now, back to the previous, *unrelated* subject," the captain said simply.

The door opened, and Frost walked in, a bandage over his broken nose, his left eye black. Frank stood up and moved to one corner, away from the big man. Frost glared at him. Van Hoeke stood, smiling, and extended his hand. Frost took it.

"Mister Frost. Please sit down, sir." Van Hoeke waved at the chair Frank had vacated and Frost sat. "First, I wish to say that Detective Inspector Burghezian should not have become involved in the dispute between you and Mrs. Burghezian," he stated.

Frank opened his mouth to protest, and Van Hoeke shook his head very gently. Frank stayed quiet.

Frost grunted. "He assaulted me. I want to press charges."

"Yes, about that." Van Hoeke smiled. He slid the sheet of paper in front of Frost. "We have a number of witnesses who reported that you assaulted Inspector Burghezian first. Now, if you wish to proceed with your complaint, then we shall, of course, do so. If it is determined, however, in the course of the investigation, that *you* first attacked *him*, then we would have no recourse but to charge you with aggravated assault. In that case, you may likely be convicted of assaulting a police officer and, under school board rules, you'd lose your job. Nonetheless, if you do still wish to proceed, as I say, we will go forward with that."

"He insulted me in front of my class. He called me names," Frost growled.

"Sticks and stones, Mr. Frost. You know that verbal slurs are no excuse for a physical assault." Van Hoeke picked up a pen and pulled an important-looking form out of his desk drawer.

Frost stared at him, his mouth open, thinking about what to do next. His eyes narrowed and he smiled. "I tell you what," Frost offered. "I'll drop the charge, if I get a letter of apology from Frank."

Frank glared at the back of Frost's head. If looks could kill, Frost would be burning in hell.

Van Hoeke nodded slowly and smiled at Frost. "Of course," he agreed. "He will gladly write you a letter of apology."

Frost sat back, smiling smugly. Frank's mouth dropped open in protest, but again he was quiet.

"That letter," the Captain continued, "will detail the facts of the incident. That's department policy, of course."

Frank shrugged at me and mouthed, "Department policy?"

I shrugged back, just as confused. Frost didn't see it.

"For instance," Van Hoeke stated, "Inspector Burghezian's letter will mention that you contributed to the altercation by causing his pregnant wife to become upset."

Frost leaned forward and pointed a finger at the captain. "You don't know what she said to me. You have no right to say anything about that," he sneered.

Van Hoeke nodded. "No, no, quite right, we will stick to the facts. Frank will admit that he, a man of smaller stature, beat up a heavyweight boxer. I'm sure he will gladly admit to that."

Frost glowered at Van Hoeke. "He better not say anything like that!" he barked.

"Sir," the captain said softly, "I will ask you to not raise your voice in my office."

Frost sat back, fuming. Van Hoeke held a pen over the form. "So," the captain continued. "Do I take it that you don't want the letter of apology?"

Frost stood up. "Screw you," he spat. He looked at Frank. "Screw you all." He stormed out and left the building.

Van Hoeke leaned back and looked at us. "Three Stooges, huh?" He shook his head and smiled. "Get the hell out of here, you stooges. We have real work to do."

Frank leaned on the captain's desk and smiled softly. "I owe you, Marty. Big time. Thank you."

I nodded. "Monopoly, huh, sir? I like it." I grinned. "Let's go, gang. We got bad guys to catch."

Frank left the office. I followed. Walsh turned back as he was leaving and did the classic Curly bit, slappomh the top of his head from behind, going, "Woo-woo-woo-woo."

Van Hoeke laughed loudly at the antics. He was still laughing as we got to my desk.

The three of us stood there, just looking at each other. Frank spoke first. "Patrick, what on earth possessed you to take a bullet for me in there?" he asked.

"You're Sergeant McBriar's senior officer, sir. I'm supposed to take the blame if I screw up."

"How did you screw up?" Frank asked.

"I told Ian," Walsh said. "He owes you. I don't. I should have stepped in."

Frank thought for a moment and smiled. "Come on, you two. Early lunch. I'm buying."

We sat in a window booth of our diner. Frank savored a bowl of stew and I had soup. Walsh chewed on a club sandwich.

We ate silently for a few minutes, then Frank cleared his throat. "I want to say how privileged I feel to work with you two," he said, softly.

"It's mutual, Frank," I replied.

Walsh nodded.

"But don't stop me if I want to beat someone up."

We all laughed.

"So." Frank leaned back. "Where are we with your case, Ian?"

I shrugged. "I spoke to the witness, Annie Ross, yesterday. She didn't want her super to know, but she's off work for a couple of weeks while her union's on strike. She figures if they knew that they'd try to kick her out."

"Why would they do that?" Frank asked.

"Rent control?" Walsh asked.

I nodded.

"She is probably paying what—ninety, ninety-five dollars a month for the apartment," Walsh explained. "But they could get one sixty for it if it was empty."

"Ah." Frank smiled. "I get it. Keep quiet or get kicked out."

"Anyway," I continued. "The first sounds she heard were Rhonda and someone arguing, then she heard the door being kicked. After that, Rhonda called her over to 'discover' Ed, who was already dead."

Frank shrugged. "So we're no farther ahead, then?"

"Right," added Walsh. "Then again, we're keeping tabs on Rhonda, Inspector."

"Frank," Frank said.

Walsh smiled. "Frank it is."

"Also," I started and breathed deeply. "Could you both do me the honor of joining me this Friday morning? Karen and I would like to get married at City Hall, if Karen agrees."

Frank stared at me for a long time. "Would she still marry you if you were unemployed?"

"She's after my body, not my money," I said.

"Fair enough," Frank said.

"Will there be food?" Walsh asked, in a hopeful voice.

I nodded. "Good point. Let's all have lunch afterwards." I smiled. "Bring a date."

❧❧❧

Karen got home just before six and came into the

kitchen quietly, without saying a word. She wrapped her arms around me and squeezed tight. "Everything go okay at work?" she asked softly.

I nodded. "We got a slap on the wrist. Van Hoeke is a good guy. He plays by the rules, but he takes care of his men."

She nuzzled the back of my neck. "Helen told me. I'm so glad for you."

That didn't make sense. I frowned. "Wait a minute. When did she find out?"

Karen smiled sheepishly. "Rebecca Van Hoeke told her. Helen told me."

I squinted, pretending to be annoyed. "Can you tell Helen to tell Rebecca to tell the captain that I want a new chair?" I joked.

She shook her head. "You'll have to go through the regular channels for that one, sweetheart."

I lifted her up and sat her on the kitchen table. Her eyes widened, unsure of what I wanted to do next.

"Hey, can you take Friday off?" I asked.

She was puzzled. "Of course. Why?"

I smiled. "Let's get married."

She grabbed my face in her hands and stared at me. "You're sure about this, right?"

"Yeah." I nodded. "Absolutely. Do you still want to marry me?"

She kissed me softly and smiled. "Shut up, you."

ഏഔഏ

I go into the dry cleaner's. Rhonda is behind the counter, reading a magazine. I look down at my hands. I don't have any laundry. She looks up at me, reaches under the counter, and smiles. She hands me a glass bottle filled with yellow liquid.

"Here you go," she says.

I say something.

She shrugs. "Dunno," she says. "Never checked."

She unscrews the cap and sniffs the bottle. She collapses, dead. The bottle falls to the ground beside her. I kneel down to sniff the pool of liquid on the floor, but there is no smell. I can't breathe and gasp for air.

෬෬෬

I sat up in bed. Karen was snoring gently. The clock said four-fifty. I was too awake to sleep. I got my robe on and made coffee. The deep gray sky, through the living room window, was dotted with clouds, soft pillows in the heavens that blanketed the world. A street-cleaning truck passed by on Keele Street. Even two blocks away I could faintly hear its brushes scraping the dirt and grime of the city into its hopper, scrubbing the streets clean for this new day.

I stepped out onto my front porch. It was cool, but not uncomfortably so. I sat down, clutched my coffee, and huddled against the side rail, enjoying the solitude and quiet.

One of my neighbors, heading off to work for an early shift somewhere, whistled softly to himself as he walked past me to a green Pinto. I raised my coffee in a salute. He smiled and nodded as he saw me, still whistling. He got into the Pinto, ran the engine till the windows cleared, then cruised down Trowell Street to meet the morning.

A sound behind me got my attention. Karen, bundled up in her robe, sat down beside me. "Is this a private party or can anyone join in?" she asked.

In the still morning air her voice, even speaking softly, penetrated the neighborhood like a shout. I leaned against her for warmth.

"Hey," I whispered.

"Hey, you," she answered. "Are you all right, hon?"

I looked up. The sky, lightening with the approaching

dawn, was still a quilt of gray, patchwork clouds, all at different heights, passing over my head in a slow procession. I felt completely, perfectly, at peace.

"I'm fine, sweetheart," I said. "I feel great. How are you?"

She took my coffee and sipped. "I'm savoring my last two days as a free woman," she joked.

"Want to change your mind?" I teased.

She shook her head. "You don't get out of it that easily. You're mine for the next fifty years."

I snickered. "Geez, you only get thirty for murder."

She laughed out loud. A paperboy, rushing through his morning delivery, stopped to examine us. I smiled and waved. He waved back.

"Come on," I said. "I'll make you breakfast."

Karen stood and reached out her hand. "Not just yet," she purred.

❧❧❧

By eight o clock, I had made lunches, Karen was getting ready in the bathroom, and Ethan was eating scrambled eggs with one hand, holding a comic book in the other.

I leaned against the sink. "What's that you're reading?" I asked, curious.

"Archie," he answered. "It's real funny, Pops."

Karen came through, hooking earrings into her ear lobes, and kissed me.

"What was that for?" I asked.

"Breakfast," she answered and glanced down at my belt. "And the other thing."

I grinned. "Thank you, too."

I waved goodbye to her as she drove off, watching her wave back through the rear window of the Beetle, and walked Ethan across the street to school. I handed him a paper bag and squatted down, facing him. "Be good, learn a lot, and eat all your lunch, okay?" I said.

"'K." He nodded. "What's for lunch?"

"Worms in Jell-O," I answered.

His face dropped.

"I'm joking," I said. "It's turkey sandwiches. You and Alan like turkey, right?"

He giggled and hugged my neck. "Yup. Bye, Pops."

He raced off into the crowd of children, searching for his friend.

᧞᧞᧞

I got to 52 Division before nine. Frank was telling a joke.

"So the priest says 'I hate playing with your dad...'"

The men all laughed.

I read my messages. Gustavo De Melo was in North Carolina, but he had left his daughter's phone number with us. Rhonda was still at her cousin's and had requested we let her get her clothes. I passed that on to a uniform and let him handle it. That left one last thing to double check. I opened my desk drawer and pulled out a small blue velour box. Inside were two smooth gold rings, one in my size and one in Karen's. I took them out of the box, rubbed my fingers over them as if to make sure they were real, then put them carefully back in my desk.

A flurry of activity by Van Hoeke's office caught my attention. Several uniforms, rushing back and forth, seemed to be doing something in a hurry. Van Hoeke poked his head out of his office and pointed at me.

"Ian! Here! Now!" he barked and waved me into his office.

I walked in as fast as I could without running. Van Hoeke was by his desk, his phone in one hand, making notes and going "U-huh," to the person at the other end. He looked up and sighed.

"Guess what, Ian? You're up." He put the phone down. "We have a bank robbery in progress at King and Spadina. Best word we have is three or four guys with shotguns, holding about a dozen customers and staff. They tried for an in-and-out, but someone tripped the silent alarm, so now they're stuck."

I nodded. "What would you like me to do?"

"You're the lead on this. Take Frank and Patrick, but you're the point man."

"Boss," I said. I never called him boss. "Frank is the senior officer on the floor."

Van Hoeke stared at me for a moment. He didn't say what we were both thinking.

"Frank isn't ready for this today. You are," he said, simply. "How soon till you head out?"

I thought for a moment. "Give me ten minutes."

I went to my desk, found the business card I was looking for, and dialed the number.

"Doctor Feldman? It's Ian McBriar," I said, short, to the point.

She seemed surprised to hear from me. "Hi, Ian, how are you doing?" she said cheerily.

I explained what I knew and asked her for advice. She got right down to business.

"First, find out who the head man is. He'll have the largest gun. I know it's stereotypical and Freudian, but it's usually true. You *can't* change his mind. He convinced the others to follow him, and he's the one they look to for direction." She paused, thinking. "Then there's the other end of the spectrum, the lackey. He may be a relative, or a friend, but he's also the weakest person in the group. He might be the easiest to sway, but he holds no power in the herd—he's nothing."

"So who should I focus on, then?" I asked.

"Go for the number two man. He has the most to gain

by challenging the leader, and he has the smarts to be one himself, or he wouldn't be the number two man."

I wrote this down in point form, nodding to myself. "How do I play this when I get there? Hard cop, nice guy, what?" I asked.

She blew her breath out slowly, apparently deciding what to tell me. "Don't act smarter than them. Don't threaten them. They know what's at stake, and they know what a tight spot they're in. Don't mention the elephant in the room. Don't use words like jail, or police. Just guide them in the direction you want them to go, but make them think it was their choice to do so, if you know what I mean."

I smiled. "Great, Colleen. I think I've got it. Anything else you can think of?"

She was quick with her answer. "This is not last year. Be careful. You aren't being ambushed in the street and, if you keep calm, you'll get farther than by barging ahead. Also, smile and let them think that this is just an average day for you, that you don't see this as dangerous."

I thought about her advice. It helped me put together my plan of action. "Colleen, thanks again. I'll let you know how it goes."

"Keep yourself safe, Ian. Call me later." She hung up.

Frank was at his desk, just staring off into space. I sat across from him., worried

"Frank, you okay?" I asked. He didn't move. "Frank? *Frank!*" He still didn't move.

Finally, he looked at me. "Hi, Ian. What?"

I looked around. Nobody else had witnessed the exchange.

"Frank," I said softly. "You were a million miles away. You were having a fit."

"Was I? Sorry, Ian, I wasn't aware." He rubbed his face and frowned. "Everything okay?"

"We've got hostages in a bank robbery at King and Spadina. There are guys holding shotguns, and Captain Hook wants me on point for this."

Frank shook his head. "I'm senior officer on watch. It's my party, not yours."

I nodded. "Yeah, but today's my day, man."

"Why?" he asked, puzzled.

"Because today you're leading from the back seat."

He smiled a sad, understanding smile. "This epilepsy sucks." He sighed. "Okay, how do you want to do this?"

Walsh drove us down to King and Spadina. His Polara flew through traffic with the gumball and the siren going. A hundred yards from the bank, he turned off the siren and cruised to a stop outside the bank.

It was in an old red brick building, the ground floor newly sheathed in pale marble to convey a sense of integrity. A small, faded Canadian flag swayed over the front window, its flagpole just an iron rod sticking out of the marble at a lazy angle. The old brass windows had been replaced with black anodized aluminum frames, and the glass was now tinted, which made it almost impossible to see inside.

I stood behind a sawhorse, looking over at the bank. A man was just inside the front door, looking nervously out at the yellow cruisers and sawhorses blocking the street.

Frank came up beside me. "What are you thinking?" he asked.

I shrugged. "Today's the eighth. Welfare checks came out last Wednesday. They're broke."

"You think their welfare money ran out? That's why they're doing this? They're broke?" Frank asked.

"Yup. That also means they didn't have a lot to spend on shotgun shells. I'm guessing whatever firepower they have is in the barrels. What do you think?"

Walsh listened to this, fascinated. "You figured all that from today's date?" He was incredulous.

"That's what the odds would favor," I said. I turned to a uniform beside me. "Officer, how long have they been in here?"

He poked his chin at the bank. "Under an hour. They burst in right after opening time. We got our information from a patron who ran out as they were ordering everyone to the floor."

I smiled. "Okay. Good." I thought for a moment. "Patrick, there's a coffee shop right over there." I pointed. "They have really good doughnuts."

Walsh looked at me, incredulous. "You're hungry?"

"No," I answered. "Get me a dozen or so doughnuts, coffees, milk, sugar. See if you can borrow a couple of cafeteria trays, too."

He nodded and turned to go.

"Get a receipt," I called. "You'll need it for expenses."

He laughed at the mundane detail and headed down the street. I still had to find a way to approach the bank without looking like Clint Eastwood. I looked down at the rail tracks by my foot. The police barricades had blocked the King Street streetcars, all the way down the block.

Behind me, a streetcar conductor was pacing back and forth on the sidewalk, sipping a coke and waiting for the road to be cleared. I waved him over.

"Hey," I said. "How would you like to tell your friends you did something incredibly brave?"

Frank stared at me. "Ian, what are you planning?"

"I need to get in there." I shrugged. "That streetcar seems like the best way to do it."

He shook his head. "With all due respect, Detective Sergeant, you're an idiot."

I grinned. "You sound like Karen. Let's just get this done without any bloodshed."

"Okay." Frank shrugged. "If you get shot this time, don't count on me saving your ass."

I draped my jacket over a sawhorse, shook the bullets out of my revolver then placed the unloaded gun back in the holster.

I told the conductor what I needed him to do. He turned pale, but he agreed to help. Walsh returned with the food, struggling to carry a loaded, yellow-plastic cafeteria tray. I got on the streetcar, with the tray of coffee and doughnuts.

A sawhorse at one end of the barricade was moved back, and the streetcar rolled through the gap.

The crowd, which had gathered behind the barricade, moved aside in a wave.

The streetcar stopped in front of the bank. Its door opened and I stepped off. A few seconds later the streetcar carried on ahead, past the far barricade. That left me standing in the street, holding a tray with coffees and two large paper bags. I inhaled deeply. *Keep calm, keep calm*, I thought.

I waited patiently, while the figure inside the bank looked back, talking animatedly to someone behind him. He was the weak link, the stupid one. I could ignore him. I stood there, smiling stupidly, till the figure in the bank opened the door a crack.

"What do you want?" he yelled out.

Yeah, that was not a question Einstein would ask.

"You guys hungry?" I said, not very loudly.

He looked behind him again and spoke to someone, shrugged, then looked back at me. "What? I can't hear you," he called out.

He'd just given me permission to approach him. I nodded and walked slowly toward him. My heart raced. I breathed deeply, trying to relax, and stopped on the road, just off the sidewalk. I didn't want him to feel threatened. I smiled again. "I brought coffee!" I lifted the tray up. "And doughnuts. Can I come in? It's cold out here."

The man glared at my revolver.

"Sorry, I forgot," I apologized.

I carefully placed the tray on the ground, held my hands up, then with my left hand, gingerly lifted the revolver and laid it on the sidewalk.

I slowly picked up the tray again and walked to the front door of the bank. The figure moved back and pulled the door open. He was holding a crowbar, a good sign—they didn't have many weapons. He was young, twenty-odd, with a three-day's growth of beard and a torn army jacket covering a skinny pair of jeans. He looked hungry and tired. He wouldn't be any trouble.

I stepped inside and nodded. "Thanks. Want a coffee?" I asked it as though I was visiting a friend.

He looked back over his shoulder, waiting for approval. A scruffy, middle-aged man in a raincoat and corduroy pants was standing on the counter, straddling two tellers' wickets, pointing a double-barreled shotgun in the air. At least he wasn't pointing it at anyone in particular.

The man with the shotgun looked around nervously. A handful of people, men and women, lay face down on the floor around me, looking anxiously at each other.

"Why are you here, cop?" the gunman barked. "What are you after?"

I smiled cheerily. "You guys want to get out of here. I'm here to drive you wherever you want to go, as long as you let these people go, okay?"

He looked around furtively, thinking it over. "Okay. Okay. No tricks, hear? No tricks."

"Suits me fine. Listen," I said, "Can we give these good folks a bite to eat? You guys, too, of course. That will be cool with everyone, right?" I said "we" intentionally, to make it feel like "we" were all part of one group. I tried not to sweat, not to look scared.

I was terrified.

The one with the gun pointed a finger at me. "You drink first," he ordered. "No tricks."

I put down the tray, took a coffee, added sugar and milk, and took a sip. "Good." I reached into a bag, pulled out a random doughnut, and took a bite. "Good," I repeated.

I handed a coffee to the one with the crowbar. He looked at the gunman for approval. Colleen had been right—this one would do whatever his leader told him to do. I had to look confident.

"Can I give out coffees to these good people, too?" I asked casually. "I'm sure they'd like some."

The gunman ran his hand up and down the barrel, a

phallic gesture to assert his dominance. "No tricks, hear? I'm watching you," he growled.

"Sure, you bet. No tricks," I agreed. I passed out some coffee to random people around the room. "Say, you want these people to sit up to drink? Otherwise, they might spill coffee on the floor," I explained. I smiled constantly, pretending that this was just a regular day for me.

The gunman moved from foot to foot and shifted his stance slightly. He was getting nervous, losing his dominance, I sensed. I needed to make him feel he was still controlling the show. "Do we want everyone all lined up against one wall?" I asked, leading him where I wanted him to go. "That will make it easier to watch them."

He looked around and nodded, nervously.

"Okay, you heard the man," I called out. "No funny business, people, just sit together against the wall. Nobody talk, and nobody make any fast moves."

The gunman relaxed slightly. He now saw me as an ally. I was controlling his hostages for him.

"Anybody want doughnuts?" I called. Nobody moved. I turned to the one with the crowbar. "So what's your favorite flavor? I got chocolate, plain, sprinkles…"

He looked into the bag, curious. I could have taken his crowbar away in a second.

I didn't—he shouldn't see me as a threat, not yet. He reached in and pulled out a gooey cream-filled bun. He took a cautious bite.

"Good choice," I complimented. "That's my favorite, too."

He smiled. He was on my side now.

The gunman grunted and stared at me. "Look, what are you stalling for? I want to get into the safe, and I want a car, right now, or I start hurting people."

I shrugged. "Okay, let's do that. We have a car outside that I can call, as soon as these people are free. You also want the vault cash, right?" I turned to the hostages. "Who is the bank manager?" I called.

I hoped the manager would follow my lead.

A slight, balding man in a dark pinstriped suit raised a hand slowly. I walked over to him and helped him up.

"Hey, what's your name?" I asked loudly.

"Marcos. Brad Marcos," he said in a whisper.

"Do what I tell you to, okay?" I mumbled. "Just agree with whatever I say."

He stared at me, a look of fear on his face, and nodded very weakly.

"Hi?" I called to the gunman. "This is Brad. He's the bank manager, okay?" I turned to the manager, frowning. "Brad, what time tomorrow will the money truck be here?"

The manager's eyes widened in panic. He understood my statement. He sucked air. "Tomorrow," he said, in a low whimper. He faced the gunman, his voice stronger, certain. "We're getting our cash tomorrow afternoon. We don't have any today."

The gunman looked around, like someone desperately looking for lost car keys. He huffed, frustrated, then pointed the shotgun at the bank manager. I stepped between them and held my hands up. I was still terrified, almost numb with fear but I kept my smile.

"Hang on," I said, slowly. "Please point that thing away from people. We don't want to hurt anyone. We'll just get ourselves into trouble."

He huffed again, thinking hard, then slowly lifted the barrel skyward. "Okay," he said, "Get me all the money you got—now."

I nodded. The leader was doing what I wanted him to do. He still felt in control, but he was cooperating with me. Up to now, though, I'd only seen two robbers. Where were the others?

"How about if this fellow helps the manager open the safe?" I pointed to the skinny kid. "Then again, it's empty, so you're better off just taking money from the tills, isn't that right, Brad?"

The manager, his hands still above his shoulders, nodded, stunned. The gunman leaned back, still watching us. "Jay! Jay! Come here!" he called.

A third man appeared from the back. He must have been rummaging through offices. He looked like the older brother of the skinny one—better fed, but still desperate-looking, still slightly unsure of himself. He was unarmed, holding only a burlap sack.

"Yeah?" he grunted. "What?"

The gunman pointed at the tills. "Empty the cash drawers into the bag—fast," he barked.

"What about the safe? We came here for the safe," the third one complained.

"Screw the safe. The safe's empty. Get the tills and let's get out of here," the gunman ordered.

The third man shook his head. "I won't leave without the *safe*, Ike. I came along on this job for the *safe*."

The gunman turned beet red and stared at him. "Do what I tell you, stupid. Just do what I tell you to do for a change. Is that so goddamned hard for you?"

I'd found my weak point. I shrugged at the third man. "Guess you should have waited and done this job tomorrow, huh, Jay?" It was risky antagonizing them, but I had to do it.

Jay pointed an accusing finger at the gunman. "Yeah, Ike. You screwed up. I told you we shoulda waited an extra day."

He was taking my side. The time for action was coming up—I had to be ready to act.

"Too bad." I shrugged. "All that planning, all that work, for a measly few bucks. It's just not fair, is it?" I walked casually over to just below where the gunman was standing.

The third one laughed like a demented parrot. "Stupid shit. I put my ass on the line for you, Ike. You got no idea what you're doing, do you? You *screwed us all*." He yelled the last bit.

The gunman pointed the gun barrel at his accomplice. "You do not tell me how to run a crew, you hear? This is my job, my decision. I tell you what we do," he hissed at the man.

The young one came up to me, not sure who to follow it seemed. He shrugged. "What now, Ike? Do we get out of here with this cop now, huh?" He gestured at me with the crowbar.

That was what I'd been waiting for. Now, the time was right. I grabbed the crowbar and jerked it away from him. The man with the gun, concentrating on the third man on his team, didn't see it until a second too late. I swung the crowbar like a baseball bat, hitting the gunman hard, just below the knees. He yelped like a dog and dropped the gun.

It clattered to the counter; the younger one panicked and reached for it. I swung the bar down and got him on the forearm. I heard a bone crack as it connected, and he fell back, screaming. He clutched his arm and knelt on the floor. The third man didn't move. "Smart choice, Jay," I said. I picked up the shotgun, broke the breech open, and looked into the barrel. It was empty. No shells at all. I shook my head. "Stupid choice, Ike," I grunted. I tucked the shotgun under my left arm and held the crowbar in my right hand, watching the three men. I called to a woman across the floor. "Miss," I said. "Walk to the door, do this, then open up."

I waved my right arm high, over my head.

She scurried to the door, gingerly waved at the street, then pulled open the door. Within seconds the room was full of uniforms. Frank walked in behind them, looking around at the scene.

One uniform nodded at him. "Anything you need here, Inspector?" he asked.

Frank smiled. "Ask Sergeant McBriar. He's the lead officer on the scene. Anybody hurt, Ian?"

"Nobody that shouldn't be."

The gunman was still curled up on the counter, groaning in agony. The younger man was on the floor, rocking back and forth to ease the pain in his arm. In groups of one and two, the patrons walked up to me, hugged me, shook my hand, thanked me for my bravery. I was embarrassed by the attention, but it helped ease my nerves. The bank manager waited till last, then he came up to me and shook my hand. "That was the bravest thing I've ever seen," he said, shaking. "We were all so scared there. I'm so glad you weren't afraid."

"Actually, I was scared to death," I said. "But somebody once said 'pretend to be brave—it's the same as being brave,' so I pretended."

He shook his head. "You did it well."

The uniforms got statements and hustled the hostages out, the medics took away the injured robbers, and I was left alone in the middle of the room. Frank and Walsh came up to join me.

"Come on, kid, you need a good meal," Frank said.

Walsh nodded agreement.

They ushered me out the main door. The sun was trying to pierce a thin cloud cover. It was windy and cool, but after the dim light in the bank even the filtered sunlight was blinding. A small gaggle of reporters, waving steno pads and microphones, leaned over the barricades, calling questions and begging for statements. I tried to ignore them, but they yelled louder, calling me by name when one of them recognized me.

Walsh turned to me. "Leave this to me," he muttered.

We watched him stroll over to his side of the sawhorses, wait for the reporters to notice him. Then he patted the air with his hand. They all went silent.

"The Toronto Police Department responded to an emergency call here this morning," he said. "We resolved the situation without any loss of life or property and with no injury to the innocent people in the bank. We have arrested three suspects, and charges will undoubtedly be laid."

He paused, and reporters barraged him with simultaneous questions. Two asked, in unison, for the name of the officer who subdued the robbers.

"That officer," he said ceremoniously, "is my partner, Detective Sergeant Ian McBriar."

A female reporter grabbed his sleeve. "Is he the one who was shot last year?" she asked.

He nodded. "Yes. Thank you for your questions. We will issue a full statement later on." He walked away, letting them shout questions at his back, taking no notice of them, and joined us, grinning. "How was that, Ian?"

Frank grinned. "You're a natural, Patrick. You did good."

ʕ·ᴥ·ʔ

We sat in the back booth of a diner on King Street, two blocks from the bank. I ate a sandwich, mindlessly chewing as I stared out the window. I was a million miles away. The anxiety and panic I had repressed in the bank came out now, making me numb.

"Ian, you okay, kid?" Frank asked.

I turned to face him. "What? Sorry?" I asked.

"Are you all right?" he reiterated. "That was a really dicey spot you were in."

I nodded. "Yeah, I was just thinking about how Karen would kill me if I got hurt," I lied.

Walsh chuckled. "Define 'oxymoron.'"

Frank leaned forward. "Do you want to quit the force?" He was dead serious.

I shook my head. "No way. This is what I was meant to do, Frank."

He smiled. "Right answer. You really are a cop."

Walsh sat back and looked at Frank and me. "Sergeant, how did you get into the force?"

"What? Was it an affirmative action thing, you mean?" I joked.

He shook his head. "It was not your first choice of career. You were going to be a priest."

I leaned back and collected my thoughts. "June thirtieth, nineteen sixty eight, the day before Dominion Day, my mother parked across from our place and walked fifty feet to our front gate. She only made it to the middle of the road. A pickup hit her and killed her on the spot. The Mounties found the driver later that night, passed out in the truck." I shrugged and sipped my coffee. "I don't really like to talk about it. Anyway, that's when I left Saint Augustine's and changed uniforms. I figured if I couldn't save sinners, at least I could punish the guilty."

"How did you get paired with Inspector Burghezian?" Walsh continued.

I chuckled. "Frank was a deputy in Ohio somewhere. He was sent on some course in Toronto taught by a young Greek girl and fell in love."

"Helen?" Walsh asked.

Frank grinned.

"Helen," I agreed. "So he moved to the big city, married her, and joined the Toronto Police Department. He worked his way up to sergeant and they put us together."

Frank laughed. "That was a match made in heaven," he joked. "Captain Hook figured we'd work well together, me and this green rookie in a cheap suit and skinny tie. We gave each other grief for about the first month. I don't think we could stand being in the same room for the longest time."

Walsh grinned at us. "What changed?" he asked.

Frank sat with his head in his hands, reminiscing.

I nodded. "About four, five weeks after we started working together—we were barely speaking at this point— Helen insisted he invite me in for coffee. She was very nice, very gracious," I continued. "She talked to me—just talk— chit-chat, mostly. I told her that I'd cooked in my dad's restaurant. She asked if I could make a dessert for her. I said sure, and brought it over the next day. That did it."

Walsh frowned. "What did it?"

"Cheesecake," Frank purred. "Delicious, marvelous strawberry chocolate cheesecake." He closed his eyes.

"Anyway," I shrugged. "We got along great after that."

છેબેઓ

Walsh dropped me back at the station house. I accepted handshakes and congratulations from the other detectives, then I sat down to finish some paperwork before I went home. I called Colleen Feldman. She'd heard the news on the radio, and she was relieved I was unhurt.

Captain Van Hoeke came out of his office and sat on the edge of my desk. "Ian, why are you here?" he asked.

"I've been asking myself that all my life," I joked. "Why is any one of us here?"

He shook his head. "Quit kidding. You just went through a traumatic incident. Go home."

"No, no," I protested. "I'm fine. Really, I'm fine."

"Bullshit. You're not," he said forcefully.

"Okay." I sighed. "Tomorrow I'll interview the bank robbers, then I'll take it easy."

"By take it easy, you mean stay home?" he pushed.

"But why? I'm fine," I protested.

"No, you're not. Go home. Don't come back until the twenty-eighth. That's an order."

I sat back. "What should I do for four weeks?"

"More like three weeks. Don't push it. Anyway, aren't you planning a honeymoon?"

My eyes widened. "Who said?"

He snickered. "Come on, do you really think you can stop that? Women talk."

I rolled my eyes. "Karen talked to Helen, who talked to Rebecca."

Van Hoeke grinned. "Mazel Tov."

CHAPTER 10

I stood in the kitchen, mechanically chopping tomatoes for a salad. I hoped that doing normal things after the morning's excitement would make it easier to calm myself down. The image of the man aiming the shotgun at me was still vivid in my mind.

Ethan was in the back yard, hanging a paper bird feeder in a tree. He'd made the feeder at school and was very proud of it.

At about five thirty, Karen's Beetle pulled into the driveway. I heard her clumping swiftly up the porch steps, then the front door opened.

I turned to face her, smiling. "Hey, hon, how are you?"

She stormed in and slapped me hard across the face. "Bastard!" she screamed.

I reeled from the assault. "Karen?" I asked, stunned.

"You risked your *life* today? Why? Why the hell would you *do* that? *Huh*?" She glared at me, her nostrils flaring. "And I have to hear it on the *radio*, driving *home*, of all things?" Her face softened, then she threw her arms around me and hugged me, hard. She started to cry. "Please be careful, okay?" she sobbed. "I almost lost you once. I couldn't stand going through that again. Just, please, please be careful." She looked up at me and kissed me, passionately.

I smiled. "Next time, can I get the kiss without the slap? I like that much better."

She sobbed with her whole body and hugged me tight, whispering, "I'm sorry," between sniffs.

I caressed her hair, waiting for her to settle down. She let out a sigh and looked up at me again.

"How about this?" I offered. "Let's celebrate the fact that I'm all right. First, let's get married."

She smiled broadly. "Deal." Then she frowned, puzzled. "First?"

"Then, can you get away? I've been ordered off work for a while. Let's go on a honeymoon."

She nodded, her face glowing. "Somewhere warm? I have a new bikini."

I grinned. "We could spend it at the cottage, except they're clearing out their personal stuff so it might get awkward."

"Want to just stay home?" She smirked. "Send Ethan off to school every day and have wild sex in the living room?"

I shook my head. "Nah, we've done that. Listen—is your passport valid?"

ᏬᏇᏬ

I went in to work the next day.

We had the three bank robbers brought up from remand and placed in an interview room. Four large uniforms guarded them.

Frank, Walsh, and I were in the next room, discussing strategy.

"Ian, you should take the lead on this part, too," Frank insisted. "It's your show, you run it."

"I can't do the Rainbow Indian on this group," I said. "They already know me."

Walsh wrinkled his nose. "Rainbow Indian?"

Frank chuckled. "We had this routine when Ian was a Constable. He'd dress like a rube, act like a dumb Native straight off a reserve, and get the suspects to spill their guts. It worked great."

"Can't I play the dummy part for you?" Walsh offered.

I shook my head. "You look like a lawyer. There's no way they'd believe you were a yokel."

"So," Frank said. "What's the plan?"

I thought for a moment then nodded. "My brother taught me this neat game. Watch."

We entered the interview room in single file. The three men were nervous. The youngest one had a cast on over his broken arm, and the oldest one, the gunman, had one on his left leg. Both men squirmed slightly when they saw me.

The last man, the number two guy, glared at me, a look of both anger and respect on his face.

I sat down and slapped a stack of manila folders on the desk beside me. It was just old trash from the bottom of my desk, but nobody else in the room knew that.

Frank and Walsh sat behind me. We were three against three, with the uniforms as backup.

I looked at the three robbers. They sat side-by-side at the table, glancing at each other and at me.

I said nothing for over a minute, then I slowly lifted the cover of one manila folder and pretended to read something inside. I closed the cover and smiled at the men. "Now," I stated, "I'm getting married tomorrow, and I don't want to be here all day. So as a today-only deal, here's a little offer for you, gentlemen."

The uniforms, standing behind the robbers, frowned.

I smiled again and continued. "You know the game 'musical chairs'? That's when there are six people dancing and only five chairs? When the music stops, the one without a chair to sit on gets kicked out. Then you take away a chair, so there are five people and four chairs, and repeat the game, and so on. Finally, the last person with a chair wins. Well, this is the same game, but backward."

The three men glanced at each other, confused. I waited a minute to let them sweat.

"Here's how it works," I said. "I will send each of you into a room with an officer. The first man who rolls over on his buddies gets a reduced sentence. *But* you must wait five minutes before you can talk. I will not listen to anything you have to say *before* the five minute mark. After the five minutes are up, whoever puts his hand up first gets a very light sentence. The other two get nailed to the wall. On average, armed robbery will get you seven to ten years in the Kingston Pen. The winner, however, goes to Mimico, where he spends eighteen months playing cards and growing tomatoes."

I stood up. "The clock starts now. Officers, take these men away, please."

The uniforms walked the three men to separate holding rooms and waited, doors closed, for the five minutes to pass.

I turned to Frank and Walsh. "I don't care who comes out first. Wait till the number two guy sticks his hand up. When he does, tell him that someone just got to me a second before, but if he has any additional information for me, I'll reconsider his offer."

Frank chuckled. "You're getting sneaky in your old age, huh, Ian?"

Right on cue, at five minutes and ten seconds, all three uniforms came out of their respective rooms; each of the men was ready to rat on the others. I had hoped for this. I instructed the one who was guarding Jay, the unarmed man, to go back in and get a better offer from him. The uniform came out a minute later, telling me that the number two man could tie our gunman to a series of convenience store robberies. He also asked if we could go easy on the young one, who, as I suspected, was his younger brother.

We worked out an agreement, and the uniforms took the men back to remand.

I returned the manila folders to my desk. Van Hoeke was sitting in my chair. "Now that you're done, will you go home?" he asked.

I shrugged sheepishly. "I had to come in, Captain. I had to get them while their emotions were running high, so they wouldn't have time to think of a way out."

He leaned back. "Good call, Ian. Good call. By the way, are you looking to sit in the inspector chair anytime soon, then?"

I shook my head. "Not yet, sir. I'm happy doing what I'm doing."

He chuckled and stood up. "We'll see. I'll meet you at City Hall."

ഇരുന

On Friday morning, we drove to City Hall and got married. Frank and Helen were our witnesses; Ethan, Van Hoeke, and Rebecca sat behind them. Walsh showed up in a crisp charcoal suit, looking very dapper. Vivian came with him, wearing a simple pants suit. It was very matter-of-fact, very businesslike. We got there at eleven and, ten minutes later, it was all done—Karen Prescott was now Karen McBriar. Everyone shook hands and kissed then we went to the King Edward Hotel for lunch.

We toasted our marriage with champagne. Frank, Walsh, Van Hoeke, and I whispered off to one side while Karen and Helen talked about us. Frank shook my hand and patted my back—we had a surprise planned for Karen, a very good one, I hoped.

Frank and Helen agreed to take Ethan for two weeks while we were gone. She would get practice at being a mother. She'd make lunches for Ethan and Alan then get the boys to and from school every day.

None of the women knew where we were going. I'd packed our luggage, so Karen had no idea where I was packing for.

ഇരുന

On Saturday afternoon, Frank and Helen picked up Ethan. Karen kissed him a tearful goodbye, as if we were going to the moon. He was thrilled to stay at Frank's for two weeks, thrilled that he could play with Frank's train layout every evening.

We were alone, waiting for our taxi, pacing the living room. Karen was anxious, excited and irritated all at once. "Ian, please, where on earth are you taking us?" she demanded.

I smirked. "You know, you took a vow to honor and obey. So obey."

She shook her head. "If you'll remember, I said 'love and honor.' I *never* said obey."

Our taxi stopped out front and honked. I locked the door behind us, and the cabbie placed our bags in the trunk while we got in the back seat.

The cab turned north on Keele Street, the driver silent till we passed Lawrence Avenue.

He tilted his head back toward me. "Where do you want to go, folks?" he asked.

I glanced at Karen. "Terminal One, please," I called.

The cabbie grunted and nodded.

"I *know* we're flying somewhere," Karen stated. "That's why you asked about my passport."

She searched my face for clues. "A beach? The Bahamas? Mexico? California."

I just grinned. She reached for the airline tickets, hidden inside my windbreaker, but I pulled away.

"Not fair," she pouted. "You have to tell me where we're going. The suspense is killing me."

I kissed her, quickly, and peeked at the tickets so she couldn't see. She fumed, frustrated.

"Okay." I broke down, smiling. "How fluent is your Italian?"

She squealed like a schoolgirl and climbed over to my side of the cab, hugged my neck, and squeezed me, cheek to cheek.

The cabbie looked at us through the rear-view mirror, amused. "Your first trip out of the country, miss?" he asked.

She waved her ring finger and smiled. "Mrs."

At the airport, we checked our cases. Karen squealed again when she saw that the tag strapped to our bags said *Rome*.

We then boarded a bright orange DC-8. The stewardess gave us the obligatory welcome speech, thanked us for flying CP Air, and wished us a pleasant flight. We would land in Rome in about seven hours, she said. Karen was beside herself with excitement, looking out the window as we taxied down the runway, gripping my arm tightly as though letting go could be lethal.

The plane climbed up into the gray overcast, jostling us as it passed through roiling clouds, then burst through into the clearest sky I had ever seen. Above us, the air was black, fading to a cobalt blue in the west. Karen settled back, more at ease now, and gratefully accepted a glass of wine from the stewardess. She also drank my wine, and by the third glass she was almost asleep.

We ate a meal on a tray and settled back for the next few hours. Karen dozed off right away. I forced myself to sleep.

I woke up when the stewardess announced that we were descending into Rome. Karen looked out the window at the Italian coastline below, creeping slowly toward us, and bounced in her seat like a child at Christmas.

I shared her excitement. I'd wanted to see Rome ever since I could remember. When I was in the seminary, I had told my friends that a pilgrimage to Rome would be my life's greatest wish. Taking this trip, having Karen with me as my bride, was as close to Heaven on Earth as I could imagine. Walsh had booked everything for me. I was somewhat suspicious of his assurances, but I would square that with him once we got back.

We took the train into town from the airport. Our hotel was listed as a five-minute walk from the Termini train station. We stepped off the train and headed across the street. I carried our bags, cautiously dodging waves of Fiats, Vespas, and buses as we crossed a series of wide and narrow roads lined with four-story buildings. Walsh had given me a map to help me find the hotel. I grinned like an idiot, delighted at just being in this magical town. Karen was still in shock. Ten hours ago we'd been in Toronto, on a cold and gray evening, and now we were here in this Roman autumn morning, the Italian sun beating down as I'd never felt sunlight before, baking me in the dust of its ancient streets.

I stopped dead on the sidewalk and stared across the street, my mouth open.

Karen smiled. "What are you thinking, hubby?" she asked, caressing my arm.

I nodded at a massive, ornate church. "That's Santa Maria Maggiore. I've seen it in photos since I was a boy. I always wondered how it would look in real life," I said. "I'm just floored at how much there is to see in this one town. I could spend a lifetime exploring it with you."

"We have two weeks," Karen offered. "How much do you think can we see in that time?"

"One week," I corrected. "Then we're going someplace else, equally exciting."

"Where?" she demanded. "I'm your wife now, you have to tell me."

She stood there with her hands on her hips, snorting. I bent down and kissed her. "Another surprise. You'll see."

Walsh had booked us into a small hotel he knew, nearly invisible behind a solid stone façade, with a square canopy over the entryway and *Hotel Doria* stenciled in gold paint over two art deco doors. We walked in, still gawking like the rank tourists that we were.

The lobby was small, intimate, furnished like I imagined a small Italian hotel lobby should be. The front desk looked like something out of a Fellini movie, all in marble, wrought iron, potted ferns, and fragrant flowers. Classical music played from a radio somewhere. Karen approached a thin young man behind the desk. He wore a jacket that was hopelessly large and said something I couldn't understand. Then he brightened up and pointed at me. "You are police, yes?" he asked. He pointed at Karen. "And you, *signora,* Mrs. Meck Beer?"

Karen stifled a laugh and nodded. The man called for a bellboy and, speaking quickly, led us into a tiny elevator, up three floors, then down a hall to a nondescript door. I had a brief irrational fear of being pushed into a broom closet and locked up for a week. The man smiled, opened the door, and waved for us to follow him in.

Karen gasped. The room was simple—small but airy— with wooden shutters to cover the window panes, both thrown open to the warm morning. Through the windows we could see the red rooftops of the city, disappearing into the distance. The light from the rising sun, shining on the eastern walls of buildings before us, illuminated them with a brilliant orange glow. Karen walked over to the window, leaned out for a long moment, then turned to me and beamed.

"Ian, my god, this is beautiful," she gushed. "Have you ever seen anything so beautiful?"

"Yes," I replied.

The young man asked her if we wanted breakfast. She nodded, thanked him, and started unpacking. Within fifteen minutes, we'd put away our clothes and set out walking shoes. A knock at the door signaled room service. We let in a pleasant, cheerful older lady who struggled to bring in a huge tray of coffee and croissants, setting them on the dressing table. She refused a tip, wished us well, and giggled as she left.

"Do we look like your typical randy honeymooners?" I asked.

"Let's not disappoint them," Karen said and locked the door.

An hour later, we sat naked on top of the crisp linen sheets. We ate pastry, sipped strong coffee, and talked about the whirlwind events of the last few days. Karen glanced at her ring every few minutes. She was still getting used to being "Mrs. Meck Beer," she said. I was just relieved she'd said "I do" to the justice of the peace.

I finished my croissant and slid under the sheets, drained. Karen rolled onto her stomach and stretched out like a cat in the sun. I leaned forward and kissed the back of her neck, moving down her spine to the small of her back.

"I could really get used to this," I said contentedly. "The food, the sex, the sunlight, the sex, the coffee, the sex…"

"Don't forget the sex," Karen joked.

❧❧❧

We spent the next six days doing the things that I'd dreamed about my whole life. We walked from the Coliseum, through the old Roman ruins, then down a set of steps into a park. Along one side of the park, fragrant bushes filled the air with the aroma of rosemary.

It took us a whole day at the Vatican. Karen had gone mostly to please me, but once there she was as awestruck as I was. We ate at sidewalk cafes and smart restaurants, Karen's language skills easing the way and her looks wooing the locals. We walked the streets hand in hand, window shopped, smelled the food as we passed doorways, and savored the warm nights. We meandered like two people without a care in the world. We made love every night, then lay there with the windows open, letting the breeze cool us, letting the sounds and smells of Rome wash over us.

On Saturday night, we lay there, listening to a woman on a balcony across the street, calling to a friend on the sidewalk. Karen translated what she could understand: two old women, discussing everyday matters, just like people everywhere, the beep-beep of traffic punctuating their words.

Karen was on her stomach, resting her head on a pillow. I leaned down and kissed the small of her back, worked my way up to her neck and back down.

She wriggled. "Hm. I like that." She rolled over and wrapped her arms around my neck. "A lot."

೮ᴣ೮ᴣ

On Sunday, we went to early mass at Santa Maria Maggiore. Throughout the service, Karen and I held hands. I took Communion and bowed to pray, and she gently kissed my neck. I felt a flush of lust and smiled at her.

We went back to the hotel, made love in that bed for the final time, ate breakfast, and packed. I still hadn't told her where we were going next.

She accepted this, saying that after all, this city *was* a good surprise. We gave our key to the front desk, and I found my wallet to pay the bill.

The desk clerk, the thin young man, shook his head. "Is paid. All paid. Thank you." He smiled, waving his hands in front of him. He turned naturally to Karen. "*Tutto pagato.*"

Karen stared at me, her mouth open. "Frank?" she asked.

I shook my head. "Patrick, I bet. I had better get him a really nice souvenir, I guess."

We strolled back to the Termini station and boarded a long train, as I clutched the two tickets the desk clerk had secured for me. This leg of the trip was still a mystery to Karen. I refused to divulge our destination, much to her frustration.

The train was about half full. Our compartment had just another couple, two young Italians who sat opposite us, discussing a book one of them was reading.

We settled into our seats. Karen stuck her head out the window and looked at the mechanical sign above the platform. She sat back down, smiling.

"We're going to Venice?" she asked slowly, in a squeaky little-girl voice.

I nodded. She threw herself onto me bodily, wrapping her arms around my neck.

"We're going to Venice!" she squealed and kissed me passionately.

The Italian couple froze, unsure of what we were going to do next.

"A good surprise, then?" I asked, coming up for air.

The train pulled slowly out of the station.

ℰᏇℰᏇ

By October, Saskatchewan usually had snow on the ground. Toronto was milder, but often it was windy and damp. I'd read about places like Rome in books, but I never dreamed I'd experience them firsthand. As we departed the station, the morning sun beat down mercilessly on the train. The ground outside, pure white in the direct sunlight, even seemed too hot for shadows to form.

Porters shuffled along, pushing wheelbarrows before them, waiting for their next fare, oblivious to us rushing by. As we accelerated, the train lost its side-to-side rocking and the rough clacking of wheels on the rails, and settled to a low, quiet rumble in the background.

The train picked up speed as we rolled though the countryside, rushing past small stations with mottled stucco walls, past splashy billboards and tall poplar trees lining the track, onto trestles over slow brown rivers, through tunnels darker than black. Each time the train emerged from the tunnels, the sun was impossibly high, impossibly bright, impossibly hot. Karen leaned against the glass, basking in the Italian daylight like a cat in a windowsill.

Our train stopped at a handful of stations, towns with exotic names I had only read about: Florence, Bologna, Ferrara, Padua. We passed vineyards and olive groves, castles so old that they had named the towns around them, cliffs cascading with unbelievable greenery, and trout streams too lazy and calm to be bothered by our passage. The sky gradually changed from a devastating, deep blue to spotty clouds to overcast then, as we rounded the top of the Adriatic, the sky cleared again, painting the train compartment with a golden light. Karen took photos, swapping film cartridges on her little Instamatic as quickly as she could.

Eventually, the train slowed, a deliberate, final kind of slowing. Karen asked a conductor how long it would be before we arrived in Venice. He indicated just ten minutes more, one last stop. The other couple got off and we were left alone. We started moving again.

Karen bounced with excitement. She grinned, looking out the window at the scenery outside, anxious to finish the final leg of the trip into Venice's Santa Lucia station. The industrial buildings, docks and warehouses fell away, and the train rolled along a causeway, a strip of land built on the water, heading for our destination. I could see the spires of churches, the bell tower in St. Mark's Square, and innumerable red tiled roofs off to the left. Karen stood, leaning her camera out the window, looking just like Katherine Hepburn in *Summertime*. I smiled, admiring her.

"What is it?" she asked.

"*Summertime*," I said.

"Feels like it," she agreed.

I shook my head. "I mean the movie—with Katherine Hepburn and Rossano Brazzi. It's a great film."

She leaned forward and kissed me, tenderly. "Shut up, you," she purred.

Santa Lucia train station in Venice looked exactly like it did in the movie. It was now after five o clock in the evening. Most of the day tourists, drained by a round of sightseeing, were headed home. They clogged the platform, clutching bags of souvenirs and bottles of cold beverages. I made my way through the crowd, with Karen following close behind, and led us into the main hall of the station. It was one large room, with a terrazzo floor and columns around the perimeter. To our right, a string of ticket windows and telephone booths ended with a smoke shop. To the left, large double doors led to a cafeteria. The smell of food, wafting through the swinging doors, was irresistible. I watched people come and go. Karen watched, too, intrigued.

"Hungry?" I asked.

"Famished," she answered.

The food car on the train only sold sandwiches in wax paper—we wanted something more substantial.

After our long trip, the cafeteria food was heavenly. We shared a plate of pasta and a glass of wine, then we walked straight out of the train station and down some steps, which led to an outdoor plaza, and ended at the Grand Canal. Karen swiveled her head slowly, her mouth open.

"Ian, do you see this?" She sighed. "Is this the most romantic view in the world, or what?" She clutched my arm tight.

"Wow," I said and put the bags down.

I looked around, as overwhelmed as Karen was. Evening was approaching, and lights came on in the houses across the canal. Everywhere, terracotta roof tiles and tall buildings were painted by the soft glow of the setting sun. The canal sparkled. As evening came, everyone seemed to slow down—even the busy water taxis appeared to be ambling. I had the name of our hotel written down on a slip of paper, and I handed it to Karen.

Karen approached a strolling policeman and showed him my piece of paper. He nodded, indicating that it was just a short boat ride, not far away. She said something I didn't understand, but even my rudimentary Italian picked up the words *marito* and *poliziotto*. He seemed impressed. He asked her something, and she nodded in my direction.

"Flash your badge," she ordered.

"You told him your husband's a policeman," I echoed.

I opened my wallet and showed him my badge. He

nodded, saluted crisply, and waved us to a spot by the canal. He motioned over a water taxi, spoke quickly to the driver, and motioned for us to come aboard. The driver, a stocky man in a thick sweater, grunted and helped us get on. He smiled at Karen, far too familiarly, I thought, and we sped away.

I stood up, leaning against the small, enclosed cabin, while Karen, looking like a movie star, rested her elbows on the top of the windshield and gazed out as the city streamed by, her hair dancing in the breeze. She turned to me and frowned.

"What?" I asked.

"We need a boat for the cottage," she called, over the sound of the engine.

The driver laughed.

"You speak English," I said.

He nodded. "Yah. I was in Quebec—ten years." His accent was mild, his voice clear.

Karen shook her head. "Now you're back here? Why?"

He laughed. "Quebec winter—I don't like snow. I work hard, I own my boat, I live good."

Karen laughed too. She leaned toward him. "Where is a good place to eat?" she asked.

He waved his arm casually. "In Venice? Everywhere."

They both laughed together.

In no time, we docked at a concrete pier. The driver unloaded our bags and accepted my money. I helped Karen out of the boat and carried the bags to a waterfront cousin of the hotel in Rome.

Inside, we entered another small lobby. This one was ornately decorated with statues and abstract paintings and had a small marble desk in the corner, where another thin young man was reading the newspaper. He looked up, surprised to see us.

"*Buona sera,*" he greeted us and smiled.

"*Buona sera,*" Karen answered back, and asked if there was a room booked in our name.

He opened a guest register, ran his finger down one column, and nodded. "Missus Mac Bree?" he asked, hopefully.

She smiled. "Close enough."

We registered, the young man crooking his neck to read the name I put on the page. Then he carried our bags up one flight of curving marble steps to a room almost directly above the lobby. He opened the door and waved us in ahead of him.

"Please," he said, expending most of his English vocabulary.

Karen went first, I trailed behind.

"Oh, Ian," she said, breathless. "And I thought Rome was stunning. Look at this."

I followed her to this room's windows. In the waning evening light, the city rooftops were silhouetted in blue-black, the canal glittered like a jeweled ribbon, and the smell of the Adriatic wafted in over it all—a delicate aroma, part salt air, part age, part mystery.

We stared out, mesmerized by the view, the sounds, and the smells of the city.

The young man waited patiently until we came back to Earth. Evidently, he was used to this reaction. He handed us our key and turned to go.

"*Scusi?*" I said. I moved my finger in a circle in the air. "*Camera, tutta pagata?*" Was this room all paid for?

He nodded, unfazed by my new linguistic skills. "*Si, tutto apposto,*" he affirmed—all in order.

"Patrick," I mumbled.

"Patrick," Karen agreed.

I handed him some cash, probably too much, and thanked him. He smiled broadly and left.

"Nice work, Casanova." Karen smiled, hugging me tight. "Full of surprises, aren't you?"

I grinned. "You ain't seen nothing yet."

We unpacked quickly and made love. It seemed the

sensible thing to do. Then we got dressed and went down-stairs. Karen asked the clerk for a good place to eat and, af-ter discussing our food preferences, he suggested a restau-rant a few doors away on the water.

We waited for our meal, watching the soft splash of waves on the canal just inches away. We agreed to two dishes that the waiter recommended and decided to share them between us. Karen accepted her food, examined it cau-tiously, and took a bite. I did the same with mine.

"Why can't I cook like this?" I grunted. "This is amaz-ing. How's yours, hon?"

She rolled her eyes. "What would it take to make this at home?" she asked.

I sighed. "Four hundred years of experience."

We took forkfuls of each other's dishes, had a second glass of wine and coffee, then we went back to the hotel and slept.

☙☙☙

Monday morning in Venice—that sounds like a great name for a movie, or a jazz album.

The sound of bustling canal traffic below woke us up. We showered, dressed, and went out to a café near the pre-vious night's restaurant for breakfast. Karen reminded me that most Italians didn't like a big breakfast, so we ordered espresso and croissants, reminiscent of our Rome experi-ence.

I wanted to see the "tourist" sights in Venice: St. Mark's Square, some churches, the Doge's Palace, the Bridge of Sighs. Karen wanted to see the glass-blowing places in Murano. She'd seen it once on TV and had always been fascinated with it.

We arranged for breakfast in our room after the first morning, and the maid who brought it must have spoken to the one in Rome. She also giggled and blushed with embarrassment when she set the tray on the night table. We spent the next five days wandering the city, seeing the sights, getting hopelessly lost, making love before dawn, then watching the sunrise.

We discovered tiny piazzas with bronze plaques to explain their importance, hidden marketplaces which only the locals knew, archways and courtyards that had seen more history than could be written, and cramped little shops whose exquisite goods seemed to tumble out into the street.

On our last full day there, I sat in bed, sipping espresso and staring out at the morning light through the open windows. I could smell the Adriatic. I sighed, wistful.

"Something wrong?" Karen asked.

"Dunno." I shrugged. "How would life be if we had this all the time? Would we get bored?"

She sat up, cross-legged. "Are you saying you're already tired of me, sir?" she joked.

"No, you know." I sighed. "It's going to be really hard to go back to work after this. Every day that I slog through a Toronto snowstorm, I'll be thinking back to this morning."

She moved the tray away and slid beside me. "Well then, let's make sure we have something special to remember this morning by." She wrapped her arms around my neck and kissed me.

⁓℮⁓

All too soon, we packed our bags of souvenirs and our luggage and checked out. We splurged on a water taxi from the hotel all the way to the airport. In the warm afternoon sun, Karen again stood up, resting against the windscreen, her sunglasses reflecting my smile.

The flight back to Toronto was pleasant, but my mind was back in those hotel rooms.

Karen was anxious to see Ethan again. From the time we crossed the Atlantic and got over Canada, she was beside herself, wondering aloud how he was, whether he'd been all right without her, and if he had missed her as much as she missed him.

The plane touched down. We sailed through customs and caught a cab. Seven at night and it was dark. The roads were cold and wet, and I clearly saw sleet on the windshield when the light was just right. In forty minutes we were at Frank's. Karen sprinted out, and I paid the cabbie. She got to the door ahead of me and opened it, not bothering to knock.

I heard Frank's voice bellow, "Welcome home," then the thunder of small feet and a squealing reunion as Ethan tackled his mother.

I entered the front door, almost unnoticed.

Frank finally turned to see me. "Holy shit, Ian, where were you—Palm Springs?" He turned to Helen. "Hey, look at this guy's California tan. Italy, my ass."

Ethan escaped his mother's grip and rushed over to me. "Hey, Pops. What did you get me?"

I hugged him with my one free arm. "Hey, sport. I missed you. Were you good?"

He nodded. "Alan had a sleepover. We played with Uncle Frank's trains. It was fun."

"How was school?" I asked.

"Fine. What did you bring me? Uncle Frank said you'd bring me a toy."

"Ah," I said, solemnly. "Let's ask Mister Pulcinello." I reached into my bag of souvenirs and came out holding a Harlequin hand puppet. I placed my arm into it and worked the mouth and hands, speaking in a squeaky voice as I did. "Hello, little boy, what's your name?" I chirped in a falsetto voice.

"Ethan," he answered, looking only at the puppet.

"You know what I like to eat?" I continued. He shook his head, puzzled. "Noses!"

Harlequin chomped on his nose. Ethan laughed hysteri-cally.

I pulled my arm out and handed him the puppet. He spent the next hour talking to it, then answering himself with a goofy voice.

I gave Frank a smooth leather wallet and a monogrammed leather notebook. He seemed to like them both. Karen had found a silk scarf and a pair of kidskin gloves she insisted Helen would love. Helen seemed genuinely touched at the thoughtfulness.

We collected Ethan, and Helen drove us all home. She had put some groceries in my fridge for the morning. We hugged everyone goodbye and went inside. Ethan, clutching his puppet, was already drowsy. He was asleep in my arms before I put him to bed. Karen and I, running on pure excitement, stayed up till nine o clock, then we fell asleep, too.

CHAPTER 11

Monday morning, I was awake by three thirty, my body still on Venice time. I made coffee and ate toast, sitting at my kitchen table. Karen shuffled through soon after, kissed me on the back of the neck, and sat down.

"Hey, you," she said softly, so as not to wake Ethan. She pulled the cup out of my hand and took a sip. Looking down sadly, she sighed. "Do you think the maid from Rome could bring us coffee in bed?"

"Yeah," I grunted, gazing at the living room window. "This view's not quite the same, either."

She sat across from me and put her feet in my lap. "Think we'll be this happy when we're old and gray?"

"You've asked me that before," I answered. "Apart from creaky bones and bifocals, I'm sure I'll feel just the same way toward you."

"Even when we're in separate nursing homes?" she joked.

"We'll always have Venice," I said, spoofing *Casablanca*.

❧❧❧

At eight-thirty, Mrs. Ian McBriar kissed me goodbye and drove her Beetle downtown; I dropped Ethan at school and headed up to the police station.

I picked up the microphone. "Dispatch, fifty-two four eight," I called.

The speaker hissed. A woman's voice came on. "Four eight, go."

"Four eight, any messages?"

"Yeah, why didn't you tell us you were getting married, Ian?" asked the woman, irritated.

I smiled. "Because I was devastated that you're already married, Nadine."

Laughter came back through the speaker. "No messages, dispatch out."

I parked and steeled myself for what I knew was coming. Entering the station, I smiled and accepted the hugs and kisses from the secretaries, then I went through to the detectives' room.

I was immediately greeted by hoots, whistles, and catcalls. I stood in the doorway, bowing theatrically, until it died down.

One detective walked up to me. "Hey, Ian," he said. "We all chipped in and got you this."

He presented me with a large cardboard box. I opened it and pulled out a black plastic ball attached to a length of plastic chain and an ankle bracelet. The men laughed.

"Thank you," I said. "How did you know my old one was broken?"

They all laughed again. After more joking and congratulations, they all went back to their desks.

Walsh sat across from me, smiling. "So, Sergeant, how was your honeymoon?"

I shook my head. "How did you manage to get those two hotels? It was wonderful. I owe you."

He grinned widely. "It was our wedding present, Ian. Enjoy."

I nodded thanks. "I have something for you." I handed him a small brown box. "From Karen."

He wrinkled his nose, puzzled. "You didn't have to. Really." He opened the box, reached in, and held up a multicolored glass ashtray and a delicate glass paperweight. He examined them, fascinated.

"They're souvenirs of Venice, from Murano," I explained. "Karen thought you'd like them."

He grinned. "Give her my sincere thanks. I love them." He carried them to his desk, still smiling.

I leaned back, waiting for Frank to join the regular Monday morning meeting.

※※

By nine fifteen, Captain Van Hoeke started talking; still no sign of Frank. Van Hoeke welcomed me back, accompanied by another round of cheers and applause, then he went through the usual routine, ordered everyone to their assignments, then looked quickly at me, specifically, and raised his eyebrows. Just for a second, ever so subtly. I nodded, equally subtly.

I turned to Walsh. "Patrick, do you mind checking on Rhonda and Gustavo's whereabouts for a few minutes? I have to talk to the Captain."

"Want me to go in there with you?" he asked.

I shook my head. "No, man. Sorry, it's a personal issue. Don't worry about it."

He shrugged and went to his desk.

I entered Van Hoeke's office and closed the door. He was studying a blank spot on his desk, as though it would reveal something if he stared long enough.

"Captain?" I said finally.

Van Hoeke slowly looked up. "Frank is out of sorts today. He's not feeling well," he said slowly and deliberately.

I sat still for a minute. "I'm sorry to hear that. Do you think it's anything to worry about?"

He paused as if formulating an answer. "No, I think Frank will be all right." He looked at the desk again and spoke carefully. "Read any good books, Ian?"

I smiled. "I'm reading a biography of Dostoyevsky."

A wave of relief swept over Van Hoeke's face. I left.

Walsh came up to me. "Gustavo's staff said he's back from North Carolina. He should be in his office later. Do we want to talk to him again?"

I shook my head. "Not just yet. What about Rhonda? Is she still at her cousin's?"

He shrugged. "She has an apartment in Gustavo's building. He moved her in while you were away."

"Is she there now?" I asked.

"She should be. Suite number two-ten." He pulled out his car keys. "Want to go see her?"

"Yes. I want to find out if she has any more to tell us since we spoke to her last. What were you up to while I was away?"

"I worked with Parker on a hit-and-run. It kept me busy. Not as meaty as this case, though."

"Not many boobs?" I joked.

"If I may say, sir," he said formally. "I think Parker is a slob. Does that make me snobbish?"

I smirked. "No, just a keen judge of character." I looked at my watch. "Can I meet you at Rhonda's? I have to make a quick detour first."

"I assume you're checking up on Inspector Burghezian?" he asked.

I looked at him, trying to read his expression. "Why would you say that?"

Walsh shrugged. "I thought maybe his epilepsy was acting up."

I looked around—nobody else had heard the comment. I repeated the question. "Why would you say that?"

"Captain Van Hoeke once asked me if I had read any good books," Walsh explained. "I had no idea what he meant. Later on, I noticed Frank's symptoms. I realized he was asking me if I knew. I should have said, 'Yes, Dickens and Tolstoy.' They were epileptics."

"I said Dostoyevsky." I smiled sadly. "He had it, too.

174 Mauro Azzano

Okay, yeah, I'm checking on Frank. You go see Rhonda. I'll meet you there in an hour."

He nodded.

"Hang on?" I asked, thinking. "How did you mean, that you noticed his symptoms?"

He shrugged. "An uncle of mine has the same kind of epilepsy as Frank. 'Petit mal seizures,' they call it now. Frank stares off at times, and he doesn't drive. I also saw his pills. At first I thought they were aspirins, but they're anti-convulsive pills, just like my uncle takes."

I sighed. "Very good, detective. Very good. Keep mum, okay?"

We walked out together. Walsh chirped his tires leaving the parking lot and I drove briskly to Frank's house.

I bounded up the front steps two at a time, pausing only for a second to knock at the front door before letting myself in.

Helen was in the easy chair, sewing something. Frank was on the sofa, reading a newspaper.

"Hi, Helen." I grinned. "Good to see you. Hi, Frank."

"Hey, Ian." He smiled. "Want fresh coffee?" He sounded more than just tired—he was weary.

I nodded. "I'll get it. Helen, you just sit." I poured two coffees and sat across from him. "So how are you feeling, man?" I asked softly, handing him a mug.

He hunched his shoulders slightly. "Fine, Ian, I'm fine. Just a little under the weather, is all." He pulled a small glass bottle out of his pocket. "I have to take this shit." He read the label. "Phenobarbital," he said slowly. "It helps the fits, but it makes me sleepy and now it makes me vomit. Worse than that, it's not working anymore." He put the bottle away. "Now there's some new wonder drug. Carbamaze-epine. They say it's the cat's ass." He sighed and shook his head. "It's all voodoo. They have no idea what to do, so they shove pills at me."

I looked down, staring at my coffee. "Listen, Frank, if there's any help you need, just say."

He frowned at his shoes. "Appreciate it, buddy. I got an offer from a corporate consultant."

"Yeah?" I asked. I had no idea what he was driving at.

"Wants to hire me. He knows all about my condition. Says it doesn't matter to him."

"Doing what?" I said stupidly.

Frank shrugged. "Corporate security—check out high-paid employees, look for industrial spies, that kind of shit. I'd drive a desk for double what the department pays me, be home every night, no bullshit trials to sit through. Sure sounds appealing. After all, I'm going to have two more mouths to feed soon. I have to think about them, too."

He looked at me with sad, sorrowful eyes. I didn't know whether he wanted me to prove him wrong or make him feel better by agreeing. "Frank, you're the best inspector this city has," I started. "If you get into trouble, though, if you're not a hundred percent when you're on the street, then you put the whole team in danger. You'd never want that—I know you—so for the good of all concerned you should consider the offer."

Helen gave a little grunt. She'd been talking to him about it as well, it seemed.

Frank shook his head and looked up at me. "I just don't like to give up, Ian. I'm not a quitter."

I leaned back, smiling. "You offered to quit for Van Hoeke, just to save my ass and Walsh's. And you don't even like Walsh."

"Hell no," Frank grunted. "He's too much like you."

I smirked. Behind Frank, Helen grinned and shook her head.

"Right," I said. "But this is not quitting. This is being the team leader. This is taking bitter medicine for the greater good. This is being the man we all aspire to be."

He stared at me for a long minute, a look of amazement on his face. "You are a real bullshit artist, Ian, you know? You can BS like I never realized before. You are so full of crap." Helen snickered softly to herself. Frank turned to look in her direction. "I can hear you. I'm not deaf. Women—hah." He sighed. "Yeah, I know you're right, Ian. I can't work a team this way. Better to quit while I'm on top." Helen said something cryptic. Frank nodded. "Yeah. Got an important question, Ian. Would you mind being the godfather for our kids?"

I smiled broadly. "I would be honored, sir."

"Do you think Karen would like to be our godmother?" he continued.

"I think it would take an army to stop her. I will ask her, though, just to confirm it."

He rubbed his face with his hands and leaned back. The fatigue and sadness were gone, replaced by resolution. "So I've been asked to close the Hereford case with you and Walsh. Captain Hook wants this case wrapped up as my send-off."

"He knows you're taking the new job?" I asked. Just saying it felt like a small death.

"Yeah, he's the one that recommended me. Figures it's a perfect fit." He nodded. "Martin has high hopes for the team, Ian. If you don't think I can cut it, don't schmooze me."

I thought for a long time. "Frank, I can think of nobody else I'd want to lead this team. That said, you don't know when you might have another fit. In a tight situation you're not doing anybody any good by being out there. Sorry, but I agree with the captain. Leave on a high point."

Frank thought for a moment then nodded. "Then it's decided. After this case wraps, I'm gone."

A piece of me died when he said that. I smiled sadly. "You'll still come over to eat, right?"

"Damn straight, kid."

❧❧❧

I parked in the laneway beside Gustavo's apartment

building, right behind Walsh's car. Opening the front door of the building by prying my key behind the latch, I walked through the lobby to a stairwell. Back in the forties, the building had been fresh, elegant, and very desirable. The aluminum railing on the staircase swept up in an arc to the second floor, an art deco holdover like something out of the *Thin Man* movies.

I could imagine Myrna Loy gliding down the steps in a satin evening gown, William Powell stepping lightly behind her in his tuxedo and bow tie, with his dog Asta on a leash beside him. The carpet, now tattered and threadbare, still had enough of its original pattern to show what had once been a very stylish floor covering. Yes, the building *had* been a desirable address.

Now, it was just a dusty echo of its former self, like an aged beauty queen who still wore her tiara for special occasions. I trudged up to the second floor and found number two ten. I knocked at the door. It creaked open.

Walsh stepped out. He wasn't happy. "Come in, Ian," he grunted. He turned and walked into the living room.

Some of the furniture from Rhonda's old apartment had been moved in to this one. It fit well. The place had the look that a home gets after someone has lived in it for a while.

Walsh walked to the far side of the sofa, where it faced the windows, and stood with his hands on his hips. Gustavo was lying on his back, his feet pointed out at an unnatural angle. His eyes were open, his mouth frozen open, mid-word, it seemed.

"The door was open and I found him like this," Walsh grunted. "Shit. There goes a witness."

"There goes a life," I corrected. "Did you call the coroner?"

"Yeah." Walsh sighed. "He should be here any time now. I'm just pissed off at him dying on us. I thought, somehow, that he was the one that killed Ed after all." He looked up at me. "How's Frank?" There was real concern in his voice.

I saw no point in being coy. "This case will be his closing act. Frank will leave the department after that."

Walsh looked down, thinking. "Does that mean you'll be moving into the inspector spot?"

I shook my head. "No, squirt. You're stuck with me."

He grinned. "Good to hear. I enjoy working with you, Ian."

Walsh went downstairs to look for the coroner, I said a quick Hail Mary for Gustavo's soul, then Walsh came back up.

A stomping of shoes in the hall caught our attention. In unison we stared at the front door. A pair of uniforms came in, unannounced, and scanned the room. One of them recognized me.

"Hey, Ian, how's it going?" he said. He was a lean, muscular man with graying sideburns.

"Doing fine, Jack," I answered. I pointed at Walsh. "Jack O'Brien, Patrick Walsh."

The two men nodded at each other.

O'Brien pointed to his partner. "Perry Greene."

Walsh and I nodded.

"Okay." I said. "Let's canvas the floor, see if anyone saw or heard anything. After that, move on to the other floors. Then tape up the hallway and wait for forensics."

The three men spread out, the uniforms taking one side of the corridor, Walsh taking the other.

I examined Gustavo's body. Natural causes didn't seem a likely cause of death, though I couldn't see any cut marks, bullet wounds, bruises, or anything else that could have killed him. Walsh and the uniforms came back a few minutes later. Most of the tenants were at work. Only two people on this floor were home, and they hadn't heard or seen anything. One of them, an old man, said he had seen the apartment door open as he walked to the garbage chute. He said people often opened their doors to get a breeze. Nobody would think that was unusual.

By then the coroner showed up, along with another

two-man cruiser. It all seemed dreadfully familiar. We cordoned off the front entrance, spoke to everyone who was home, took notes, made measurements, and stood around, waiting as the photographer got done so the coroner's men could remove the body.

I stood in the hall, off to one side. The coroner walked up to me. He was a bookish man with Clark Kent glasses and a wrinkled brown suit.

He grunted as he approached. "I hear congratulations are in order," he said. "You recently got married?"

I nodded. "Thanks. Yep, we just got back from the honeymoon. No rest for the wicked, I guess."

He glanced at the open apartment door. "So I suppose you're wondering what killed him?"

"Right. I couldn't see anything obvious."

"I'm not surprised." He grinned. "It's the first time I've seen this used as a weapon."

I stared at him.

"A hatpin," he said smugly.

"A hatpin," I repeated.

"Just as likely they used a thin knitting needle. In any case, it was pushed through his heart."

I thought for a moment. "That would explain the lack of blood. It would suggest a woman killer, I'm guessing."

He nodded. "Likely. There are precedents for this, you know, and not just in Agatha Christie stories. There's a woman called Doss, who died recently in jail, then there was Minnie Dean in New Zealand, some eighty years ago, I think. Both women killed their victims with hatpins."

"Any idea on time of death?" I asked.

"Around eight this morning, I'd say. Rigor hasn't set in yet, and the body is still warm."

I let out a long breath. "Hatpin. Okay, Doc, keep me informed."

Walsh came up the stairs, flipping through his notebook.

"I finished going through the building—no help so far.

I'll come back this evening and knock on doors. Maybe somebody saw something as they left for work?"

"Good idea, Patrick," I agreed. "Let me know tomorrow."

The forensic team arrived next, carrying cases full of equipment, measuring tapes, and boxes of chemicals, two of them wearing big clunky cameras around their necks. They spoke in their own language, ignoring us as they worked. Walsh and I walked down to our cars, talking softly.

"Listen," I said. "Let's ditch my car at my house and go to the Flaherty's. If Rhonda's not here, she must be there."

We dropped the Fury off and Walsh drove the Polara, weaving quickly through traffic.

A cop looks like a cop, whether he's in uniform or in a suit. Two of them together even more so.

A dark blue Polara looks like an undercover car, no matter what, and when occupied by two guys in suits, you don't need to look for the little police antenna or the dog dish hubcaps to tell who's inside. Early afternoon traffic, not usually accommodating, got out of our way as Walsh blipped his siren for a second whenever he felt boxed in.

We got to the Flaherty's house. Paulette Flaherty's Maverick sat in the driveway, and we parked, blocking it— just in case.

We worked as a team. Walsh quietly went through the garage to the back yard and waited out back while I rang the front doorbell. If anyone tried to avoid us by running out the back door, they would be disappointed. A moment later, a young woman, very slim, very pretty, opened the door.

"Hi?" she asked.

I got out my badge. "Is Rhonda here?"

The woman stared through me, not seeing me at all. "Who are you?"

I held my card higher, a foot from her face. She ignored it.

From the kitchen, I heard a padding of slippers on the

hardwood floor. Paulette's voice yelled out from around the corner. "Cynthia! Cyn. Who is it, dear?"

"I don't know, Mom," the young woman said. "Who are you?" she repeated.

I looked into the young woman's face. "I'm sorry, but you're blind?"

"No, I've got poor eyesight, but I'm not blind," she answered firmly. "Who are you, then?"

"I'm Detective Sergeant McBriar. I'm here to see Rhonda."

Paulette came up behind the young woman, placed a hand on her arm, and gently led her aside. "That's all right, love, I'm here," she said softly. "Hi, Ian. You're here to see Rhonda? She's not here anymore. She's living at that apartment the Portuguese fella got her."

I sighed. "No, she isn't. Do you know where she could be then?"

She shrugged. "Maybe out with that fella, I suppose."

"I don't think so," I said sharply. "He's dead—in that apartment."

Paulette shrank back, shocked. "Oh, my stars. What has that stupid girl done?"

I got out my notebook. Walsh came in through the back door, unnoticed. He walked past a frowning Paulette and joined me. He saw the young woman and did a quick double-take. "Hi; what's your name?" he purred.

The young woman blushed. "Cynthia."

Walsh held a hand out. She stared off, ignoring it. He frowned, puzzled at the snub.

"The young lady can't see too well," I explained. "Cynthia, did you want to shake my constable's hand?"

She reached out in the direction of Walsh's voice. "Hello."

Walsh took her hand in both of his and shook it daintily. "A pleasure," he sang.

"She's not here," I told him simply. "Paulette, do you know where Rhonda might have gone?"

Cynthia leaned toward her mother. "Aunt Rhonda said she wanted to get away. She misses home, she said. Said she di'nt feel safe here no more."

Paulette shook her head and tsk'ed.

"Home, you mean Newfoundland?" I asked.

Cynthia nodded. It seemed an unnecessary gesture. "Back to Corner Brook."

"Did she leave any personal belongings here when she moved?" Walsh asked hopefully.

"Some," Paulette answered. "Let me check."

She walked to the back of the house and returned a moment later. "Her clothes is gone. She had some here, but now they's gone." She shrugged. "Silly girl. Why would she run off like that?"

"Maybe to avoid being arrested for murder?" Walsh said dryly.

I sighed. "Where would she go in Corner Brook? She has family there, I'm guessing?"

"Yeah." Paulette sighed. "She got uncles and cousins all over town, of course."

"Could we get names and addresses for them?" Walsh asked.

"Sure, love," Paulette said.

She went to her telephone table and retrieved a tattered address book. Walsh noted some names and addresses, with the three or four phone numbers she had written down beside them, and closed his notebook.

"Thanks," he said. "Of course, if you hear from her, please call us."

Paulette shrugged. "Jim's a police officer. I know the routine. I'll call you."

Walsh reached out and touched Cynthia's arm. The girl jumped slightly at the familiarity. "Nice to meet you, Cynthia," he cooed. "I hope to see you again soon."

Cynthia snickered. "You sound cute."

"Hey, you better believe it." Walsh smiled. "Bye again, ladies."

We headed back to the station, called the phone numbers Walsh took down for Corner Brook, and looked up some others from the names Paulette had given us. Nobody had heard from Rhonda lately.

"I'm not surprised," I said. "Given how cheesy her place looked, I bet she's traveling by bus, not by airplane. She won't surface for a couple of days at least."

Walsh sighed and leaned back in his chair. "So we're stuck until we get more news, huh?"

"Yeah," I grunted. "Go home, Patrick. Enjoy the quiet time while you can."

He shrugged and walked off, whistling.

I called Karen's office. "Can I speak with Karen Prescott, please?" I asked.

"No," said the woman. I recognized the voice. "But you can speak with Karen McBriar, Ian."

I slapped my forehead and chuckled. "I knew I'd do that someday."

I asked Karen if she minded me having Frank and Helen for dinner. She'd be delighted, she said.

I then asked Frank if he and Helen would like to join us for dinner. They'd love to, he said.

I checked my watch. A quarter to three. Plenty of time to cook.

Captain Van Hoeke leaned out of his office and waved a finger at me. I followed him in. He held the door until I sat down, then he closed it behind me.

"Ian, how do you like your job?" he asked out of the blue.

I frowned. "Are you unhappy with my performance, Captain?"

"Quite the opposite." He inhaled deeply and stared at me. "You're good with the men under you, witness young Walsh, and you ask intelligent questions. What about you moving up to inspector?"

"Geez, boss," I said with a smile. "Frank's chair is still moving. Don't you think we should wait a while?"

Van Hoeke shook his head. "Frank is like a brother to me. You know that. When he leaves, though, I want someone in his place that I can trust. What do you say? Do you want the job?"

"He told you he's leaving?" I asked.

"He did. He respects you, Ian, and he respects your judgment. You've always looked out for him. I want to run this office as best I can, and to do that I need your help. So, what do you say?"

I looked at my shoes and thought for a moment. "Can I let you know tomorrow?"

"Suits me fine. See you then."

We both stood up. Van Hoeke held his hand out. That felt like he was getting a definite commitment. I took his hand, out of courtesy, but not firmly.

"We'll talk tomorrow, sir," I said.

A uniform dropped me off at my house. I bought groceries, put dinner on, changed into jeans and a sweater, then went into my back yard and raked up the leaves scattered by the wind. It was a very calming activity. I could rake and think at the same time. Should I take the job? Would Frank approve if I did? Would he be upset if I didn't? How about Karen? I was sure she would be thrilled. It would mean fewer chances of being hurt on the job, shorter hours, and better pay. Still, I would miss the detecting part of my job.

I put away my tools and went inside. Ethan came home and went downstairs to watch cartoons.

Around five-thirty, Karen's Beetle pulled into the driveway behind my Fury, and I heard her skipping up the porch steps to the front door. She opened the door and yelled, "Hi."

"Kitchen," I called.

She dropped her purse on the telephone table and wrapped her arms around me from behind.

"Hey, you." She nuzzled my ear. "What's for dinner?"

I turned around and kissed her. "Beef bourguignon. I hope you like it."

She stepped back, frowned. "What's wrong? Something's wrong, isn't it?"

I sighed. "How on earth do you do that?" I went back to preparing dinner. "Frank will be leaving soon. He decided today."

"I know," she stated flatly. "Helen told me."

I nodded. "Captain Hook offered me Frank's spot. He thinks I'd be good at it."

"Is that good?" She searched my face. "That's good, right?"

I shrugged. "It's mostly admin work, less grunting and running. It's the first rung on the big ladder, so that's good, but I still feel funny about taking Frank's place."

"You took his place when he was promoted. You got sergeant when he moved up." She said.

I sighed. "But he was still working with me in the department. I was still under him. I could still buy him doughnuts every morning."

"He's not dead, you know. You can talk to him every day, just like now," she pointed out.

"I guess. Anyway, let me think about it. After all, it's not like we need the money."

She smiled. "No, not like."

❧❦❧

Helen and Frank showed up just after six. Ethan helped set the table, then watched with curiosity as I assembled the dishes—a bed of hot wild rice on the bottom then a ladle of beef and vegetables over it. Together we carried the steaming plates through to the dining room.

Frank was into his second helping of French bread when I placed a plate in front of him.

He wrinkled his nose and tilted his head. "What is this?" he mumbled.

"Oh, jeez, Frank," I groaned. "Do we have to go

through this every time you have a dish for the first time? Just try it then spit it out if it sucks, all right?"

Helen and Karen snickered. Frank shrugged, embarrassed. "Sorry. Just asking."

He bit into a cube of beef. "Oh, dear goodness," he whispered. He took another, much larger bite, and nodded enthusiastically. "Real good. Real good," he said, patting his mouth with a napkin. He nodded again.

I rolled my eyes and smiled. Ethan was less subtle. He ate noisily, finishing most of his food before stopping to sip his milk.

Helen lifted her head and smiled. "Very, very good, Ian, delicious. So, are you going to take the promotion?"

I huffed in mock irritation. "Does everybody want me to change jobs? Honestly, I just get back from my honeymoon, and you're all nagging me already."

She leaned toward me. "What do you want to do when you're forty, Ian? Do you think you'll still want to run down the bad guys? Do you really want Karen to worry every night?"

I thought about that for a minute. "True, got me there. Still, I've only been a sergeant for a year. I still need to learn some things."

"You learned from me," Frank drawled. He grinned. "You learned from the best."

We finished the meal then had coffee in the living room. Helen drank a glass of milk then stretched out on my sofa, her feet in Frank's lap. Ethan went downstairs to watch TV. Karen talked about our trip, the sights we'd seen, the places we went. Helen nodded, attentive, then all at once she sat up, her eyes wide, holding her stomach.

Frank stared at her, worried. "What is it, hon? Are you all right?"

She shook her head. "I don't know. I'm not sure." She breathed deeply and winced.

Frank turned to me. "Let's get her to emergency. Now," he said and started to slide out from under her feet.

"No, no, it's not like that." Helen waved her hand. "It's, oh, I don't know."

Karen looked into her eyes. "Feels like intestinal hiccups?" she asked.

Helen nodded, unsure. "Yes, kind of."

Karen grinned. "You're being kicked."

"Kicked?"

Karen smiled at Helen's stomach. "Kicked. Twice."

Helen frowned, not understanding for a moment, then her eyes opened wide. "Oh." She gently rubbed her stomach, tilting her head as if to listen, and smiled. "Oh, you're right."

Frank, totally lost, frowned. "Right? What's right? Right how? What?"

Helen took Frank's hand and placed it on her stomach. He waited, puzzled, for a moment, then his face lit up. "You're being kicked," he gasped. He repeated it, softly, beaming. "You're being kicked. Oh, sweetheart."

I had never seen him be so openly affectionate. I decided to bring up a subject that had been in on my mind for a while. "Hey, Frank, would this be a good time to call your folks?" I asked.

He looked at me, a mixture of joy and fear in his eyes. "I dunno, man. I mean, my dad and me were never close. And after Woody died, things got real cold." He sighed. "I dunno."

"Don't you think you should tell him you're going to become a father?" I asked.

Frank stared down at his feet. "We left a lot unsaid, Ian, a lot unsaid. Maybe it's too late."

"Was it too late for you to have kids?" I challenged.

Helen slipped away from Frank and padded to the kitchen phone. I heard her talking softly. "Hello, long distance, please. For Confluence, Pennsylvania."

Frank and I were talking intently. He wasn't listening to what she said.

I heard her voice, soft and low, around the corner.

"Yes, I'd like the number for Theo Burghezian. I'll hold."

Frank shook his head and leaned. "Water under the bridge, Ian, that's all. We move on and live our lives."

Helen continued. "Yes, operator, please connect me."

She spoke softly at first, then louder. "Hi, Theo? It's Helen." A pause. "Your daughter-in-law."

Frank sat bolt upright, realizing what she was doing. He froze, unsure whether to be angry or embarrassed by her brashness. We listened silently to her side of the phone call.

"No, no, he's just fine. Listen, we thought you should know. You're going to be a grandfather."

At that word, Frank started to shake with emotion. It occurred to me that he'd never thought of her pregnancy like that before.

Helen listened for a moment then spoke again. "Uh-huh. Yes, he's excited. That's why we wanted to let you know." A pause then she laughed. "Well, it could be both. I'm expecting twins." She was quiet for a long time. "No, don't cry, Theo. Listen, Frank's here with me. One sec." She leaned around the corner to face us, covering the mouthpiece. "Frank, get over here," she ordered.

Frank walked meekly to the phone and took the out-stretched receiver as though it might bite him.

He held it to his ear. "Hey, Dad? How are you?" he whispered. He sat on a kitchen chair and quietly wept as he spoke. They talked for over an hour. Frank laughed, told stories, recounted what he'd been doing, and described the cases that we had worked together. Helen, Karen, and I sat, far off in the living room, as the two men spoke. After a long time, Frank finally said he'd call on the weekend, and I heard "I love you too, Dad." He hung up and came back, wiping his eyes. He pointed a finger at Helen. "You! I'll get you for this."

She patted her stomach. "I thought you already did," she joked.

Frank turned to me. "I'll pay you for the long distance, Ian."

I shook my head. "Don't you dare try. I'll never forgive you." I grinned. "So, what did he say?"

Frank smiled meekly. "It was a misunderstanding. My brother signed up because of Dad, not me. Dad didn't talk to me afterward because he felt guilty that Woody died. If we'd only talked back then…" He shook his head.

"At least you talked now." Helen smiled. "How is your dad? Is your mom excited too?"

Frank nodded. "They're coming to visit us at Christmas, him and Mom. It's going to be a good time." He leaned back and rubbed his face. "So, Ian, are you going to take my job?"

I rolled my eyes. "Everybody wants me to take your job. Why can't I just be a plain old super sergeant for a while yet?"

Frank nodded. "Okay, Sergeant, what are you doing this week?"

"Sorry?" I asked.

"This week," he repeated. "Where are we with your case?"

I sighed. "Rhonda, Ed's live-in, took an apartment that her boyfriend Gustavo got her. Gustavo DeMelo owned the building."

"Owned?" he asked, picking up on the past tense.

"Yeah, it was a love nest for them. Walsh and I went to see her there, and we found Gustavo, dead. Probably stabbed with a knitting needle, of all things."

"So it was a woman that did it?" Frank ventured.

"We figure," I agreed.

Helen frowned. "It was premeditated, planned, then?"

Frank looked at her. "How do you figure, hon?"

She smiled. "If she tried to kill him with a plastic needle, it would probably break. When I carry knitting needles around with me, I carry the plastic kind. Otherwise they'd poke through my bag. Besides, even if I did bring metal needles with me, I'd probably have some knitting already started on them, right?"

Frank and I nodded.

"Well," she continued. "Imagine pulling a needle out after you've done a bunch of work. That would be very frustrating, don't you think? All that yarn unraveling. I bet she brought a needle with her just to kill him."

I shook my head. "I want to kill someone, the first thought in my mind isn't 'Hey, I don't want to unravel my knitting,' is it?"

She laughed. "I agree, but think of the routine. Knitters are creatures of habit. They are fastidious about how they work, where they do their knitting, what they talk about when they knit, it's all connected. That's why she had an metal needle with her."

I wasn't convinced. "Really?"

She leaned forward. "I came over once and moved one of your kitchen knives. You were livid that it was left the wrong way in the knife block, remember?"

I nodded. "That was my Henckels carving knife. You put it in the paring knife slot. I remember."

"You remember the exact knife." She grinned. "Years later, and you remember the exact knife."

"But," I argued, "I wouldn't grab that knife to kill someone. I'd use a different one."

"Exactly," she agreed. "And if you *went* somewhere to kill someone, you'd bring along a different knife. Even if I had brought along my knitting, I would look for another way to kill the person, not with those same needles. I wouldn't think of them as weapons.

"But if I went somewhere to kill someone with a knitting needle, I would bring one along with me, just one metal needle, and no yarn."

Frank went, "Hmmm. So, do you think the killer thinks of her plastic needles like that—as hobby items?"

"Hey," Helen protested. "It's not just a hobby, it's a serious craft. Let me ask you. Didn't you once tell me that when most suicides jump off a bridge, they take off their shoes?"

"Yeah, that's supposed to be true," I agreed. "A psychological need to be neat or something."

"So," she concluded. "I'm right. I bet a woman planned it, and she used a metal needle."

"Do you think his girlfriend did it? Rhonda?" I asked.

Frank stared at us, fascinated.

"No, why would she?" Helen shook her head. "She was already sleeping with him, so she wasn't being pressured into sex. She had moved into his apartment, so she didn't feel in danger. But someone was upset with him for some reason, just him—and not upset with her."

"Why do you say that?" I asked.

Frank looked as if he had wondered the same thing.

"Simple." Helen smiled. "He was stabbed, but you haven't mentioned that there was a struggle, or if the apartment was ransacked. What was it like in there?"

I shook my head. "No, you're right. The place was neat, nothing broken, no signs of a struggle. It's like they just walked in, stabbed him, and left."

She grinned. "Told you."

Frank and Helen went home. Ethan had fallen asleep in front of the downstairs TV. I carried his limp form over my shoulder and tucked him into bed.

I went to bed. Karen slid under the sheets beside me then propped herself up and reached over me to turn off my desk lamp. Her breasts brushed my face. I caressed her back, expectantly.

"Don't get your hopes up," she said. "I'm tired—it's been a long day."

I chuckled and wrapped my arms around her. "Good night, Mrs. Mack Beer."

She laughed and hugged me tight. "Good night, Pops."

CHAPTER 12

I enter the dry cleaner's.
Rhonda is behind the counter, holding a bottle of yellow liquid. "Nice to see you again," she says.
I say something.
"I been in Corner Brook," she answers. "Visiting family."
She holds up the bottle of yellow liquid and starts unscrewing the cap. I stop her and take the bottle away. I open the bottle myself and smell it. She screams and covers her eyes.

❧❧❧

I woke up.

I was dressed and making breakfast by seven. I dreaded going in this morning. I had to tell Captain Van Hoeke whether I would take Frank's job, and I still had no idea what I'd say.

Karen shuffled up to me, wrapped in her robe, and hugged me from behind. "Hey, you." She kissed my neck. "You were talking in your sleep."

"Really? Did I mention anyone by name?" I joked.

"Yes. I never knew you felt that way about Frank," she joked back.

I chuckled. "I was dreaming about our missing woman, Rhonda. Same dream as before—I was in a dry cleaner's and she handed me a bottle of liquid. It's some kind of poison. I don't know how it relates, but I think it's crucial to the case."

"So," she asked. "Will I be Mrs. Sergeant or Mrs. Inspector?" She smiled, but it was forced.

"I don't know." I shook my head. "I'm tempted, but I'm not sure I'm ready. What do you think?"

She frowned. "Helen told me about how you acted in that bank. That sounds to me like you're good at handling people. That's what the job takes, right?"

"Frank told Helen?" I asked.

"Martin told Rebecca," she answered.

"Ah, and she told Helen, who told you." I sighed. "Should we get Rebecca her own office?"

"No need. Martin is under strict orders to report to her," Karen said.

I thought for a moment then grinned. "You know, if she'd known I was going to become an Inspector, my old girlfriend just might have stayed with me."

"Too late. She had her chance." Karen poked me in the chest, smirking. "By the way, if you ever mention her again I'll scratch your eyes out."

I wrapped my arms around her shoulders. "Hey, I married you, not her."

She kissed me. "And don't ever forget it."

☙❧☙

I parked next to Walsh's Polara in the station lot. He was sitting in his car, reading something. I got out and nodded at him. He got out of his car and nodded back.

"Morning, boss," he said with a smile. "So, any idea where you'll be sitting next week?"

"Why does everyone want to tell me what I should do?" I groaned. "I'll let you know."

I walked into the detectives' room, and the low rumble

of men talking, immediately went silent. I was reminded of the scene in *Gone With The Wind* where Vivien Leigh shows up at a fancy ball wearing the gaudy dress. I suddenly felt very naked, very much on display.

Frank came out of Van Hoeke's office, looking puzzled by the silence, and spotted me. "Ian, come here," he bellowed. Walsh followed me at a slight distance. Frank pointed at him. "Sit. Stay," he ordered.

Walsh sat meekly at my desk. I sat across from Van Hoeke and waited patiently as Frank dragged a chair beside mine.

Frank smiled at us. "Carry on, Captain."

Van Hoeke nodded at me. "Well, Ian, what do you say? Do you want the job?"

I nodded back. "Yes, I do. But not yet. I won't accept the position until at least a month after Frank has left."

Both men were silent. Van Hoeke leaned back and spoke slowly. "Go on, then."

I leaned forward. "I don't want anyone saying I took Frank's job. No matter how long we worked together, I don't want there to be any rumors that I edged him out of the Department."

Van Hoeke thought for a moment and smiled. "That one statement, Ian, tells me that you are the right man for this position."

He picked up a pen and scribbled something. "We have a floating Inspector; right now he's at 53 Division, but he wants out of the field. He's going into a job with the OPP as a high mucky-muck, but this keeps him busy until that desk is free."

He turned to Frank. "So, do you agree? Do we have your blessing on this arrangement, Frank?"

Frank smiled. "Why are you asking me? Ian knows as much as I do about policing. Besides, I'm out of here as soon as this case closes."

The two men looked at each other, silent, for a long moment.

I decided to break the ice. "Does somebody need a hug?" I joked.

They both laughed nervously.

We all walked out into the detectives' room. Van Hoeke gave me a look that I understood. Walsh got out of my chair, I sat at my desk, and he and Frank sat on the corners of it. Van Hoeke walked to the chalkboard.

"Can I get your attention?" he yelled. Everyone went quiet. He nodded our way. "As some of you already know," he started, "Frank Burghezian has been given the opportunity to explore a different path in life."

There was no mumbling, no surprise. Everybody knew. Of course, they knew.

Van Hoeke continued. "I've known Frank for seven years. For seven years now, I've worked with him. It has been a privilege, an honor, and frequently a pain in the ass."

Everyone laughed.

"Frank's last assignment will be to close this case he's overseeing. That means that, as soon as the investigation is concluded, Frank will leave the department."

The silence in the room was as thick as soup. Van Hoeke waved my way. "For the time being, Ian will continue as sergeant. In the future, this may change, but for now Ian has asked to remain in that role. Fifty-Three Division has offered to lend us an inspector, and he will temporarily take over Frank's duties when that time comes."

He paused, and I looked around. Through the room, heads were nodding approval. These men didn't see me as an opportunist. I wasn't taking Frank's job or pushing him out. That was good. They also saw me as a member of the team. That was good, too.

"So, without further ado," Van Hoeke said. "Let me thank Frank for his service. We wish him well and we will arrange an appropriate sendoff when the date is decided. Any questions?"

An arm waved in the back. "Can we have the sendoff party at Ian's again?"

A rumble rose up. I blushed. Not only was I part of the team, but they enjoyed my company, too. That cinched my position for the future.

Frank looked over at me, asking a silent question. I shrugged and nodded. Of course I'd host his farewell party. More happy grunting from the men.

"Okay, all of you." Van Hoeke growled. "Back to work, everybody. We're not paying you to gossip."

In groups of two and three, the men came over to Frank and wished him well. They came over to me next, as protocol determined that they should, and offered me their best wishes as well. I accepted them all cordially. I would need their cooperation once I was an inspector.

Inspector. Just thinking of the title in front of my name gave me a tingle. Five years ago, I was a beat cop, a twenty-three-year-old Metis kid who just wanted to fit in. A month from now I would be Detective Inspector Ian McBriar, responsible for a squad of police detectives.

Once all the hand-shaking and well-wishing was over, the men scattered, heading off to work on whatever they had to do.

I stretched back and sipped my coffee, taking pleasure in the approval from the group.

Around ten-thirty, one of the secretaries dropped a manila folder on my desk.

"The pathologist's report for you, '*Sergeant,*'" she smirked, enjoying a private joke. Obviously, word had gotten around.

I thanked her, opened the folder, and read the highlights. Gustavo De Melo had died from a sharp object, probably a knitting needle, penetrating his heart. Before that, however, he had ingested the equivalent of several scotches and cola, laced with a sedative. He had died the same way that Ed Hereford had died. Somebody had gotten him drunk, drugged him, then stabbed him.

The pathologist who did the post-mortem on Ed had also done one on Gustavo. I was uneasy, nagged by something. I needed to be sure I wasn't going off into left field on this thought so I picked up the phone and called the pathologist.

"Yes?" said the man's voice, direct and to the point.

"Hey, Ian McBriar here," I stated amiably.

"Oh, hello, Inspector," he responded cheerily.

I sighed. "Not yet. I haven't taken the job," I said, not a total lie.

"Fine. Have it your way." He snorted. "How can I help you?"

"The two post-mortems you did, Ed Hereford and Gustavo De Melo? Both men had cold medicine in their systems, right?"

"It seems so. Apparently. Yes," he answered.

I raised my eyebrows, curious. "Apparently?"

"Well," he explained. "There were narcotics in their systems that are present in over-the-counter medication, yes."

"You're hedging," I said. "What aren't you saying?"

He chuckled. "You sound more like Frank every day. Okay, what we found *could* have been from cold medication, but the level of opiate was way too high."

I grabbed a pen and pulled a pad close. "What opiate?"

"Codeine. There was far too much present in both men to have been just a component. I think it was added to whatever else they ingested."

"Someone spiked their cold medicine?" I asked. "Why would they do that?" It was a rhetorical question.

"No, they ingested no cold medicine, but it was in their food or something they drank," he corrected.

"Why not in cold medicine? It contains codeine, doesn't it?" I was intrigued now.

"It was codeine sulfate. It's water soluble, and it would have been put into a glass of water, or a cola, something like that."

"Or a bowl of soup?" I asked.

"Yes, that would do it."

"What effect would it have on our victims?" I pressed.

"It would slow heart rate and respiration, and it would make the victim groggy and confused," he said.

I sighed. "Where would I get codeine sulfate? Is it available over the counter?"

"Codeine is available in low doses, like the 'two-twenty-two' painkillers, but in higher strength it's by prescription only," he explained. "I've prescribed it myself for certain conditions."

"What would you prescribe it for?" I asked.

He grunted. "Muscle pains, abdominal pain, headaches, especially when the patient is allergic to aspirin, things like that."

I scribbled some notes as he spoke. "So, in your opinion, would this be used more by a woman than a man?" I asked. "As a way to subdue him before killing him, I mean?"

He laughed. "You're the detective. I leave the speculation up to you."

I smiled. "Okay, how's this? I've met your wife—lovely lady—but if she ever wanted to bump you off, do you think she'd drug you this way before she stabbed you?"

"I'd certainly hope so," he answered seriously. "I probably wouldn't feel much if she did." He was silent for a moment, thinking. "Actually, if I was drinking scotch and soup, like the first man was, I probably wouldn't notice the taste of the codeine, either. That would explain why he was given the alcohol."

I thought back to Rhonda's first dead boyfriend. "Both men were given scotch, right?"

The pathologist grabbed something—a stack of papers, from the rustling sounds—and read out loud, "Alcohol, specifically scotch, probably a cheap blend, from our analysis, and it looks like the same kind that was found in Mr. De Melo's stomach. Hard to tell. It metabolizes fairly quickly, but we did get some trace residue."

I thought back to De Melo in the maintenance office of

his apartment building. There were rum bottles around him. "He preferred rum," I said. "Could this have been rum?"

"No way," he answered. "It's a different chemical makeup. It's definitely scotch, not rum."

I thanked him and hung up. That detail bothered me. Gustavo drinking whisky seemed all wrong.

Walsh sat down across from me, waiting for me to finish the call. "Boss," he said. "I canvassed the building last night, where we found Gustavo."

I leaned forward, attentive. "Right, what did you find out?"

He opened his notebook. "Most of the tenants are older. Most didn't hear or see anything—they said. One of them, though, was this really cute blonde. She was a gymnast in college, and she—" He looked at my expression and stopped. "Anyway, she lives below that apartment and she heard someone walking around just before eight in the morning. That was unusual, she said, because she knew the old tenant had moved. It only went on for a few minutes, anyway. Then she had to leave for work."

"Well done," I told him. "A trifle over-zealous, but well done."

"That's not all." He flipped a page on the notebook. "Did you notice that there is a building across the laneway from Gustavo's apartment? It has living room windows that face Gustavo's. I spoke to three people who were home when he was killed. One of them, an older lady, saw him playing grope and grab with some woman."

I sat up straight. "Very good. Did she give you a description of the woman?"

He shook his head. "They have those crappy lacy curtains in all the apartments. You can see shapes through them, but not enough to recognize faces or anything. I looked across, and I could see the people in the unit beside Gustavo's apartment moving around, but I could only tell if they were tall or short, skinny or fat."

"How did she know it was a woman?" I asked.

"She saw a bra come off. That got her attention, especially at eight in the morning. It was someone slim and average height. That pretty well means it was a woman, I guess."

I smirked. "Yeah, I think that's a safe bet."

"You think it was Rhonda?" he asked matter-of-factly.

I shook my head. "Frank's wife figures she had no reason to do it. I tend to agree, but still, if it walks like a duck and quacks like a duck…" I shrugged.

"It could be a small goose," he quipped.

ⲉⲟⲉⲟ

We called the Newfoundland Constabulary. They had sent a car to interview Rhonda's relatives in Corner Brook, and they had spoken to the neighbors. Nobody had seen or heard from Rhonda since she'd moved to Toronto, apart from Christmas cards and the like. They promised to contact us as soon as they had any news.

Frank sat on the corner of my desk. "Hey, can I buy you both lunch?"

Walsh chuckled. "I never say no to free food either, Frank."

"Good," Frank said. "I need to talk to you guys."

We sat in the booth of our favorite diner. Our waitress, an older woman with a beehive hairdo and Catwoman glasses, handed out menus as though she was dealing poker cards.

Walsh smiled at her. "Hi. Does your mom know you're out all by yourself?" he cooed.

For the first time I could remember, she blushed. She leaned forward and purred at Walsh. "Would you like some *hot* coffee?"

"If it's from you," he answered, "it's *got* to be hot."

She giggled like a schoolgirl and left. Frank and I sat, speechless.

"What is it with you?" I finally said, exasperated. "Do you have no limits at all?"

Walsh thought for a moment. "You ever read much Dashiell Hammett, Ian?"

"I've seen the movies," I answered.

Frank watched our conversation with amusement.

Walsh grinned. "He once said, 'I like women. I *really* like women.'"

We waited patiently for our food to arrive. I turned to Frank and smiled. "How's Helen feeling?"

He grinned. "She was asleep behind me, and the twins were kicking me all night."

"Sorry," I said. "Didn't sleep well, then?"

He shook his head. "I've never felt so happy." He looked down, embarrassed by the admission.

"You know you are all in my prayers, right?" I said.

"Appreciate it, padre," Frank said. "Take all the help we can get."

The waitress brought us our burgers. Walsh's plate had a much taller stack of French fries than ours. Frank stared, irritated.

"What?" Walsh asked.

Frank shook his head. "You and women," he grunted. "It'll get you in trouble, some day."

The waitress came back and asked if everything was okay. That was also a first.

Walsh smirked at her. "If I feel funny later, can you come over and discuss it?"

She blushed again. "I—I'm married, you know," she stammered.

Walsh beamed sweetly at her. "Yeah, all the good ones are."

She giggled and left, smiling.

Frank snorted. "That's a lot of work just for some extra fries," he joked.

Walsh smiled. "I don't do it for the fries, Frank, I do it for the thrill."

Frank grunted. "Anyway, where are we with the case?"

I got him up to speed with Rhonda's disappearance, the pathologist's report on the codeine, and Walsh's interviews at the crime scene.

Frank nodded, listening with one ear, the way Van Hoeke did, then leaned back.

"Okay, you've got this one under control, carry on and run the show, Ian."

"Fine, so we'll just sit tight till we find Rhonda?" I asked.

Frank shrugged. "Yeah, nothing you can do, really. Halloween's in two days, you can get ready for trick-or-treaters, decorate the house, do dad stuff."

"Dad stuff?" I asked. "I've been wondering, how will you be if Helen has a girl?"

"How do you mean?" Frank asked.

"I mean—" I squinted. "—the first time a boy comes to take her out on a date, what will you do?"

"Show him my gun collection," Frank said casually. "And fire a warning shot."

CHAPTER 13

I went home early, changed to casual clothes, and finished getting my back yard ready for winter. It was almost November. The grass had stopped growing weeks ago, the bank of Echinacea along the garage had wilted to brown twigs, and the vegetable garden needed to be turned under before the snow came.

I worked silently, humming some jazz tunes to myself as I did. This was an activity I enjoyed. It was peaceful and let me concentrate. And I could feel the stress of the day evaporate away as I dug. By four-thirty, I had cleaned up the small back yard, draped burlap over the flower bushes, and covered the vegetable patch with a canvas tarp. Now I could cook dinner.

Karen got home at her usual time, and Ethan thundered up from the basement to greet her. He was reading Archie comics at a furious rate and wanted to show her just how well he could read.

Before she had her shoes off, he thrust an open page under her nose and pointed to the words on the page, reading them aloud one by one.

She waited good-naturedly at the doorway and let him read two pages to her, laughing with him at the joke on the final page. After that, she smiled at me apologetically.

"Hi," she said and kissed me warmly. "Sorry, hello, hon. How was your day?"

"Slow." I hugged her. "We're in a holding pattern till we get more news on a missing suspect."

"What's for dinner?" she asked, sniffing the air.

"Grilled chicken breast and wild rice," I answered.

"Again?" she joked.

I chuckled. "I just felt like rib-sticking food, that's all. By the way, I cleaned up the yard. We're all set for winter."

Her eyes widened slightly. "Industrious, weren't we? If this keeps up, I'll have to fire my other husbands." She grinned and kissed me again. "I appreciate it, sweetheart."

I called Walsh after dinner and told him to cool it till we heard from the Newfoundland police.

He didn't complain. I imagined his Polara, parked outside Vivian's place all day.

On Wednesday, Ethan and Karen headed off, then I called the pathologist and the forensics lab. Neither had anything new to report.

That gave me the day to myself. What to do? I pulled the Fiat out of the garage and went for a drive around town. This might be the last nice day I could do this before next spring.

On a whim, I went out to the cottage, the brisk wind making the drive feel like a fun adventure. To my surprise, the lavender Buick was in the driveway.

I revved the Fiat's engine, rolled to a stop beside the Buick, and went up the front porch.

I knocked at the partly open door and waited politely. A voice called out, "Hello?"

"Hi?" I answered. "It's Ian McBriar."

The squeak of rubber on hardwood came closer and the door opened wide. The realtor was wearing a lavender velour track suit and a pair of lavender running shoes. She stretched out her hand. "Hi. Nice to see you again, Sergeant."

"Hello, Audrey. Nice to see you, too." I shook her hand, warmly. "Still packing up, I see?"

She shrugged. "We're about done. Actually, could I

ask you to put a heavy box into my trunk? It's the last of the books. My dad wants to keep them all, of course."

"I'd be delighted," I said.

I lifted the box up, staggered out to the Buick, and placed the books dead center in the trunk. She slammed it shut. "There," she pronounced firmly. "All done." She looked around her and sighed. "You know, I'll really miss this place. I do hope you'll be as happy here as we have been."

"I'm sure we will," I said. "Does this mean that I can move some things in before January?"

She nodded. "What the hell? It's all yours, Ian. Enjoy."

The sudden casual tone made me smile. "You missed our wedding," I joked. "It was on the fly, an ad hoc affair, but we're planning a large ceremony later on."

She tilted her head and looked at me. "You're really set on this girl, huh?"

"My old partner asked me the same thing a year ago," I said.

"What made him say that?" she asked.

It was an insightful question.

I thought over my answer. "Karen didn't know it, but I owned the house we're living in now. I said it was for rent and asked if she'd move in with me. Later on, she guessed it was mine, but I wanted her to love me for me, not my possessions."

"She does, believe me," Audrey said sincerely.

"Why would you say that?" I asked.

"After you bought the cottage, she and I spoke a few times, about various paperwork issues. She asked if there wasn't some way that she could pay for part of it. I told her that since you'd written a check for the whole amount, she should talk to you about it, but she still wanted to pay for part of it out of her savings, without you knowing. That was sweet of her."

I smiled warmly. "Thank you, Audrey, that really made my day."

"Anyway, Ian, the place is pretty well empty now, so if you want to move in early, at least it won't be left vacant." She handed me a second house key. "Here," she said. "All yours."

I nodded. "Great. Listen, if you're in the neighborhood, drop in for coffee."

"Karen said you're a great cook."

I looked around and smiled at a memory. "I do okay."

"What's funny?" she asked, curious.

"We went to Venice for our honeymoon. We rented a water taxi, and Karen said it made her want to buy a boat."

Audrey laughed. "Funny how that happens. That's how I met my husband. He sold us our boat."

I walked her out to her car and she drove off, leaving me alone at the cottage. I checked my watch—not quite noon. I would treat myself to a luxurious day out. I drove to Jackson's Point and picked up some fish and chips from the local diner. Then I drove back to my cottage and found the coffee maker. I had lunch on the sofa, watching the waves out the window with my feet on the coffee table, the radio tuned to the Buffalo jazz station as I ate. This was glorious. It wasn't quite breakfast in bed with Karen on the Grand Canal, but it was very pleasant. I stretched out on the sofa, feeling completely relaxed.

I woke up with a start. It was four in the afternoon. I'd been asleep for three hours. I scrambled upright, put away the lunch things, and closed up the cottage. I drove the hour to get home. Ethan was playing at Alan's house, so he wouldn't be home yet, anyway. I had the irrational thought that I should make dinner before anyone realized I had gone to the cottage without them.

I drove the Fiat straight into the garage, closed the overhead door, and went up the porch steps and through my front door. I thought I heard Ethan, but when I called out nobody answered.

As soon as I walked into the living room, I knew something was wrong. It wasn't anything obvious. It was a feeling, more than anything. The side door was ajar, but it hadn't been a minute earlier.

I went into the kitchen. The chairs had been moved. I took a large meat knife and, holding it by my side, I went from room to room. My shirt drawer had been gone through, as had Karen's sweaters and underwear. The books on our night tables had been moved aside to lift the top and rummage the contents, then put back, not quite right.

I suddenly panicked. I went to the spot in my closet where I hid my service revolver, and sighed with relief. It was still there, untouched.

The question was, who would break into my house? Of course, I thought, the two stupid shits who had tried to rip off my Fiat radio. I probably scared them off when I came in.

I called Walsh. He was home, but the giggling sound I heard behind him indicated that I got him just before he became "indisposed."

"Patrick, I have a question," I stated. "Those two punks who were stealing my Fiat's radio, do you have their names and addresses?"

"Sure, Ian," he slurred. I heard syrupy saxophone make-out music played in the background then paper rustling. "Okay, got one, the older one; Gino Monetti. But he won't be home now. He works at his dad's hardware store on Rogers Road."

I got the store's address, thanked Walsh, assured him it was nothing serious, and hung up.

I was still in jeans and a sweater. That would help keep everyone relaxed when I spoke to the kid.

I parked the Fury outside a hardware store, below a sign that read, *Monetti Hardware and Building Supply*. The store was just a hundred feet from a railway overpass, on a particularly drab block, even for Rogers Road and was within walking distance from my old apartment. I had been in there a few times to buy things for my house, but apart from that I'd had no dealings with the business. Old bathtubs, sheets of peeling plywood and miles of used pipe were scattered in the side yard, while the front door, flaking and in desperate need of paint, bore multiple scars from work boots kicking it open.

I walked into the store. It was a labyrinth of shelves, tall racks of tubing and buckets of nails, screws and hinges.

I approached a man in a faded denim apron over an old striped shirt.

"Hi." I smiled. "I'm looking for Gino Monetti?"

"Yeah?" he answered eloquently.

I waited a few seconds for him to add something more to the statement. He didn't.

"And," I added. "Where can I find him?" I smiled again, less convincingly this time.

"'At's me."

This man could fit the Bible on a postcard, I thought. "Okay, I guess I'm looking for your son, Gino junior?" I pressed, guessing.

"What about?" he barked. A thick Italian accent came through, evident after more than two syllables.

I nodded politely and held up my badge. "I have a few questions for him, that's all."

He grunted at the ID then leaned over my left shoulder, yelling so loud it hurt. "*Gino!*" He turned back to me. "He's coming."

He just stood there, watching me, as I waited. I heard footsteps behind me and turned in time to see the youth I'd chased walking toward me, his head down. He got to within five feet of me and looked up.

His eyes widened, and he turned in the narrow aisle to run away. Too slow, too late again. By the time he'd done an about-face, I had hold of his elbow. He was shaking his arm, trying to break free, so I just squeezed a little tighter until he stopped shaking.

I turned to the boy's father. "Where can we talk privately?" I asked, no longer polite.

The man waved at a plywood box, an office constructed of scraps and a half-glassed door in one corner, the glass long-ago painted black.

I pushed the youth ahead of me through the door into the office. It had just two swivel chairs crammed into it. I kicked the seat of the chair farthest from the door, and it swung into position for someone to sit in it. The boy's father tried to follow, but I closed the door behind me before he could come in with us.

"Sit down," I ordered and guided the youth's arm to sit him in the far chair, then I sat in the other, blocking the exit. "Would you tell me, why it's a smart idea to break into my house after I went easy on you?"

He shook his head. "What are you on, man? How stupid do you think I am?"

"I caught you in my garage. I'd say that's the mark of a low IQ," I answered.

The doorknob turned behind me, and the boy's father poked his head in.

"What's going on? What did he do?" the man asked, defiantly.

I stood up. For the first time, the man realized I was a head taller than him. I leaned in, nose to nose, and stared down at him. "Five minutes. Wait outside," I ordered.

He shook a finger at me. "You can't do this to him. You got no right," he argued.

"I can arrest him on suspicion of burglary," I answered. "Or you can wait five minutes."

He grumbled something in Italian and closed the door behind him as he left. I sat back down. "Once again, why did you break into my house?" I stared at the boy, waiting for him to answer.

He shook his head, definite. "Me and Vinnie was stupid, but that's all. It was a dumb thing to do, but I would never break into a house, man, never. That gets you jail time."

"What's the difference, in your view? Breaking in is breaking in," I challenged.

"There is no break and enter into a car in Canada, man. It's not a domicile." He pronounced those last words carefully. "It's only a property crime, just a fine, max."

I sighed. "That's a very sophisticated point in law, Gino. But why should I believe you didn't break into my house?" He shrugged, less fearful now. "Like I said, man, that's serious jail time. We was just having fun before. It was stupid, you know."

He poked his chin out the door. "My old man was real pissed at us. Besides, you got those cops watching your house now."

A cold wave washed over me when he said that. "What cops?" I asked.

He seemed surprised by the question. "You didn't know?" He grinned, his teeth a mouthful of Chiclets happy to be out in the air. He laughed. "Son of a bitch."

I rested my elbows on my knees. "Okay, Gino, here's your chance to win a whole bunch of brownie points. What cops?"

He shrugged. "One is a big fat bugger. They wear cop suits—both guys. They were on Kane Avenue three school days. I seen them when I biked to work, around the corner from your place. I figured they worked with you. They're cops. They got to be cops."

"No," I said softly. "No, they aren't. Can you describe the car? The color, at least?"

The boy grinned again. "'Seventy three Dart—baby-shit brown. I think it's been stroked."

"Stroked?" I wasn't familiar with the term.

"Souped up. I saw them take off once, and they left a long patch of rubber."

"What time did you see them parked there?" I asked.

"Dunno," he answered. "I got to be at work by four. They were there at three thirty those days when I biked past them."

I nodded. "Okay. You've just won the good citizen award. I'll let your dad know you're in the clear." I stood up. The youth smiled cheerily. "I do have one question," I said, an afterthought coming to mind. "If you see them to-morrow, would you call my house?"

The boy grinned, amused by the request. "Sure."

I wrote down my phone number and handed him a pile of change. "Listen, don't stare at them. Just ride past their car, take down the license plate, find a pay phone, and call me, okay?"

He chuckled at the irony. "Sure. I'm happy to help the law."

I opened the door and let him out. His father and two other men were standing in the middle of the store, whispering, not sure what to expect. I smiled and walked up to them.

"Good news," I said. "This was a case of mistaken identity, and your son has helped us out in an investigation. He's a good kid." At that, the men relaxed visibly. I turned to the boy again. "So, Gino, you have my number, right?" He nodded. "Great, thanks again."

I left the shop and went home. Karen's Beetle was in the driveway. It suddenly occurred to me that she'd walk into the mess I had found. I ran into the house, calling her name.

"Karen! Karen, where are you?" I yelled anxiously.

"In here." Her voice, soft and sad, came from the bed-room.

I ran to the bedroom door. She was sitting on the bed, a pile of papers on her lap, others scattered all around her. She had tears in her eyes.

"Why would anyone do this?" she whimpered. She held up the pieces of our marriage license. "What have we done to anyone to deserve this?" She put the papers down, curled up on the bed, and cried.

"I have a lead on who did this," I said.

She looked up at me, surprised and hopeful.

"Those boys who tried to take my radio? They didn't do it, but one of them saw a car parked around the corner, watching us. He described it very clearly. I don't know how this relates to the case I'm working, but it can't be a coincidence." I stood up. "You pick up Ethan, I'll check out the rest of the house. We are not going to let these assholes do this to us."

She looked down at her hands, stood up slowly, gritted her teeth, and stared at me. "When you find them, Ian—" she started.

"Don't worry, I will." I promised.

"I know," she said, her voice suddenly sharp. "But when you do, you beat the shit out of them."

"Whatever the law allows," I promised. "Approximately."

☙❧☙

Wednesday, October 30th, 1974. I wrote that down very precisely on the page of my Moleskine notebook. Karen stormed around the house, getting ready for work, while I made lunch for Ethan and Alan. She kissed me goodbye. It was perfunctory—she was in a foul mood—then I got my suit on and walked Ethan across the street to school.

I got in my car and drove off. As I turned right toward Keele Street I saw a tan-colored Dart, parked on Kane Avenue. It was right in my rear-view, sitting at the side of the road. I drove onto Keele, then made a quick U-turn and looped back to Donald, a street that paralleled mine, one block over. I parked on Donald, facing my backyard neighbor.

My street does not have a back lane. My back yard butts against the back yard of a house owned by another family. I knocked on their front door. Nobody was home. I walked around to their back yard and hopped their back fence into my own back yard, then climbed into my basement, through a small window I always left unlocked, and went upstairs. Now all I had to do was sit quietly and wait.

As it happened, I didn't have to wait long. Within a few minutes, the rumble of a fat V8 sounded outside my living room windows. I peeked through a slit in the nearly closed drapes and listened as the car's engine stopped two doors away.

Perhaps I was wrong. Perhaps they were just visiting a neighbor down the street. Perhaps. A minute later, two men in suits, walking slowly, stopped on the sidewalk in front of my house. They spoke softly, looked around to see that nobody was watching, then they came up the driveway to the side door.

I looked around, wondering where to hide. I wanted to nab them inside the house, to catch them red-handed, and not just chase them off. I needed to know why they were in my house, what they wanted. These were not kids and they were not common thugs. These men were here with a purpose.

I pressed my body against the kitchen wall, out of sight of the front entry and the side door. Whichever way they came in, they wouldn't see me right away. I inhaled deeply and forced myself to breathe slowly, silently.

I listened. The side door made a clicking noise as someone expertly jimmied the latch. The door opened, softly and slowly. Footsteps sounded on the landing inside the side door—four feet, two men—then the door closed.

One man's voice, strong and certain, called out. "Hello? Hello, is anyone home?"

I held my breath and stayed quiet.

The voice said, "Wait outside. I'll be right there."

I waited, silent. My left wrist pressed against my coat pocket. Damn, I'd left my gun in the bedroom. I looked around, scanning the kitchen counter for something to use. My gaze landed on the knife block. Sticking up, high in the middle of the block, was my Henckels carving knife.

I leaned over slowly and pulled the knife out of the block. I clutched it, the blade pointing down, flat against my side. I heard footsteps go downstairs into the basement. I waited. A minute later, the feet came back upstairs. I took a deep breath and waited as the man rounded the stairs up from the basement, past the side door landing.

He walked right past me into the living room. He hadn't seen me. I followed him, the knife in my hand. I raced in behind him and placed the knife blade under his chin. He froze.

"Give me an excuse," I snarled. "You move, and you're a dead man."

He shook his head. I backed up and he turned slowly around, smiling faintly.

He was well-dressed, slim, but looked like he could hold his own in a fight. He didn't show any fear or panic. He glanced at the blade and then back at my face, as if deciding what to do. I didn't want to wait for him, so I stepped back, weighing whether or not to slice him open.

There are two basic ways to hold a knife in a fight. You can hold it so it points straight out like a bayonet and jab at your opponent, or you can hold it like Anthony Perkins did in *Psycho* when he stabbed Janet Leigh. That way, you can swipe, stab, or slash without getting it kicked out of your hands by your opponent. I went for the *Psycho* grip. I spun the knife around to point right, away from me, and watched the man's eyes for his next move.

"Why are you in my house? What do you want?" I barked.

"This was a mistake, Sergeant. We won't be back. No trouble, now let me go," he said, firmly. He held his hands up, indicating he held no weapon.

"Bullshit," I snapped. "You're one minute away from bleeding to death in my living room, and no one will blame me for killing you. Talk fast."

He lowered his arms, clasped his hands in front of him, and smiled at me. "You wouldn't two-seventy me, would you?"

He looked behind me and frowned. I turned just in time to see the other man, a scowl on his face, swing something

at me. The room spun around, and I fell to my knees. The
second man had a sap, a simple leather pouch filled with a
couple of pool balls. The blow made the world go hazy. I
fought to get up, but I was only half-conscious. He brought
his foot up and rammed it into my gut, knocking the wind
out of me. I fell to the floor, gasping for breath.

He bent down and sneered at me. "Not so tough, are
you, copper? Huh?" he barked.

He spat on me, covering my cheek and neck with sali-
va. The first one was still off to one side, watching us.

The first one moved in close. "What are you thinking,
Larry! You're beating up a cop!" He sighed. "I told you to
stay outside. Come on, let's go." He grabbed the man's arm.
"We're busted, come on, let's go."

"Sure," said the second one.

He swung his foot back and kicked me in the stomach,
hard. I rolled onto my face involuntarily, and he drove his
heel into my back.

"Let's go, Larry, come on. The cops are coming.
They're on the way," the first one pleaded.

"Yeah, okay, we're going," Larry said.

They went back down the steps to the side door. I heard
them open it slowly, then the one who didn't hit me said,
"Clear," and they left.

I had the irrational worry that they might have left my
door open after they'd gone. I lay there for a few minutes,
partly to catch my breath, partly playing possum, in case
they came back.

A car pulled into my driveway and I sat up, readying
myself for a fight. Everything hurt. The side door opened,
and I struggled to stand, but my legs were rubber. I crawled
to the kitchen table and pulled myself upright. Behind me I
heard footsteps—they were back. I turned to face the in-
truders again with had one hand on the kitchen table, one
hand holding the knife. It was the best I could do.

A face poked quickly around the corner then just as
quickly retreated. It reappeared, slowly. I recognized Walsh

and relaxed. He came around the corner, eyeing my knife with suspicion.

He had his revolver in his outstretched hands. I shook my head and put the knife on the table.

"Hey, boss, what happened?" he asked. He looked around, scanning the area for anyone else.

"I'm alone." I assured him. "They left."

"They?" he asked and holstered his gun.

I nodded. "Two bruisers. I hid out. They broke in and I tried to jump one of them. I got sloppy. I was stupid."

"Were you expecting them to come back, then?" he asked.

I explained the events of the last day. He nodded. "That's why I'm here." He shrugged. "I got a call from Frank. He wanted me to check on you. He was worried."

I chuckled, despite the pain, and shook my head. "Karen called Helen, who spoke to Frank."

Walsh snickered. "The Wonder Bra Telegraph," he smirked. "No offence, boss."

I shook my head. "None taken, Patrick."

He nodded. "S'cuse me." He picked up my phone and dialed a familiar number. "Hi, yeah, it's Patrick." A long pause. "He says two guys came in and jumped him. He got roughed up, but he's okay." Another pause. "Tell you what, I'll come get you."

He hung up and faced me. "Be right back. Do you need anything?"

"Beer and pizza?" I said.

"Really?" he asked.

I rolled my eyes. "No, I'm just kidding, Patrick. Hurry it up though, okay?"

I went to the bathroom, washed my face, then changed into clean clothes. As I walked back into the kitchen, I heard footsteps in the driveway. Walsh came back in, opening the door for Frank. Frank barged past him and hurried up to me. "Are you all right, Ian?" he asked. There was real worry in his face.

I was suddenly furious, angry that my home had been violated, angry that I'd been overpowered, angry that Karen no longer felt safe in our home. I was also angry that Frank had to come to help me for a second time now. At least this time I hadn't been shot, but I was still furious. I stared at the floor, trying not to explode.

"Ian," he repeated, "are you all right?"

I opened a cupboard door to get a glass, changed my mind, and slammed the door shut, hard. Both men jumped.

"All right? *Am I all right*? No, I am *not* goddamned *all right*!" I yelled. I kicked the refrigerator. "Who the hell were they? What did they want? I am sure as *hell* going to find them and tear their frigging *balls* off!" I growled.

Frank smiled slightly. I didn't understand, at first, that he was trying to calm me down. "Hey, Ian, can you make me a coffee, man?" he asked calmly, watching my expression.

I looked down bashfully. "Oh, yeah, sorry, man. What was I thinking?"

I mechanically filled up the coffee pot. Frank sat at my kitchen table. Walsh sat beside him, wondering just what I would do next. He looked back and forth between Frank and me, ready to jump in between us if things got rough, it seemed. I put the coffee things down, sat down, cradled my head in my hands, and sniffled, the morning overwhelming me.

Frank put his hand on my shoulder. "It's okay, Ian, it's okay."

I sighed, rubbed my eyes, and sat back. I would not let this get to me. I would hunt them down and find out exactly who they were and just how these men were connected to the Hereford case. I would not let them wreck my home.

We heard the sound of a Beetle's engine racing up the street. It stopped abruptly in the driveway. All three of us turned to face the front door, in unison.

Familiar heels stomped up the porch steps, and the front door flew open. Karen raced into the house, looked around, and froze as soon as she saw me. Her shoulders slumped. She rushed over to me and squatted beside my chair. She wrapped her arms around my shoulders and kissed my cheek.

"Ian, sweetheart, are you all right?" she asked, fighting the urge to weep.

"Yeah, hon, I'm fine." I smiled and looked at her, curious. "Helen called you?"

She nodded. "Right away. She said you'd been attacked. I had to make sure you were all right." She caressed my face. "Are you hurt very badly?"

"Only my pride," I lied. My right eye was swollen and my cheek was bloody. She squatted down beside me, stroking my hair. I wanted her to feel better. "You know," I said, "from this angle I can see right down your blouse."

She stood and bent forward, staring at me nose to nose. "Dumbass," she said softly and kissed me.

We did the things we were supposed to do as police officers. Walsh and Frank took my statement, noting time, place, date, and particulars of the incident, along with a description of the men and the car as described by the youth. Karen went through the house, checking once again on what was disturbed the first time. Nothing had been taken. Nothing was missing.

That in itself was puzzling. I sat on the edge of our bed and went through our jewelry box, picking at the few gold and silver pieces Karen possessed, my good watch, and a couple of American twenty dollar bills from our last trip to Buffalo. They hadn't been touched. Whoever these men were, they were not after our valuables. They were after something, but what?

Frank insisted we eat dinner at his place, and Walsh offered to sleep in our basement overnight. It was more symbolic than anything, but Karen and I were grateful for the concern. Helen made dinner for all six of us, her tummy now noticeably swelling, to Frank's immense pride. Karen and I helped set and serve, and Walsh kept Ethan amused.

We left at the end of the evening, unsure about what to do next. Walsh, luckily, took the lead and drove us home, then came back a half-hour later with an overnight bag and made himself comfortable in the basement. He slept with the door open, mostly so we'd feel more secure. I double checked all the doors and windows then went to bed.

I slept fretfully, tossing and turning all night. Karen slept soundly, her leg draped over a pillow beside her. It was an alluring image. I felt lucky to be married to her, and at the same time, furious that our home's security was being taken away from me.

෴

Next morning, I dressed, made breakfasts and lunches, then I walked Ethan to school. On a hunch, I walked toward where the youth told me he'd seen the Dart parked. A long block away, I thought I saw it—a light brown roofline at the side of the road, so I kept walking in that direction.

I told myself I must be wrong, that there was no reason they'd still be hanging around, but when I was five telephone poles away from the intersection, one of the car's doors opened, and I recognized the man who'd slugged me. He got a newspaper from the back seat and got back in the front. I ducked behind a fence and made my way back to my house, keeping cars between me and him.

Patrick was finishing his second coffee and reading the newspaper. I raced up the side entry to the kitchen. He leaned back, startled by my angry expression.

"I found them," I spat. "Light brown Dart, parked at the corner of Kane and Trowell. Those two weasels are watching this place." I raced through to my bedroom, collected my badge and revolver, and strapped on my holster as I spoke.

"Good," Walsh said. "What do you want to do, boss?" He stood up and dusted toast crumbs off his pants.

I thought for a moment. The Fury was parked a block away, on Donald. I smiled. "I've an idea."

I ran through my back yard and over my neighbor's fence again. I walked out to the Fury and looked at my watch. Walsh approved of my plan, but we needed perfect timing to make it work.

At the agreed time, he got into his car and backed out of my driveway, very slowly. I started up my Fury and drove along Donald to where it met Kane, the street the Dart was on. Kane was a one-way street. If the Dart wanted to drive off to Keele Street, they'd have to drive right past me.

Peeking around the corner, I could see the Dart. I saw the men, looking in the direction of my house. As Walsh pulled out of the driveway, they said something to each other and one of them started the engine. They pulled away from the curb and rolled toward me. I had them.

I put the gumball on the roof and stopped in the middle of the intersection, blocking the road. The Dart was mid-block, between Trowell and Donald, before they saw me. They screeched to a stop, and the driver looked over his shoulder to back up. That's when they saw Patrick behind them. Patrick did a quick half-turn in the street, blocking the road behind them. He got out of his car, aiming his revolver at the ground, and I did the same.

This was not what I wanted to do as a policeman. I wanted to catch bad guys. I wanted to do the right thing. I didn't expect a gunfight on the streets of Toronto.

The driver of the Dart was the first man in my house, the one who hadn't hit me. His expression was cold, irritated, like this was an annoyance, but all in a day's work. The man sitting beside him, the one who'd hit me, looked furious. I had a brief urge to shoot him, but it passed.

Our two police cars were about fifty feet apart, both with gumballs flashing. Walsh moved closer to the Dart, slowly, and aimed his revolver at the Dart's trunk. I raised mine as well, pointing at the driver.

"Shut off the engine. Hands in the air! *Now!*" Walsh

called out. The driver looked at Walsh through the rear-view and said something to his passenger.

Walsh cocked the hammer on his revolver and pointed it directly at the driver's head. "Get out! *Now!*" he repeated.

I heard a clunk as the transmission shifted, and the tires started to smoke. Backward. The Dart backed up the street, did a neat one eighty and slammed into drive. Walsh leaped aside to avoid being hit. The Dart mounted the sidewalk, just missing Walsh's Polara, drove the wrong way along the one way street, then made a quick right, and took off down Trowell.

Walsh and I jumped into our cars and gave chase. Walsh was ahead of me. He drove very well, very fast. He tried to cut off the Dart, but it zigzagged to stop him from getting alongside. Walsh stayed on him, though, and managed to stay a few yards behind the Dart until just before Keele Street. At Keele, the Dart tapped its brakes. Walsh screeched to a stop to avoid hitting it, but the Dart slowed just enough to check for cross traffic then shot across all four lanes. A bus and a line of cars blocked us from following. Walsh shifted into park and got out. Turning on the siren to get across would have been pointless. They were long gone.

I stopped beside Walsh's car, both blocking the road, both our gumballs flashing. Walsh slammed his car door.

"*Shit!*" he screamed. "Frigging shit! *Shit! Shit!*" He kicked his front wheel. "*Damn!*"

I got out of my car and watched the traffic whiz by, as if that could tell me something, then I shook my head. "Well, now how do we find them?" I grumbled.

"We could run the plate." Walsh held up a notepad and smiled. "I got the license number."

Walsh drove me to 52 Division. I walked into the detectives' room, still bruised from being beaten up. The men in the room stared silently at us. Van Hoeke waved us into his office and closed the door. "What the hell happened to you, Ian?" he asked.

"I was attacked in my house by two men," I said. "We saw them later, and—"

Van Hoeke held his hand up to stop me. "That's not what I mean. You're one of the good guys. You are supposed to play by the rules. You're not John Wayne." His voice rose to a growl as he spoke. "I'd expect this from Frank, but I would not expect this from you. You had a shoot-out in the street? Come on, Ian, *what were you thinking*?" He bellowed out the last four words. Everyone in our end of the building stopped as they heard them. Van Hoeke was beet red now, furious.

I sat back, digesting his words. "I made this personal," I said. "That's where I went wrong."

Van Hoeke gave an exaggerated nod. "That's right. Very *good*, Sergeant. Now you *get* it. Every day, we talk to people who are poor, innocent victims. We ask them to let us do our job, to let us work within the system, but what do you do? You play Dirty Harry in the street. A block from Ethan's school, for god's sake. Does that hit home, Ian? Does it make you think? Huh?"

My mouth dropped open and I looked down, embarrassed. He was right, of course.

Van Hoeke was less red now. He took a deep breath. "Give me your revolver."

I handed over my gun. He flipped open the chamber and counted bullets, then he sniffed the barrel. He did the same with Walsh's gun. He handed them back to us.

"What do you want, Captain?" I asked. "Walsh was just following my orders. If you want to kick me off the force, I understand, but Walsh was not responsible for any of this."

"Bullshit," Van Hoeke said flatly. "He shaves and he wears long pants. He knew perfectly well what he was doing. If you'd fired a shot, you'd both be out on your asses right now. As it is, consider yourselves extremely lucky. You will both be officially reprimanded. Get out."

I thanked him, Walsh thanked him, and we left his office. Other detectives walked past my desk, wearing the expression of men who sympathized, but didn't dare help.

I sat, fuming, wondering how I could get these guys without running afoul of Van Hoeke. A secretary faced me, silently holding a slip of paper. She'd been there for a while, I guess.

"What?" I barked.

She jumped back. "You wanted a license plate checked?" she asked meekly.

I grunted a "Yes."

"You're sure that this is the right car?" She frowned and handed me the paper. "Okay."

I looked at it and stared at her. "Really?" I asked.

She nodded and turned to leave.

"Hey," I called. "Sorry about yelling. I'm really upset, I apologize. Sorry."

She smiled sadly. "I heard," she said.

I went into Van Hoeke's office and sat down. He looked up at me, irritated. "Yes?"

I handed him the slip of paper. "The wheel man was good, very good," I said. "I thought he was a getaway driver, but look at this."

Van Hoeke read the paper and looked up at me, intrigued. "Well, this does put a different spin on things, doesn't it?" He handed it back.

Walsh walked past Van Hoeke's door. I waved him in and handed him the same slip.

He read it quickly. "Really? The car is registered to the RCMP? That explains the trick driving."

"You know," I said, "the driver said something that I'd forgotten. He said, 'You wouldn't two-seventy me.' I think he wanted to identify himself without his friend knowing he was a cop."

Walsh wrinkled his nose. "How do you mean?"

Van Hoeke grinned. "Criminal code, section two - seventy, 'assaulting a police officer.'"

We were all quiet for a minute. "Why would they break

into my house?" I asked. "All my case files are here, anyway."

Walsh shook his head. "Why would they even care about the Hereford case? They could just call the station and ask us, right? But break into your house? Something's not right."

Van Hoeke leaned back. "Is there anything else you're working on, besides the Hereford thing?"

"No, nothing I can think of, Captain, nothing at all."

"Keep me posted," Van Hoeke said. He pointed his pen at us. "And keep it in the holster."

Walsh and I went to our desks. I had to find out what the Mounties were up to. Was it something to do with Ed's murder or with Gustavo's, and how would that concern the RCMP? I went through the file folders on my desk. My phone rang.

"Sergeant McBriar," I answered, mechanically.

"Hello," a man's voice said pleasantly. "You met me on Kane Avenue."

I recognized it at once. "We met in my house, too," I added coldly. "What do you want?"

"You ran my car's plate. I'd like to come by and explain myself."

"All by yourself, or will your friend be coming with you as well?" I asked.

"No, just me. Will you be in the office all day?" His voice was detached, professional, and businesslike. He could have been setting up an appointment to install carpeting.

I leaned back. "I'll be here for another hour."

"I'll see you shortly, then." He hung up.

I called Walsh over and told him about the phone call. We figured that this must be a courtesy call, possibly to tell me to back off, but back off from what? And if so, why didn't the RCMP just tell me to back off earlier, rather than break in? I wanted to call Karen, to tell her everything was going to be all right, and our home was safe again, but first I needed to hear from this Mountie why he'd broken into my house in the first place. Then I could call her.

I told Van Hoeke about the call. He was intrigued. That was certainly an understatement. Half an hour later, one of the secretaries walked up to my desk. She did not smile.

"There's an RCMP officer to see you, Sergeant," she said coldly. She knew—everyone knew.

I stood up. "Send him in."

The man I'd held a knife to in my living room walked up to me. Today he was dressed in a navy three-piece suit and carried a thin black binder under his left arm. He reached out his hand. "Sergeant McBriar, I'm Constable Smith." He smiled and kept the hand out.

I ignored it. "Come," I said simply.

I walked into Van Hoeke's office, the Mountie trailing me. Captain Van Hoeke stood up; the man looked at him.

"Who are you?" the captain asked bluntly.

"Constable John Smith," the man said. He didn't bother extending his hand.

"Really?" Van Hoeke said. "John Smith? That's the best your people could come up with?"

The man chuckled. "Let's all go with that name for now, shall we?"

Van Hoeke looked at his watch, theatrically. "Ian, I have to do something important. Can you speak to—" He sneered. "Constable Smith' while I'm gone?" He left abruptly.

I sat in the captain's chair and the man in the navy suit sat across from me. "I can imagine you're somewhat upset."

"No," I answered. "When I get a flat tire in the rain, I'm upset. When I drop my wallet down the toilet, I'm upset. When someone from our side of the blue line breaks into my house and beats me up, then I am way beyond upset."

The man cringed a little at that. "Listen," he said. "The best I can hope for here is to make you understand why I did what I did. I realize that."

"No," I corrected. "The best you can hope for is that you leave this room on your own two feet. Second best is if I don't get you thrown out of the RCMP. Anything beyond that is pure luck."

He scowled, leaned forward, and placed the binder on the table.

"Did the captain leave us alone so we could talk off the record?" he asked, matter-of-fact.

"No. He left because if I kick the shit out of you, he can swear that he didn't see me do it."

He didn't wince at that. He nodded slightly. "I checked up on you. You have the reputation of being a good cop. You play by-the-book. Everything I found says you always color within the lines. I believe you'll give me a chance to explain myself?"

I leaned back. "Go on."

He opened the binder to a series of documents—deeds, invoices, forms in several languages; I had no idea what they were. He slid the binder my way. I didn't examine the documents too closely.

I pushed the binder back his way. "What does this all have to do with me?" I asked.

"You and your girlfriend are trying to adopt Ethan," he said.

"Wife," I corrected. "We got married last month. You should update your facts. This mess is about Ethan? That makes you even more likely to leave here in an ambulance. Talk fast."

He smiled again. That was brave. "I have been working undercover for the last four months," he said firmly. "We are following some financial fraud that goes quite deep. Our target is a small fish in a very big pond. His money is noth-ing compared to what we're going after, but he's our open-ing into the bigger case. Our investigation is nearly con-cluded, but with you trying to adopt the boy, it could all go down the drain. Marchand could walk away from this mess scot free."

"Marchand? Pierre Guy Marchand? What kind of investigation is this?" I growled.

He thought for a moment. "You want to buy some property, so you borrow the money from an investor. The investor lends you the purchase price. You buy the property and resell it a month later to somebody else. You keep the money and you never pay back the loan."

"Wouldn't that be a simple civil issue?" I asked. "One best settled in a lawsuit?"

He leaned forward. "Let's say your investor's money is overseas. Nassau, Lichtenstein, Columbia. We can't verify their side of the transaction. We only have your word for how the money was actually borrowed. As well, the same real estate has been bought and sold a half dozen times in a decade. It's an old shell game. Marchand wins, we lose. We all pay."

I shook my head. "You expect me to believe that the RCMP put you under cover for a stupid real estate swindle? You guys have bean counters for that."

He smirked, as if amused at my perceptiveness. "You cut to the quick, I see. Okay. Now, same scenario, but let's say you're doing it for a fee, as an agent for a third party." He leaned forward and stared at me. "You're doing it for someone who shouldn't have the money in the first place, someone who got rich selling kilos of white powder." He paused, as if thinking about what to say. "You act as an agent for this 'someone.' You find a property worth ten million dollars and they lend you the purchase price from their account in Argentina. You buy the property then later you sell it and place the proceeds into an account in Toronto, minus your considerable fee. You've just laundered the value of the real estate and your client now owns clean money."

"So?" I asked. "Again, how does this concern me in any way?"

"There is a running joke among his staff," he continued. "They say 'PM for PM.' Pierre Guy Marchand wants to become the leader of the Liberal Party and the next prime minister." He rested his hand on the desk. I glared at it, and he slowly pulled it back. "He has been very wary of getting caught with dirty cash. He looks like Mister Clean to most of the world. If his opponents find out that he has an illegitimate son, then that would destroy his chances of getting elected to parliament and if he can't become an MP, then he'll never be PM. That's why he sent us to your house, so you'd back off. We were looking for information we could use against you, to stop you adopting Ethan. If there was a custody fight it would get ugly—his enemies would use that knowledge against him. I needed to go along with him, because if he suspects the RCMP is onto him, he'll hide all the evidence we're trying to get."

I thought about this for a moment. "Does that mean that I'm supposed to keep my life on hold while you build a case against him? What do we tell Ethan—I can't adopt him, I can't give him my name, I can't become his father, because some criminal is running for parliament?"

He smiled politely. "You're trivializing a complicated situation," he said dismissively.

"Like I give a shit about your situation," I countered.

"Hey, man." The Mountie shrugged. "I came in here as a courtesy. I didn't have to do this."

"You came here because I found out who you are. Who are we kidding? It wasn't an act of altruism," I sneered.

Walsh came into the office, closed the door behind him, and nodded at the Mountie.

The Mountie nodded back. "Constable John Smith," he said.

"I don't think so. Try Warren Bancroft." Walsh grinned. "You bought gas with a credit card. The Chargex slip had your name on it. You really should be more careful. And lock your glove box."

Walsh held out a piece of paper, shorter than a dollar bill.

The man's mouth opened silently. He snatched the pa-

per, sneering at Walsh. "You went through my car?" he
barked angrily.

Walsh laughed. "Yeah. Tell me how that feels. Getting
broken into is a real piss-off, right?"

The man crumpled the charge card receipt and put it in
his pocket.

"You probably needed that for your records." Walsh
smiled sweetly. "So I made copies." He handed the man a
Xeroxed page. "I got more, if you need them."

The man glowered at us, furious at being on the receiv-
ing end of intrusion.

I leaned forward. "Thanks, Patrick. Good work. Now,
'John,' it's my turn. I can destroy your investigation with
one phone call to Marchand. I can tell your superiors you
helped rough up a detective sergeant, and finally, I can
make sure you spend the next decade shoveling snow in
North Bay. Then I can tell the media, so everyone feels my
pain. Or you can make it right for everyone."

He sneered at me. The anger in his face was palpable.
"What do you want?" he growled.

"Me?" I smiled, acting surprised. "For myself, I want
nothing. What I do want is to be sure that you bozos won't
bother me, ever again. I also want to know that you and
'Larry' won't interfere if I do contact Marchand."

"Marchand? Pierre Guy Marchand?" Walsh snapped.

The Mountie nodded, surprised at his reaction.

"That shmuck cheated us out of a fortune," Walsh
grunted. "I hate his guts."

The Mountie turned to face me. "Why should I believe
that you'd do any of this?"

I pointed over his shoulder. Outside the office, a half-
dozen detectives stared through the glass at him. They did
not look happy.

"See them? These guys will find out *everything* about
you," I snapped. "If you have a girlfriend on the side, or if
you have a drinking problem, or gambling debts, or you
steal apples, or you beat your dog, or anything else, *any-*

thing, they will find out. And do you know why? Because, if some asshole cop broke into their home, we'd do that for any one of them. We are a family here. You are screwing with guys who always look out for each other."

The men outside the room grumbled in agreement.

The Mountie shrugged, defeated. "Fine," he snarled. "We won't bother you again. You have my word. I'll go even further. Call it my wedding present to you." He pulled out a sheet of paper from his jacket and laid it on the desk. "Marchand will be in the area next week. He will have the evidence we need with him. You help us nab him, and I'll help solve your problem. That way, we both win."

"I smell bullshit," I said. "This is the real reason you came here to see me, not to be a good guy."

He laughed. "No fooling you. Okay, here's the offer. Next week, Tuesday, November fifth, Marchand will be in Hamilton. He's finalizing the sale of a building project in the area. Anyway, he has a house on Ravenscliffe. Here's his address." He slid the paper toward me.

"Ah," Walsh said. "I know it. We own some property on that street."

The Mountie shook his head, astonished. "Anyway, as I say, he'll be there Tuesday. He has a seven o clock meeting with his lawyer. I heard him make the appointment. You storm in, all piss-and-vinegar, and demand he let you adopt Ethan."

"Why would I do that?" I asked.

"He'll yell and scream, which he always does, then he'll tell you to get out. You tell him that you have something on him, a zoning report, regarding his Hamilton sale. He'll say you're lying, so you tell him you have the original document, and you leave. Once you do, he'll open his safe and check that he still has the original. When he does, the safe will no longer be a 'legally protected' location. I will confiscate the contents and arrest him."

"The Canada Criminal Code, part nine, section three forty-eight," I recited. "Breaking into a legally protected location to retrieve evidence would get it thrown out of court, but reaching into an open safe wouldn't. Then again, you could just get a warrant for the contents," I suggested.

"He has friends in court. They'd warn him and he'd burn the evidence. This way, when I arrest him I'll get him to cut a deal for less jail time in exchange for letting you adopt Ethan," he said.

"Why do you need me for this game?" I asked. "You could get anyone to act as bait. Why me?"

"Your actions would be believable. Plus, he had you roughed up. I owe you," the Mountie said.

I thought for a moment. "Seven o clock on Ravenscliffe. You will be there when I show up?"

The Mountie nodded, got up, and opened the office door. A cluster of detectives blocked his way. The Mountie looked back at me, and I slowly nodded my head. The detectives fell back and the Mountie left.

Walsh watched him go. "I don't trust what he said for a second," he hissed.

"Me neither, Patrick," I agreed. "I don't think they'll come back to my house, though."

I called Karen to tell her that we'd been broken into by mistake. It wasn't a total lie. I assured her it wouldn't happen again. She was relieved at that.

Van Hoeke reappeared as soon as the Mountie left. I smiled. He understood me completely.

ベンベン

Thursday was Halloween. Ethan dressed up as a cowboy, much to my dismay, and went up and down the street with his Stetson and plastic six-guns, collecting candy in an old pillowcase. I followed him at a discreet distance, making sure he was all right as he went door to door. By eight o clock he was exhausted, full of cheap chocolate, and ready for bed. Karen and I were grateful that he wasn't aware of

the events of the week. He was barely aware that we'd rear-
ranged some papers, and most of my bruises were under my
shirt, anyway.

I climbed into bed, pleased that my home felt safe and
secure again. Karen slid down beside me.

"So, hubby, what are you thinking?" she asked.

"I have to make everything right for Ethan," I said.

She sat up. "Really? How?" She searched my face,
scrutinizing me. "What are you going to do, Ian?"

I told her about the Mountie's visit. I explained that in
exchange for my help, the RCMP would go easy on
Marchand, if he'd let me adopt Ethan.

She frowned and shook her head. "I don't know, love,
it sounds flaky," she said. "I think you're being used here."

I sat back. "That's a very cynical view, don't you think,
hon?"

She shook her head again. "Pierre has delusions of
grandeur. He's a narcissist. He is also without any scruples.
Someone once said that he's the only man they knew who
could follow you through a revolving door and come out
ahead."

She sighed, obviously weighing how she wanted to say
what she was thinking. "When I knew him in University, he
was suave, charming, and completely amoral. The reason I
moved to Toronto, the reason I left Ottawa, was to get as far
from him as I possibly could.

"After Ethan was born, he'd call me just to torment me,
no other reason. My parents helped me move here and get
settled, because they saw how he was destroying my life.
He's evil, but you're not. I think he's got tricks up his
sleeve that you're not even aware of."

I thought about that statement. She was probably right,
of course.

I was going into this from the perspective of being an
honest, straightforward man, dealing with another straightforward man, and that put me at a huge disadvantage. I lay
back, thoughtful, and fell asleep.

∽∾

I am lying in the bush near Smeaton, Saskatchewan, beside my mother's father and my uncle. My grandfather is very old, almost eighty, and his hands are wrinkled leather. Still, he holds his rifle with the precision of a surgeon's scalpel. He is a small man, wearing a brown buckskin jacket and black denim pants, his intricately beaded sleeves recounting the story of his time in World War One in the trenches of France. He was over thirty then, a father who enlisted to show his loyalty to the country that he loved, even though it treated his people badly.

My uncle, less than half his age, is a towering oak of a man who smiles easily. He came up from Montana for this hunt, taking time off from his construction job. He has promised to let me drive his truck, now that I am sixteen, as long as I am careful with the clutch.

I raise my head to talk to my uncle, but my grandfather places his hand on my arm.

I lie perfectly still. Soon, a white-tail deer jumps out of a small stand of trees, looks around cautiously and trots past us, heading toward another stand of trees. In one smooth motion, my grandfather points his rifle, aims, and fires.

The rifle makes a "PIW" sound and the bullet strikes the deer in the chest. It drops to the ground, dead. Wordlessly, my grandfather and uncle lead me to where the animal lies, check that it was a clean kill, then my uncle lifts the animal onto his massive shoulders and carries it back to the truck.

I turn to ask my grandfather how he knew the deer was going to come out of the trees at that time.

"You got to know about your quarry, little Abukcheech. You got to know what it wants to do." He smiled, his Cree tongue making his English speech a staccato. "It does what it knows, even if it knows in its heart that it is not right."

CRCR

I woke up. That was the answer. I knew what to do on Tuesday night.

I called the station house on Friday morning. There was still no word on Rhonda. She had vanished, it seemed. Walsh was tracking down the last few residents of the building where Gustavo died, as well as in the building across the laneway, but there was little hope for any new information there.

I invited Frank, Helen, and Walsh to dinner then went out to pick up some groceries. Instinctively, I looked for the light brown Dart but it was nowhere to be seen. Bancroft had kept his word, it seemed.

I made lasagna. Helen and Frank liked lasagna, and I hadn't made it for them in a long time. At four in the afternoon, I picked up Ethan from school and walked him home. He helped me set the table. Then Walsh called to ask if Vivian and Alan could join us for dinner. I would be pleased to have the company, I said.

CRCR

By six, Karen had changed out of her work clothes and into stretchy pants and a sweater. Helen and Frank wandered in. Helen was noticeably more pregnant every day, it seemed, and Frank shadowed her like the secret service protecting the president. Walsh, Vivian, and Alan came by shortly after, and the two boys immediately ran downstairs to play with Ethan's Hot Wheels.

We sat in the living room as dinner cooked, just relaxing and talking about hockey. The Leafs were on the road, playing the Atlanta Flames later in the evening. It didn't look good for the season since the Leafs were in yet another slump. Walsh spoke casually, but his attention wandered to the kitchen from time to time.

"Something wrong, Patrick?" I asked.

"I'm trying to place the smell, boss. Italian food?"

"Lasagna," I stated.

Frank's eyes opened wide. "For real?" he said. He stared off, inhaling deeply, winding up to ask what I knew was on his mind.

"Yes, Frank, I made one for you to take home as well," I said. I turned to Vivian. "In case you like it, there's one for you to take home, too."

She blushed, embarrassed at my thoughtfulness.

We had dinner and our guests left, sated. All the food went to good homes, as Karen quipped. Ethan fell asleep on the floor in front of the TV, and we put the floppy boy into his bed.

Karen climbed into bed beside me. I was lying back, looking at the ceiling. The sparkly effect from the texture made it look like thousands of stars twinkling in the light from the bedside lamp.

She rubbed my moustache. "Whatcha thinking?" she asked.

"Ever think, when you were a kid, about what fun it would be to walk on the ceiling?" I said.

She laughed out loud then shushed herself. "You idiot. I haven't thought of that in years. What brought that to mind?"

"I was thinking about Tuesday night," I said. "I dreamt about one time I was just a kid, and I went hunting with my grandfather. I think he was trying to tell me what to do Tuesday night."

She sat up. "What will you do?"

I slid under the sheets. "I will let the quarry come to me," I said. "Good night."

CHAPTER 14

On Saturday, I suggested we should take a break and go out to the cottage. I mentioned that I'd gone there mid-week, and Audrey, the realtor, had finished clearing out her personal things.

We drove out to Georgina, then up Woodbine Avenue. The moment I pulled into our driveway, I could feel myself calm down. Ethan jumped around in the back seat, delirious at being back at "his farm," as he still called it.

I got out of the Fury, let Ethan drag Karen and me up the steps to the front door, and Karen let us in. The things that Audrey had taken were few, mostly family mementoes, so the cottage was still functionally complete. I'd bought some groceries for the drive up, made sandwiches, and sat on the sofa, watching the lake beyond the lawn as Ethan played with a toy on the floor. It started to rain lightly. Even that felt cozy. I lit a fire in the wood stove, and the warmth spread through the house in minutes. Karen stretched lazily on the sofa, her feet in my lap.

"Remember Venice?" she said.

"Gosh, yes." I smirked. "Feeling frisky, are we?"

"No, not that, silly," she chided. "I mean, remember when I said we should get a boat."

At that, Ethan's head popped up. He smiled broadly.

"Did you really?" I teased. "Since you mention it, I did go to Jackson's Point for lunch on Wednesday, and I noticed the marina next door. We can check it out if you like."

With Ethan pleading and dragging us along, we drove to Jackson's Point, met with a man who had a boat for sale, and accepted his offer to take us out for a run on the lake.

It was a cool day and the first real hint of winter was in the air, the light drizzle giving a misty haze to everything outside the marina office.

The man proudly showed us his boat. It was very small—an aluminum speedboat, barely the length of the Fury, with a tiny outboard motor and just four seats, but it was tremendous fun. We bounced up and down over the choppy waves. Ethan laughed hysterically at the ride, dipping his hand in the lake, Karen smiling the whole time. She happily took the wheel at one point, biting her lip and nodding at the man's instructions on how to throttle and steer. Once the boat got up to speed, her smile widened and she skipped over the water, confident, pleased with herself.

Watching her happy expression, seeing the wind whip her hair around her face and her delight at being in the boat, I felt a surge of warmth and love for her as strong as any I'd ever felt.

We tied up back at the marina, and I offered to pay for the gas we'd used. The man refused, saying it was his pleasure, but we agreed that if the boat was still available in the spring, we would settle on a price and I'd buy it then. We shook hands and drove off.

Ethan was beside himself with glee. He hugged me and his mother, delirious at actually being on a real live boat, and bombarded Karen with questions about our trip to Venice, and the boats there. Did they go this fast? What was a canal, anyway?

Karen was quiet through the short drive back to the cottage. Ethan ran in and immediately began exploring his bedroom, looking for any other toys and things left behind that he could play with. I took my coat off and poked the fire, enjoying the warm embers before we had to douse it and go back to Toronto. Karen sat still, leaning against me.

"What is it, hon?" I asked.

She spoke softly but firmly. "Do you have any idea how much I love you?"

I grinned. "You can show me later."

She shook her head. "No, I mean it, Ian. You didn't need to help me out last year. You committed yourself to me and Ethan. You didn't need to take us into your home, and you certainly didn't need to buy this for us." She waved her hand around the cottage.

"You deserve it, all of it," I answered. "You and Ethan. And don't ever think that I see you as a consolation prize. I'm the lucky one in this family, not you two."

"Family?" She grinned and wrapped her arms around me, pinching my elbows to my sides. She kissed me passionately, then lifted her arms to wrap around my neck. She kissed me again.

"What was that for?" I asked stupidly.

She grinned again. "Shut up, you."

ᥱᠵᥱᠵ

It was early evening by the time we got back to town. I didn't feel like cooking, but we were all hungry, so I took us to a diner downtown for soup and a sandwich. I had a specific reason for choosing that place.

It was the restaurant on King Street where I'd gone after the bank robbery. Karen's face went hard when I told her where we were.

We ordered and handed the menus back to the waitress, then Karen leaned forward and glared at me.

"Ian, why did you bring us here?" she asked.

There was no point being flip or evading the question. I took a sip of coffee. "You wanted to know why I take the risks I took in that bank," I said. "Look around. These people are eating, talking, having a good time. They feel safe because of me and the guys I work with. If it wasn't for us, there would be chaos—no rules, no law. We keep the world secure for people like you and Ethan. That's why I do what I do, and that's why I wanted to show you this place."

She looked around the restaurant, seeing it with fresh eyes. The waitress laughed at something the cook had said, and the man behind the counter smiled at someone as he poured coffee. A patron was talking animatedly while his date nodded and ate her food. It was an absolutely average scene, but she now saw that it could also only happen because of guys like me. She smiled. I saw the understanding in her face.

"Puts my lousy job in a whole new light, doesn't it?" I asked.

"You keep the peace." She smiled again. "You keep us safe—I get it now."

We finished the meal and got up to leave. Karen mentioned to the man at the cash register that I was the one who'd stopped the bank robbery. He thought he recognized me, he said. It took a lot of persuading to get him to accept my cash. I scowled at Karen and we headed for the car.

She huffed. "Don't you want people to know what you do for a living?"

"I do, but I don't do it to get free food—I do it because it's the right thing to do." I sighed, collecting my thoughts. "I say my prayers every night. I pray for you, for Ethan, for my friends and relatives—hell, I even pray for those I've put in jail. I don't do it for any goodie points, and certainly not for the glory. I do it because it's right," I reiterated.

She looked up at me, sheepish. "Sorry. I didn't quite see it that way before."

I patted her bum. "Dumbass," I joked.

℘℘℘

On Sunday morning, I got up early and went to church. I sat in the back, in my usual pew, and thought long and hard before the Mass started.

Was my plan for Tuesday reasonable? Was I outsmarting myself? Would it work? Marchand was not stupid, so if I was too obvious he'd smell a trap and walk away. If I was too subtle, he'd ignore me. All that was immaterial—I could only do what was right. That message, that ray of hope I'd given Karen, bolstered me. I told myself that my plan would work. It had to work.

ℰↃℰↃ

On Monday, I went into the station house for the weekly meeting. After the usual messages and tasks, I called the Newfoundland Constabulary to ask them about Rhonda Clark. A woman's voice answered and I introduced myself.

She brightened upon hearing my name. "Just a moment, love, they's a constable needs to talk wi'ya."

I listened as the phone was placed on a table and footsteps walked away, then others, heavier, slower shoes, came close.

A man picked up the phone and spoke to me. "Sergeant McBriar?" he asked, his voice sounding like Jim Flaherty. "We got some information about your missing lass, Rhonda."

I sat up. "Yes?"

He was firm, to the point. "She called her favorite aunt here, in Corner Brook, last week. Said she was stayin' low since you found some dead fella, 'cause she figures you'd blame her for it."

"Does her aunt know where she is?" I asked.

"She only says it were a collect call. She took the call, of course, it being family, but she says she don't know nothing about where her Rhonda might be."

"Can you have the call traced?" I asked. "Let me know what authorization you need for that."

"I will so," he replied. "I'll call you with the details today then."

I thanked him and hung up.

Walsh stood across from me and watched my expression. "Everything okay, boss?" he asked.

"Rhonda popped up. She called an aunt in Corner Brook, collect. We're tracing the call."

He leaned back. "Hmm. So she *is* in hiding, but I still don't think she did it."

"Why do you say that?" I asked.

"Why phone her aunt? If you were hiding out after killing someone, wouldn't you just vanish? Run off to Peterborough and work in a store, or sneak south into the States? But if you call an aunt, that's sending up a flare. That's a plea for help."

I nodded. "Right. I agree. Now let's find out just where she is. We'll get that later today or tomorrow, I guess."

Walsh stared at me. "About tomorrow night. Where do we want to meet?"

"We?" I asked, incredulous. "We, paleface? What do you mean, we?"

He smirked. "Look, I can't let you go it alone to get the shit kicked out of you again. I need to cover your back."

"Thanks for the vote of confidence," I joked. "Fine. You can drive me there, but you will stay in the car, all right?"

He nodded firmly. "You got it, Ian."

⁊∕ᴈ⁊∕ᴈ

I made dinner and we had a quiet evening. Ethan went to sleep early. Karen dragged me through to our room, kissed me passionately, and undressed me.

She seemed desperate, frenzied, as though she was getting in this one last act of lovemaking before I went off to war.

Afterward, I went through to the kitchen and got something cold to drink. I came back with a glass for each of us.

She was sitting up in bed, her knees against her chest. "Ian, what do you have planned for tomorrow?" she asked bluntly.

I smiled. "Nothing dangerous, nothing illegal, nothing stupid. But I want to keep an edge, to be able to spring this plan fresh, for the first time. When I come back, I'll tell you everything."

"Really?" she asked.

"Honest," I confirmed.

∽∾∽

My grandfather and uncle walk ahead of me, leading me out of the bush. The thick grass is waist-high, and my grandfather goes first, intuitively dodging gopher holes and rocks. My uncle follows him, the large deer over his shoulders bouncing in time with his footfalls. My grandfather, pleased by the successful hunt, does a dance on the walk back to the truck. He taps his left foot twice, then his right foot twice, singing a song in an old Plains Cree language.

My uncle smiles and sings along.

I do not know their language. I turn to my grandfather. "How did you get the deer to come to you?" I ask him.

My grandfather laughs. "That is your mistake, young Abukcheech." He calls me by my Cree name, meaning mouse, and points to my forehead. "You should ask yourself, where should I sit to watch the deer go by?"

∽∾∽

I woke up.

The plan was sound, unorthodox, but sound. I watched Karen go to work, walked Ethan to school, and waited at home. I wanted to check on the trace of the phone call to Rhonda's aunt, so I called Walsh.

He was at his desk and he'd done some digging he

wanted to tell me about. "Apparently, the phones in Corner Brook are not run by Bell, like in the civilized world, but by the 'Newfoundland Telephone Company,'" he said. "They used to be called 'Avalon Telephone.' Anyway, they have a reciprocal deal with Bell for long distance billing, so when the aunt took the collect call, both telephone companies got the number that Rhonda called from."

"Good work, Patrick. Where is she?" I asked.

"Well, she called from a pay phone at the corner of Barrington and Danforth. I figure she probably rented a room in one of the old houses in the area. She could hide out there for a while until she felt safe enough to come back, don't you think?"

"Yeah," I grunted. I had a sudden flash of inspiration. "Can you contact Gustavo's cleaning company? Get the home addresses of the people she used to work with at True-Bright Janitorial. Let's see if any of them lives near Barrington and Danforth."

I heard him scribbling furiously. "Right—good idea." He paused. "So, tonight, we'll meet at your place about five-thirty?"

I sighed, resigned to having him come along with me. "Five-thirty it is," I agreed.

I took a nap in the afternoon and woke up around three. It was important not to go into battle tired.

I showered, took out my best suit, and wore my best watch. I put on my pants and shirt then casually reached for my holster.

No. I wasn't going as a policeman. I was going as Ethan's father. That didn't mean I was going empty-handed, though. I had planned for this, too.

It was now five-twenty-five. I had told Ethan to play at Alan's until Karen got home, so I locked my front door, walked down the steps, and waited on the sidewalk.

Walsh's Polara was not there. Great, not only had he invited himself on this trip, but he was going to be late, as usual.

A moment later, a large burgundy Jaguar sedan cruised silently to a stop in front of my house and Walsh got out.

"Hi. Are you eady?" he asked cheerfully.

"Where did this come from?" I asked. I got into the Jaguar, eyeing it suspiciously.

"Hmm? Oh, it's mine," he said and slid behind the wheel. "Shall we go?"

He chirped the tires and zoomed out into the road. We glided noiselessly up Keele Street to the highway, then joined the other seven lanes of busy traffic headed west toward Hamilton.

I looked around the interior of the car now, admiring it. "This is very plush, Patrick. Why did you decide to take this car tonight, though?"

He shrugged. "It will blend in better in that neighborhood. A cruiser would stand out, even an unmarked one. Besides, it's not cool to bring a Toronto cruiser to Hamilton. It just feels wrong."

I nodded. "That's why I left my badge and revolver at home."

Toronto had some exclusive addresses, places where the name alone tells people who you are. The poor lived in Scarborough. The rich lived in Rosedale. The wealthy lived on The Bridle Path.

Hamilton, though, was a grittier, dirtier, working-class city on the edge of the rust belt. It was built around steel mills and railroads, a hub at the end of Lake Ontario that shipped goods to the rest of the country. Still, it had its areas that said "money" without having to say it out loud. At the south end of town, in an area called Durand, bordered by Queen Street and James Street, was a small corner of Hamilton that whispered "old money."

We turned off the highway, drove through the town of Burlington and on to Hamilton, then went south on Queen Street. Queen Street started off as a sterile road lined with small bungalows and cracker-box walk-up apartment blocks to the north, but it became a tree-lined avenue of elegant baronial estates and restored Victorian mansions by the south end of the street.

⌀⌀⌀

It was now six-twenty. I wanted to arrive early. Constable Bancroft was expecting me there at seven. I didn't want him to be ready for me. It would be better for both of us.

Walsh, clearly familiar with the area, turned left onto Aberdeen, another street that exuded wealth. Its houses were as well-kept, as elegant and lovely as those on Queen Street, but not so ostentatious. I could imagine surgeons and executives dining behind its leaded glass windows.

By six-thirty, it was quite dark. Walsh stopped the Jaguar on the street, just down from a mansion with the pale brown Dart in the driveway. He gripped the wheel, winding up to ask a question.

I cut him off, reading his mind. "No," I said. "Absolutely not. You will wait here—period."

He nodded, disappointed. "Fine. Okay. How long do I give you before I come after you?"

"If anything goes wrong, you'll know about it soon enough," I said.

He shrugged agreement.

The address Bancroft had given me—a red brick three-story house where the Dart was parked—looked like a small version of a castle from a vampire movie. The irony was not lost on me.

I walked up to the massive oak front door and turned the handle. It was locked so I rang the bell and waited. In the frosted glass panel in the door, I could see a figure approaching. The door opened, and the second man—the one who beat me up—opened it. I had a chance to see him properly, now. He looked like a wrestler, muscular, tough, with a buzz cut and stubble of beard.

He gasped in surprise. "What are you doing here?" he barked.

"I'm here to see Pierre." I said simply.

"He's not here. Go away," the man grunted. He reached out and placed a fat hand on my chest.

"We both know that's not true." I smiled. "Move aside." I pushed his arm away.

"I said get lost," the man barked.

I wanted to provoke him into doing something stupid. "Piss off and die, Larry."

He grabbed my forearm, growled, and hauled back to punch me. I gave my arm a twist and broke free, but he swung the punch at me anyway.

I ducked and threw a hard kick into his knee. He groaned and bent over, clutching his leg.

I suppose it was not the charitable thing to do, but I really wanted to return his beating so I swung my leg back and tried to kick his genitals into his throat. I came very close.

He folded over. Bending his head way down, he held his crotch and gasped in agony. I felt good about that. It repaid him for sapping me. Besides, I needed him out of my way.

The front foyer of the house was huge, filled with expensive-looking antique furniture. A spindly wooden chair sat against one wall. I picked it up and swung it high and fast over Larry's back, smacking him hard on his neck and shoulder. To my surprise, it didn't break.

He fell over onto his right side, swimming sideways as he tried to get back on his feet. I grabbed his jacket and stared into his eyes. "Now, I'm going to go through *your* house, Larry," I hissed. "And there's not a damn thing you can do to stop me."

I looked around for somewhere to restrain him. The foyer ended at a curving, ornate mahogany staircase, like in an old movie I once saw, branching up in two stairways to the second floor. I slapped one end of my handcuffs on Larry's right ankle then dragged him by his left arm to the base of the staircase, backed him up against a thick newel post, and wrapped his handcuffed leg behind it. I poked his left hand behind the post and clapped the other end of the handcuff to it.

He was still groggy, and now he was back-tied to the stairs, and out of my way. He struggled, trying to get up, despite the handcuffs. He rolled around, looking for a way to stand, still dazed, not quite comprehending how restrained he was.

I squatted down and looked into his face. "You want to walk away from this? Don't speak, don't move," I sneered. I pulled my fist back fast, and he cringed, shying away from it. "Not so tough now, are you, Larry?" I mocked him. I reached into my jacket and produced a huge, shiny Bowie knife, pressing it against his nose. "If you make a sound, I break your fingers. If you warn Marchand, I cut them off. Understand?"

He glanced at the knife then back at me and nodded silently. I put the knife away.

At the other end of the foyer was a double set of oak doors. I saw a sliver of light under them, with shadows moving around. I walked up to the doors and listened. Right away, I recognized Pierre Marchand's voice.

I opened the door and stepped in. The Mountie was sitting in the corner, reading a newspaper. Another man stood at one end of a conference table. He was short, plump, with a Cesar Romero moustache that barely touched his lip and thick wire-rimmed glasses that were too large, like swimming goggles on his face. *That's his lawyer*, I thought.

Across from him stood a man that looked like Errol Flynn. This was Pierre Guy Marchand. He was tall, handsome, fluid, and impeccably dressed. It was obvious how he could snare impressionable young women. My anger toward him rose up, but I stayed calm. "Marchand!" I barked.

The Mountie looked away from his newspaper and stood up, startled.

Marchand sneered. "Get out. Get out now," he said dismissively.

"I'm Ian McBriar," I said.

He turned his back to me and casually moved a pen on his desk. "I know. Get out of my house."

I stood my ground. "I want your signed permission. I'm going to adopt Ethan," I said.

He turned to face me and leaned against a carved desk. "No," he sneered. He leaned for a long time.

I watched his fingers, wrapped under the edge of the desk, twitching furiously. "Keep pressing that button all you want," I said. "Your goon is rather tied up just now."

His expression melted from one of disdain to one of fear, then it turned to anger. "I told you to get out. You're trespassing," he barked.

"And I said you will sign the permission form for me to adopt Ethan," I replied.

He sat down and pulled out a ledger book. "Fine," he snapped. "How much do you want?"

He opened the book at a page of checks and looked up expectantly.

I shook my head. "You think I want money? I don't want money. I just want to adopt Ethan—period."

"Everyone wants money," he spat back. "You do, too. How much do you want?" He waited for an answer.

"I have no desire to take any money from you. I just want your permission to adopt Ethan. Otherwise, I will have you arrested. Then I won't need your permission," I bluffed.

Marchand laughed. "This is Hamilton, not Toronto. You're not a cop here, boy. You're just another small man who wants something. The answer is no," he sneered and closed the ledger.

"Wrong. You're going to sign that permission form to-night," I said firmly.

He leaned back, an amused look on his face. "Really. And why should I give away something which is clearly mine?"

"He's not a 'something.' He's a little boy who deserves to be part of a family. That's all I'm after for him."

Marchand snickered. "Living with a slut and an Indian—that's a great life for him, isn't it?"

That sent me over the edge. I reached into my jacket, grasped the knife, and pulled my arm down. The Bowie knife made a piercing "zing" sound as I drew it out of its sheath.

The Mountie jumped back against the wall. Marchand's lawyer shuffled slowly away from us, terrified.

"You've insulted my wife and you've insulted me," I growled. "I won't let you get away with that."

Marchand waved a finger in my face. "Do you think you can just threaten me, boy? Do you think that scaring me with that thing will get you what you want? Forget it."

"You and your goons broke into my house. I can send you to jail for that. It doesn't matter what town you're in, I can still have you arrested." I tilted my head back. "Fat boy Larry in the other room will give you up in exchange for a free pass." I leaned forward. "*He doesn't like you.*" I nodded at the Mountie. "Joe Slick here will gladly save his own ass, too, long before he saves yours."

The Mountie stifled a smirk.

"Here's a game I know," I said. "Let's see how you like it."

I reached out, grabbed Marchand's hand, and slapped it palm down on the table. His fingers naturally splayed out. I held his wrist, tight. This was just a simple magic trick I knew, one that my brother taught me, but it was a very effective trick. I stared at Marchand's face, raised the knife high in the air, and plunged it down blindly. The knifepoint stuck in the table, just missing his index finger. He yelped in panic and tried to pull his hand away. I held it tight.

"Are you out of your mind? What are you doing? Let me go!" he screamed.

I shook my head. The Mountie and the lawyer gasped, worried that I would spear Marchand's hand.

"No?" I said. "Two out of three."

I looked back at the other men. They stayed far away from me. I raised the knife even higher over my head, gave a Cree war howl, and plunged it down again. This time, it just missed Marchand's thumb. He wrenched back and forth even more forcefully, trying to break free.

"Stop! You can't do this! What are you doing? You're a police officer!" he screamed.

"No." I laughed. "In Hamilton, I'm just a man who wants something from you, remember?" I lifted the knife once more. "You better hope I miss a third time." I hesitated, the knife high over my head, and stared at him. "I tell you what," I said. "I'll make you a deal."

He stopped squirming and looked at me. A deal—this was something he understood.

"Go on," he said, breathing heavily. His eyes moved back and forth from my knife to his hand.

"You sign Ethan's adoption consent form, and I'll go right out that door, for good. You will never see or hear from me again and I will not tell the newspapers or anyone else that you abandoned *your own son* for *six years*. I will say nothing. You will be able to run for parliament without any hint of scandal."

"You know about that?" He sounded surprised. "What else can you offer?" he asked, wanting more from me.

"I don't press charges against you for sending your two thugs here to rough me up and ransack my house. It all goes away. It never happened."

The lawyer came forward slowly. "Do it, Par. Do it. It's a good offer. Do it," he mumbled.

Marchand stared at me, scanning my face for deception. "I have your word? No tricks?"

I was annoyed that he would ask me that, considering his behavior, but I nodded my agreement. "You have my word. The Toronto Police Department will not have any further interest in you. As a matter of fact, I have a written promise to that effect. I'll sign it when you sign the adoption consent." I took two sheets of paper from my jacket and laid them in front of him. One was the adoption form, the other a promise to leave him alone, absolving him of any previous actions.

Marchand looked them over quickly. "Agreed."

The casual way he gave up any interest in Ethan's future made me hate him even more. He signed the adoption consent form and thrust the document at me. My heart raced, but I had to stay calm for a while yet.

His lawyer ceremoniously attached a legal seal and witnessed the document. I nodded my acceptance, signed the agreement to not prosecute, and slid the Bowie knife back into my jacket. "Keep that document very safe. It's valuable," I said casually and folded up my precious sheet of paper.

Marchand looked at my written promise, grunted, and turned around. He swung a low panel away from the wall, revealing a safe behind it. He grasped the combination lock and stopped.

The Mountie leaned forward, anxious, ready to jump in, but I frowned at him and he waited.

"No tricks, none at all. I have your word?" Marchand said cautiously.

"The Toronto Police Department does not have any further business with you."

He grunted, satisfied, and opened the safe. The Mountie rushed forward, pushed Marchand away, and stuck his hand into the open cavity.

Marchand snapped at him. "Smith, what the hell are you doing?"

"Mister Marchand, I am confiscating this material in connection with a matter of criminal fraud," the Mountie said smugly.

"What are you talking about, you idiot? Smith, get out of there." Marchand struggled to pull the Mountie's hand away. Too late—he had the safe's contents out on the desk.

Marchand glared at me. "You lied! You said no tricks!"

I shook my head. "No. I said that the *Toronto* police were done with you. I made no promises concerning anyone else. I said nothing at all about any other police force."

The Mountie scooped up the papers from the desk and stuffed them in his coat pocket.

"I'm Constable Bancroft of the RCMP," he barked. He picked up the telephone and quickly dialed a number. "Now," he said and hung up.

I turned to leave but remembered something. "Sorry about the table. Get it repaired and send me the bill."

Marchand roared with anger and swore loudly at me.

I turned back to face the Mountie and pulled a small key out of my pocket. "Ah, you'll need this to free Larry. He's kind of tied up."

I tossed him the key. He grinned broadly. He was enjoying this. I turned to leave again.

"Sergeant?" he called. "Nice work, sir. Well done. Well done."

I smiled and went back out to the foyer. The big guy was still handcuffed, still wrapped around the stairs. He shrank back when I came close.

I leaned down, sneering. "Better look for a new job, Larry," I whispered. "Your boss is going to jail, and if you don't want to join him, stay out of Toronto."

I walked down the driveway toward Walsh's Jaguar. In the distance, I heard an approaching police siren. Marchand was screwed. I smiled to myself.

Walsh dropped me off at home. He joked that he only came along so I'd invite him to dinner again, then he took off, chirping the tires once more.

The drapes parted briefly as Karen peeked out to see me. I stepped through the front door, and she leaned against the kitchen wall, afraid to ask the obvious question.

She sighed. "How did it go?" She almost cringed as she said the words.

I smiled, held up the signed piece of paper, handed it to her.

She read it over and over, to make sure she hadn't mis-read it. She sat down in a chair, stunned. "Oh, my," she said. She covered her mouth and looked up at me. "Oh, my."

Covering her face with her hands, she started to cry softly. I squatted down and hugged her, gently. She wrapped her arms around me and squeezed tight.

I winced and gave out a slight yelp. She leaned back, startled.

"Sorry, hon. Sore ribs, still."

She smiled gently and kissed my forehead. "Thank you," she whispered.

✌✍✌

Early the next morning, Steven Machtinger let me into his office and closed the door. "Good morning. You have a resolution to your dilemma." It was a statement, not a question.

I quietly handed him the signed form. He looked it over and nodded then placed it to one side. "Was any coercion used to obtain this agreement?" he asked.

"Why do you ask?" I countered. I wasn't expecting that question.

"If he disputes this, it could drag out for months. If he was coerced into signing this document, if this agreement was signed under duress, then it would of course be deemed invalid."

"That won't be the case." I smiled. "He has other legal issues on his mind right now, and fighting me is not on his to-do list."

He nodded, satisfied.

"What happens now?" I asked.

"We present this to the Province this morning, and a family court judge issues an order for adoption. Then we will get a new birth certificate for Ethan. I expect we can have this concluded before Christmas. How is your lovely wife feeling?"

I smiled. "Karen is very happy."

He picked up the permission form and leaned forward. "Good. Now that that's settled, I'd like to know. How did you get him to sign it?"

I grinned. "Have you ever examined witnesses in court?"

Machtinger shrugged. "Of course."

"Then you know not to ask a question when you don't want to know the answer."

He smiled. "Point taken. Good day, Ian."

I left his office, clutching a bundle of Xeroxed forms, along with a copy of Marchand's consent, drove to fifty-two division, and sat at my desk, feeling happy.

One of the secretaries handed me a stack of papers. I thanked her and started reading through them.

Twenty minutes later, Walsh sat across from me, watching my expression. "Something wrong, boss?" he asked.

I shook my head. "Maybe we were wrong about Rhonda. Maybe she really did kill Ed." I handed him the papers. "The Newfoundland police say that her second husband, the one who died? Cameron Wilkins," I said, rubbing my eyes. "Anyway, he was a heavy smoker, he had cancer, and he was dying, but he went all of a sudden. You interviewed the doctor that looked after him, right?"

"Sure, and he said the death seemed suspicious at the time." Walsh agreed.

"Right." I nodded. "Well, apparently there were questions somebody posed after he died, as to whether they'd overdosed him with the cancer medications. The courts had him exhumed to do some tests." I smiled. "Have you ever heard of the Comte de Bocarmé?"

Walsh shrugged. "That's another one of your old movies, right? Basil Rathbone?"

"Nope." I shook my head. "I read about his case years

ago. He was a French count who was executed in 1851 for killing a man he owed a fortune to. The count was an amateur chemist, and he made a poison that was untraceable."

"Okay, and the punch line is?" Walsh asked, expectantly.

"Nicotine," I said. "In 1850, a very determined investigator spent three months proving that the nicotine in the dead man's tissues was from intentional poisoning. Just the year before, a prosecutor in Paris had complained in open court that if someone wanted to get away with murder all they had to do was use a plant-based poison, since they had no way to detect that."

Walsh grinned. "The crap you remember, boss. Are you telling me that the count poisoned his victim with cigarettes?"

"Makes you rethink your filthy habit, does it?" I chuckled. "No, it was concentrated nicotine. In 1850, Bocarmé purchased a whole shed full of tobacco leaves and boiled them down to a bottle of pure nicotine. It takes less than a spoonful to kill a grown man.

"Our dead guy, Mr. Wilkins, had a lifelong smoking habit. They found nicotine in his system, of course, but there was also a trace of it in his stomach, even after a year in the ground."

Walsh frowned, thinking. "When I interviewed the doctor, he didn't mention that at all."

"Of course," I agreed. "You said he was in Africa or something for a few years right after the death. He was gone during the exhumation, so they didn't bother notifying him about it." I leaned back and sighed. "I wanted to see if that was also the case for the other guy that died, back in the fifties, but he was cremated, so we'll never know."

Walsh bent forward and knitted his fingers together, thinking. He looked down at his shoes. "If we believe that Rhonda did it, that she killed all four men, then when her first victim died, the cremated guy, she would have been what—twelve, fourteen? Does that seem likely?" he asked.

"I wondered that myself." I rubbed my moustache. "Also, why would she kill them in the first place? And then why kill Ed and Gustavo? What did they do that could have set her off that much?" I stood up. "I dunno, Patrick, it smells funny. I just don't get it. First thing, we have to find Rhonda. Then we have to find out just what the hell happened."

He smiled. "Right. You'd asked if any of True-Bright's staff lived near that phone booth that Rhonda called from." He pulled out his notebook. "Two women do. One is Carmen Figueira. She's Portuguese, like De Melo. She lives right on Danforth, over a store. The other one is Marta Petricic, a Yugoslavian gal, they told me. They said she's a good worker, a nice lady. Anyway, Mrs. Figueira lives with her husband and kids, but Marta lives alone. I figure if Rhonda was hiding out with anyone, Marta's our best bet."

"Where does Marta live?" I asked.

Walsh flipped his notepad over. "They gave me an address on Coleman Avenue, across from Coleman Park."

I scratched my head. I knew the area, sort of. "That's about a hundred yards or so from the pay phone intersection, right?"

"Yeah, boss. A two minute walk, tops."

I stood and grabbed my coat. "Let's go visit Miss Petricic."

Walsh drove up Keele Street and joined the highway headed east, picking his way through traffic. I watched him. He was stone-faced and silent, looking straight ahead. He went right past the Don Valley Parkway exit and turned down Victoria Park instead.

"Taking the scenic route?" I asked, curious.

"The Don is a parking lot at this time of day. Victoria Park is faster," he said solemnly.

I frowned. "Is anything wrong, Patrick? You seem really gloomy all of a sudden."

"Um." He glanced my way. "About Rhonda."

"Yeah?" I asked.

He grinned an embarrassed grin and hunched up his shoulders. I understood the silent admission. "Oh, for god's sake, Patrick. Really?" I groaned.

"Well, you saw her, boss. You know, when she's all dressed up, she's a very pretty woman."

"Jeez, Patrick." I sighed. "Can't you keep it in your pants even for a murder suspect? What in heaven's name were you thinking?"

He shrugged. "I didn't mean for it to go that far, boss. It just happened, that's all."

"No. Tornados just happen. Thunderstorms just happen. But sleeping with a suspect doesn't 'just happen.'" I waved my arms in front of me, showing my irritation. "Unless you both walked naked down a dark hall and bumped into each other, it didn't 'just happen.'"

He started to laugh at the statement then caught himself and shook his head sheepishly.

"I'm sorry, boss. It's just that you were on your honeymoon, I went to check on her at her new place, and I helped her move some furniture. One thing led to another. You know how it goes."

"No, I don't know," I said coldly. "Why don't you explain it to me? Hi, Rhonda, let me move your sofa, then I'll jump into your pants. Is that the way it went?"

He was silent for a minute. "Actually, that's pretty well right on, yeah," he admitted.

I rubbed my forehead. "This really throws shit at the fan, you know? What can we do now, without it coming back to bite us?"

"How do you mean?" he asked stupidly.

"May it please the court, I didn't do it," I said in a small Newfie voice. "I'm innocent. I slept with Patrick once and I wouldn't keep on sleeping with him, so now he's gone and accused me."

"Oh, yeah. Right," Walsh said meekly. "Hadn't occurred to me." He blew air out the sides of his mouth. "Sorry, boss."

I shook my head. "Look, you just used up all your brownie points. When we find Rhonda, you will come in with me, but one whiff of favoritism or wink-wink on your part and you will sit in the car. Are we clear on that, Constable?" I growled.

"Loud and clear, Sergeant," he mumbled.

The address we had for Marta Petricic was across the street from a small green field named Coleman Park. It was a red brick duplex facing the park, and she lived in apartment C.

I didn't see how there could be more than two apartments in it. It was only a two-story building. The front door didn't seem to be used at all. A worn cocoanut mat was flipped up, blocking the screen door, with a small pile of dust and leaves wedged under it, almost as if to emphasize that this door was never opened. I walked around to the side door, Walsh dogging me bashfully. The side door had three buttons screwed to the wooden door frame. I pushed the one with a metal letter C beside it.

From a slim window in the basement, I heard a sound like a distant fire alarm—the doorbell.

Thirty seconds later, I didn't hear, so much as feel, footsteps in the basement plodding up wooden stairs, and the door opened. Rhonda stood there, wearing a pair of jeans, a plaid lumberjack shirt, and slippers, an apple in her hand.

She looked up at us and her face fell. "Oh, shit. Ya found me."

"Tag, you're it," I said. "May we come in and talk to you, Rhonda?"

She sighed, took a bite of apple, and slinked back down the stairs, her slippers scuffing the polished stairs. We followed her.

She opened a plain wooden door and walked into a basement apartment. It was just one large room, taking up most of the downstairs, with a galley kitchen against one wall and a curtained-off area shielding a bed. There was a narrow, high window that faced the street with a TV set under it.

A sofa sat across from the TV, with a telephone table beside it.

"You're staying here with Marta?" I asked.

Rhonda sighed. "Yeah, she lets me sleep on her divan. She's nice, she is. Took me in and all."

I looked around the apartment. It wasn't fancy, but it was neat and clean. "Where's Marta now?"

"She's off at her other job. She works in the cafeteria at Gledhill Public School."

"So, you're just hanging around, killing time, then?" I wanted to make her feel uneasy.

"I suppose you're wonderin' why I run off, huh?" she said, flopping onto the sofa.

Walsh and I pulled out a pair of vinyl-covered chairs and sat facing her.

She bit into her apple again.

"It had crossed my mind," I said. "Why did you run away?"

She shrugged. "Gus were dead. I got nowhere to go, now. Marta were good enough to help me."

"Did you move in here before or after you killed Gustavo?"

She waved the apple at me. "Hey. I never done nothin' to Gus. He were dead when I went into the apartment. All I done were put his pants on him, is all."

Walsh and I stared at each other. Rhonda noticed the reaction. She looked back and forth at us. "What did I say?" she asked.

"You dressed him?" I asked. "Why would you do that?"

"Weren't polite to see him in the altogether like that." She shrugged. "So I puts his pants back on him. Just like him and me did for Ed."

Walsh shook his head, astonished. "Rhonda, what do you mean by 'like for Ed'?"

Her eyes darted to me then to back to Walsh again. She shrugged. "When me and Gus found Ed, he had that knife stickin' in him. He were wearin' his shirt, but he di'nt have no pants. Gus says that was wrong, so he helps me get Ed's pants on. We figured that was the decent thing to do."

"Then you called on Annie Ross, your next door neighbor, to witness the scene," I said.

She nodded. "Yeah, that were so."

I sighed. "Rhonda, assuming that you're telling me the entire truth—and frankly, I think this would be the first time you have—then at best you've contaminated a crime scene, and at worst you have destroyed important clues that could have identified the killer."

When I said that, her face dropped. She covered her mouth. "Oh, lord," she said softly. "It never went through my brain, you know. I never even realized."

Walsh leaned forward. "Listen, hon," he started.

I stared at him. "Hon?" I mouthed.

He shrugged apologetically. "Who'd want to hurt Ed or Gustavo? Anyone you can think of?"

She shook her head firmly. "They di'nt do nothin' to no one. They just was nice to me, is all."

"Did they know each other, do you think?" I asked. "Before you knew Ed, I mean?"

She thought for a moment. "Don't think so. Gustavo always lived in Toronto, since he moved from Portugal as a boy, and Ed only come out from The Rock maybe five, six years ago."

I sighed, frustrated. "Did you not think to tell us that Ed was from Newfoundland?"

She shrugged. "Why? Half the folks I know is from Newfoundland. So Ed were from Newfoundland too—so what?"

"Was he from Corner Brook, like you?" Walsh asked.

Rhonda smiled. "Oh, no, sweets."

Walsh squirmed slightly at "sweets."

"He were from Deer Lake," she said.

I scribbled notes in my book. "Where is that relative to Corner Brook?"

She wrinkled her nose. "Dunno. A half hour away, maybe?"

"So about the same as here to our police station." I sighed. "What did Ed do in Deer Lake?"

She nodded, definite. "He worked for a bakery, but it were in Corner Brook, not in Deer Lake."

It must have occurred to her how stupid that statement made her sound. She winced.

I rolled my eyes. "So, Ed and you both worked in Corner Brook, but you didn't know each other?" I challenged.

She frowned, irritated. "Don't make it sound like I was keepin' stuff from you. I never knew Ed till I come here. Honest."

I sat back and rubbed my face, frustrated. I had a another thought. "What about your cousin, Paulette? Did she know Ed in Corner Brook?"

"No, I don't think so. She were a housewife. She didn't get out much." She scratched her cheek, then absentmindedly reached into her shirt and scratched under her bra strap. Walsh's eyes followed her hand. "Mind you," she said, "After the funeral, I think, she did go to work with Jim."

"After the funeral?" I asked.

She tossed her half-eaten apple into a wastebasket beside the sofa and reached into her breast pocket for a pack of cigarettes.

I waited patiently as she tapped out one from the pack, stuck it between her lips, and gratefully accepted the flame from Walsh's slim gold lighter.

She smiled at Walsh and gave him a conspiratorial wink.

I repeated the question. "You said 'after the funeral.' What did you mean?"

She tapped ash into the wastebasket, onto the apple. "Paulette's sister got sick. Lucy, she were named. She were young, just ten or eleven, and she got some illness they couldn't fix." She looked down, dead serious. "She were a lovely child, but she were sick for months, and the doctors couldn't find nothin'. Jim took her all the way to Charlotte-town once to find out what were wrong with the lass, but she just weren't long for this earth, and we lost her. Paulette never got over it. She figured it were Jim's work what made her sick, them chemicals and all."

That sent a chill up my spine. "What chemicals do you mean, Rhonda?"

My dream—Rhonda, the dry cleaner's, the bottle of yellow liquid, all seemed as solid right now as the chair I was sitting on.

Rhonda shrugged. "Jim's family had this business what cleaned out septic tanks and the like."

"I remember—Jim mentioned that," I said. "Go on."

"Anyways, they had this other business. They used these chemicals to clean up engines. Jim and Paulette was courting, and Lucy would come along when Paulette visited Jim's work. She'd play around them vats of stuff. Smelled terrible. Then Lucy started to cough, all the time."

She looked down at her feet and flicked more ash into the wastebasket. "I never thought about it back then, but it were the same stuff what I used when I were working at the dry cleaners. We called it 'gold can,' cause it come in this gallon tin that were a gold color, and I tell ya, it gave me headaches like the good Lord himself couldn't cure. I were sure glad when I moved to Toronto. "I don't know what they was using here, but I liked it way better. Didn't give me no headaches nor back pains or nothin'."

She stretched out and pointed her toes like a ballerina, arching her back.

Walsh followed her body's curve from her neck to her ankles.

She shook her head, oblivious to him. "Like I said, lit-tle Lucy were a sweet girl. It killed Paulette's folks when she passed. It killed Paulette, too." She hung her head slightly and examined the filter end of her cigarette.

I rubbed my eyes, thinking. "Okay, back to the part where Paulette went to work with Jim. What did she do there, exactly?"

Rhonda nodded. "Jim and Paulette gets married in fifty-two. She were just nineteen. Lucy passed in fifty-three. Jim wouldn't let Paulette into the back shop no more," she said. "He were worried that maybe she'd get sick, too, just like Lucy. So she was in the front office with another gal, forget her name, and she worked there till she had Cynthia. Cynthia gots this thing." She rubbed her belly. "It gives her stomach pains all the time. Had it since she were a girl. Paulette stayed home after that."

She flicked more ash onto the apple and tucked her feet under her. "Then Jim decides he wants to go somewheres different. He knows they's no jobs on The Rock, but he's got this friend who moved out here years back. The friend became a copper in the OPP, and he tells Jim about the good life he's got here. So in 'sixty-three, they says goodbye to Corner Brook and comes to Toronto. Paulette writes me letters, tells me how much she likes livin' is in the big city. My Cam passed the year before, so I figure I got nothing to lose, and I come out here shortly after."

She blew a cone of smoke up to the ceiling, as if to punctuate her statement.

Walsh leaned forward, serious now. "Rhonda, I have to ask you. Did you kill your husband, Cameron?"

She shook her head. She wasn't upset by the question. "They done ask me that over and over, the Constabulary did. Like if they asked me enough times, or in enough ways, I'd tell them I did it." She nonchalantly butted out her cigarette on the underside of her slipper and tossed it into the wastebasket. "Cam were smoking from when he were a boy. He got sick after we got married, and for months he were dragging himself around, but he still went to work every day. The doctors say it were only a matter of time."

She sighed. "One day, he come home feelin' terrible, he says, and takes the next day off. I comes home from the dry cleaner's and he's curled up in the toilet, lyin' dead on the floor." Her eyes welled up. She shrugged away the emotion. "Oh well, it ain't like he were nothing special, you know, not like…" She glanced at Walsh.

He turned bright red then looked away.

I ignored the remark and looked her in the eyes. "Rhonda, do you know how Cameron died?"

She shook her head. "They asked me if I done somewhat to him. I never done nothin'. I come home and he were dead, is all."

"Would it surprise you to learn that he was poisoned?" I asked.

Walsh leaned back, staying out of the conversation as much as possible.

She sighed and shook her head sadly. "Jesus, Lord," she muttered. "They asked me that over and over, too. I remember he said he were too sick to eat, on account of his gut were a mess. I never thought about poison till they asked me."

"So, you didn't do it, huh?" I asked.

She looked down at her cigarette. "It never seemed like you was thinking of me as guilty, you know."

"No," I sighed. "I don't think you did it."

Walsh leaned forward. "Rhonda, you called your aunt in Corner Brook. Why did you do that?"

She shrugged. "I wanted to let her know I were all right. My family worries. I wanted her to let them all know, is all."

"So," I said, smiling. "I repeat. Can think of anyone who would have wanted to hurt Gustavo?"

She shook her head. "Gus were a nice man. I don't know nobody wished him harm."

I leaned back and sighed. "So are you going back to the Flaherty's now, or will you stay here?"

She shook her head. "I like it here—closer to shops and such. Besides, Marta says she likes the company. It's nice bein' around someone, she says."

Walsh scribbled notes and smiled. "Listen, hon, what was Paulette's maiden name?"

That was good—I'd forgotten that it would not be Flaherty, of course.

"O'Dowd. Her name were O'Dowd," she said.

He thanked her and we both stood up. She glanced my way and grinned at Walsh. "So are you gonna come by and visit me?" she asked.

Walsh shot me a nervous look. "We'll have to see, Rhonda. We can call you here though, right?"

She grinned, her eyes scanning Walsh up and down. "I'll talk to you soon, then," she said.

I noted down the number from the dial on the phone, and we left.

Walsh was smiling now, relieved that he had avoided getting into deeper trouble.

"You got lucky, Patrick," I said. "I don't think she did it. You're out of the shit."

He nodded. "Who did it, then? And did the same person kill all four people? It doesn't make sense."

I shook my head. "A bakery, dry cleaners, a janitorial company. Let's talk to the people who worked with Ed and Gustavo, see what they have in common."

Walsh reached into his jacket and pulled out a pack of cigarettes. He raised the pack slightly and glanced over at me for approval to smoke.

I shook my head. "Don't push your luck."

He sighed and sadly put the cigarettes away.

CHAPTER 15

The True-Bright Janitorial Company operated out of an address on Merton Street, a quiet, residential street which crossed Mount Pleasant then continued east to Bayview. True-Bright was on the corner with Mount Pleasant, in a row of dingy buildings housing everything from a hardware store to a dress shop. It made sense that they would be there. It was a low-rent area, and it was walking distance to De Melo's apartment. A pair of uniforms had already spoken to the staff, told them that Gustavo had been killed, but only said that it was a suspicious death.

We parked at the address listed and stared at the number above the door for a minute. It was the right place, according to our notes, but this was a grocery store.

We walked in, anyway. The store was not much larger than my living room. It had a row of produce on a high counter along the front window, and two small aisles of canned goods filling out the rest of the space. At the back of the store a doorway was covered by a curtain remnant. Beside that sat a homemade desk with a dirty NCR cash register perched on it.

Behind the desk sat a tiny person. I couldn't tell if it was male or female. He/she was Chinese or Japanese, wearing a Mao suit, with a withered, leathery face perforated by a cigarette poking out at a downward angle. It was sitting hunched over, reading a newspaper.

I walked up to the desk. "Hello." I smiled and held out

my ID. "We're with the police. Where can we find the True-Bright Janitorial Company?"

The person lifted its head and spoke. "De Melo dead."

I realized from the voice it was female. "Yes, we know," I said. "True-Bright? Where is their office, please?"

She waved out the front door. "Back lane. Go back lane." She returned to her newspaper.

We walked back outside and down a narrow alleyway beside the store, to the back lane.

"Well," Walsh quipped, "I thought she'd never shut up. Yak, yak, yak, that one."

I smiled. "You didn't want to ask her for a date, though?"

There was a door in the back wall of the grocery building, a dark brown painted metal slab with a postage-stamp sized window at eye level. It reminded me of those old speakeasies. I almost felt I should give a secret knock and say, "Joe sent me" when they slid open the peephole.

A corrugated metal garbage can beside the door reeked of rotten cabbage and fish. We avoided the can and stood on a narrow concrete slab which poked out from under the door. I pulled on the door and, to my surprise, it was not locked. We now found ourselves in a small anteroom, maybe five by eight feet, with a rickety wooden staircase on one side leading up to a storage loft. Straight ahead was another metal door, this one with a large frosted window.

I glanced up at the loft, worried whether it was safe to walk under it. It was piled high with barrels of floor cleaner, mops, and boxes of paper towels stacked to the dusty ceiling. Looking at the metal door, I could see shadows moving in the frosted glass. We walked up to the door and knocked.

Inside, the movement stopped. A voice called out tentatively. "Hello?"

It sounded like a child's voice.

"We're with the Toronto Police," I said firmly. "We'd like to ask you some questions."

The door opened slowly, with a loud creak. Inside, two

women sat at a pair of what looked like battleship-gray teacher's desks, pushed together to face each other.

One woman looked like an Okie farm wife from *The Grapes of Wrath*. She was painfully gaunt, with a look of either perpetual wonder or sheer desperation on her face. The other one was the complete opposite, squat and round, like a large watermelon.

The thin one was organizing papers on one of the desks, stacking them carefully into piles. She eyed us with suspicion. "Who are you?" she asked, her voice crackling like dry bread.

We held up our warrant cards. "We need to ask you about Gustavo," I said, firmly. "And you are?"

The thin one spoke. "Agnes De Souza," She nodded at the other woman. "And Rita West."

"So can we talk to you about your boss?" I asked.

"He's not my boss," the skinny woman said flatly.

Walsh and I looked at each other. "You're his wife?" I asked. "We were told you'd gone back to Portugal."

She laughed. Her voice cackled, and when she inhaled it sounded like a weak vacuum cleaner. "You're thinking of my sister." She snorted. "She isn't in Portugal, either. Nah, she moved to North Carolina, to be with her daughter. He tells all his women 'My wife left me. Poor me. I'm all alone.' That's his come-on line."

"Don't you mean all that in the past tense?" Walsh frowned.

She laughed again. "Yeah, you're right. I shouldn't speak ill of the dead, after all."

"You don't seem terribly broken up about it," I remarked.

She shrugged. "What can I say? Gus is—Gus was, always looking for greener pastures, always a new conquest. He always cheated on her—as far back as their honeymoon." She reached up to an ashtray on top of a file cabinet, grabbed a lit cigarette, and inhaled it deeply.

The other woman tilted her head up. She looked like a

beach ball with a head stuck on it. She swiveled her chair on its pedestal, by pushing her tiptoes against the floor, until she faced me. She sighed and grunted when she breathed, wrinkling her nose as she did.

"Gus was a nice man," she said. This was the little girl voice I'd heard, sounding like Shirley Temple with asthma. "He was nice to work for. He bought us lunch lots of times. He was nice." The skinny one sneered. "Yeah, he could be real nice—when he wanted."

I pulled out my notepad. "Why would he say that his wife was in Portugal?" I asked, knowing the answer already. I just wanted her to open up to me.

Agnes shrugged. "I asked one of them once, after he ditched her. She thought he was alone, that my sister was gone, and he was all on his own. I guess that's his pickup line. 'Poor me, running this company all by myself, and no wife at home.'"

Walsh frowned and flipped open a page on his notebook. "Did he have many…" He paused as if searching for a nice term. "…female friends he left behind?"

Agnes wrinkled her nose. "Yeah, a whole busload. This last one, though, she was something special to him. He told us about her. He never did that before."

"Do you know her name?" I asked, trying to look innocent.

"Yeah. Rhonda. She works here. At least, until I find her." She snickered. "Then she's fired."

"You still own part of the company?" I asked.

"All of it," she snapped. "It was my father's before Gus married my sister, it was half mine after my father died, and it's all mine again now that Gus is dead."

I looked behind her. The two desks filled the main office, but an open door lead to a smaller office at the back. I remembered hearing Gustavo close that door as I called him, so he could speak in confidence.

"May we see what's back there?" I asked, pointing to the door.

"Yeah, help yourself," she grunted and went back to sorting papers.

I shimmied around the two desks and opened the door to the back area. It was tight, a closet-sized space for one with a desk, a chair and a file cabinet. I stepped in, barely able to squeeze between the file cabinet and the desk. Walsh stayed back in the main doorway.

By comparison to the front office, Gustavo's desk was neat, tidy, with just a few papers out, and a calendar with a date circled on it and "staff payroll" written beside it. Behind the desk were two boxes of paper towels and a cardboard box with the name of a chemical company.

I opened the box; inside were six rectangular yellow tins, similar to the one-gallon olive oil tins my grocer sold. I lifted one up and read the label.

"What's that?" Walsh called from the doorway.

"Perchloroethylene," I read. I unscrewed the metal cap and took a tentative sniff, remembering the yellow bottle in my dream.

Walsh walked up to me. "Getting high, boss?"

I shook my head. "Sniff this." I held out the can.

He sniffed carefully and sneered. "Dry cleaning fluid," he pronounced. "Smells terrible."

"Dry cleaning fluid," I repeated. "I've been thinking about this stuff a lot lately. Why would I be thinking about this stuff?" The skinny woman was still organizing paper into piles. I held up the can. "I'm curious," I stated. "Why do you have dry cleaning fluid in the back office?"

She seemed puzzled by the question. "We use it to take out spots—carpets, drapes, stuff like that. It's used a lot in our business."

"Do you usually keep it here? I mean, where do you store it to use on the job?"

She frowned, nodding at the can. "Gus kept it in the supply closet. Sometimes there would be a food stain or spilled paint smudge he had to remove. Like I said, that stuff works well to get them out."

"Where were you on Sunday night and Monday morning?"

She grinned. "I was up in Collingwood, with my boyfriend. We have the hotel and restaurant receipts, if you want."

I was surprised that she was so blunt about that. "Collingwood?" I repeated.

She laughed, sounding like the witch from *The Wizard of Oz*, and sat on the edge of the desk. "Yeah, when Gus got killed, I was a hundred miles away, getting laid."

"You still haven't asked me how Gustavo died," I pointed out. I tilted my head. "Why is that?"

She shrugged her shoulders. "He's dead. How doesn't matter to me. I figure he pissed off a husband or one of his old girlfriends or other, that's all. What was he—shot?"

"Stabbed," I corrected. "Drugged and stabbed."

She looked down. "Would he have felt much pain?" I shook my head. She shrugged. "Too bad."

Walsh snickered. "No love lost between you, huh?"

"Not really," she said. "He was a good father, good businessman, lousy husband to my sister."

"About that," I said. "He was just in North Carolina, visiting his daughter, right?"

She nodded. "He was always good with his girl. I'll give him that. His son-in-law moved the family down there because of work, so Gus went to visit pretty often. Actually, I think he was screwing the mother—the son in law's mother. She's a widow. Easy pickings." She said it casually, like discussing the color of his hair or his shoes.

I lifted up the can of dry cleaning fluid and showed it to the woman. "Can I buy this from you?" I asked.

She grinned. "Take it. It's my gift to you." She waved her hand, brushing me away.

"Actually, it could be evidence. Can I still have it?" I asked.

She shrugged and went back to sorting papers. "Yeah, sure. Souvenir."

I put the can in the trunk of the Polara and got in the passenger seat. Walsh got behind the wheel and shook his head. "Man, and I thought *my* love life was wild," he joked. "This guy's a blast."

"Yes," I agreed. "He *was*."

"Was." Walsh corrected himself. "Think that's what got him killed?"

I shook my head. "I dunno. I mean, if his ex-wife didn't kill him, and Rhonda didn't kill him, then who did? Was it because of his womanizing? If it was, why was Ed Hereford killed? He wasn't a cheater, by Rhonda's account. He was just boring."

"Oh," Walsh said. "I meant to tell you. I already checked with Ed Hereford's coworkers while you were off. They all said the same thing. Good guy, no trouble, worked hard, got pissed to the gills on weekends, but always came in sober. Dead end there, too."

Walsh headed west along Danforth Avenue, driving through downtown.

I frowned, thinking. "Why did she put his pants back on?"

Walsh glanced at me. "Sorry?"

"Rhonda said that she put Ed's pants back on. Why would she do that? It's not the kind of thing you'd lie about, so it must be the truth. Why would she do that?"

"Because his pants were off," Walsh said, stating the obvious.

"We found him in the kitchen. Why would his pants be off in the kitchen?" I mumbled.

"I could give you some personal examples?" Walsh offered. "Some girls like different...locales." He shrugged. "Maybe he had a girl there who liked it in the kitchen."

"Is that a euphemism for something I would rather not know about?" I asked gingerly.

"No. In this case kitchen means kitchen," he said. "Unless he was in the middle of doing it and had to run to the kitchen to turn off the gas or something?"

I thought about that. "That gives me something to check out, Patrick."

We parked at the station house and walked in together. Walsh observed the unwritten protocol that said I should go through the doorway first.

Frank was at his desk, on the phone, scribbling furiously. He said, "Uh huh," and nodded. After a minute, he smiled and put his pen down. "Listen," he said into the phone. "I owe you. If you're ever in Toronto, I'll buy you dinner." He listened for a moment and laughed. "Yeah, bring her too. She cute?" He paused. "Whatever. Like I said, I owe you, Inspector. Bye."

I sat across from him and Walsh sat on the edge of the next desk.

"Who was that?" I asked.

Frank grinned like the Cheshire cat. "That was the Newfoundland Constabulary," He said. "I had a thought. What if there was a connection between Cameron Wilkins, Rhonda's dead husband, and the first guy who died." He put a thick manila folder on the desk. "I read the progress report. Good work, both of you." He tilted up his notepad. "The first guy who died, twenty years ago, was one Barry Hanlon. His widow is Irene O Dowd Hanlon."

Walsh and I looked at each other. Frank sat up, interested. "What? What is it?" he asked.

"Frank," I said. "We just spoke to Rhonda. Her cousin's maiden name is O Dowd."

Frank shook his head. "Okay, Ian, I'll bite. Where does that lead us?"

Walsh stepped in. "Rhonda said that Paulette had a younger sister, Lucy O Dowd, who died when she was ten or so, but she never mentioned another sister. Could that possibly be Irene?"

Frank shrugged. "Irene Hanlon remarried after Barry died. She still lives in Corner Brook. My contact there says she was happy to talk about her first husband, Barry. Barry had a medical condition. It caused him to bend his elbow when passing a bar and it had a side effect that made him stray, too. Irene got tired of him wandering so she basically lived apart from him for the last years of his life. When he died, it was a minor hiccup for her, no more."

I sat back, thinking. "This is the guy who owned a dry cleaner's, right? Irene's first husband?"

"Right," Frank said. "I don't know if Irene is Paulette's older sister or not, but I'll check."

"Cameron Wilkins worked for Highways in Newfoundland," I said. "Doing what?"

Walsh pulled out his notebook. "He repaired the road signs for the Department. Cleaned and repainted them." He looked up for a moment then closed his eyes tight. "Degreaser."

"Huh?" Frank asked.

Walsh leaned forward. "You're looking for a common bond. I'm thinking it's the degreaser. When they bring old signs in for repair, they wash and degrease them first. Otherwise, the new paint won't stick."

"What do they use to degrease them?" I asked.

"The stuff they use at True-Bright: Perchloroethylene," Walsh replied.

Frank shook his head. "How do you even know this?"

Walsh smiled. "I had a summer job with Ministry of Transport in college. I did a lot of traffic control and flagging but, when they needed us to, we worked in the paint shop, fixing road signs. If there was a sign to be repaired, we used Perchloroethylene to degrease it before painting."

I buried my head in my hands. "I knew it. I've been having strange dreams about that stuff. I couldn't figure out why, and it drove me crazy. Now I get it. That's the common link."

Sighing, I sat up. "Both the dead men in Corner Brook worked with the stuff—Perchloroethylene. That's the one link between them. Barry used it at his dry cleaner's, Cameron used it at the paint shop, and here in Toronto, Gus worked with it, too. The question is, did Ed Hereford also work with it? If he did, then that links all four dead men together."

Frank frowned, his mouth slightly open. "How is that a link? What if they all hated broccoli? Isn't that just as good a link? I don't get it."

"Okay, how about this?" I said. "The other three men used Perchloroethylene in their jobs, but Ed didn't. He worked in a bakery. Is there another common link, something else we're missing?"

Walsh frowned. "Maybe there is more than one link. Are we looking at something bigger?"

Frank nodded. "Could be. Three of them slept with Rhonda. Is that a good enough link?"

Walsh's eyes widened at that statement. Frank didn't seem to notice.

"Next question then," Frank continued. "Are we done at four deaths, or will there be more?"

"I hadn't thought of that," I mumbled. "We might end up with a higher body count."

Frank smiled at Walsh. "Listen, squirt, can you get us a couple of Danish and coffees?"

Walsh nodded. "Sure thing, Frank. The coffee truck should be here any minute."

Walsh walked out to the front desk and looked out, waiting for the truck to come. Frank watched him go then turned to face at me.

His face went hard. "So Patrick is screwing Rhonda?" he asked sharply.

I winced. "I only found out today. He says it was a one-time thing. I don't think he's lying."

"Will it hurt the investigation?" He was matter-of-fact, straightforward.

I sighed. "I doubt it. I'm pretty sure Rhonda is innocent."

"Still…" Frank frowned. "If it even only *smells* like she's guilty, Patrick is off this case. You know that, right?"

I scratched my chin. "Got it, Inspector. What tipped you off?"

Frank shrugged. "Whenever anyone mentioned her before, his eyes would glaze over, like a teenager in heat. Today, though, every time he said her name, he squirmed. You didn't notice?"

I shook my head.

He smiled. "You don't have very many old girlfriends, do you, Ian?"

Walsh came back with a pair of pastries and handed them to us.

Frank stared at him. "So, Patrick, was she worth it?"

Walsh glanced my way then grinned, embarrassed. "No, Frank, it was not worth the risk I took."

Frank chuckled. "Remember that for next time. And count yourself lucky that Ian is your boss and not me."

Walsh glanced my way again and shrugged. "I've already been told I used up all my credits with Ian." He sat down. "Something else. You mentioned we could have more bodies?"

Frank nodded. "Worried you might me next?"

Walsh shook his head. "Not really, but I wonder what the trigger was for the deaths."

Frank frowned. "Trigger?"

"Sure," Walsh said. "Nobody gets up one morning and says, 'Hey, I think I'll kill someone.' There must have been something these men did to set off the killer. Did they pick a bar fight? Or call someone's sister a dirty name? What?"

"You sound like Helen." Frank grinned. "Still, I bet you're right. So, squirt, what do *you* think they did that set the killer off?"

Walsh sighed. "No idea." He rubbed his nose, thinking. "You had a thought, right, Ian?"

I stared at the floor for a few seconds, trying to recall something that was way down in my memory. It would come to me in time if I stopped looking for it. "Okay," I said. "The two men here died after they were drugged with codeine. Cameron Wilkins was probably given a lethal dose of nicotine. We don't know about the first man, Barry Hanlon, because he was cremated and they never looked into his death too deeply. I have to think, though, if he really *was* married to Paulette's older sister, there's a connection there. Can we get the family history from your friends in Newfoundland?"

Frank nodded. "Leave it with me." He looked at his watch. "Let's grab lunch. You're buying, squirt," he said and pointed at Walsh.

ↄ◠ↄ◠ↄ

At four-thirty in the afternoon, Steven Machtinger called and asked me to come to his office. I knew why he wanted to see me and drove there as quickly as I could without being reckless.

I waited patiently in the anteroom. Machtinger was speaking with a client, and through the closed door I could hear him discussing the law regarding wills and trusts. The other voice, a woman's, came through the door shrill and loud, complaining about the ungrateful nature of her children.

After a few minutes and more murmured conversation by both parties, I heard chairs scraping on wooden floors, then the inner office door opened and a woman came through it.

She was large, matronly, dressed in a navy blue dress, a white coat, and a large blue hat. She reminded me of the society matron all the Marx Brothers movies. She walked gingerly, as though the floor was buttered, her ivory high-heeled shoes wobbling as she took a step. She looked me over dismissively then marched past me to the elevator.

Machtinger ushered me into his office and sat across from me. He reached down into his desk, came out with a large flat envelope, placed it on the desk, and looked at me, watching my expression. I wanted to pick it up to see the contents, but I was somehow afraid that if I touched it before I was supposed to, it would disappear. Scratch a Catholic and you'll get superstition, someone once told me.

"Well," he said. "As I mentioned to you, we *had* expected to have resolution by Christmas."

My heart sank slightly at those words. He opened the flap on the envelope and slid out three letter sized pages.

"It normally takes weeks for this to be resolved. This is unprecedented." He smiled. Stapled to the envelope was a square piece of paper. Written on it was simply: "Thanks. WB."

Machtinger read the pages, one by one. "You have friends in high places, it seems. Here is the certificate of adoption, the new birth certificate, and the judge's order for both." He placed them gently on the desk in front of me and pointed to a line on one page. "You decided on the name 'Ethan Prescott McBriar.'" He read upside down. "Are you happy with that name?"

I nodded, stunned. "I'm very happy," I whispered. "Very happy. Thank you very much, very, very much."

He smiled and placed the papers back in the envelope. "Congratulations on your new son."

He stretched his hand out. I took it warmly in both of mine and shook it for a long time.

"You know, if I had a bottle of cream, we'd be making butter," he joked.

I let his hand go and blushed, embarrassed. "Sorry. Thank you, thank you very much," I repeated. "Thank you. Thanks again."

He grinned broadly. "Go home, Ian. Go home to your wife and son." He waved me out the door.

∽∾∾

At a quarter to six, Karen's Beetle whistled louder and

louder then stopped as she parked in the driveway. I heard her footsteps clop up the steps to the porch, then she opened the door.

"Hi?" she called. "I'm home."

"Here," I called from the bedroom.

She kicked off her shoes—they clunked as they hit the front closet door—and padded through to join me. "Hey, you," she said. I was sorting papers in the corner file cabinet. "What are you doing, Ian?"

"Oh," I said casually. "We just got some paperwork that I wanted to put away."

I handed her the envelope. She opened it, frowning, and then saw what it was. Her eyes opened wide and she flopped down onto the bed, stunned. "Oh, dear god," she whispered. "Oh, dear god." She started to cry softly, tears running down her cheek and onto the pages.

"Here," I said, moving the papers away. "You okay, hon?"

She wrapped her arms around me and gave me a long, passionate kiss. "Better than okay."

☙☙☙

Thursday morning was glorious. I can't remember what the weather was. It was still glorious. Karen and I walked Ethan to the school office. He proudly told the school secretary that his name was now Ethan Prescott McBriar and that he now had a real dad.

He slowly, carefully spelled his name, standing on his tiptoes as he leaned over the counter and faced the woman. He handed her his birth certificate as proof, warning her not to wrinkle it at all.

She dutifully wrote the new name on an index card and placed it in a long wooden box with the letters *Mc-P* on the front, then slid that into a wooden cabinet.

The principal patted Ethan's shoulder and accompanied

him to class, as Karen and I followed. The principal opened the classroom door and stepped in. The teacher was not yet there and twenty or so young boys and girls were playing noisily, waiting for her to show up. As soon as they saw who was in the doorway, they stopped dead and the room went quiet. "Good morning, boys and girls," the principal said, in a CBC radio announcer's voice.

"Good morning, Mister Charlton," they all chimed in unison.

"As some of you may know," he intoned, "Our Ethan here was waiting for some good news. That news has come. He has been adopted by Detective Sergeant McBriar, here." He nodded my way and I nodded at the class. "The only change for Ethan, is that instead of being Ethan Prescott, his name is now Ethan Prescott McBriar."

The principal looked at me—I was clearly blushing—the he turned back to the children. "Does anyone have any questions?"

The class was silent for a moment, then one hand went up—a boy slightly taller than Ethan, with curly red hair. "Mister McBriar, are you a real policeman?" he asked, almost pleading.

The class giggled.

"Yes, yes, I am." I pulled out my police badge and held it high.

"How come you don't have a police uniform?" he challenged.

"That's a very good question. When I joined the police force as a constable, I drove a patrol car, and I wore a uniform. I later became a detective, and that means that I wear a suit. In a way, this is my new uniform. Thank you."

A girl stuck her hand up, waving furiously. "Do you still have your uniform?"

I nodded. "On special occasions, like parades, or funerals, things like that, I still wear it, yes."

Another boy stuck his hand up desperately. "Do you have a gun?" he called.

The class giggled again.

"All Toronto police officers are issued firearms," I said diplomatically. "However, I wouldn't normally bring a gun into a school." I opened out my jacket to show I was unarmed.

The principal nodded. "No other questions? Good. Please be quiet until Miss Graff comes in."

Karen gave Ethan a hug.

He hugged back quickly, embarrassed at the public display of affection, and we followed the principal back to his office.

He turned my way and lowered his voice to a whisper. "I was speaking to Mr. Taggart this week."

"And?" I asked.

"He says you 'beat the crap out of Mister Frost'?" The words came out carefully, softly.

"I never touched him. But my old partner was in an argument with Mr. Frost. He was struck first and defended himself. Is there a problem there?"

He smirked. "I would have paid fifty dollars to see that."

"Frost is not one of your favorite people on the planet, then?"

"You could say that. I used to be his principal. I've had him in my office on several occasions over his behavior. He is not a nice man—he managed to upset my staff quite often."

"He managed to really upset my old partner, too."

"Is he also a boxer?" he asked. "Is he a large man as well?"

"He's five foot seven." I grinned. "A Green Beret beats a pair of fists, every time."

The principal smiled broadly and shook our hands, and we left.

Karen kissed me firmly and got into her Beetle. She cranked up the radio, bouncing along to some dance number, revved up the engine, and backed out into the street. I watched her sing along with the tune as she drove down-town.

I hummed to myself, something jazzier, and got into the Fury. I turned on the police radio and called in, mechan-ically. "Fifty-two-four-eight, to dispatch?"

"Go, four-eight," the answer came back.

"Four eight, any messages?" I waited for the response.

"Four-eight, please come in soonest possible, meet with Inspector."

What did Frank want with me now? "Four-eight, rog-er." I hung up the mic.

෬෬෬

I pulled into the 52 division parking lot and walked in. A group of detectives was clustered around Frank's desk, listening quietly to someone I couldn't see. They all laughed loudly and then scattered slowly.

Frank stayed behind, sitting on the edge of a desk, as Captain Van Hoeke leaned against an adjacent desk. A very pretty woman sat in Frank's seat. She was petite, thirtyish, a June Allyson with curly brown hair, in a tight gray skirt and a snug white blouse.

She stood up, smiled like a movie star, and reached a hand out to me. "Hi," she said. "Nancy Coogan."

I shook her hand. "Wow," I mumbled. "Sorry, that just slipped out."

She shrugged. "I get that a lot. It takes a while for men to get past the woman and see the cop."

I shook my head. "Who are you, exactly?"

Van Hoeke nodded. "Inspector Coogan will fill in as Frank winds down his duties. The other inspector from fif-ty-three division was called up early by the OPP, so Nancy came over instead."

Frank stood up. "Tradition holds that I should buy you lunch on your first day," he crooned.

"Shouldn't I buy you lunch instead?" she countered.

Frank nodded. "Never say no to free food."

Coogan leaned back on the edge of the desk and faced me. Frank, just behind her, scanned her bust line. "Where are you with the Hereford case?" she asked. "How close are you to an arrest?"

"We're still chasing down clues," I said. "We don't think his girlfriend did it, but we can't find a smoking gun. I have a niggling hunch about something, but it doesn't make any sense at all. It's just a hunch."

Frank was still visually tracing her figure.

"What's your hunch about?" she asked, glancing off to her right. "Cut it out, Frank. I'm a black belt."

"Are you married?" he asked, without missing a beat.

"Yes. He's a black belt, too." She turned back to me. "Go on."

I smirked. "Perc—Perchloroethylene, is a degreaser. Three of the four dead men worked with it."

"Four?" she asked.

It occurred to me that our notes focused on the local deaths. "Ed Hereford's body was discovered by his girl-friend, Rhonda, and her boss. Her boss, Gustavo De Melo—her *other* boyfriend—was found dead in an apartment he'd given her and—"

"You've pretty well ruled her out for De Melo's death, right?" Coogan interrupted. "I read that in the notes. Why kill the meal ticket?"

"Exactly," I said. "Meanwhile, it turns out that Rhonda was once married to a Cameron Wilkins back in Newfound-land, who probably died as a result of nicotine poisoning. Another man, Barry Hanlon, died some years before, but was cremated and we couldn't find out what killed him. Hanlon was married to Rhonda's cousin, we think. That's where we sit now."

"So what connects all these deaths together?" She was direct, focused, straightforward.

"Three of the dead guys used Perchloroethylene in their

jobs," I said. "A different three were from Newfoundland. None of the men, except maybe the first one, died of natural causes. It's one of these math things where you've got intersecting circles—you know—showing common traits?" I waved my hands, making ovals in the air to explain my thoughts.

"They're called Venn diagrams," she said. She leaned forward, tapping her foot. "You've got two guilty parties. One did the deed, one helped. Work from that angle."

Frank was still examining her figure. She ignored him and held her hands out, explaining. "Look," she said. "If all four men died in Newfoundland, I figure we'd be looking at one person. If they all died here, same thing. I've seen this kind of thing before, though. The way I see it, one person killed the men in Newfoundland, for some reason that made sense to him, and the other person helped them finish the job here, as it were. If I were to bet, I'd say it was a husband and wife team."

"The only couples in this mess are Gustavo and his wife, and Paulette and Jim Flaherty. But Gustavo's dead," I said. "Then there's Rhonda and Ed, but he's dead."

"Flaherty's a cop," Coogan answered. "But it could still be him. What about Gustavo's wife?"

"We checked. She's in North Carolina. She has been this whole time. It certainly wasn't her."

"What's your hunch? What about this Perc?" she probed.

I was quickly seeing her as a good investigator, not just a pretty woman. "Something about the smell, something I sort of remember. I've had dreams about Rhonda and bottles of Perc, and I have no idea why."

"What happens in the dreams?"

I felt self-conscious talking about this and took a deep breath. "In my dream, I walk into a dry cleaner's. Rhonda is behind the counter and hands me a bottle of Perc. In one dream she asks me not to open it, in another she smells it and dies. I dunno. It could be nothing."

"You've only dreamed about the victims before this, right?" she asked.

I nodded.

"I read your file. It's an occupational hazard, like free doughnuts. Still, I bet there's a reason it's a recurring dream. A lot of us get inspiration from unlikely sources."

Walsh came into the room, his mouth slightly open, and stared at Coogan.

She stretch her hand. "Patrick, it's nice to finally see you."

"Hey," he purred. "Have we met before?"

"No." She grinned. "I'm Inspector Coogan." Her voice went cold. "I'm your new boss."

I watched him visibly deflate at those words.

"Shit," he said softly.

CHAPTER 16

Frank called the Newfoundland police again. His contacts would dig deeper on the O'Dowd family. Frank also asked for their help on why anyone would want to kill Barry Hanlon and Cameron Wilkins. They would get back to him in a day or two, they said.

We took Nancy to lunch and Frank agreed to spend the afternoon getting her up to speed.

Walsh and I excused ourselves after the meal and went to visit Rhonda again. We stopped across from Coleman Park and watched her basement window for a few minutes. The curtain covering the window moved back and forth, as though someone was brushing against it. Then a light went on and off again. Walsh followed me up the side path and stood back as I pushed the button by the letter C on the door frame.

Feet pounded up the stairs in the house, and the door opened.

Rhonda stood there, this timedressed in a smart skirt suit and high heels. Her hair was done, her makeup tastefully applied. She smiled, turned, and headed back down the stairs. Picking up a stack of clothes on the bed, she placed them in a suitcase. "Come in. I'm almost packed."

"Why? Are you moving to another apartment?" I asked. I didn't think it that was what she had planned, but I played dumb.

"Nah. I got me a job in Ottawa. It's a good job, an office job, where I gets to answer phones and talk to people and stuff. I'm lookin' forward to that, I tell you."

Walsh frowned. "When do you start?"

"Ten days. I got me a friend I can stay with till I get a place."

"Rhonda, we have two deaths connected to you," I said. "You can't leave until we find out who's responsible for them. You must know that."

"But I di'nt kill nobody. I di'nt do nothin. Why can't I go then?"

Walsh sighed. "Look, until we make an arrest, you're a suspect. You must realize that."

She huffed, sat on the bed, and glared back and forth between us.

I decided to change the subject. "I have something to ask you." I sat on one of the vinyl dinner chairs and slid close to her. "Your cousin, Paulette—her sister Lucy passed away, you said. Does she have any other brothers and sisters?"

"She has a brother Kelly. He moved to Alberta years and years ago. We ain't heard from him much. And a sister, Irene. She lives in Corner Brook still."

"Is Irene married?" I asked.

"Sure is. She married Barry Hanlon way back, but he done died of consumption, and then she took up with her new husband."

Walsh glanced back and forth at us, curious at the questions.

"Was there anything about Barry that made you…" I searched for the right word. "Uncomfortable around him, or nervous?"

"How d'ya mean?"

"Some men have a roving eye. Did he ever make advances toward you?"

She laughed. "Barry were ugly and fat. The only way he could get tail were to pay for it. He were lucky his business did good."

"What business was that, Rhonda?" Walsh asked.

She grabbed her purse and rummaged through it for a minute, coming up with a pack of cigarettes, pulled out one cigarette, and placed it gently between her lips.

Walsh leaned forward and extended his lighter, the flame illuminating the underside of her face.

She took the light and inhaled deeply. "He had a dry cleaner's and he ran a wholesale warehouse."

"Like wholesale food, furniture, what?" I asked, getting impatient.

"No, love, it were wholesale chemicals—fluids and oils and stuff what them car places use," she said, sucking on the cigarette. "He di'nt sell gas or diesel. Just other stuff they used for cars, I think."

"Rhonda," Walsh said. "Did you ever visit him with Cameron, your husband?"

"Oh, sure. Me and Cam went to his house lots of times. Cam got some of his chemicals from Barry's company. Dunno what it were used for. Never asked."

"Did Paulette know him? I'm just curious," Walsh asked casually.

I began to see his skill in getting people to open up without being pushy.

She nodded. "Sure. Jim used them chemicals, same as Cam. With the car engine business, I guess."

"You never spent much time around the shop area, I guess," he purred.

"Nah. Even Paulette stayed away from it all after we lost Lucy." She waved the cigarette in a circle around her face." Said the smell done somethin' to her head."

"Like what? Like it gave her watery eyes or some-thing?"

"No, it made her brain pound. Really upset her."

"Okay," I said, stepping in. "Listen, you have to stay here for a few days yet. When we get this case resolved, I will personally see that you get to Ottawa on time, all right?"

She sighed. "Yeah, sure." Pulling her clothes out of the suitcase, she placed them on the sofa. "But you promise I'll get there before the job starts, right?"

"When we get this case solved, Patrick or I will personally drive you there, if needs be."

She grunted her approval and sat back down. "Fine, but I really needs that job, ya know."

♥♥♥

Walsh took me back to the station and I drove home. I would go in early the next day, Friday, and clean up any paperwork before the weekend. Meanwhile, I wanted to relax and make dinner.

I tuned to the Buffalo jazz station on the living room stereo, turned it up so I could hear it in the kitchen, and started dinner. Just before five-thirty, the whistle of Karen's Beetle's motor echoed up the driveway, and she stepped up onto the porch. I chopped vegetables, deep in thought. The front door opened, and she walked into the kitchen. Wordlessly, she wrapped her arms around me and squeezed me tight.

"Hey, you," she said softly.

I leaned my head back. "Hi, wifey," I said.

"What's for dinner, Pops?"

"Stew."

She leaned against the kitchen counter, facing me, and frowned. "What's up, Ian? Something wrong?"

"We interviewed the girlfriend of the two dead guys this afternoon. I don't think she did it, but we don't have any other leads. Still, there is something she said that I need to check out. I'll do that tomorrow."

After dinner, we watched some television; Ethan watched *The Odd Couple*, laughing at the jokes, then yawned wide and fell asleep on the carpet.

Karen smiled at me, resting her feet in my lap, the way

Helen had with Frank. Within a half-hour, she was asleep. I turned down the bed and slipped Karen on top of the sheets. She woke up and undressed, then she fell back to sleep.

I undressed, climbed into bed beside her, and wrapped my arms around her. A minute later, I was also asleep.

୧୬୧

I walk into the dry cleaner's. Rhonda, dressed in a smart skirt suit, stands behind the counter, sorting through a pile of clothes. "I need to find my clothes," she says. "I'm going to Ottawa."

I say something.

She nods, reaches under the counter, brings out a square yellow can and hands it to me. "Here ya go,"' she says. "Now ya got all ya need."

I ask a question, and she just laughs.

"That's why they died." She lights a cigarette and blows smoke into the air. "Yup, that's why they died."

୧୬୧

I sat up in bed, wide awake, and dripping with sweat. I rested my elbows on my knees and breathed deeply. Dear Lord—that was it. *I must be wrong*, I thought. I hoped that I was wrong, but I doubted it. I slid back down and tried to sleep.

Twenty minutes later, I was still wide awake. I looked at the clock. It said five in the morning. Karen was sleeping peacefully, it seemed. I hadn't disturbed her.

I moved a leg out the side of the bed, placed my foot on the floor, and slid the other leg out to follow.

Karen coughed. "Still can't sleep, hon?"

I kissed her forehead. "Sorry," I whispered. "Bad dream. Go back to sleep."

"I see." She sat up. "Now that we're married, you think

you can get away with just a quick smooch on the forehead, huh?"

I chuckled, leaned down, kissed her gently on the lips, and moved down, kissing her chin, her neck, then her cleavage.

She giggled and playfully pushed me away. "Make breakfast, you nut."

I pulled on my bathrobe and shuffled through to the kitchen and put on the coffee.

Karen came in soon after and watched me, fascinated, as I made lunches for Ethan and Alan. "Do you usually think as you cook?" she asked, tugging her robe tight around her.

"I cook because cooking lets me concentrate," I said. "It's backward, but the act of cooking helps me think better, not tune out. It's not just my way of relieving stress, how I turn my mind on."

Karen put her elbows on the table and rested her head in her hands. "What got to you today?"

I sighed. "Remember when we got broken into?"

"I vaguely remember that, yes," she joked.

I grimaced. "I didn't tell you the whole story."

She sat up straight. "Well?" she barked.

I explained all about the Mountie and the hired thug. I told her about running the plate on the Mountie's car, getting to Marchand, and beating up the hired thug in Hamilton.

She listened with her mouth open.

"So that's everything," I finished.

She shook her head. "Why didn't you tell me everything before? You kept important facts from me. Is that how you want our life to be? Lying to each other?"

"I wasn't lying," I argued. "I was trying to spare you worry. I told you the truth. It was a mistake that they broke in, and they wouldn't be back. That was true."

"But it wasn't the whole truth," she moaned. "I need to trust you, Ian. We're married." She poked her finger into the table, punctuating her statement. "How can we go ahead, how can I trust you, if you aren't completely honest with me?"

I kissed her, gently. "Deal," I agreed. "No more half-truths. I promise."

"So is that what gave you the sweats this morning? The lying?"

I shook my head. "That wasn't it, but I wanted to tell you the truth because this morning I realized how easy it is for a man to get caught up in his lies, and how it can snow-ball."

She frowned. "I don't understand."

"The Mountie pretended to be a thug. That was a lie. I think the person who killed our victims also lied. That's what I want to find out today."

She shook her head. "I don't get it."

"I'll tell you later."

℣ℤ℣ℤ

I got into the station parking lot by eight in the morning.

To my surprise, Walsh's Polara was already there. I sat at my desk and read through the pink telephone message slips from overnight, then I waited.

Five minutes later, Walsh came into the room, holding a bunch of papers. "Morning, boss. Good to see you here."

"Patrick, you're in early," I said.

"Newfoundland time. It's after nine-thirty there." He sat across from me. "Remember how Barry Hanlon had a chemical wholesale company? Guess what they sold to both Cameron Wilkins and Jim Flaherty."

"Perchloroethylene?"

"Bingo. He also used it himself at his dry cleaner's, of course. Now, trick question. What did Paulette Flaherty do before she was married?"

I shook my head. "No idea. She went to work with Jim after they got married, right?"

He nodded. "I called Rhonda's aunt. Before she got married, Paulette worked for the local hospital as a nurse's aide."

I was very impressed with him at this point. "Go on."

"Paulette was assigned to Barry Hanlon. Guess what?" He grinned a movie star grin. "Barry was taking codeine for his cancer pain. If he'd overdosed on it, nobody would have suspected foul play. If some of his pain pills went missing, who'd know? Besides, he had one foot in the grave anyway. Why bother digging too deep?"

"What about Cameron Wilkins? He wasn't drugged with codeine."

Walsh smiled again, a cat-with-the-canary smile. "He was allergic to codeine. He vomited when he took it. It was in his notes. And the nurse's aide who visited him? Paulette. She knew she couldn't drug him with it, and she would have had access to nicotine from the dispensary, like she would have had access to codeine from the same place."

It made sense. "But why kill them in the first place?"

"No idea. That's what has me stumped. Also, if she is our black widow, why would she kill Ed Hereford and Gustavo De Melo?"

I thought for a moment. "Colleen Feldman."

"I hear she's cute." Walsh said.

"Forget that. The department sent me for counseling last year, and I read those psych magazines in her waiting room. There was one article that stuck in my mind; I couldn't quite place the context. Now I get it."

I found the business card I wanted, picked up the phone and dialed the number. A familiar voice answered. "Colleen Feldman."

"Hey, Colleen, Ian McBriar here."

"Do we have another bank robbery, Sergeant?" she asked.

She was smiling, I could tell.

"Not today. You have some old magazines in your waiting area, right?"

"Yes, it's mandatory. If they were current, I could be charged with malpractice."

I grinned. "I read an article last year, about things that can set off schizophrenic episodes."

"Do you want to borrow it? I'm sure it's still here," she said. "But I suspect there's a more pressing reason for your call?"

"Do you know of any triggers that would make someone wacky, push them over the edge?"

"That's not very scientific, Ian. The technical term is 'loopy' or 'zany.'"

"Sorry. I'm being quite serious here. I need to know what might cause someone to go crazy enough to kill."

She was silent for a minute, then I heard paper rustling. "There were some articles about a condition called 'deep psychosis.' That may have been what you read."

"That sounds familiar. Do you remember what the article said?"

"Do you read every one of your memos?" she asked. "As it happens, it was written by one of my old psychology professors, so I did read it. You're lucky." More rustling of paper. "Found it. Okay, I thought so. I do remember this one. Yes, deep psychosis can be triggered by a number of stimuli. What did you want to know?"

I found a pen and started making notes. "What kind of stimuli?"

"It could be any one of several things. One person I once interviewed had been assaulted by a man with a beard. He went catatonic every time he saw a beard. Another was slashed by his wife as she listened to Dean Martin music. Every time it came on in a store or on the radio, he would start to shake and cry."

"What about smell? Could that do it?" I asked.

"Very powerful olfactory triggers are underrated by many therapists. Did you have a particular smell in mind?"

"Dry cleaning fluid," I said. "I suspect it's a common factor in the crimes I'm investigating."

"That's totally possible. Chemical aromas are purer, more concentrated. If they trigger a memory, or an unpleasant association, then that could certainly cause a psychotic reaction in the right person. I've heard of it with floor wax, bread, gasoline, all sorts of things."

"Could this person plan and execute something complicated, over a period of time, while in deep psychosis? I mean, beyond just going bonkers and shooting someone?" I asked.

"Certainly. In their mind, it all makes sense. The fact that they're hurting another human being is immaterial All they want to do is take away the stimulus. If that means an act or series of acts that hurts someone, then it's still well within the realm of possibility."

"Okay, thanks, Colleen. Can I contact you later for specific advice?"

"Sure. Listen, be careful, all right? People like that can snap if cornered," she warned.

"Thanks, Mom," I said and hung up.

Walsh wanted to go back to where Gustavo had died to knock on some more doors. That was a good idea so I asked him to join me at Ed's apartment in an hour. I thought I might find some more clues there.

Right after Walsh left, the Newfoundland Constabulary called me back. They had some details for me, and I quickly wrote them down. They would send me a printed copy of their report, they said. That required me to make another phone call to Colleen Feldman and it confirmed what I was afraid of—Flattery was probably the killer.

I parked at Ed Hereford's and paced the sidewalk outside the apartment building. This case was almost over. I had all the answers now. I just needed a few more details to wrap it up neatly.

Across the street, another apartment building—a copy of Ed's—reflected my car in the lobby windows. I walked up to the front door. It was locked, but down the street I saw an older man in a gray shirt and pants sweeping the sidewalk. I walked slowly over to him and smiled.

He looked me over, sizing me up. "No vacancy," he said, shaking his head. and went back to his sweeping.

I coughed and held out my badged. He examined it carefully, nodded, and rested the broom on a shrub. "Yeah?" he asked, irritated. "What?"

"We're investigating the recent death, across the street," I said. "Can I ask you a few quick questions?"

He gave an exaggerated sigh and looked at his watch. "I'm busy. You gotta be quick. I'm busy."

"Just a few questions, as I say."

He looked me over, sneered, and put his hands on his hips. "Look, I got work to do. What do you want, Geronimo?"

My smile vanished. "Okay, Pops, how about this? You're a material witness, and I think you're hindering a police investigation into a homicide. I can hold you for obstruction of justice. I can lock you in a cell for two days and stick you with a criminal record for life. How about that?"

His face dropped. "Sorry, officer. I didn't mean, you know—"

"Not officer," I growled. "It's *Detective Sergeant* McBriar. Now, can we start over?"

His hands fell to his sides, the signal for defeat, and nodded.

"Fine," I snapped. "Have you seen any strange people around here, especially just before the death?"

He shook his head.

"Nobody out of the ordinary? You saw nothing strange, no matter how insignificant it seems?"

He shook his head again. "A couple of cars, that's all."

"What cars?" I asked, not very hopeful.

"One of your guys', a cop—police officer, I mean." He was almost whispering now.

"Our guys?"

"Yeah, but not a Toronto cop," he said. "Policeman. I meant policeman," he added quickly. "He was an OPP or something."

"Huh?" I said. "How do you know he was OPP?"

He shrugged. "You know, his uniform was different. It didn't have a red stripe on the pants."

"What about his cruiser? What did it say on the door?"

"It wasn't a cop car—police car. It was a little Ford, a Comet or something."

That confirmed what I was afraid of. "What color?" I asked.

"Light blue. Yeah, but it was a Maverick, not a Comet. I saw them funny horns on the badge," he said, remembering. "Someone you know?"

"Yeah. Someone I know," I mumbled. "Thanks for your cooperation, sir. I appreciate your help."

I walked back across the road to Ed's apartment building. I knew I was right. It was Flattery. Down the street, I spotted a York Regional Police cruiser—Jim's car. Right behind that was Walsh's Polara. I had to hurry. I didn't know what he might do, so I raced up the stairs to Ed's apartment. Walsh was at the kitchen table, talking pleasantly to Flaherty. Flaherty was in full uniform. He sat across from Walsh, resting his elbows on the table as they chatted.

I walked in as casually as I could and sat facing Flattery. "Hi, Jim. What are you doing here?"

He nodded at Walsh. "I were in the area, so I figured I'd pick up whatever Rhonda left behind, if it were all right by you, and hold them for her till she needs them."

"Don't you know where she is?" I asked.

Walsh started to speak and I glared at him. Flaherty didn't see it.

"No idea. Where's she at, then?" He asked it casually, but his expression was too earnest.

"She's gone, moved to Manitoba, went to find a better life," I said.

Walsh stiffened at the lie and stared at me.

Flaherty looked down at his shoes. "Ah."

"Ah," I repeated. I looked at the ceiling and sighed. This hurt me, right down to my soul. "Officer Flaherty, can I ask you to put your gun on the counter?"

He looked at me and smiled—a sad, resigned smile. "You know, huh?"

Walsh's eyes widened. He looked back and forth between us, wondering what was going on.

"I'm sorry, Jim," I said. "Yeah, we know."

Flaherty lifted his revolver out by the butt, placing it in my hand. I flipped open the cylinder, shook out the bullets and handed the gun to Walsh, who looked at it like it might explode. He put it gingerly on the counter behind him.

"Well, it were just a matter of time," Flaherty said. "Can I call Paulette to say I'll be missing supper?"

"Sorry," I said. "Not just yet."

Walsh stared at me, then Flaherty, then back at me, bewildered. "Ian, what the hell is going on?" he barked.

"It was bad luck," Flaherty said. "Rhonda met someone that I knew from Corner Brook."

Walsh looked back and forth between Flaherty and me, apparently still puzzled.

Flaherty stretched out and rubbed his face. "Paulette had a real bad experience as a young woman. Barry Hanlon was scum, pure scum who assaulted young women. He got away with it. We couldn't touch him. He doped them gals up and had his way with them." He shook his head, remembering. "Paulette were just sixteen. She were a lovely young gal then, the kind of gal that scum like that just loves to go after…" His voice trailed off.

"But I got my own back," he said, his voice stronger now. "Paulette was a nurse's aide, and she tended Hanlon on a home visit. He didn't remember her. She was just another nurse to him. But now—now that he was dying—she sure remembered him. She told me about him. I got him back." He smiled at me. "They said you was good. I see they was right. What gave you the idea I done it?"

I sighed. "Dry cleaning fluid. I read an article once about smells triggering schizophrenic episodes. Barry took those girls to his dry cleaner's to rape them. The smell of the cleaning fluid must have been a powerful reminder. What about Cameron Wilkins?"

Flaherty cradled one knee in his hands. "You're a smart fella, Sergeant. Why do you suppose I would have done him in, then? Cam never done nothin' bad to Paulette."

"No," I said. "But he always smelled of cleaning fluid. I imagine visiting Rhonda and finding Cam covered in that smell from the paint shop, smelling like Barry Hanlon, Paulette must have been beside herself, especially after poor Lucy passed away. It must have driven her crazy."

He winced slightly at that word. "She ain't crazy," he growled.

"No," I agreed. "But she does get upset over certain smells. Your house smelled of cinnamon the first time I went there, and nutmeg the second time. Those aromas keep her calm, don't they?"

He nodded. "When I gets my uniform cleaned, I got to leave it in the garage for days till the smell goes. I got fans going and everything, just to take the odor away. Cameron Wilkins was dying of cancer," he continued. "I thought I could dope him up with codeine, like Barry, then suffocate him, but he was allergic to codeine. It made him vomit. So I found another way to kill him. I got nicotine from the hospital dispensary and I spiked his food. I knew a man in his condition wouldn't notice the taste. He died real quick. He probably didn't feel a thing."

"What about Ed Hereford?" I asked. "Why did you kill him?"

Flaherty sighed. "He were a friend of Hanlon's. When Barry died, he were at Barry's bedside. He remembered seeing Paulette come visit Barry. Couple months back, he had a jacket dry cleaned.

"Paulette came to see Rhonda. She smelled the suit and made a terrible fuss. Ed put two and two together and he was going to tell everybody. He wouldn't shut up, so I shut him up, all right."

"That's why you came here in the first place, to leave the past behind?" I asked.

He nodded.

"How did you kill Ed?" I asked.

"Stabbed him." He nodded at the kitchen drawer. "With one of them knives."

"Did he struggle much?" I asked.

"You bet. He were a strong fella. Had a dickens of a time with him."

I shook my head. "Sorry, you just blew it. He was drugged with scotch and large amounts of codeine. He couldn't struggle at all. I doubt he could stand up straight, let alone fight back."

Flaherty looked down, defeated. "Sorry. I were mistaken. I guess I forgot how I did it."

Walsh stared at me. "Ian, what the hell is going on?"

I looked sadly over at him. "Jim didn't do any of this. He's a cop and he's a good man. Paulette killed them all. She killed them for exactly the reasons that Jim said, but it was her that did it, not him."

"No, you're wrong," Flaherty argued. "I'm the one what done it, not her."

I shook my head. "Paulette gets upset over certain smells. She had a rough time getting over Barry Hanlon's assault. Perchloroethylene has a unique smell and he must have smelled of it all the time. When Lucy got sick, it would have been all over your shop. I bet it drove Paulette into a frenzy to smell it. There's even a name for the condition. It's called 'deep psychosis.' I spoke with the New-foundland Constabulary and they told me that the week Cameron Wilkins died, Paulette was at home, but you were in Charlottetown with Lucy, taking her to a specialist. You couldn't have killed Cameron, but Paulette did."

He looked up at me, pleading, wanting me to shut up. I wasn't enjoying this either.

"Finally," I said, "When Gustavo was killed you were on patrol outside Toronto. I checked."

Flaherty shook his head. "We got a daughter, Cynthia. She's got a handicap. She can't live alone, without her mother and me. We can't leave her—she'd be sent to a home."

"I know," I said. "She's almost blind, and she has a bowel condition. They told me so today. They also said she needs to take codeine for her stomach pain. Paulette believes that the chemicals from your old work caused Cynthia's birth defects and killed Lucy, isn't that right?"

He nodded.

"Meeting Ed here after all those years, having him fawn over Paulette when she came to visit Rhonda, was just too much," I continued. "I bet he mentioned Barry, and that just pushed her over the edge. When Rhonda found him, his pants were off. He was home sick that day, so Paulette got him drunk and fed him soup laced with codeine, then when he tried to have sex with her she stabbed him. Getting rid of him was the last loose end from the old days."

Walsh was silent, listening. "Boss," he said, softly. "What about Gustavo?"

"A witness saw Gustavo undressing a woman. She only saw outlines through the drapes. We thought it was Rhonda, but it was Paulette, wasn't it? Paulette came over to find out if Ed had said anything, or if Rhonda suspected her. Rhonda wasn't there, but Gustavo was, and he reeked of cleaning fluid. We know he used it a lot, too."

I paused but Flaherty didn't deny anything.

"He put his moves on Paulette," I continued. "After all, she looks a lot like Rhonda. But to Paulette, he must have seemed like Barry Hanlon all over again. He was gruff, pushy, and a slob. Except this time she had some of Cynthia's codeine with her. She led Gustavo on, gave him a couple of scotches, then maybe a soft drink with codeine, and when he was unconscious she stabbed him with a knitting needle. He was also discovered with no pants on. Pretty well nails it for the same person in both cases. How am I doing so far?"

Jim Flaherty's face was stony, expressionless. That told me I was right.

"We have to arrest Paulette, Jim. We'll have to charge her with manslaughter."

I sat still, waiting for that to sink in.

"Manslaughter?" he asked carefully. "Not murder?"

"She will go to jail, but not for life. She'll get out in time. You and Cynthia can live your lives and wait until then."

He looked at his hands. "I lied to you. What will happen to me?"

"How do you mean?" Walsh asked.

"Cynthia needs me. Please, I can't leave her alone. She needs me," Flattery pleaded.

It seemed like a question intended for me.

"You helped our investigation," I said. "That's all you did. Go home. Go be with your daughter."

"Can I come along when you take Paulette away?" he asked. "She gets very upset when her routine changes."

I nodded. "I would appreciate your assistance, Constable Flaherty."

We got a pair of detectives in an unmarked car to meet us at the Flaherty home. Jim walked in with us and explained to Paulette what was happening. She wasn't angry, or violent, or even surprised—just sad at leaving her home, yet relieved that it was all over.

Paulette sat in the back seat with Walsh. Jim sat in the back seat of the other car with Cynthia. We were low key, casual. A few neighbors walked past us and didn't even stop to gawk. We were quiet, polite, smiling. Paulette insisted on bringing along an overnight case with spare clothes and cosmetics for her stay in jail. Despite everything, I felt sorry for her.

As I drove, I watched her through the rearview mirror, enjoying the scenery, smiling faintly.

Walsh touched her arm and she turned to face him, still smiling a polite smile.

"Paulette. I'd just like to know. Why did you do it?"

"Do what, love?"

"You killed four men. Why did you do it?" he asked again.

She leaned back in her seat and inhaled deeply, collecting her thoughts. "It's important to keep things in order, don't you think?"

"Order?" Walsh asked. "What do you mean, order?"

"Well, lad, they was grand bothers. They upset my life, and Cynthia's life, and poor Lucy's life too. I just wanted to clean up the mess, is all. I just wanted order back."

She smiled and went back to gazing out the window.

Walsh looked down at his shoes, trying to figure out, it seemed, what to ask next.

Paulette frowned. "They's going to ask me lots of questions then, aren't they?"

Walsh nodded. "Yes, hon, I'm afraid they are. Is there anything I can do for you when we get there?"

She looked slightly afraid. "What should I tell them?"

Walsh took her hand. "Tell them the truth."

We walked her into the remand center and Walsh made her comfortable. He brought her a mug of tea and some biscuits and stayed with her through the booking process. Jim Flaherty took Cynthia home and explained what had happened, in a way that she could understand.

After the weeks of work, and the digging, it was a huge anticlimax. There were few pats on the back, few congratulatory handshakes, no offers of cigars or meals.

I had arrested another cop's wife and split up his family. I had flipped over a rock and exposed the slime underneath. Nobody wanted to see that, least of all me. I went home.

❧❧❧

On Saturday, November thirtieth, we all went into the station. It was Frank's last official day in the department and most of the detectives were there. They wanted to send him off in style.

Champagne flowed, and everyone made jokes, read speeches, and told funny stories about Frank, mostly at his expense. Helen came in with him, now noticeably pregnant. Frank shielded her from any possible bump, protecting her furiously until he sat her safely at his old desk.

Van Hoeke and his wife showed up, with flowers for Helen and a bottle of scotch for Frank.

Karen and I sat near them, watching Frank accept the accolades.

After the Captain had spoken, everyone yelled, "Speech, speech," and Frank held his hands out, waving them to be quiet.

He climbed on top of the desk and looked around. "Hey, so this is how Ian sees it," he joked. Everyone laughed. He looked down at Karen, Helen, and me and smiled. "I will miss each and every one of you." He scanned the room. "You will all forever be a part of me, and I will cherish the time we worked together for all my days. Thank you all."

He got back down. There was applause, smiling faces, and moist eyes all around. The next hour was quieter. Everyone wished him well, and everyone told him how much they would miss him. Then we put his personal things in the trunk of Helen's Nova.

Karen asked Frank and Helen over for dinner. I promised there would be apple pie for dessert. At six in the evening, the sky turned black and light sleet shower dusted the driveway with a powdered sugar coating of ice particles. Ethan was in the basement, watching TV.

Frank and Helen stomped carefully up the porch steps, knocked at the door, and let themselves in. They shook their coats dry and hung them up. Then we sat in the kitchen, chatting like we always did.

I prepared beef bourguignon, Frank's new favorite, as Helen and Karen whispered to each other, giggling and gesturing our way. Gradually, like a candle glowing to life, it dawned on me that I was a cop, but Frank wasn't, not anymore. He wasn't Sergeant Something, Detective Something, or Inspector Anything. He was now Frank, just Frank. That realization made my heart sink.

"Frank," I said, "Are you all right?"

He looked up from listening to Helen. "What do you mean, kid?"

"I mean, how are you about leaving the force?"

Helen and Karen stopped talking.

He glanced at them. "I have had the privilege to work with some of the best and most dedicated men in the department. And with you, too," he joked. "Seriously, how can I complain? I got paid good money, I got good time off, and I got to boss you around."

I smiled. "Well, it will be great outranking you for a change."

We ate everything I brought out. Frank ate half of Helen's dessert while she pretended not to notice. Karen and Helen whispered together until it got late and Helen drove Frank home. It seemed like the typical ending to a typical day, except that Frank wasn't working with me anymore.

Ethan was fast asleep on the carpet. We lifted him up and slid him into his bed, then got ready for bed ourselves and slid under the sheets. I was not tired but I was too listless to do anything, too bleary-eyed to read, and too wound up from the day to sleep.

Karen sat up and stared at me. "So, hubby, what's wrong?"

"I feel strange—about Frank," I said. "I'm glad I have him as a friend. I know we'll visit as often as ever, but it still feels strange, knowing that I won't see him at work every day."

"But you're still going to take the Inspector job, right?" she asked.

"Yeah, I suppose. Everyone's good with that. That helps my decision a lot."

"Plus you'll get a pay raise," she said. "That's good too, right?"

"We don't really need it, though," I said. "Frank needs the money, now. I'm glad he'll get that in his new job, at least."

Her eyes twinkled. "Why does he need it more than us?"

"Well," I said, speaking very slowly, "For one thing, Helen's pregnant, and you're not."

She took my hand and pressed it against her stomach. Her smile lit up the room.

"Actually…"

The End

About the Author

Mauro Azzano was born in Italy, north of Venice. He grew up in Italy, Australia and finally Canada, settling on the west coast outside Vancouver, Canada. He has a broad experience to call on as a writer, having worked as a college instructor, commercial pilot and a number of other unusual occupations. Currently, he is working on the Ian McBriar Murder Mystery series and training as a distance runner.